# OPERATION MILLENNIUM

Also by Shaun Clarke

*The Exit Club*
*Dragon Light*
*Underworld*
*Red Hand*
*The Opium Road*

# OPERATION MILLENNIUM

SHAUN CLARKE

POCKET
BOOKS

LONDON · SYDNEY · NEW YORK · TOKYO · SINGAPORE · TORONTO

First published in Great Britain by Simon & Schuster UK Ltd, 1999
Published simultaneously by Pocket Books, 1999
An imprint of Simon & Schuster UK Ltd
A Viacom Company

1 3 5 7 9 10 8 6 4 2

Simon & Schuster UK Ltd
Africa House
64–78 Kingsway
London WC2B 6AH

Simon & Schuster Australia
Sydney

A CIP catalogue record for this book is available
from the British Library

Hardback ISBN 0-684-86082-1
Paperback ISBN 0-671-01592-3

Typeset in Century Old Style by SX Composing DTP, Rayleigh, Essex
Printed and bound in Great Britain by
Caledonian International Book Manufacturing Ltd, Glasgow

For
George Sturrock

# CHAPTER ONE

It was a long, dark tunnel into hell. The walls were mildewed, gleaming with drops of water, as if dripping sweat. But it was Cusack who was dripping real sweat as he advanced through the gloom, holding his sub-machine gun at the ready.

Though alone down here, he was not alone in the building. He could hear the sounds of combat – the sharp crack of pistols, the savage roar of other weapons, exploding hand grenades and shattering glass – as his fellow troopers cleared the floor upstairs. They would soon be finished, but in the meantime he was on his own, hoping to clear the basement where that lunatic kept his prisoners. He tried to imagine what it must have been like for the captives, chained up and tortured on a daily basis in this damp, dark hole. But the concept was simply beyond imagining, eluding rational thought.

Though this was actually the basement of a vast, ruined building in a disused waterworks in south London, it certainly *seemed* like a catacomb of hell with its cracked, cobwebbed walls, rubbish-strewn concrete floors, rusty manhole covers over foul-smelling drains, and leaking, incessantly dripping taps. Even as Cusack advanced farther along what he assumed was the central corridor, moving down a series of soaked steps that took him ever deeper into the catacomb, checking the other corridors that disappeared into the darkness on both sides, looking for the prisoners and the lunatic who had incarcerated them, he heard the continuing battle above and was only slightly consoled. Rats, fat and fearless, crawled over his booted feet while bats, disturbed by his movement, launched themselves from pipes criss-crossing the ceiling to fly over his head.

*Shit*, he thought, *this place is starting to spook me. Let's get it over and done with. Where are you, you bastard?*

His feeling of being spooked was increased by the fact that he was seeing the dimly lit basement through his PNG night-vision goggles, which lent an eerie green glow to a darkness only fractionally illuminated by infrequently spaced overhead lights, none of which were bright. Though wearing only his standard-issue army jacket and trousers, Danner boots with Gore-Tex lining, and a soft-peaked cap without its customary SAS badge, he was sweating more than usual and straining desperately to hear any sound other than the scuffling of rats and the flapping of bats' wings. He had been expecting to hear the lamentations of the monster's victims, and the fact that he had heard nothing so far only made him sweat more.

*He's either gagged them or killed them*, he thought, *and now it's just him or me. Another Satanist who likes playing games. Where's God when you need Him?*

It was a blasphemous question, shocking even though unspoken, and Cusack wondered at how far he had fallen in such a short time. Once a deeply religious man, always questioning himself, he now questioned the nature of his Creator – and had yet to find answers.

Not that he needed an answer to that question down here, where there was only one question that had relevance:

*Where* is *that lunatic?*

Cusack strained to hear the movements of the man he had come to kill, but heard only the noises of the rats and the bats. The bats were flying above his head, drawn from darkness to light, sometimes brushing him with their wing-tips, making his flesh creep, and the rats were scuttling across the concrete floor, hidden by darkness. As the sounds of the battle upstairs had tapered off, indicating that the ground floor had been cleared, these noises were the only ones that Cusack could hear, apart from his own tense, heavy breathing. The fact that he could still not hear the hostages filled him with dread.

*I don't want to see what's down here*, he thought. *I've had enough for one lifetime.*

Which was true enough, he realized, as he advanced along the gloomy corridor, moving his weapon left and right, covering an arc of fire to both sides, wishing that his quarry would appear and let him put an end to it. During the past couple of years he had been on many operations like this, so-called 'cleansing ops' mounted to neutralize one or other of the growing number of Millennialist freaks who were turning the country into a war zone. He had not only killed his fair share in the process but had also witnessed the torments of the damned. Each of those experiences had sliced a little more out of him, reducing him further each time, and this particular one, given its especially vile nature, could only do him more damage. Now he sensed that he had reached the end of the line and would soon have to give it all up. It was time to retire.

Right now, however, he had no choice but to advance ever deeper into the vast basement, keeping his weapon at the ready, preparing to fire, but anxious not to kill any of the prisoners by mistake if they were used as a human shield, as they were so often these days. The prisoners down here, whether still alive or already dead, were victims of a 'religious terrorist' who called himself 'Joshua'. Joshua had taken it into his head to rid the country of AIDS by abducting young people at gunpoint, mostly when he found them necking in cars parked in secluded areas, then holding them captive, torturing them to death and sending photos of their mutilated bodies to the press, along with dire warnings about what would happen to similar 'AIDS-spreading fornicators'. The

Metropolitan Police had been pursuing Joshua for the past year, becoming ever more desperate as the death toll mounted. But it was only when they had finally discovered where he was hiding out, where he was holding, torturing and eventually killing his prisoners, that they had called in the SAS Quick Reaction Force.

Tasked with neutralizing this latest in a growing number of religious terrorists – or 'Millennialist freaks', as some would have it – Cusack had formed a six-man QRF team and mounted an assault on the derelict building, giving his men the job of clearing the top floor, which Joshua's gang of heavily armed maniacs had been protecting, while he entered the basement alone to confront the ringleader. Now, as the battle above was clearly coming to an end, he was reaching the far end of the basement from which, as he knew, there was no exit. Joshua couldn't be far away.

In the event, Cusack saw the hostages first.

The far end of the central corridor led into a rectangular, brick-walled, partially lit space, once used as a boiler room and still littered with rusty equipment and tools. There, handcuffed and chained together, were the eight people, all young men and women, whom Cusack had come to save.

He was too late. Some of the youngsters were still propped up against the massive steel boiler where they had originally been placed and the rest were slumping either to the left or to the right, prevented from falling the whole way to the floor by the chains that were binding them together. They had all had their throats cut. In most cases, the blood was still pumping out of them, drenching their filthy clothing, and the limbs of some were still twitching as their lives drained away. It was evident, from the nauseating smell of shit and piss, that they had been chained there for a long time and that Joshua, knowing that his own end had come, had slashed their throats mere minutes ago. Now they formed a hideous tableau that reminded Cusack of the worst of his nightmares. He looked away instantly.

Scanning the dimly lit boiler room, holding his weapon at

the ready, he saw no sign of movement and deduced that Joshua could only be behind the boiler, waiting for the right moment to open fire. That moment would be when Cusack advanced into the shaft of light that fell obliquely from an overhead bulb to illuminate the area of floor that he would have to cross.

Realizing this, Cusack did not advance. Instead, he took a few steps backwards and to the side until he was against the wall of the corridor, hidden by the darkness. Clearly, Joshua was depending on the boiler's steel sides to protect him and was assuming that Cusack would, sooner or later, have to advance across that exposed ground to locate him. Cusack, however, had other ideas.

Quietly, he lowered his sub-machine gun to the floor and withdrew his more powerful Herstal Five-seveN pistol from its holster. While Joshua would be aware that the MP5 sub-machine gun, like most of the SAS's old weapons, would not be able to puncture the boiler with its orthodox firepower, he was not to know that this particular lightweight handgun fired what were essentially scaled-down rifle shells with 5.7mm rounds that could punch holes in brick walls, pass through tree trunks or pierce forty-eight layers of laminated Kevlar armour at 200 metres. The weapon also held four times as many bullets as the .44 Magnum: more than enough, Cusack thought with satisfaction, to complete this particular task.

Spreading his legs in the classic firing position, holding the weapon in the regulation two-handed grip and taking aim at the large, rusty boiler about midway up its vertical, just above the heads of the upright bloody corpses in that hideous tableau of death, Cusack called out, 'I know you're there, Joshua. You can't get away, so why not come out with your hands up? Otherwise you'll be finished.'

There was silence for a moment. Then Joshua made the mistake of replying, thereby giving Cusack a rough idea of his target's position behind the high boiler.

'Who are you?' Joshua asked, his voice reverberating eerily from behind the left end of the boiler, where clearly he was preparing to leap out and fire his weapon as soon as Cusack advanced into the light.

'SAS,' Cusack replied.

'A sanctioned killer for the Establishment,' Joshua said. 'A disciple of Satan. Go fuck yourself, you shit-eating pig.'

'If you come out with your hands up,' Cusack replied, 'I promise to take you in. If you don't, I'll have no choice but to kill you.'

'If you want me, you'll have to come and get me. Let's do this face to face, scumbag.'

'No, thanks,' Cusack said.

He fired several rapid shots, moving the Herstal's barrel from left to right, cutting a line across where he had gauged that Joshua was standing. The noise was appalling, reverberating around the basement as bullets slammed through the front of the boiler and came out the other side, some ricocheting off the high wall to send pieces of splintered brick flying out in all directions from boiling clouds of pulverized mortar. Cusack heard a brief scream, the metallic clatter of a falling weapon, a breathless curse, then more rattling from the dropped weapon. Not waiting for the silence to return, assuming that he had at least wounded his target and that the injured man was now groping about on the floor, he launched himself across that area of exposed ground into the obliquely falling shaft of light, firing his pistol two-handed while on the move. This time he heard a high-pitched metallic drumming as his 5.7mm bullets went straight through the boiler, more exploding of bricks, the whining of other rounds when they ricocheted off the wall, and the raining down of shattered plaster and mortar. Cusack only stopped, nearly choking in the dust, when he reached the right-hand end of the boiler, mere inches from the booted foot of one of the slumping, dead, blood-soaked hostages.

Placing his back to the boiler, still holding the lightweight, powerful pistol in a two-handed grip, though now with the weapon's barrel pointing up vertically in front of his face, he listened keenly and heard ragged gasping coming from behind the boiler's far end.

Breathing as quietly and as evenly as possible, Cusack lowered his pistol to the firing position and inched his way around until he had reached the boiler's other side. Its back was about a metre away from the high brick wall off which some of his bullets had ricocheted. He could hear the spasmodic gasping more clearly now, and could judge from it that Joshua had indeed been badly wounded and was now stretched out on the floor, possibly with his weapon back in his hands. However, knowing that Joshua would be expecting him to come around the other end of the boiler, where he had aimed his first burst of fire, Cusack carefully moved his head out from behind the boiler to glance along the dimly lit space between it and the wall.

Wearing blue denims, suede sneakers and what had once been a white shirt, his dark hair cropped short on his straining neck, Joshua was stretched out on his belly on the floor. His back was bloody and torn: Cusack's bullets had gone in one side and out the other to smash his ribcage and cause even worse damage. More ominously, at least for Joshua, blood was seeping out from beneath him to form a blackish-red pool around his prone body. Though a mangled and terminal mess, he was still painfully trying to reach the Glock 9mm semi-automatic handgun that he had dropped when Cusack's bullets had slammed into him.

'Don't bother,' Cusack said, stepping out from behind the boiler, still holding his Five-seveN pistol in the two-handed firing position and aiming it at Joshua's shattered, bloody spine.

Joshua stiffened automatically at the sound of Cusack's voice. Then he cursed hoarsely and rolled on to his back, wincing with pain as his open wounds pressed against the hard ground. He strained to raise his head and look directly at Cusack as the SAS man, still aiming his pistol, advanced along the walkway between the boiler and the wall. When Cusack reached the wounded man, he spread his legs over him to plant one foot on either side and aimed the pistol at his head. Joshua was only about thirty years old and had ascetic, almost handsome features and a steely-grey, psychotic, perceptive gaze. Though clearly mortally wounded and in terrible pain, he managed to offer Cusack a mocking smile.

'So what happens now?' he asked.

'What do you want to happen?' Cusack replied. 'Either you die or you spend the rest of your life in prison. The choice is all yours.'

'Do I really have a choice?'

'Yes, you do,' Cusack said.

'Up yours, motherfucker,' Joshua said. 'I don't have to choose at all. When I look at you, at the helpless decency in your face, the Christian values etched there, I know you're not the kind to kill an unarmed man, much less one who's wounded. You're too soft for that, you reamed-out arsehole.'

'You really think so?' Cusack said.

'Yes, I think so.'

Cusack blew the cunt's brains out.

# CHAPTER TWO

He was, outwardly, yet another of the growing number of those who preferred to live in shadowy isolation while communicating with the outer world via fax, e-mail and the World Wide Web, eschewing most forms of human contact except when he was the one in charge. His personal dark place was a dingy flat in an old conversion in Cricklewood, north London, an area swarming with working-class Paddies, whom he could use, but also with the Indians, Pakis, Chinks, Greeks, Turks, Jews, Muslims and assorted Blacks that he hated so much. In truth, his hatreds were many – and increasing with each passing day of his thirty-fifth year.

He looked his age and then some. Sitting at his work table, which was cluttered with old newspapers and political magazines, CD-ROMs, boxed and loose computer diskettes, and a wide variety of software packages, gazing into his upgraded Dell 310 computer system, with its helpful 640MB hard disk, he was temporarily lost in cyberspace, that on-line world of possibilities for the dispossessed and the paranoid. He was pale, gaunt and intense, eyes as green and fathomless as a cat's, blond hair almost golden and hanging to his shoulders, features coarsened by early deprivation and subsequent depravity, though oddly softened by a hint of femininity that many women found dangerously attractive.

He had been up most of the night, surfing the Internet, interacting passionately with its newbies and perns, hackers and crackers, flamers and thrashers, surfers and posters and lurkers and ghouls, its group-mind fundamentalists and cyber-terrorists, all keeping in touch through their news-groups, chat groups, bulletin boards and mailing lists, some-times even communicating as avatars in three-dimensional environments, living ghosts in the system. What most of them had in common, he knew, was a distaste for f2f (face-to-face) encounters and IRL (in real life) relationships. What mostly linked them together, he also knew, was their fascination with what cyberspace had to offer in place of real time's tedium: sex-and-violence movies, soft and hard pornography, every kind of bizarre religion, New Age politics, Millennialist philosophies, paranoid conspiracy theories, general subver-sion, revolution and, most important, illegal information on the purchase and manufacture of conventional weapons, explosives, bombs, poisons and various kinds of biological warfare, all of which interested him greatly.

Now it was close to noon. Surprisingly alert for one so sleepless, he completed his surfing, culling the last of the information he needed for the next stage of his master plan, then escaped from the Net. He clicked on his colourful screen saver (a constantly repeating cosmic explosion that he felt was appropriate to him), then spun around in his swivelling chair and stood up to face his poky flat – a dark, dirty hole.

*I'm worth a lot more than this,* he thought bitterly, *and soon the whole world will know it. My time is coming at last.*

This thought was encouraged by his distaste for his flat, which consisted of two rooms: a cramped combined bedroom and living room with hideously flowered, stained wallpaper, unwashed lace curtains, threadbare carpets and junk-shop furniture, and an even smaller room with a makeshift shower and toilet and walls of fake pine. What little space there had been was now taken up with his computer workstation and with the high piles of propaganda leaflets that lined all four walls. The propaganda was racially orientated and filled with paranoid conspiracy theories that included evil plots being woven by the British government, the Royal Family, the Jews, the Blacks and other 'immigrants' to destroy what was left of the former 'Great' Britain. Ironically, the flat was situated above an Indian restaurant in Cricklewood Lane and the stench of curry had wafted up through the floorboards for many years as a permanent reminder to him of just how 'foreign' his country had become. The British Empire had gathered in its flock to swamp the English in aliens.

*Ethnic cleansing is the only cure*, he thought, *and it will come in good time. But the first task is to bring down the government. And that starts today.*

Too excited to be affected by his lack of sleep, he shucked off his filthy white-towelling dressing gown, had a hot shower and washed his hair, then put on an open-necked shirt, blue denims and black leather boots. After drying and combing his long blond hair, which looked even more golden when washed, he sat down to a light breakfast of shredded wheat with milk, followed by a cup of hot tea. When he had finished, he put on a black leather jacket and left the flat. After locking the door carefully behind him, he descended the stairs to go out through a doorway at the side of the Indian restaurant. As always, the stink of last night's curries made him bristle with anger.

'Filthy wogs!' he muttered.

Turning into Cricklewood Lane, which was as busy as ever, the pavements packed with polyglot pedestrians and wet from a recent rainfall, the roads jammed with noisy traffic and swept by a cold wind, the sky low and leaden, he walked a short distance, past the usual mixture of English cafés, kebab houses and African vegetable shops, to enter the first pub he came to. A small and informal Irish place with a giant TV at one end and a dartboard at the other, it was already busy at ten minutes before noon, with some of the drunken Paddies singing maudlin songs and the air wreathed in unhealthy cigarette smoke. Disgusted by the sight of them, but mindful of the fact that they were at least white and that the younger ones could be recruited if required, he went to the bar, brushing his hair from his high forehead and smiling at Mary, the middle-aged, softly rounded and usually sharp-tongued barmaid – though with him she was always the soul of kindness.

Returning his smile, she said, 'Mornin', love. Still teetotal, are you? Coke with ice as usual?'

'You've got it,' he said.

'No wonder you look so healthy.'

'Pure in body and mind,' he responded, smiling once more. 'I quote from the good book: *Look to your health; and if you have it, praise God, and value it next to a good conscience.*'

'Sure, it's nice to know that some still read their Bible,' Mary said, though clearly she herself had not read hers in years since the quotation was, in fact, from *The Compleat Angler* by Izaak Walton, who had died in 1683 at ninety years of age, thus proving that he had practised what he preached. 'Sure, these days, with all the filth that's goin' on, we could do with more religion, not less, like.'

'Amen to that, Mary.'

Charmed to have a Christian gentleman in this bar of old soaks, turned on by the superficial warmth in his voice, by his clear green gaze that had already seduced so many, Mary went to fetch his drink, briefly leaving him free with his thoughts which were, had she but known it, apocalyptic. Surveying the other customers in the mirror above the bar, he was appalled at the number of empty pint mugs already on the tables taken over by groups of working-class Irishmen in their gabardines, grey or black coats, open-necked shirts under woollen pullovers, black shoes and soft peaked caps. Clearly, they had started drinking at eleven in the morning and were already well on the way to being legless. By two o'clock, when most decent people would just be finishing their lunch, this lot would be in their beds, resting before returning for another booze-up in the late afternoon. It was a pitifully narrow way of life, a form of living suicide of the kind that could make him choke up with anger. He felt that way right now.

*From the cradle to the grave*, he thought, *without doing one worthy thing in between. They might as well be the walking dead for all the use they are to society. They should have been put down at birth.*

When Mary brought his drink, he paid her immediately and gave her another winning smile, charming her totally whilst studying her face and deciding that she was, if pleasant and lively, not much brighter than most of her dumb customers. Another wasted life, in fact. No doubt she would have benefited from what he had to offer, but he preferred those he chose to be younger, more impressionable, less prone to revolt, ready to be putty in his hands, ripe to be moulded.

He checked his wristwatch. Where the fuck was Simmonds? He should have been here by now. Any kind of delay would be intolerable. Having to listen to these drunken Paddies singing was enough to ruin any day, let alone this important one.

'So what are you up to?' Mary asked him, pressing her large breasts against the counter to make them bulge up under his nose. 'Still lookin' for work?'

He nodded. 'Never stop looking, Mary. No luck so far, though.'

'Sure, these aren't the best of times at all for those wanting to work. Jobs are scarce all round.'

'Quite right,' he said, thinking bitterly of the growing number of unemployed, of the widening gap between rich and poor, the rising crime and increasing racial disharmony that was turning the country into a war zone. He had suffered like a lot of the others, but those days were over now.

'Must be hard,' Mary said sympathetically, 'for someone still as young as you to have no work and be deprived of life's little luxuries.'

'I don't complain, Mary. I turn again to the good book: *He raiseth up the poor out of the dust, and lifteth the needy out of the dunghill* . . . In other words, the Lord will reward me. Of this I'm quite sure.'

'He will,' Mary said, nodding agreement, deeply touched to find someone so religious. 'Sure, faith like yours can move mountains. But you should think of getting yourself a nice wee girl and making a life for yourself. You're too old to be single, like.'

'I'm too poor to be married,' he lied. 'And thirty-five isn't too old.'

'You'll be forty before you know it,' Mary responded, 'and that's when the going gets really rough.'

'I'll survive. Don't you worry.'

At that moment, the door behind him opened and he glanced back over his shoulder to see Tom Simmonds entering the pub. In his late twenties, Simmonds was short and barrel-chested, with a broken nose, thinning brown hair cropped close to the skull, a penetrating brown-eyed gaze and a square block of a face flushed with constant drinking and scarred from a lot of fist fights. Now wrapped in a ski jacket that made him look even shorter and broader than he was, he nodded curtly in recognition and walked up to the bar.

'Hi, boss,' he said. 'Sorry I'm late. Got held up in the traffic. A five-mile tailback on the fucking M4. Almost drove me crazy, I can tell you.'

'No problem,' the blond-haired man said, though again he checked his wristwatch. 'Any time this afternoon will be fine, so we've a good bit of leeway. No time for a drink, though. We'll have to leave right now, Tom.'

Simmonds cast a yearning look at the bar, but nodded agreement. 'The sooner the better, as far as I'm concerned. That stuff makes me nervous.'

'What stuff?' Mary asked automatically, having overheard the conversation.

'The pints of Guinness he sees all around him,' the blond man lied. 'Mr Simmonds is off the drink, so he gets nervous in the presence of temptation. I think I'd best take him out of here.' He finished his own drink and put the glass back on the counter. 'Thanks, Mary. I'll see you anon.'

'Cheers,' Mary said.

The two men left the bar. Once outside, standing on the crowded pavement and buffeted by a strong wind, the blond man said, 'So where's the truck parked?'

'In a side street along the Broadway,' Simmonds replied. 'Three or four blocks down.'

'Good. Let's get to it.'

As they made their way along the wintry Broadway, in a tide of jostling pedestrians of many races, the blond man, glancing repeatedly about him, had his every prejudice confirmed.

'Just look at this place,' he said disgustedly. 'It's supposed to be England, *our* country, and what do we have here? Irish pubs, American hamburger joints, kebab houses, halal meat shops, Indian, Chinese, Italian, Turkish, African, Caribbean and even Abyssinian restaurants. Christ, even the bookies, taxi companies and second-hand furniture shops have been taken over by swarthies. If we're not careful, if we don't put a stop to it, we'll end up as a minority in our own country. Well, that's not going to happen!'

'Yeah,' Simmonds replied. 'We should follow the line of that Swedish group . . . what's its name?'

'The White Aryan Resistance.'

'Right. I mean, for years they've been shooting and bombing the shit out of all those Somalis, Kurds, Assyrians, Turks and Lebanese – even the refugees from Kosovo and Bosnia. And Sweden's supposed to be the most law-abiding country in Europe – so if *they*'re agitated about their immigrants, why can't we be?'

'Exactly. We're now inundated with the scum of the earth, immigrants from everywhere, from all the shitholes of the world – blackies and swarthies and half-castes and conspiring Jews, professional beggars and diseased whores, AIDS-carriers and born criminals, fanatical Muslims and all the others who despise our Western values – so we have to add

them to the list of our legitimate enemies and embark on
some cleansing operations. We have to exterminate them like
the vermin they are and build the country anew.'

'I'm with you there, boss,' Simmonds said in his mild,
mindless way. 'But right now, as you correctly pointed out,
we've got more important fish to fry.'

'Yes, indeed,' the blond man said.

In truth, while he and Simmonds agreed on certain
matters, notably those to do with race, the blond man had
little respect for his colleague, viewing him as just another of
the dumb bastards, cannon fodder, that he was forced to use
for certain – usually dangerous – tasks. In fact, he had only
taken Simmonds on when, during one of his own illegal
recruiting meetings at the old flying school in Wiltshire,
Simmonds, obviously none too bright but clearly keen to
create some mayhem, had confessed that he was holding in
storage at his small farm just outside Calne a compact
arsenal. This lethal cache included a wide variety of firearms,
a 60mm anti-tank rocket launcher, three 50-pound bags of
ammonium nitrate and dozens of 55-gallon plastic drums of
the kind often used for large bombs. Asked why he had
acquired such material, Simmonds, who was in regular
contact with the wide range of right-wing extremists on the
Internet in this, the year of Our Lord 2003, had explained that
he was preparing for the day when a sinister cabal of wealthy
bankers, politicians, media manipulators and highly placed
Jews would use British Special Service forces, probably the
SAS, to sweep across the country and eliminate covert anti-
government activists such as himself. This belief was enough
to ensure that Simmonds, no matter how dumb, was
recruited to the cause.

'It's just up here,' Simmonds said when he and the blond
man had walked two or three blocks, passing innumerable
establishments all run by the foreigners they both despised.
'Just a few yards along.'

'Parked legally, I hope?' the blond man said.

'On a meter,' Simmonds replied, turning into the side street and walking on with the blond man beside him. 'I was real careful, boss.'

They walked for another minute along the narrow, wind-blown street, packed with cars parked nose to tail on either side of the road, and stopped when they came to a battered Ford truck.

'This is it,' Simmonds said.

'And you did it exactly as I said?'

'Yes, boss. The rear's packed with nearly 5,000 pounds of ammonium nitrate fertilizer mixed with fuel oil, boosted with metal containers of acetylene to make it even more lethal and contained in twenty 55-gallon plastic drums. Wired to an electrical initiator and a control clock that can be set to any time you see fit.'

'No more than five minutes,' the blond man said.

'No problem,' Simmonds said. 'So how do we do it?'

'We simply drive there, park the truck a good way away from the killing zone – far enough away for the security guards not to be suspicious – then set the device for five minutes and get the hell out of there. Five minutes should be long enough for us to get out of reach of the blast while being short enough to ensure that the truck won't be checked. Are you happy to drive?'

'It's my truck,' Simmonds said.

'Good. Let's get going.'

They climbed into the truck. Simmonds turned on the ignition, then released the handbrake and started off. He drove to the far end of the narrow street, turned down the next street, then cut back into Cricklewood Broadway and headed for the West End. Not one word was spoken between them throughout the rest of the journey, doubtless due to mounting tension, though the blond man was certainly less tense than his companion. Being more experienced in this kind of operation, he distracted himself from his lingering doubts by gazing keenly about him as they crawled through the eternal traffic jam of Kilburn, filled with more Paddies and swarthies, then along Edgware Road, which might as well have been Kuwait, and then into Park Lane which, though still dominated by native whites, was also given over to tourists. The blond man did not disdain the tourists, who aided the economy and then departed. But he certainly resented the sight of the wealthy Arabs entering and leaving those expensive Park Lane hotels or, even worse, emerging from the streets of Mayfair which, just as they had done with Edgware, they were beginning to colonize. Naturally the present government let it happen, he believed, because, in these materialistic times, only money had value.

*A stern punishment is due*, the blond man thought, *and it will soon be administered . . . within minutes, in fact.*

To avoid the dense traffic of Piccadilly, Simmonds had driven around Hyde Park Corner to go along Constitution Hill and the Mall. Now, as Simmonds turned off the Mall and circled around Trafalgar Square, the blond man looked out and saw the tourists swarming like larvae on the steps of the National Gallery and forming a sea of bobbing heads in the square itself. As usual, they were feeding the pigeons that flocked around Nelson's Column and clambering disrespectfully on to Landseer's bronze lions to have their pictures taken, littering the ground with the cartons and wrappings of food purchased in American-style 'fast food' joints. The blond man was disgusted.

'Take the first space you see,' he said as Simmonds drove the truck into Whitehall. 'If you've made the bomb properly, the blast should do everything we want, no matter how far we are from the forecourt of Horse Guards Parade – and we won't be that far.'

'Why not park at the far end?' Simmonds responded. 'That way we might at least get Ten Downing Street.'

'It's not worth the risk. If we parked anywhere near Downing Street or the Cenotaph, the police would check us immediately. Up this end, with the theatre, pubs and restaurants, they won't take any notice until it's too late. Lots of vehicles park here temporarily when they make their deliveries, so we should be okay.'

'That makes sense,' Simmonds said.

He found a space almost immediately, between two other illegally parked delivery trucks, directly opposite the Whitehall Theatre, close to Great Scotland Yard and obliquely across the road from the old Admiralty. Tourists were photographing the winged sea horses on the central Admiralty arch, packing the pavement on that side of the road. Farther along, below the middle arch and clock tower of Horse Guards Parade, an immense crowd of yet more tourists was filling the space in front of the forecourt entrance, where they were photographing and otherwise tormenting the two rigidly immobile Blue and Royal Life Guards of the Household Cavalry Mounted Regiment.

After turning off the truck's ignition, Simmonds applied the handbrake and licked his dry lips. 'Well,' he said, 'here we are. The control clock is by my right hand, just under the dashboard. Do I set it right now?'

'Yes,' the blond man said. 'To go off in precisely five minutes.'

Simmonds licked his lips, wiped beads of sweat from his forehead, then leaned forward, tilting slightly sideways, to turn the dial on the control clock, setting the timer for five minutes ahead. When he was finished, he straightened up again and started opening the door on his side of the cabin.

'Okay,' he said anxiously. 'Let's go.'

'Not yet,' the blond man said.

Simmonds turned back, surprised. Before he could register what was happening, the blond man had jabbed a hypodermic needle through Simmonds's trousers and into his fleshy thigh. Feeling the sharp prick of the needle, Simmonds looked down in surprise and watched in a seeming trance as the blond man emptied the syringe, poisoning Simmonds's bloodstream, then just as quickly withdrew the needle. In a state of disbelief, Simmonds looked up again. But even before he could ask the obvious question, he felt the paralysis numbing his limbs and racing up to his heart. He died seconds later, sitting upright, his limbs still frozen, his eyes open but unseeing. The blond man propped him gently against the seat.

'God bless you,' the blond man said.

Knowing that the truck would be totally destroyed in the forthcoming explosion, he put the empty syringe on to the seat beside the lifeless Simmonds, then opened the passenger door and dropped down to the pavement. Closing the door, leaving Simmonds sitting up there, looking as if he was still alive, the blond man walked at a normal pace back to Trafalgar Square, went right around the square, then mingled with the tourists crowding the steps of the National Gallery. From there he could look straight across the square, his view of Whitehall only partially blocked by the soaring fluted granite of Nelson's Column.

A minute later, as he and the unsuspecting tourists looked on, the large bomb in the parked truck exploded, creating a hellish, unreal din, streaking the growing gloom with red and yellow flames, filling half of Whitehall with flying debris and billowing black smoke, covering the road with a nightmarish hail of smashed glass, broken bricks, pulverized concrete, red-hot metal fragments, smouldering pieces of burned wood – and dismembered, scorched human limbs.

As sirens started wailing, as the full extent of the appalling devastation was revealed, as the tourists around the blond man screamed and shook and sobbed, he smiled and went down the steps of the National Gallery to make his way back to the dark, dirty hole he would soon be leaving for good.

*I am a prince*, he thought.

# CHAPTER THREE

'"Prince"?' the Secretary of COBR asked wearily. 'What kind of name is that? "Satan" or "Jesus" or "Joshua" I'd understand – invariably the Millennialists go for those biblical connections – but . . . *Prince*? I'm sorry. I'm confused.'

'That's all his signature says,' Daniel Edmondson, the MI5 representative, replied, sounding almost as weary as the Secretary. Edmondson was approaching retirement age and starting to yearn for it. 'Prince. He may have taken it from that rock singer of a few years back – the guy who dropped his name altogether, replaced it with some weird symbol and then dropped out of sight.'

'Any connection?'

'Only in the sense that the original Prince's act was fairly outrageous and this Prince seems determined to be out-rageous too, though in a vastly more destructive, dangerous manner. In other words, he does more than sing songs.'

'Damned right,' the Secretary said, now tight-lipped, his gaze brightened by anger under his thatch of silvery-grey hair. 'He blew up half of Whitehall with a bomb so big that its blast reached almost all the way from Trafalgar Square to Downing Street. The very building in which we sit, this very basement, also received damage, admittedly minor. So, yes, this Prince *certainly* does more than sing.'

'So what *was* the damage?' asked Brigadier Leonard Wesley Moorland, Supreme Commander of the Combined Services. 'Do we have an official report yet?'

'Alas, yes,' said William Hargreaves, the surprisingly mild and softly spoken Commissioner for the Metropolitan Police. 'I have it right here.'

These men and others were gathered together in a wood-panelled basement room in the Old Home Office in Whitehall, a building that had escaped most of the blast from the recent bombing, though it had received some minor damage, as had the buildings in Downing Street. The men formed a top-level management team known oddly as COBR, though this was really just an acronym for 'Cabinet Office Briefing Room'. All of them, including the Police Commissioner and Lieutenant Colonel Maurice Blackwell, the present Commanding Officer of the Special Forces Group, wore pinstriped suits and public-school ties. They were all Establishment figures, now enjoying Courvoisier brandy and Havana cigars at the taxpayers' expense. Above the long table, above the Secretary's head, was a rather grim painting of the Queen, Elizabeth II. Her dead gaze fell upon them.

'So?' Brigadier Moorland asked pointedly, after too long a pause. 'What does it say?'

The Police Commissioner looked down at his report and paraphrased from it. 'The bomb is believed to be of the type first used in the Oklahoma City bombing of 1995 and currently favoured by terrorist groups of all kinds, though it was larger than any used before. Judging by the size of the blast, we must assume that it was composed of at least five thousand pounds of explosive, almost certainly ammonium nitrate fertilizer mixed with fuel oil in plastic drums and boosted with metal containers of hydrogen or acetylene. The epicentre of the explosion was near the pavement directly facing the Whitehall Theatre. Examination of the resultant debris has confirmed that the bomb was carried there by truck and that the truck, with the explosives in the rear, was then parked and the bomb was set off with a timing device. Bodily remains indicate that the driver of the truck was killed in the blast.'

'Dumb bastard!' Brigadier Moorland snorted contemptuously. 'Probably mistimed the explosion and blew himself up by accident. Bloody amateur!'

'This particular "bloody amateur",' the Police Commissioner continued sardonically, while still staring down at his notes, 'managed with his home-made bomb to devastate the southern side of Trafalgar Square, causing serious damage to Nelson's Column, which will now have to be pulled down, the destruction of two of the Landseer bronze lions, the complete obliteration of the Charles I statue and major damage to the buildings in that area. With regard to Whitehall itself, everything within a one-hundred-metre area of the epicentre of the blast was completely destroyed, including the old Admiralty, a lot of Great Scotland Yard, the old War Office, the entrance and forecourt to Horse Guards Parade, the Scottish Office right beside it, the Banqueting House directly opposite, and the Welsh Office. There was minor damage to parts of the old Treasury, the Ministry of Defence, Downing Street and even this very building. The cost in human terms has been appalling, with a couple of hundred dead and many more wounded or badly burned. The bombing was, in short, the most damaging terrorist attack this city has ever known. Even the IRA at their worst never came close to it.'

'God Almighty,' the Senior Foreign Affairs minister, Anthony Courtland-Smith, exclaimed softly, shaking his head from side to side in disbelief.

The Police Commissioner looked up from the papers and glanced at the others around the table. 'So,' he said, 'this mysterious Mister Prince is clearly a man to be reckoned with. Especially when you consider what he has stated in the letter he sent us, claiming responsibility for the bombing. This letter is more than a simple confession: it's a statement of intent.'

'I don't think I want to hear this,' Edmondson said.

'I do,' Brigadier Moorland said. 'I want to hear every word.'

'So do I,' the Secretary said, 'so please read it, William.'

The Police Commissioner nodded. 'Right.' He picked up Prince's letter, which he had virtually memorized, reminded himself of what was in it, then put it down again, though he glanced frequently at it as he talked. 'The letter came to us from Paris, with a French stamp on it, but it's on the letterhead paper of the British Millennialist Movement.'

'I've never heard of it,' Lieutenant Colonel Blackwell said. 'Over the past three years or so, ever since the Millennium, I've fought a wide variety of right-wing extremists and religious terrorists – most of them in so-called Millennialist movements – but I've never heard of that particular one.'

'Me neither,' said Daniel Edmondson, 'and MI5 is keeping tabs on every group of that kind. It's a new one on me. You think it's Paris-based?'

'We doubt it,' Hargreaves said, speaking on behalf of his Metropolitan Police intelligence officers. 'We believe the letter was taken by hand to Paris and posted from there to ensure that we couldn't trace its true source from the postmark. We believe that this organization, the British Millennialist Movement, is based right here in Britain.'

'God, not another one!' Courtland-Smith exclaimed, expressing the committee's common frustration at the sheer number of so-called Millennialist groups that had sprung up in the country as the year 2000 approached. At the time, it had been assumed that once the year 2000 had passed without any sign of a great, magical event (either a Second Coming or an extraterrestrial invasion, both of which had been hotly favoured by the Millennium freaks) the disillusioned Millennialists would have dispersed. But such had not been the case. In fact, once they'd got their excuse to get together – in which they'd been aided greatly by the ever-expanding Internet – membership of the Millennialist groups had increased dramatically. Now, three years after the disappointingly mundane reality of the actual Millennium, they had found any number of new beliefs to replace the old and the number of individual groups had multiplied so greatly that the Millennialist movement had become a separate, highly dangerous subculture. Having found plenty of new beliefs to replace the old, mainly a mind-boggling variety of paranoid conspiracy theories, all of which were supported by easy access via the Internet to fellow conspiracy freaks worldwide, the Millennialists were immune to reason and increasingly anti-authoritarian and subversive. Also, given easy access on the Internet to the purchase of ex-Soviet Bloc weapons and explosives, as well as instructions for the manufacture of home-made bombs, they were becoming increasingly well armed and dangerously motivated. The past five years had seen a dramatic increase in terrorist atrocities by Millennialist terrorists, so this latest outrage, falling as it did into that category, had to be taken seriously.

'So what does Prince, or his damned organization, want?' the Secretary asked impatiently.

'It's worse than you can imagine, Mr Secretary.'

'Just read the letter.'

Hargreaves sighed, then picked up the letter and read from it. '"This is a declaration of war. I write as the Head of the British Millennialist Movement to inform you that we were responsible for the bomb that went off in Whitehall yesterday. That bombing was intended as a statement of intent and our intention is to bring down the corrupt British government and, more importantly, to get rid of the satanic Royal Family. Our former 'Great Britain' is now in terminal decline, both materially and spiritually, and has clearly become the Babylon of our sinful times, headed by a secretive, degenerate Royal Family. Despite this secrecy the following facts are known to us: (1) Elizabeth II is the Queen of Babylon and the patroness of English Freemasonry. (2) The followers of the Queen of Babylon are entrenched in the civil service, in the police force, in the judiciary and even in MI5 and other British intelligence organizations. (3) It is from London, England, that the Antichrist is coming because the Royal Family is part of the ancient Illuminati society, dedicated to the ultimate dominion of the whole world. Knowing these facts, the British Millennialist Movement is bestowing the ultimate blessing on British society by dedicating itself to the physical obliteration of the satanic Royal Family through a campaign of righteous terrorism that will, ultimately, clear the way for the coming of the Lord of Light, our Saviour, on Judgement Day, the day after Doomsday. I, Prince, am a disciple of our Saviour, the Lord of Light, sitting at His right hand, and I personally will lead the British Millennialist Movement to victory. Yesterday's bombing was merely the commencement of our religious, just war. There is much more to come. War has now been officially declared. Yours faithfully, Prince . . ."'

A lengthy, shocked silence followed the Police Commissioner's reading. The men filled it with the distraction of minor activities, such as the relighting of cigars and the pouring of more brandy. Eventually, when the smokers were all puffing nervously and the drinkers had sipped more brandy, the Secretary glanced up at the painting of Queen Elizabeth, looked briefly, pointedly, at each of the men around the long table, then cleared his throat by coughing into his clenched fist.

'Clearly,' he said, 'our excellent Police Commissioner did not exaggerate when he said that this was worse than we were expecting. It certainly is.' He sighed and had a sip of his brandy, then turned to Daniel Edmondson, his silvery-haired, still handsome and always urbane MI5 representative. 'Do you have any comment to make about this?'

'Yes, Mr Secretary. The ideas expressed by this so-called Prince have been bandied about for years by the American Patriot, or Millennarian, Movement, which is why we've been trying to keep that organization out of England. However, given that most of these movements now communicate via the World Wide Web, the Internet, and that they are using that medium of communication to swap ideas, recruit new members, and gain access to information on everything from weaponry and explosives to biological warfare, the possibility of keeping them out is minuscule and we now believe them to be operating here through their British members. This British Millennialist Movement, headed by this so-called Prince, is either connected to its American counterpart or is merely picking up its paranoid ideas from them. Either way, since the American movement, essentially a white supremacist movement with religious overtones, believes in violent means of social change and may, indeed, have been tied to the notorious Oklahoma City bombing, I believe we have to use all means at our disposal to find out just who this so-called Prince is, then track him down and neutralize him *and* his organization.'

'Neutralize?' the Secretary asked. 'How?'

'By any means at our disposal – and with extreme prejudice if necessary.'

The Secretary looked doubtful. 'You think this British movement will be that bad?'

Edmondson nodded affirmatively. 'Judging by what we've just heard, I'd say they would be. The tone of the letter is essentially religious and that's always a bad sign. The number of terrorist groups driven by religious rather than political zeal is on the rise. Right now, even here in England, we're dealing with our own brand of Christian white supremacists – of whom this Prince sounds like one – as well as messianic Jews, radical Sikhs and Muslim fundamentalists. This particular brand of terrorist isn't out merely to score political points but to wipe out entire classes of those he deems to be enemies; and it's this kind of terrorist, more than any other, who's into chemical and biological weapons because his religion can justify . . .' Here Edmondson shrugged as if defeated, then added: '*Anything*.'

'Right,' William Hargreaves said. 'If God's telling you to do it, any means to an end is acceptable, no matter how obscene.'

Edmondson nodded affirmatively, smiling at the Police Commissioner by way of thanks for his support. Then he returned his steady gaze to the Secretary. 'William has just said it: for religious terrorists, anything goes. And judging by the tone of Prince's letter – the references to Doomsday and

Judgement Day and so forth – I'd say we're dealing with some kind of religious nut who's been influenced, at least in his view of the Royal Family, by this crazed American movement. That means he's an extremist of the worst kind who'll do just what he says.'

Another uneasy, lingering silence led to more sipping of brandy and the inhaling and exhaling of cigar smoke. Eventually, however, the Secretary broke the silence by looking at each of the others in turn, then addressing them all with the single question, 'Any ideas?'

Eyes flicked this way and that – at brandy glasses, the burning tips of cigars, the ghastly painting of Queen Elizabeth on the wall behind the Secretary, the walls themselves, the ceiling and the floor.

'I asked a question,' the Secretary said eventually, 'and I expect an answer. William, what about you?'

The Police Commissioner shook his head from side to side, saying, 'I don't think the endgame is a police job. I think we're faced with an armed force here. Millennialist movements are invariably large in numbers, always well armed and prepared to fight to the death with God on their side, despite the fact that He didn't materialize, as they had imagined He would, during the year 2000. Given my past experience with this kind of business – dealing with religious fanatics who wish to change the political spectrum and assume that God is on their side – I'm convinced that we work best when kept out of the political arena. We should stay in the background, quietly get on with our investigations, and then call in the Special Forces when force is required. I think that's the situation we have here, so I'm willing to extend all the help I can during the initial stages, though I won't involve my men in an actual conflict. I'd lose more than I'd gain.'

'I agree,' Daniel Edmondson said. 'The police, particularly in London, are already stretched to their limit. This particular job could be time-consuming and end in violence, so they should be excused.'

'Leonard?' the Secretary said, turning to Brigadier Moorland.

'Not a straightforward army job. Not the paratroopers, either. It needs soldiers who specialize in undercover work and that certainly suggests the Special Forces, the SAS in particular. Would you not agree, Maurice?'

He had addressed the question to Lieutenant Colonel Blackwell, the 45-year-old commander of 22 SAS, still based in Stirling Lines, Hereford. Because a particular regimental restriction had been lifted in 2001, Blackwell was the first officer to be allowed to serve in the regiment for more than three years at a stretch. This had given him an edge over his predecessors, lending him more authority, and it showed now in his calm self-possession. His gaze was steady and fearless.

'Yes,' he said to Brigadier Moorland, 'I do agree. This job can't be done solely by the police and it can't be done with conventional forces.'

'Why not?' the senior Foreign Affairs minister, Anthony Courtland-Smith, asked in his ignorance.

'Because the Millennialists don't wage war in a conventional manner,' Lieutenant Colonel Blackwell replied without hesitation. 'Being absolutely fanatical – with God on their side, as William here put it – they wage war not only with ordinary firearms, but also with home-made bombs or chemical and biological weapons. As we've heard, they obtain the information they need from similar groups and individuals through the seemingly uncontrollable Internet and from private radio stations, including the notorious Radio Free World and many other short-wave and FM stations that are loosely or directly tied to rightist military and cultist organizations around the world. For this very reason, it was reckoned that even the conventional – for want of a better word – SAS wouldn't be up to the task and a specially trained SAS-based QRF had to be formed.'

'Pardon?' Courtland-Smith asked. 'What was that?'

'QRF. Quick Reaction Force.'

'Oh. Sorry. *Do* continue.'

'Formed in the year 2000, the SAS QRF was specially trained to identify, locate and neutralize the lunatic fringe of activists – the Millennialists and so forth – with every means at their disposal, including the very latest weapons and state-of-the-art surveillance systems. They *were* successful. In fact, the QRF has already become a legend in its own time, far surpassing its parent organization, the SAS. It's tackled every kind of Millennialist threat, including fanatical arsonists, anti-government bombers, violent Jesus-freak motorcycle gangs and religious terrorists of every denomination, many holed up in heavily defended bunker camps in the countryside. So, yes, I think the QRF could do the job.'

'But have they done anything recently?' Courtland-Smith asked.

'Yes,' Blackwell replied. 'Only a week ago, a QRF led by Sergeant Lenny Cusack cleaned out a booby-trapped underground complex right here in London, in a disused East End waterworks, and neutralized a religious terrorist known as Joshua. In that instance, the Metropolitan Police –' at this point Blackwell nodded in the direction of Police Commissioner Hargreaves '– identified and located the target for us before we moved in, mainly because he was known to be operating out of this city. But certainly, in most cases, the QRF were involved from the start, albeit initially receiving aid from the police. I think Police Commissioner Hargreaves would agree that this worked fine for both of us.'

'I agree,' Hargreaves said.

'So we're all agreed,' the Secretary said, 'that the QRF is the best choice for this task?'

'Not *quite* agreed,' Brigadier Moorland said, surprising them. The Secretary raised his fine eyebrows, looking quizzical. The Brigadier glanced at Lieutenant Colonel Blackwell, then turned back to the Secretary. 'I have to remind you, Mr Secretary, that in recent years the SAS has come under fire from many quarters as a regiment that is, on the one hand, out of date and, on the other, increasingly engaged in activities that are not entirely in keeping with its former high ideals. This criticism is bound to reflect on its QRF and it *could* give us problems.'

Raising his eyebrows again, the Secretary turned his glacial gaze upon Lieutenant Colonel Blackwell. 'Maurice?'

'I agree that the regiment has had its problems in recent years,' Blackwell rejoindered, casting a glance of contempt in the direction of Brigadier Moorland, then giving the Secretary his full attention. 'But these have mostly arisen because the Combined Services Directorate, under the command of Brigadier Moorland, has repeatedly reduced our financial resources while at the same time insisting that we take on jobs that we've consistently tried – in vain – to refuse. The charge that the SAS is out of date is clearly rendered redundant in view of the many tasks that we've carried out successfully in the past decade, both at home and overseas. The second charge has virtually been created by the media and it's based on a fact that I can't deny: namely, that for about the past five years the regiment's original ideals have been compromised by the kind of work it has been ordered – I repeat: *ordered* – to do. Those orders came directly from the Combined Services Directorate and so we couldn't refuse them.'

This time the silence was one of embarrassment, though Brigadier Moorland did not share in this particular feeling. Unfazed, even amused, he simply smiled and nodded, as if agreeing with the SAS CO, then turned back to the Secretary and said, 'Whatever the rights or wrongs of this matter, Mr Secretary, I was obliged, given my own position, to express my doubts to you.'

'Your doubts have been noted,' the Secretary said frigidly, 'and despite them, it seems clear to me that the SAS should be given this important task.' He turned back to Lieutenant Colonel Blackwell. 'Obviously, given the significance of this operation, an exceptional man will have to be placed in charge. Do you have that man?'

'Yes,' Blackwell replied without hesitation, 'and I've already named him.'

'Sergeant Cusack is trouble,' Brigadier Moorland said.

'That's why I want him,' Blackwell said.

Sergeant Cusack was voted in.

# CHAPTER FOUR

Chloe was desperate. She had run out of money again, she wouldn't be able to pick up her benefits for another two days, and she hadn't had the daily dose of smack that she needed to keep her sane. Sniffling miserably, she wiped her runny nose, rolled off the creaking bed in her small, spartan room in the seedy hostel, examined herself in the cracked mirror above the stained enamel sink, and was shocked by what she saw – the dark rings under her big brown eyes, the chapped, adolescent lips, the pale, unhealthily hollow cheeks, the shoulders slumped in instinctive shame. She instantly turned away in self-disgust.

Nevertheless, she *was* desperate. Already, she could feel the first twitchings of deprivation, the electric shocks from her shattered nerves, the silent screaming of her need for another fix that she could not afford. She had no money for food, let alone for a fix, and the darkness was closing in fast. She simply had to get out.

Sitting wearily on the edge of the bed, she tugged black leather boots on over her stockings, then stood up to put on a bright blue ski jacket. Under the jacket she was wearing a cotton jumper, buttoned up the front to allow easy access to groping male hands, and a tight miniskirt that showed off her long, shapely legs. She wore no panties or brassiere. After zipping up the jacket and wiping her runny nose again, she left the room, locking the door carefully behind her. She made her way down the stairs, sighing with relief when she saw that the degenerate bastard who ran the place was not seated behind his desk in the small booth used as 'reception', then hurried out into the street, where darkness was falling and the cold was setting in. Shivering, she glanced left and right, hoping to see a potential client, but she saw only distracted pedestrians taking no notice of her as they made their way past piles of uncollected garbage. Disappointed, feeling worse every second, she decided to head for King's Cross Station to try to pick up someone there.

The area around the station was depressing, filled with cheap cafés, seedy pubs and a proliferation of run-down hostels used mostly by the growing number of unemployed who subsisted on ever-shrinking state benefits. Unemployed herself since coming to London about eighteen months ago, addicted to drugs and slowly but surely being mentally destroyed by them, Chloe could look back on her former life in Birmingham only with the utmost distress. Like so many young people, she had come to London to find the work denied her in the Midlands, but had found only a similar lack of work in the south and even worse conditions for the jobless. She had left home without informing her parents: two decent, deeply religious, uninspiring people, both of them also unemployed for too long. Now, as she made her way through the mean streets around King's Cross Station, thinking with woe about what she was going to do, she remembered them and knew that, despite her love for them, she could never let them know what had happened to her.

An only child, not born until her parents were well into their thirties, which made them older than most parents, Chloe had been overprotected until she had come to London. Smothered by their exaggerated concern for their only child, failing to find gainful employment upon leaving school at sixteen, becoming pregnant by her first boyfriend and then having a secret abortion, she had fled to London hoping to find a new life, determined not to tell her parents where she was until she succeeded.

In fact, her new life had soon turned into a nightmare. Arriving in London with her pitiful savings, she had been so overwhelmed and frightened that she had trusted the first young man she had met when she got off the train. Clearly seeing her confusion as she stood on the station concourse uncertain about what to do, the young man had introduced himself as David Peel, a worker with the Young Persons' Shelter, a charitable organization devoted to helping the increasing number of young people arriving from the provinces who, like Chloe, hoped to find work. Chloe had believed him. When he had invited her to accompany him to a nearby boarding house where, he said, she could have cheap lodging for the night, she had agreed to go with him. The following morning, he assured her, he would take her to the Young Persons' Shelter and get her fixed up with a job and proper accommodation. Upon arrival at the boarding house, which had struck even the naive Chloe as being particularly seedy, he had booked her in, telling her that his organization would take care of the bill, and then escorted her up to a tiny room. Once she had been unburdened of her luggage, which David had placed on the bed for her, he had invited her out for a meal and a drink.

The meal, which Chloe had insisted on paying for, was in a McDonald's and after that they had retired to a nearby pub where Chloe soon became drunk on too many neat vodkas. She did not recall making her way back to the boarding house, but clearly she had done so because the next morning, when she woke up, she had a blinding hangover and a vague memory of having sex with David. Even worse, she discovered that someone, obviously David, had stolen all her savings, leaving her with no money at all.

Confessing to the burly middle-aged landlord of the boarding house that she could not pay her bill, she had been threatened with the police who would, so the landlord informed her, throw her in jail. Terrified not only of jail but by the thought that the police, if called, would inform her parents of her whereabouts, she had broken down into tears and begged the man not to report her. He had agreed on condition that she let him have sex with her, which she did, trembling fearfully throughout the sordid encounter. From that point on, it was all downhill.

Now, as Chloe made her way to the station, passing seedy pubs and cafés and more piles of uncollected garbage, whipped by a cold wind that blew papers around her feet, she avoided looking at the beggars, drunks and prostitutes on the wet, lamplit pavements, not wishing to be reminded of her own condition, of how low she had sunk. While refusing to think of herself as a whore, telling herself that what she was doing was only temporary, a vital, brief necessity, she knew in her secret heart that this was what she was becoming and was aware that if her parents found out their hearts would be broken.

*This is definitely the last time*, she thought. *Just one more to get me through the night and let me make a fresh start in the morning. Tomorrow I'll find someone to help me and then start a new life. No more after this.*

This was, of course, a resolution that Chloe had made many times before though had never managed to keep. This she realized with despair as she turned out of a side street and saw the Great Northern terminus of King's Cross Station, brightly lit within, people pouring in and out of the concourse, scrambling for the taxis arriving and departing constantly or queuing up for the double-decker buses which, also brightly lit inside, looked warm and inviting. Shivering, Chloe crossed the road and took up a position at the side of the station, in the shadow of the high wall, and started smiling automatically at every man who passed by, inviting each to stop and make an offer.

Drifting out of herself, divorcing herself from her own actions, she still could not avoid recalling her slide down the slippery slope, beginning with that first night in the bed of her landlord and continuing when he encouraged her to try some marijuana. Over the next few days, he had introduced her to smack and then, when she was regularly sharing his bed in return for food, accommodation and the drug she now needed, had recommended, when she pleaded for another fix, that she earn the money she required by walking the streets. Hopelessly addicted by then, she did as he suggested, despite her revulsion, and from that point on she was doomed.

Now, standing in the shadows, trying to smile coquettishly with her badly chapped lips, Chloe sensed that at eighteen years of age her life was practically over. There would be no fresh start tomorrow. It was too late for that. Already every nerve in her body was shrieking for smack, for another urgent fix, and the need for it was so overwhelming that she wanted to die. Instead she sold herself again. The man guided her up an alleyway. He took her standing upright, pressed against a damp brick wall, one hand unbuttoning her jumper, the other hitching up her miniskirt, then frantically squeezing her rump with both hands as he thrust up inside her, his cock encased in a condom. He came, gasping and groaning, shuddering convulsively for some time. Then he released her and let her feet settle back on the ground before, instead of handing her money, throwing his first punch.

Chloe was stunned by that first blow, the clenched fist against her belly, and was doubling up when the other blows came in rapid succession to hammer her ribcage. She opened her mouth to scream but the breath had been knocked out of her, so she simply threw her hands up to protect her face as the beating continued. 'Cunt!' he muttered. 'Whore!' He hammered harder and harder, quickly, repeatedly, as if working out with a punchbag, breathing harshly, obscenely excited. She felt sharp, stabbing pains, the snapping of some ribs, and then, knocking her hands aside, he went for her face, punching one cheek, then the other, splitting her lower lip before she dropped on to her knees and leaned her head forward protectively. He punched the back of her head and neck, accompanying each blow with a grunt, then, when she fell face down on the pavement, he put the boot in. One kick, then a second, a pause and heavy breathing, then a third kick, another rib snapping, and then his footsteps receding. When the moaning of the wind was all she could hear, Chloe sobbed and passed out.

Regaining consciousness, she found herself still lying on the damp ground, still being whipped by the wind, numbed with cold and shivering. Forcing herself to sit upright, she was pierced by fierce pains in her ribcage and recalled just how badly she had been beaten. Her lower lip had stopped bleeding but felt torn and bruised, though luckily, when she nervously checked her teeth, they all seemed to be in place.

Awash in self-pity and, even worse, recalling that the man had not paid her before attacking her, Chloe felt the rising panic of an addict desperate for a fix. Sobbing again, feeling as if she was living a nightmare, she climbed back to her feet, holding on to the wall for balance, then awkwardly made her way out of the dark alleyway, instinctively drawn to the comforting lights and noise of King's Cross Station. In the back of her mind was the thought that, despite her appearance, the dried blood and the bruising, even despite her broken ribs, she might find another customer, someone to give her the money for the fix she so badly craved. But it was obvious, as she made her way on to the concourse, that the men who glanced at her as she passed were startled by her appearance.

Understanding within minutes that she did not have a hope in hell, that no client would be forthcoming, Chloe leaned against a wall by the telephone booths, burst into tears once more and then slid to the floor to rest her forehead on her raised knees and cover her head with her hands. She sobbed wretchedly, in despair, her body shaking as she broke down completely. Then, to her surprise, she felt a hand resting gently on her shoulder.

Looking up, she saw a man with long blond hair and a steady, green-eyed, reassuring gaze.

'You need help,' he said.

# CHAPTER FIVE

Cusack was in a cell in Hereford police station. He had been locked up for the night after getting involved in a brawl with a trio of local hoodlums who had learned that he was in the SAS and had drunkenly challenged him to show them how tough he was.

Cusack had showed them. The first hoodlum was knocked by his sharp right-handed punch over the nearest table, which was packed with respectable customers who scattered in all directions. The second was thrown over the counter in a cacophony of smashing bottles and glasses, and the third was just about to get some of the same when two other men, excited beyond control, leaped into the fray.

Within seconds, the whole pub had turned into one noisy brawl, with men swinging wildly at each other, women screaming, and the landlord phoning for the police while trying to duck flying bottles. Hereford being a small place, the police were there within minutes and Cusack, pointed out as the instigator of the brawl and already known as a local troublemaker, was taken in a paddy wagon to the police station and thrown into a cell. The following morning, his friend, SAS Sergeant Jack Lewis, broad-shouldered, barrel-chested, red-haired and green-eyed, came to pay Cusack's fine and take him back to Stirling Lines.

'You're hardly a sight for sore eyes,' Jack said, 'but you look like you'll live. Just how much did you drink?'

'Enough,' Cusack said.

'Come on, let's get out of here.'

In order to leave, they had to pass through a caged-in security area of the kind that had been introduced a few years back when police stations in even the quietest backwaters had become targets for violent teenage gangs. Composed of the perennially unemployed and unemployable, the gangs travelled the country in hot rods or on motorcycles, slept in derelict houses, terrorized local communities, lived off the proceeds of crime – usually mugging and the robbing of post offices or small stores – and took a particular pleasure in attacking police stations and army camps, preferably with stolen firearms and home-made bombs. Cusack had particular reason to loathe such gangs and was reminded of them when he passed through the security area to get back to the street.

'It's like living in Colombia,' he said. 'It might even be worse.'

'Nothing's worse than Colombia,' Jack replied, 'but give us time and we'll get there. We're halfway there already.'

Cusack smiled ruefully at that. Jack was referring to the many times they had been sent to Colombia during the past five or six years to train secretly the vile Colombian army and security police in counter-insurgency tactics on British-owned oil rigs. As the Colombian army and police were known to use torture routinely in their interrogations and to be responsible for hundreds of murders and atrocities, the SAS had not been keen to get involved. Nevertheless, despite their protests SAS troopers had been sent frequently to Colombia and now knew from direct experience that it was hopelessly corrupt and violent – indeed, virtually lawless. Though Great Britain was clearly not that bad yet, it was certainly changing fast, filled now with fanatical Millennialist organizations and violent gangs of the disenfranchised, who were chiefly motivated by paranoid conspiracy theories and a subsequent hatred for any organizations representing authority, such as the police and the army. This was turning Great Britain into a war zone – disturbingly like Colombia, if not yet as corrupt.

'Here we are,' Jack said, stopping at a battered old red Ford Cortina parked against the kerb a few yards from the police station. As he opened the driver's door and slipped in to open the passenger door, Cusack mused on the fact that a few years back his friend would have come to collect him in a regimental jeep, whereas now that was considered too dangerous. Army servicemen, including the SAS, were fair game for the growing number of street gangs and even here, in the historic town of Hereford where for years the SAS had walked with impunity, it was no longer advisable to be seen either in uniform or in army vehicles. Jack had come here in his own car for that reason.

Intrigued by this thought, Cusack went around the front of the vehicle and slipped in beside Jack. When Jack had pulled away from the kerb and was heading out of town, Cusack said, 'I guess I'm in shit this time. Was the CO mad when he sent you to bail me out?'

'Well, given that this is about the fourth time in a month – the joke's going round that you should move your bed into the cop shop – no, he wasn't as mad as he should have been. Lucky for you, he'd asked me to find you before the cops actually called to say they were holding you. Seems to me that he's got a job for you. If he has, you'll be off the hook.'

'I don't want another job,' Cusack said. 'I want to retire.'

'You'll get over it,' Jack told him. 'You're not the retiring kind. Besides, I *want* you to be given another job. I'm so bored already, I'll take any shit they hand down. So if Blackwell offers you a job, you bring me in on it. Understand?'

'Yes, I understand,' Cusack said. 'But I'm seriously thinking of calling it quits when my time is up, which is only five months from now. Between now and then I'd really rather not take another job. That last one was enough for me.'

'Joshua?'

'Correct.'

'You did a good job on Joshua. Nailed the fucker to the cross. A lot of us cheered when you did that.'

'Not the boss,' Cusack said.

He meant their commanding officer, Lieutenant Colonel Blackwell, who had wanted Joshua brought in alive and believed, correctly, that Cusack could have done that very thing but had deliberately killed the terrorist instead. This was, of course, true. Cusack had not brought anyone in alive since . . . Well, even now, he could barely think about it, but certainly not since that particular time. He didn't bring them in alive because there wasn't an ounce of forgiveness in his heart; he hated all of the scumbags. Particularly the ones like Joshua who used religion to excuse their vile deeds. Now he drank to ease the pain of his stark memories and to kill the shame he always felt in knowing that he was motivated by hatred. He had once been a religious man himself, but all of that was gone now. What he had now was guilt.

'The boss wanted Joshua alive,' Jack said, 'because he thought he could give us a lot of info on other loonies. Then you double-tapped the bastard to oblivion, shutting his mouth for all time. Why did you do that?'

'You know why,' Cusack said.

Jack sighed. 'Yes, I guess so.'

The journey to Stirling Lines did not take long and soon they were driving through the main gates of the camp. As Cusack was wearing civilian clothing, now badly messed up from the brawl of the previous evening, Jack dropped him off at the Spider, the eight-legged SAS barracks, so he could have a shower and put on his uniform. Twenty minutes later, in full uniform, including his beret with the regimental winged-dagger badge, he was standing before Lieutenant Colonel Blackwell's desk. Blackwell looked serious.

'At ease, Sergeant,' he said. Cusack certainly didn't feel at ease when he saw the stony glint in Blackwell's eyes. 'You had to be hauled out of the brig again, so I'm informed.'

'Yes, boss,' Cusack admitted.

'How many times in the past month is that?'

'I'm not sure, boss.' Cusack shrugged. 'Three or four.'

'Four, to be precise,' Blackwell said.

'No argument, boss.'

'So what the hell's going on, Sergeant? You used to be one of the best men I've got; now you're drinking and fighting all the time. Is there a problem that we still have to work out?'

'Maybe there is, boss. Maybe it's time for me to quit. I've done more than my fair share, maybe too much, and it's all gone stale on me. I don't want to do any more. I think that's my problem.'

'Oh, really?'

'Yes, really.'

A silence fell between the two men as Blackwell stared steadily, thoughtfully at Cusack, taking his measure or, perhaps more accurately, trying to think of what he should say next, how hard he could push. Blackwell was an officer who respected his men and would not willingly ride roughshod over their feelings. He was, on the other hand, an officer who knew just what he wanted and would stop at nothing to get it. Eventually, as if having made up his mind, he nodded and leaned forward slightly, his gaze steady and bold.

'Would it be fair to say that what's gone stale on you is your private life?'

'I don't think I want to –'

'You don't want to discuss it, but you're going to have to because I'm fed up with hauling you out of the local brig. I'm also fed up with asking you to bring people in alive only to have you tell me that they gave you no choice but to neutralize them. As I happen to think these two subjects are closely related, I'm afraid we'll just *have* to discuss them . . . It's still your wife and daughter, isn't it, Sergeant? You can't put them behind you. Isn't that the truth of it?'

Though Cusack normally respected his CO, right now he wanted to leap across the desk and strangle him. Instead, practically grinding his teeth, he replied as evenly as he could manage: 'Certain things aren't that easy to forget and I certainly can't put what happened behind me. And my drinking and fighting . . . Well, what can I say, boss? It's something I can't seem to control and I won't pretend otherwise. I think the only solution is not to sign on again when my time is up.'

'You're planning on going back to Civvie Street?'

'I'm certainly giving it serious consideration.'

Blackwell looked sceptical. 'What civilian job would a man like you do? Who'd even hire you? You've been a regular soldier for most of your life – you've no experience of anything else – and your time in the SAS will only make things more difficult. The only work you're likely to get in Civvie Street is with a security firm or, even worse, as a mercenary. Is that what you want?'

'No, it's not,' Cusack replied, thinking of all the former SAS men whom he had met in Colombia where they were serving as mercenaries working for a filthy regime. That kind of shit had started back in 1998 when the United States had asked a private mercenary firm to provide the American military contingent of an international mission to verify the withdrawal of Serb forces from Kosovo, thus allowing the US government to avoid the political risk of having regular American troops lose their lives in active service in the Balkans. Once that was sanctioned, it opened the floodgates for other countries, including Britain, to do the same. From there it was but a short step to the legitimization of private armies that worked either for their own government or for the highest bidder, no matter how corrupt. The knowledge that many of these mercenaries were former SAS men had earned the regiment no credit and, indeed, had badly tarnished its reputation, perhaps for all time. So, no, Cusack didn't want to be a mercenary. He simply wanted some kind of oblivion, though he didn't know which kind.

'Sergeant, listen to me,' Blackwell said in a tone of voice that brooked no interruption. 'We all know what happened to your wife and daughter last year and we all know that it sent you off the rails. Nevertheless, you're still one of the best soldiers we have and I can't sit back and watch you ruin yourself. They're dead, Sergeant. They died brutally and they're not coming back and you'll simply have to live with those facts and learn to accept them. Nothing you do will change things for the better and your present behaviour won't help you at all. So why not put the whole mess behind you and look to the future?'

'Easier said than done, boss.' Even now, Cusack had only to close his eyes briefly to see vividly what he had come home to: the bodies of his wife Mary and 15-year-old daughter Jennifer, both battered and broken, lying in pools of their own blood on the living-room floor of the small house in Redhill, both raped and beaten up before being stabbed to death, their panties stuffed into their mouths to prevent them screaming. Cusack had found them in that condition when he had returned, on an otherwise perfectly normal day, from the SAS base at Stirling Lines just over a year ago. That nightmarish scene was now burned into his mind and could not be erased.

'Is that self-pity, Sergeant?' Blackwell asked sarcastically. 'If so, it's disgusting.'

'It's not self-pity, boss. I'm just stating a fact of life. Some things you just can't forget and I can't forget that.'

'I'm not saying you can forget it,' Blackwell continued remorselessly. 'What I'm saying is that you've got to put it firmly behind you and accept that life must go on. You've got to stop drowning your sorrows in a bottle and venting your anger in drunken brawling. If you want revenge – and I'm sure you do – you can get it another way.'

'I don't want revenge,' Cusack said.

'Yes, you do. Of *course* you do. Every time you get into a brawl you're venting your frustration over the fact that the people who turned your life into a nightmare are still on the loose – somewhere out there.'

'That's right,' Cusack said. 'Those cunts are still on the loose and there isn't a thing I can do about it. So, yes, I get angry pretty quickly – and I just can't control it. I don't *want* to control it.'

'No, you don't want to control it. You want to strike out at someone. You want revenge against those bastards, but you don't know who they are and so you need surrogate figures to attack – hence the fist fights in pubs.'

Cusack shrugged. 'I suppose so.'

'No "suppose" about it, Sergeant. And does this not also explain the fact that you seem to be incapable of bringing anyone in alive, even when specifically ordered to do so?'

'You can't bring a man in alive if he's trying to kill you.'

'You managed to do so before and you could do it again if you really wanted to. The truth of the matter, Sergeant, is that your anger's got the better of you. It's made you hate all the scumbags you have to track down, and when you go after them, you're thinking they might be the same men, the exact same bastards who broke into your house to kill your wife and daughter. Consumed with that possibility, you don't give them the chance to surrender; it's a double tap every time. Now isn't that the truth, Sergeant?'

'Yes, boss, I reckon.'

'So how many do you have to kill, Sergeant, before your need for vengeance is satisfied and you can apply objectivity once more in your work?'

'My rage *can't* be satisfied, boss. It's become a disease. That's why I want to get out.'

'Well, your time isn't up for another five months. Even then, if you still decide to go, what good would it do you? Those brutes would still be out there, doing to others what they did to your wife and daughter, and you'd know that and be even more tormented than you are right now. At least, while you're still in the regiment, you're in a position to do something about the others out there – all the Millennialists and religious terrorists and stoned psychopaths – but once in Civvie Street, you'll be even more impotent than you've been feeling lately . . . Incorrectly, I think.'

'Why incorrectly?'

'Because as long as you're with the regiment – in particular, as long as you're with the QRF – you'll be tasked with cleaning up the same kind of vermin who broke into your house and destroyed your life. That means that sooner or later – if you haven't already done so without even knowing it – you might come across the very people you want to find. At least, there's a chance – a slim chance. There'll be no chance at all in Civvie Street.'

Realizing that what Blackwell was saying was true, Cusack felt trapped. On the one hand, he couldn't bear the thought of staying on in the service, of being reminded with each new task, each new psychopath to be pursued and neutralized, of the kind of scum who had murdered Mary and Jennifer. On the other hand, he couldn't ignore what the CO had said: that in Civvie Street he would not only be considered unemployable, except as an armed security guard or mercenary, but would also be removed from any remote possibility of finding the men who had made his life hell. Caught between these conflicting positions, he hardly knew what to do. Blackwell, obviously sensing his dilemma, moved in to exploit it.

'I have another job for you,' he said.

'Excuse me, boss, but you told me the last job *was* the last. You said that after that job was completed I could drop out of the QRF and become a member of the Training Wing DS for the rest of my time. You *promised* me, boss.'

'*You* promised to bring Joshua in alive, and instead you shot him. You owe me one, Cusack.'

'I don't want to do it, boss.'

'I think you might,' Blackwell insisted, 'when you hear what I have to tell you.'

'Oh? What's that?'

'For a start, we *don't* want this one brought in alive. We want him terminated. This is the man responsible for the Whitehall atrocity and it's our belief that he's planning something even worse. Judging by the letter he sent us, he's obviously a religious terrorist of the most dangerous kind and he's not going to stop until he's dead. So we want you to kill him.'

'I still don't want to do it, boss.'

Blackwell sighed. 'At the risk of causing you further pain,' he said, speaking with calm deliberation, 'I wish to remind you that the leader of the brutes who killed your wife and daughter left a note that he signed as the Prince of Darkness, head of a group called the Second Coming Movement. In that note he also stated that what had been done to your wife and daughter was *your* punishment for being, I quote, "a trained government assassin" – in other words, a member of the SAS. Our subsequent investigation of that group revealed that according to their propaganda, put out on the World Wide Web, they believed that the British government was dominated by disciples of the Antichrist, the Prime Minister was actually a resurrected Pontius Pilate, and the British Army, particularly the SAS QRF, had been instructed by him to seek out covertly and destroy all true Christians. The Prince of Darkness and his disciples, the members of his so-called Second Coming Movement, were therefore dedicated to punishing, if necessary by termination, anyone connected to the army, particularly the SAS QRF. Thus, having observed your daily movements between this camp and your home, they broke into your house in your absence and *punished* you in the worst way they could imagine – something worse than getting a bullet in your brain. Instead, by doing what they did to your wife and daughter, they turned your life into hell on earth. *That* was your punishment.'

'I know all this, boss,' Cusack said impatiently, not wanting to be reminded of what had happened, feeling punished enough, but 'I don't see the relevance.'

'The relevance,' Blackwell said pointedly, moving in for the kill, 'is that we believe there's a connection between the people who broke into your home and the person, or persons, who bombed Whitehall.'

Cusack felt as if he had been sandbagged. His heart started racing. Helplessly, he lowered his eyes to meet Blackwell's remorseless gaze. 'How come?' he asked, trying to keep his voice steady but not quite succeeding.

'The man responsible for the Whitehall bombing sent us a note that he signed, simply, as Prince. Not the Prince of

Darkness – just Prince. However, a second investigation into the Prince of Darkness and his Second Coming Movement revealed that they were no longer advertising themselves on the Internet and, indeed, appeared to have vanished entirely. Last but by no means least, the contents of the letter we received from Prince shortly after the Whitehall atrocity suggested that his beliefs – or his paranoid delusions – were uncomfortably similar to those of the so-called Prince of Darkness, though since embellished with contributions from the reprehensible Millennarian Movement in the United States. It is very possible, therefore, that the Prince of Darkness has simply abbreviated his name to Prince and that his Second Coming group has evolved into the British Millennialist Movement. In short, they could be one and the same. What do you think?'

'Jesus Christ!' Cusack exclaimed automatically.

Blackwell smiled thinly, victoriously. 'We don't want this man brought in alive. We want this man dead. *Now* do you want the job?'

'Yes,' Cusack said.

# CHAPTER SIX

---

Prince was, in a real sense, saying farewell to London, though he was keeping the small flat in Cricklewood as a stopover for future visits. Those visits, he hoped, would be few and far between, as he now detested the city for a large number of reasons: its ever-growing ethnic population, its accelerating crime rate, its gross materialism, its noisy, gridlocked roads and its polluted atmosphere. The level of pollution, he was convinced, had risen to dangerous levels, and it was best to live out in the countryside where the air, if not exactly pure, would at least be less poisonous. For those reasons and others, then, he would, in the future, spend most of his time in the renovated flying school in Wiltshire and visit London only when strictly necessary. His new life was beginning.

'All right in the back, are you?' he asked, speaking over his shoulder from where he was sitting up front in the Land Rover beside Andy Pitt, who was driving. They were on their way to the old airfield with three newcomers: the girl, Chloe, and two male adolescents, both of whom he had found begging at separate locations in Oxford Street, both frozen and hungry and, like Chloe, desperate for a fix. He had steadied them temporarily by giving them some smack but would start weaning them off it once they were with the others in the community. Right now, with their craving temporarily satisfied, they were sitting silently, expectantly, in the rear, pressed tightly together.

'Yeah,' one of the boys, Jim Bleakly, said.

'Cool,' the second boy, Mark Sayers, concurred.

'What about you, Chloe?' Prince asked when he received no response from her.

'Groovy,' she said. 'A bit hungry, maybe. Are we getting near this place you're taking us to?'

'We're practically there,' Prince informed her, glancing left and right to see the lush green fields and low hills of Wiltshire spread out on both sides of the winding road under a low, cloudy sky. 'About five minutes or so.'

'Groovy,' Chloe said again.

Prince smiled. It amused him to note how everything in the world appeared to move in circles: Chloe's use of language was proof of it. Words like 'cool' and 'groovy', commonplace in the 1950s and 1960s movies still shown on television, were now back in vogue with the young, as were black leather jackets and, for the girls, skintight sweaters. Indeed, when Prince was trawling the West End of London for new recruits to his cause he often felt, when studying the young people in the streets, that he was caught in a time warp, transported back to the days of rock 'n' roll, which he personally only knew through old magazines, TV documentaries and the vinyl collection of his parents who, when not brutalizing him, had grooved on Elvis Presley and Gene Vincent. The music of those 1950s icons was making a comeback along with the clothes. Prince was not displeased. Appalled by the decadence of the present day, with its almost total lack of religious or philosophical values, its crass, materialistic concerns, he liked the thought of that more innocent age having an influence on contemporary white youth. The thought that rock 'n' roll had its roots in black music did not enter his head.

'How many other kids are out there?' Jim said, referring to what Prince had informed him was a 'non-denominational religious community' of young people located in the buildings of an abandoned airfield in Wiltshire. Prince had, of course, emphasized that the community was entirely self-sufficient, did not have anything to do with the government, was connected to no church and did not insist that those who stayed there take part in its various beneficial activities. The aim of the community, he had glibly explained, was to help homeless or unemployed young people, including those addicted to drink or drugs, by letting them find themselves through counselling. Naturally, it was the precise nature of the counselling that he had chosen not to explain.

'A little over fifty so far,' he replied. 'We only opened the establishment a couple of months back and we're still renovating some of the buildings. But it's all worked out beautifully so far and we're growing bigger every week. You certainly won't feel lonesome.'

'I'm used to feeling that way,' Mark Sayers said. 'It's pretty lonely when you're begging on the streets and that's all I've done for the past year or so, ever since leaving home. I'm not sure if I can mix with a lot of other kids. I might not stay long.'

'All we ask is that you give it a try,' Prince said smoothly. 'Naturally, if you really don't like it, you can leave any time.'

'Great,' Mark said. 'Groovy.'

Deciding that Mark had a strictly limited vocabulary, his brain doubtless gutted by too much smack, Prince, feeling impatient, tried to draw the taciturn Chloe out of herself. 'So what about you, Chloe? Now that you're calmer and have had time to think, what are your feelings?'

'About what?' she responded in a tone of voice that made it clear she was still suspicious of him. Indeed, she had only come along because he had promised to wean her off her drug addiction in easy stages. In other words, by giving her regular doses of smack, though in smaller amounts every time, gradually replacing it with methadone, then gradually weaning her off that as well. It was the lure of free smack, no matter what the circumstances, that made a lot of the young addicts come with him, since even a cure involved a fix. Few could see beyond that.

'About interacting with a lot of other young people,' Prince clarified, 'and possibly becoming part of our community.'

'I don't know what I think. I can't really think about it. I just wanna stop depending on smack and I'm willing to try anything that might work. I can't think past that.'

'A positive attitude,' Prince told her, 'and one that bodes well for your future.'

'Yeah, right,' Chloe said, sounding despondent, doubtless itching for another hit of skag, even if it was offered in return for her commitment to a gradual, painful withdrawal process. 'Christ, when do we get there?'

'We've arrived,' Prince said as Andy Pitt turned the Land Rover off the main road to enter a narrow lane lined on both sides with hedgerows. He drove along the lane for another couple of minutes, passing the occasional tree, well-spaced telegraph poles, then a barbed-wire fence separating the lane from a wide, open field. Looking across that field, which was surrounded by low green hills, Prince saw the corrugated-iron hangars once used to house the small aircraft of a commercial flying school. That business had closed down long ago and the extensive fenced-in property – including the aircraft hangars, administration buildings, control tower and Portakabins used to house trainee pilots, instructors and equipment – had been locked up and left to rot. Coming across it just over a year ago, Prince had been impressed by its isolated location. Situated well away from the nearest main road and practically hidden from sight by the surrounding hills, it was perfect for what he was planning.

He did not buy it. Instead, learning that the property had been neglected for years, he simply moved into it with a gang of teenage volunteers, the first members of his recently formed British Millennialist Movement. Under his supervision, they renovated the crumbling buildings, fixed the plumbing and wiring, brought in computers, communications and surveillance equipment and weapons, and stocked up with food and drink, gradually turning the place into a self-sustaining community with living accommodation, stores, laundry, motor pool, administrative buildings, canteen, sick bay, lecture rooms and a military-style Operations Room. Armed guards had been placed in guard boxes at the main gates, others patrolled the barbed-wire perimeter, and yet others took turns as long-distance observers and machine-gun teams in what had formerly been the air traffic control tower.

In short, the former flying school had been turned into a heavily defended armed camp of the kind that had been springing up all over the country ever since the Millennium. This was Prince's domain.

The three newcomers, however, did not comprehend this when the Land Rover passed through the main gates. First, they saw only the heads and shoulders of the guards on either side, both bare-headed and wearing jungle-green overalls, so they were not to know that the guards were armed with SIG-Sauer 9mm handguns and had Radio Systems Inc walkie-talkies for instant communication with the Operations Room in the event of any threat from outsiders. Next, when they were driven farther into the establishment, they saw only the old aircraft hangars, recently repainted in a bright, cheerful red, then, just past the hangars, a collection of Portakabins, all freshly painted in a soothing lime green that merged perfectly with the well-kept lawns around them. Finally, when they climbed out of the Land Rover, which had parked by one of the Portakabins, they gazed about them and saw only perfectly normal people, all wearing jungle-green army overalls, walking this way and that. True, they saw a couple of men up in the old air traffic control tower, but from the ground they could not see the 5.45mm RPK-74 machine-gun, which was carefully hidden from view. Thus, apart from the novelty of finding themselves standing near an old aircraft runway, the newcomers saw nothing unusual and had no cause for nervousness.

'So,' Prince said when he too had stepped out of the Land Rover, 'here we are. Over there,' he continued, pointing to some of the lime-green Portakabins, 'is where you'll be sleeping. As newcomers, you'll each have your own room until you decide if you want to remain here or leave. However, each building contains a dormitory of ten beds with toilets, baths and showers, so if you decide to stay on you'll move into one of those, sharing the place with nine others. We think it's easier if initially you stay on your own until you get used to the place.'

'What are the other buildings?' Mark asked.

'That's the canteen to the right,' Prince said, still pointing with his index finger, 'and that's the sick bay farther on. Those other buildings, the ones near the perimeter fence, are used for group therapy meetings, as lecture rooms and classrooms, and for various creative activities.'

'*Creative* activities?' Chloe asked dubiously.

Prince smiled reassuringly at her. 'We finance the running of this place by making a wide variety of artefacts that we sell to local shops and in local markets.'

'Do *we* have to do that?' Chloe asked, glancing doubtfully at the two male newcomers.

'No,' Prince lied. 'Naturally, we encourage you to try it, but you don't have to do it if you don't want to – we prefer volunteers. Now let's get you signed in and kitted out with all you'll need while you're here. Bedclothes and so forth. After that, you can have a meal and then rest up for the evening or, if you prefer, watch a movie, listen to music, or read in one or other of the three community halls. We *do* insist on lights out at ten p.m. Apart from that, things are loose here.'

'I won't get through the night without my fix,' Chloe said bluntly.

'Just report to the sick bay when you need it and they'll make sure you get it.'

'That's it?'

'That's it. We'll start reducing the amount we give you as from tomorrow, but tonight you'll get all you need. Okay, let's go inside.'

As Andy Pitt drove the Land Rover to the motor pool located near the old runway, Prince led the three newcomers into the nearest Portakabin. Obviously the administration centre, it had a counter running along most of its length, with four desks behind it, each supporting a state-of-the-art Compaq computer system and operated by a young woman. There were various maps and photographs pinned to the walls, mostly of London and Wiltshire. All the women were wearing the same army-style overalls and either had their hair cropped short or pinned up on their heads. Smiling, one of them, a blonde with short-cropped hair, pushed her chair back, stood up and approached the counter. Her glance in Prince's direction was reverential, then she gazed at the three newcomers in turn, saying, 'Hi. Welcome.'

Jim and Mark nodded and mumbled greetings in return, but Chloe said nothing. She merely looked on suspiciously as the girl behind the counter, still smiling, spread three forms out on the counter and placed ballpoint pens on top of them.

'I'm Lorna Peterson,' she said. 'The chief administrator. I'd be grateful if you'd each fill in this registration form. Name, date of birth, your educational qualifications or professional skills, the names of your parents and their home address. That's all we want to know.'

Jim and Mark immediately started filling in the forms, but Chloe – a potential troublemaker, Prince thought – stopped writing and glanced up, looking suspicious again.

'Why do you want details of our parents?' she asked. 'Are you going to contact them?'

'Only in an emergency,' Prince said quickly, 'and even then, only with your permission.'

'What kind of an emergency?'

'A medical emergency,' Prince said. 'And it would have to be something very serious before we'd consider contacting them.'

'I'd rather die than have you contact my folks and tell them where I am,' Chloe said.

'We don't insist on those details,' Prince replied smoothly, 'so if you want to leave them out, then by all means do so.'

'I will,' Chloe said.

*This one will need some serious attention,* Prince thought as he studied Chloe's once pretty, now gaunt features and sullen expression. *She might be more resistant than the others and could give us trouble. I must bear this in mind . . .*

When Chloe had filled in the rest of her form, leaving out, as she had said she would, the details about her parents, she slid the form across to Lorna Peterson. The two boys had already handed theirs back and were now looking expectantly at Prince. Smiling, gazing at each of them in turn, he said, 'Well, now that you're registered with us, Lorna will take you out, help you collect all you'll need while you're here – blankets and pillows, toiletries, clothing – then show you to your rooms. When you've deposited the kit in your individual rooms, Lorna will show you around the rest of the community, introduce you to some people and, finally, leave you in the canteen. Once you've eaten, you can do what you like – until lights out, of course. Any questions?'

'Yeah,' Chloe said. 'Everyone here seems to be wearing the same gear – those vomit-green army overalls. Do we have to wear the same while we're here?'

'If you don't mind,' Prince said. 'We prefer it, but we don't insist upon it. The choice is yours alone, dear.'

'So how come I haven't seen a single soul here dressed in anything else? You're trying to tell me that, given the choice, they *all* chose that shit?'

Though experiencing a sudden urge to throw her into solitary, commencing her treatment immediately, Prince managed to control himself and merely said, 'Yes, surprisingly enough they did. At least, they all did in the end. A lot, like you, were resistant in the beginning, but wearing their own clothing tended to isolate them from the majority, making them feel different, so in the end, I suppose, they simply felt more comfortable being like the others. I can assure you, however, that none of them were forced. They all made their own choice.'

'I'd feel embarrassed *not* wearing the overalls,' Mark said, 'when everyone else here is wearing 'em. I'd feel like the odd man out. So I'm gonna wear them.'

'Me too,' Jim said.

Chloe shrugged. 'What the fuck's the difference? They're no worse than what I'm wearin' already, so I guess I can play ball. And even *I* don't want to be stared at.' She turned her sullen gaze on Prince. 'So what happens tomorrow, Mister Prince?'

'Please call me Prince. Just Prince.'

'I thought that was your surname.'

'Here I'm called only by that name,' Prince informed her, realizing that his voice was sounding strained and that he suddenly felt unreasonably agitated. 'Just Prince. No "mister".'

'I just think it's kinda funny saying "Prince". I mean, unless it's your surname and, from the way you're carrying on, I guess it isn't.'

'I must *insist* that you call me "Prince",' Prince said, now feeling hot and bothered, wanting to strangle her. 'So let's not argue about it.'

Chloe shrugged. 'No skin off my nose. Anything you want, Prince. I'm just here to be cured.'

*You're here*, Prince thought, calming down again, *because you think you'll get an endless supply of smack and can light out as soon as we withdraw it. But you won't light out anywhere. You'll soon be one of us, girl.*

'Right,' he said, turning to Lorna Peterson. 'Please take care of them, Lorna.'

The glacially pretty blonde woman nodded, her gaze still reverential. 'Yes, Prince.'

She was just about to lead them out of the office when Chloe stopped her with, 'What happens tomorrow?'

The blonde woman glanced nervously at Prince.

'You breakfast in the canteen at seven a.m.,' he said quickly. 'Then you return to your individual rooms no later than eight. Someone will come to collect you shortly after that and escort you to a lecture room to commence your counselling and prepare you psychologically for your gradual withdrawal from drug dependency. You'll also be told about our community – what motivates us, what we can do for you and, hopefully, if you decide to stay on, what *you* can do for *us*. Now, are there any *more* questions?'

'Just one,' Chloe said. 'Are you sure we won't have any problem if we go to the sick bay and ask for a fix?'

'No. The sick bay will be told that you're coming and they'll give you enough of a fix to get you through the night. Just make sure you don't go there before nine-thirty. Go about fifteen minutes before lights out and you won't have a problem. Okay?'

'Okay,' Chloe said.

Relieved that she was shutting up at last, Prince forced a smile, then nodded at Lorna Peterson who led the newcomers out of the building. Prince watched them through the window until they had disappeared into the supply store, then he too left the building and made his way to the Portakabin containing his personal accommodation and the Operations Room.

The accommodation consisted of a spacious living room, a small study, a bedroom with double bed, a kitchen, and a bathroom with bath, shower and toilet. Though the other accommodations in the community were spartan, his own were luxurious, with thick pile carpets on the floors, Italian tiles on the kitchen and bathroom walls, lights with dimmer switches, black leather couches and other furniture, all modern, purchased at Harrods. There was a wide-screen stereo television set with video recorder in the living room and a smaller set, also with video recorder, at the foot of his bed. Music from a state-of-the-art Sony music centre – CD player and double-cassette deck – could be piped into the kitchen, study and bedroom. An upgraded Dell 310 computer system with a 640 MB hard disk was on the desk in the study, along with an inkjet printer, a flatbed scanner and a digital camera. The only luxury not included was alcohol, because Prince did not drink.

Entering the kitchen, he made himself a light pasta dish, followed by a cup of herbal tea. When the meal was finished, he placed the dishes in the dishwasher, then went into the bathroom for a hot shower. After the shower, he dried himself, sprayed deodorant into his armpits, then put on a pair of light blue cotton pyjamas and, over them, a white towelling bathrobe. He then left the bedroom, crossed the living room and entered the adjoining Operations Room.

From this room, with the aid of hi-tech surveillance systems, including CCTV, he could survey the rest of the community, inside and outside, every building and every room. He could see and hear everything.

Checking his wristwatch and noting that it was just turning 9.00 p.m., he sank into a chair in front of the CCTV and turned on the system. Using a remote-control handset, he switched from one part of the community to another, first checking the exterior areas – the old runway, the motor pool, the main gates, the barbed-wire perimeter fence, his armed security guards – and then moving inside the buildings. Switching to the canteen, he saw the newcomers eating, zoomed in on them, and kept the scene on the screen until, about thirty-five minutes later, the three of them got up from the table and then left the building. Switching to the exterior of the canteen, he saw them emerge and tracked them all the way to the sick bay. When they entered the building, he switched to inside and saw them gathered around the receptionist's desk. He stayed on them until the first of them, Chloe, was ushered into the surgery of one of the medics. He switched to the surgery and watched the medic prepare a disposable syringe. When Chloe had injected the smack into her arm, she left the room and was replaced by Mark Sayers. Prince waited until he had seen both Mark Sayers and Jim Bleakly shoot up their skag, then he switched to outside the building and waited until the three newcomers emerged and made their way, looking happier, to the Portakabin selected for their indoctrination. He watched them enter the building, then switched to the corridor inside and observed them entering their separate rooms. Satisfied, but bored also, he distracted himself by retiring to his kitchen, where he had some toast with butter and another herbal tea.

Just after ten, when the lights in the community had all winked out, he returned to the CCTV, seated himself in front of the system, and switched to the interior of each newcomer's room, one after the other. Jim Bleakly and Mark Sayers were both asleep, but Chloe was still awake. Prince zoomed in on Chloe. Clearly rolling on the high of her recent injection of smack, she was stretched out on the bed, smiling and fingering herself, approaching a climax. Prince watched her and felt the stirrings of an erection. When she came, he grew fully hard. When she subsided and eventually fell asleep, he turned off the CCTV system and returned to his bedroom. Lying back on the bed, he picked up the walkie-talkie beside his pillow and called Lorna Peterson. He told her to come over immediately, then he put the instrument down.

Obedient as always, her gaze reverential, Lorna arrived five minutes later and came straight to his bed. He still had his erection. She saw it and was impressed. She had been indoctrinated, was now a total believer, and clearly viewed him as Christ resurrected. Her purpose in life was to serve him.

'Do you love me?' Prince asked.

'You know I do,' she replied.

'Prove it,' he said.

Lorna knelt at the altar of her Lord and drank of His essence. When He came, spilling into her, filling her mouth and throat, then smiling with satisfaction, her own satisfaction sprang solely from the knowledge that she had pleased Him by doing His bidding. Having seen His wrath, she knew that it was fearsome and not inclined to forgiveness. Her love and terror were one.

'Bless you, my child,' Prince said, stroking the back of her head.

'The Lord be praised,' she replied.

# CHAPTER SEVEN

Given a free hand, Cusack began casually enough by inviting his buddy, SAS Sergeant Jack Lewis, for a couple of beers in the Booth Hall pub in Hereford. While ostensibly this seemed like a crazy thing to do, Cusack had learned long ago that you could discuss anything in a pub, given a reasonable amount of elbow room, because drinkers were, in general, only interested in their own conversations. He safeguarded matters by taking a corner table, but he wasn't really concerned.

'I'd fuck that for a start,' Jack Lewis said, indicating with a nod of his head a middle-aged woman seated at the bar, her tan clearly obtained from a sunlamp, her blonde hair obviously dyed, her streamlined body enhanced with a skintight sweater, denims and high-heeled boots. 'Just let me get my paws on her.'

'You sound like an animal,' Cusack responded, 'and I doubt that she'd go for the beastly type. Drink up and accept defeat.'

'Who dares wins,' Jack said, quoting the regimental motto as he ran his fingers through his shock of red hair and let his green eyes widen in mock madness. 'I guarantee that when I walk out of this pub, I'll walk out with her.'

'What's the bet?'

'My selection as your other half for whatever the CO conned you into.'

'What makes you think he conned me into anything?'

'The fact that you called me for this piss-up. So don't fuck me around.'

Cusack grinned. 'Smart boy.'

'So what's coming down?'

'We're after the guy who planted that bomb in Whitehall.'

Jack gave a low whistle while keeping his eye on the woman at the bar. 'Oh, boy!' he exclaimed. 'Sounds good to me. What have you got?'

'Nothing so far. Only a letter that makes him sound like just another Millennialist nut. He thinks the Queen is the Queen of Babylon and the patroness of English Freemasonry. The Royal Family as a whole is part of the ancient Illuminati society.'

'I've heard of that,' Jack said, 'but I can't recall exactly what it is – or was.'

'A mixed bag,' Cusack said, 'from which anyone can pull out anything they fancy.'

'Like the Bible.'

'Correct.'

'Tell me about it.'

'One version of the story is that the Illuminati was founded by a former Jesuit in Bavaria in the seventeenth century. It was a secret society devoted to republican free thought and its ultimate aim was to replace Christianity with a religion of reason. It was soon banned, however, by the Bavarian government. The name "Illuminati" was also given to the followers of a Spanish mystical movement during the sixteenth and seventeenth centuries. Its adherents, mostly reformed Franciscans and, again, Jesuits, claimed that they were in direct communication with the Holy Spirit. For this reason, they did *not* have to participate in the liturgy, good works and observance of the exterior forms of normal religious life.'

'Nice for them,' Jack said sardonically.

'Quite. Though their extravagant claims for their visions

and revelations made the Inquisition issue edicts against them at least two or three times.'

'You've obviously done your homework.'

'The *Encyclopaedia Britannica*. On the Internet.'

'Great. Anything else?'

'Yes. Certain aspects of the Illuminati can be traced back to the Rosicrucians, a secret worldwide brotherhood claiming to possess esoteric wisdom handed down from ancient times. The name derives from the order's symbol: a combination of a rose and a cross. Lots of occultism is mixed in with their teachings. No one really knows where they came from, but the earliest document that mentions the order, the *Fama Fraternitatis*, or *Account of the Brotherhood*, was published in 1614 and claims that the founder of the order, Christian Rosenkreuz, who reportedly lived to be 106 years old, acquired secret, occult wisdom on trips to Egypt, Damascus, Damcar in Arabia, and Fez in Morocco. Others, however, claim that Paracelsus, the notorious Swiss alchemist, was the order's true founder. Yet others insist that the order actually originated in ancient Egypt and was espoused by the likes of Plato and Jesus. Whatever way you look at it, those who presently believe in the existence of the Illuminati certainly reckon them to be a secret order in possession of secret wisdom.'

'And our nutter believes that the Royal Family are members of the Illuminati?'

'Right.'

'Anything else?'

'Yes. He believes that the Illuminati is dedicated to the ultimate dominion of the whole world, that the Royal Family, being in the Illuminati, is satanic, and that he therefore has to dedicate himself to destroying them and their cohorts, the elected British government, through a campaign of righteous terror. The first step in that campaign was the bombing of Whitehall. Almost certainly, then, his ultimate aim will be Buckingham Palace.'

'Might not be a bad idea,' Jack said sardonically. 'The

Royals aren't too popular any more, even with the hoi polloi.'

'They're certainly not popular with our bomber, and I think he means what he says.'

'Most nutcases do.' Jack glanced at the woman by the bar just as she turned her head to look about her. She caught his glance and quickly looked away, though her gaze was fixed on the mirror on the wall above the bar. 'That's it, sweetheart,' Jack murmured, smiling. 'Check me out in the mirror. What I've got, you can have.' Sighing, he turned back to Cusack. 'All that shit, my friend . . . Well, it sounds like it's millennial. The Millennialists, they're all into that kind of thing – they picked it up from the Yanks. Extreme paranoid right-wing politics mixed up with fundamentalist Christianity and a lot of mystical shit. This guy sounds made to order.'

'No doubt about *that*,' Cusack said. 'His organization is called the British Millennialist Movement. Given what he stated in his letter following the bombing, I'd say that his thoughts were warped by millennial fervour back around the year 2000 and, like a lot of the Millennialists, he's mixed up his own brand of right-wing extremism with a hotchpotch of religious and other mystical beliefs. I mean, he calls himself *Prince*.'

'A prince of fucking darkness, right?'

'More a Prince of Light, I'd think. If he's against the Illuminati, he'll be into some kind of Christianity, no matter how bizarre or warped. And judging by his thoughts on the Royal Family, I'd say he imagines that he's engaged in a war against Satan.'

Jack glanced at the woman across the room, looking her up and down admiringly, assuming she would see his hungry glance in that mirror above the bar. Nevertheless, for all his interest in the woman, he was listening carefully to Cusack.

'Christ,' he said, 'we certainly get 'em these days. They're all over the country, holed up in their armed camps, still waiting for the Second Coming or extraterrestrials or some- thing, and ready to fight to the death to defend their so-called rights. They're true believers for sure. So what else do you have on this Prince guy?'

'Nothing so far. I'm being helped in these initial stages by Scotland Yard, whose forensic boys are examining the debris of the Whitehall bombing, hoping to find out something about the truck that the explosives were transported in. They already know that the bomb was the kind first used in the Oklahoma City bombing of 1995. This suggests that Prince may have been influenced by the American Millennarian Movement and is probably running a British version of the same. They've also found enough body parts mixed in with the widespread debris of the truck to indicate that the driver was killed in the blast. They're hoping that they can, by forensic examination of any pieces of teeth that can be found, ascertain through computerized dental records just who that guy was.'

'Well, whoever the fuck he was,' Jack said impatiently, 'he certainly wasn't Prince himself, since Prince sent his letter the day *after* the blast.'

'Correct. But if we can find out who the driver was or where that truck came from, we could be at the beginning of the narrow, winding track that leads us to our man.'

'What happens if we manage to track him down?'

'The police drop out of the picture and we put together a QRF of the size required for whatever we have to deal with.'

'That could be a fortified camp, heavily armed and fanatical.'

'I suspect it will be,' Cusack said. 'God knows, there are enough of them around these days. It's just like Middle America.'

'Let's have another pint,' Jack said.

He pushed his chair back and stood up, tall, broad-shouldered, barrel-chested, and started across the room.

'You want to talk to that woman,' Cusack said.

'I want to win my bet,' Jack replied.

Cusack looked on with interest as his red-haired friend walked up to the counter, deliberately stopping right beside the woman he was virtually sniffing out, almost shoulder to shoulder with her. He spoke to the barman, obviously placing his order, then turned his head to smile warmly at the woman.

It was a smile of considerable charm; the same kind Jack had used to charm his way out of trouble when he and Cusack were trapped behind enemy lines in Scud Alley in Iraq. That was way back in 1991, when Cusack and Jack had been only twenty-two years old and on their first mission with D Squadron, 22 SAS, taking part in Operation Desert Storm. Tasked with tracking the mobile Scud missile launchers that were causing havoc to the Coalition war effort, they had roamed the desert in heavily armed Land Rovers, the famous 'Pink Panthers', engaging in deep-penetration hit-and-run raids behind enemy lines, destroying the enemy's aircraft on the ground, attacking their lines of communication, ambushing their patrols and, when not able to complete the job themselves, using their SATCOM communications systems to vector F-15 strike aircraft on to the Scuds.

During one such raid, Cusack's Pink Panther had been badly damaged, one of his three-man team had been killed, and he and Jack had been compelled to make a hellish forced march through enemy territory – a march that took four days – seeking sanctuary across the Syrian border. En route they had come across a wide variety of locals, including Bedouin traders on camels, and it was then that Jack's easy grin had come in useful, enabling him to charm the nomadic Arabs both into not handing them over to the vengeful Iraqis and into giving them some more positive help.

Now, as Cusack could see, that same easy grin was working its charms on the lady at the bar. She was smiling and nodding in return, obviously agreeing to something. Also, as Cusack noticed, she did not move away when Jack casually let his hand rest on her shoulder. Satisfied, Jack picked up his two pints and returned to the table.

'Got her in hand, have you?' Cusack asked when Jack had sat down again.

'I promised to join her for a drink when you and I finish

discussing business. I also ascertained that she hasn't eaten yet and is keen on Chinese. From Chinese it's but a short hop to her bed. I'm in like Flynn, buddy. You lose. I win. So count me in with regard to Operation Millennium.'

'That's what we'll call it,' Cusack said.

They touched glasses and drank. Then Jack, having had his sport, returned to the business at hand.

'He just signed himself Prince?'

'Yes,' Cusack said.

'Not *the* Prince – as in *the King* or whatever? Not the Prince of Darkness?'

'No, neither. He probably imagines that a member of the Royal Family is the Prince of Darkness. Now what are you *really* asking, Jack?'

'This is delicate,' Jack said.

'Just spit it out, pal.'

'Well,' Jack began in a hesitant, embarrassed manner, 'you *have* been talking in a pretty determined way about not volunteering for any more cleansing ops and, more specifically, about leaving the army when your time is up next year. So what I'm trying to find out, I guess, is how the CO conned you into taking on this particular task. Can I take it, then, to answer my own intended question, that there may be some link between this Prince and the so-called Prince of Darkness who . . .' Jack shrugged and turned away, this time studying the woman at the bar only in order to avoid Cusack's gaze. 'Well, you know . . .'

'Yes, I know.' Cusack understood his friend's embarrassment, which was overlaid with concern, as Jack had been like a member of Cusack's own family, adored by both his wife and his daughter and responding in kind. Their brutal fate at the hands of a so-called Prince of Darkness had therefore shocked him deeply, perhaps nearly as much as it had shocked Cusack. Ever since then, like most friends in such circumstances, Jack had been embarrassed to even raise the subject.

'Okay,' Cusack said, his hatred for those unknown

assailants welling up once more to consume him, just as the horror of that nightmarish event threatened to destroy him. 'Let's spread the whole mess out on the table. The animal responsible for what happened in my home *did* call himself the Prince of Darkness and he headed a group called the Second Coming Movement. This virtually confirms that it had to be yet another of those mad movements formed just before the year 2000. Both the Prince of Darkness and his Second Coming Movement advertised themselves boldly on the Internet, relentlessly spewing out the customary paranoid conspiracy theories. Though in their case, instead of alien bodies in Roswell or elsewhere, it was the Royal Family and the Antichrist emerging from London in general and, presumably, from Buckingham Palace in particular.

'However, at the end of the year 2000, which came and went without a Second Coming or extraterrestrial invasion, the Prince of Darkness's Second Coming Movement, like a lot of other Millennialist movements, abruptly dropped out of sight. As we now know, a lot of those movements simply collapsed when their adherents, disillusioned that no great apocalyptic event had come to pass, that the earth had remained as normal, faded away and never returned. However, other movements, obviously the more fanatical, simply rewrote their previous scenarios to explain away what had happened – or, more precisely, what had *not* happened – and kept going on the strength of their new creeds.'

'I'm with you so far,' Jack said.

'Stick with me,' Cusack replied. 'It's possible that this Prince of the British Millennialist Movement was formerly the Prince of Darkness of the Second Coming Movement and he simply revamped his title – *and* his scenario – when the year 2000 passed without event.'

'You mean Prince and the former Prince of Darkness are one and the same?'

'Like I said, I think it's certainly possible.'

'And the CO believes that?'

'Yes.'

'So?'

'So I think that despite all the best efforts of Scotland Yard, the only way we'll find our Prince is by letting him find *me* again.'

Adroit at keeping two serious matters in his head at once, Jack raised his glass to the woman at the bar, gave her that charming grin, then turned back to Cusack. 'What makes you think he wants to do that?'

'Because the former Prince of Darkness believed that the British government was controlled by the Antichrist. He also believed that the British Army, particularly the SAS Quick Reaction Force, had been instructed by the Prime Minister, standing in for Pontius Pilate, to covertly seek out and destroy all true Christians. Knowing this, Prince decided to rigorously punish members of the SAS, either by killing them or, even worse, by doing to their families what he did to mine – and he could only have done that, the fucker, by placing his intended victims under surveillance.'

'Jesus!' Jack whispered automatically, briefly forgetting the woman at the bar and intending no irony. 'So the bastard knows you personally.'

'Yes. He knows where I live and work – he's seen me travelling between my home and Stirling Lines – so if we leak the news that I've been tasked with tracking him down, I'm sure we'll draw his attention.'

'But now you're living in the Spider,' Jack said, referring to the eight-legged barracks in the SAS camp.

'I *was*,' Cusack emphasized. 'Because I'd put the house on the market. But I'm now going to take it off the market and move back into it. That should be pretty easy to do, since all the furniture's still there.'

'But do you think you can actually *live* there again, given your memories?'

'I can try,' Cusack said.

*Nothing else is guaranteed*, he thought. For, indeed, he wasn't at all sure that he *could* manage it, given that he still remembered too clearly, in precise, soul-destroying detail, what he had found in the house that evening when he'd returned from Stirling Lines. Cusack had, in fact, moved out of the house because every room in it, every stick of furniture, every photograph and painting, even the CDs, had reminded him painfully of Mary and Jennifer, as they had once been, beautiful and carefree, but also, horrifically, of how he had found them, all bloody and torn.

There had been times, too, when Cusack had awoken at night to find himself reaching out for Mary, imagining that she was still beside him – and other times, even worse, when he had imagined that he could hear Jennifer, tossing and turning in her bed in the adjoining room. Indeed, so strong had been this conviction that he had often clambered out of his own bed and gone into that next room, half expecting to find Jennifer there. Instead, he found only the stripped bed, its bloody mattress long since taken away, all signs of the horrors wrought upon his daughter removed by the police.

Finally, when he had suffered too many nights like that, Cusack decided that he couldn't live in the house any more, so he had placed it on the market and moved back into the Spider at Stirling Lines. Despite his own fears, he would now move out of the Spider and back into his own house. If he still had problems, he would find the strength to endure by dwelling on the possibility of catching Prince. Nothing else was guaranteed.

'So when do I enter the picture?' Jack asked.

'Immediately,' Cusack told him. 'Initially, at least, I want a six-man QRF team fully trained and on standby. We'll pick the men between us, then I'll let you get on with the training while I liaise with the Metropolitan Police *and* leak the news that we're out to get Prince.'

'The Head Sheds won't like that,' Jack said, using the SAS slang for senior officers.

'Fuck them,' Cusack said. 'Even if they guess that I made the leak, they won't be able to prove it. I'm not going to use one of our favoured journalists; instead, I'll put it out on the Internet. That's where all the conspiracy freaks trade information, so that's where Prince and the British Millennialist Movement are most likely to see it. I'll post the news as a lurker.'

'*Parfait*,' Jack said. 'So when do we start looking for volunteers?'

'Next week,' Cusack said. 'I want to get out of the Spider and back into my house before we make our first move.'

'Sounds good to me.' Jack glanced across the room, in the direction of the blonde woman at the bar. She caught his glance and smiled reassuringly at him. 'Anything else?' he asked.

'No, that's it for tonight. I'll head back to the base now and leave you elbow room for that lady.'

'You're so kind,' Jack said, grinning.

Cusack finished off his pint, then pushed his chair back and stood up. 'I'll call you and we'll arrange to meet next week.'

'I'm your man,' Jack said, also pushing his chair back to stand up and cross the room to the waiting lady, casting Cusack another wicked grin just before moving off. Cusack tried not to stare as he left the pub, but he couldn't help but see Jack signalling to the barman, clearly about to order drinks for himself and the lady, whose smile was already radiant.

*Never bet against him,* Cusack thought. *The bastard wins every time.*

Leaving the pub, he only had to walk a short distance along the lamplit street to reach his car, a green Volkswagen Golf. He had just slid into the driver's seat and closed the door when his mobile beeped. After turning it on and announcing himself, he heard the familiar voice of his CO, Lieutenant Colonel Blackwell.

'You'd better get over here straight away,' Blackwell said tersely. 'I've just had a call from Scotland Yard. Prince has struck again.'

'I'm on my way,' Cusack said.

# CHAPTER EIGHT

It was so easy to do. Each of the six small, green-painted cardboard boxes, resembling lunch boxes and soft-drink containers, held sealed plastic tubes filled with the deadly nerve poison Sarin (GB). At five in the morning, the six young people chosen for the task were called into the Portakabin used by Prince as a combined conference room and chapel. There they were each given a box or carton and then invited to take one of the chairs in front of the raised wooden dais while Prince, wearing a white robe, his gold-blond hair resplendent in the overhead strip lighting, gave them a pep talk.

'What I'm asking you to do, you can do with a good conscience,' he began persuasively, 'because the city you're about to attack is a Babylon headed by high priests – the Royal Family and politicians – whose souls are branded with the Number of the Beast. You all know that number. It is the number 666. It is stated so, clearly, in the book of Revelation: *Let him that hath understanding count the number of the Beast: for it is the number of a man; and his number is six hundred three score and six* ... This number, then, is the number of those who rule Babylon and that city is the one we know as London. Therefore heed the words of the Good Book once more: *Babylon is fallen, is fallen, that great city, because she made all nations drink of the wine of the wrath of her fornication* . . . So! You are about to punish the fornicators and strike at the very heart of the Beast. For this, you will be rewarded on Earth, as you will be in Heaven. You will sit by my right hand.'

Pausing to let his disciples drink in his words, Prince gazed through the window of the Portakabin and saw that darkness was still upon the face of the earth and stars could be glimpsed between the clouds. Life seemed so beautiful at that moment, so far removed from the pale horse of death soon to gallop into Babylon, that he had to place a check on his emotions when he returned his gaze to his flock.

'I understand the concerns of some of you – concerns based on Christian charity – that I am asking you to do to the sinners of Babylon what that Muslim beast, Saddam Hussein, did to the Kurdish civilians in northern Iraq a few years ago. Bear in mind, however, that some of Saddam's most deadly germ cultures were produced in Fort Detrick, Maryland, the US Army's so-called *defensive* germ-research centre, that many of them were shipped to Baghdad from a company based in Rockville, also in Maryland, and that the production and selling of those deadly biological agents were carried out with the explicit approval of the US government. Does the American president stand alone in his guilt? No, he does not! A vast arsenal of vile biological weapons is presently being produced in Iran, Libya, Syria, North Korea, Taiwan, Israel, Egypt, Vietnam, Laos, Cuba, Bulgaria, India, South Korea, South Africa, China and Russia. More importantly, right here in Great Britain, where the Antichrist rules, the researching and stockpiling of even worse biological weapons – anthrax, botulinum, aflatoxin and other plague-inducing germs – are proceeding rapidly to ensure, when the time comes, that the Queen of Babylon and her satanic cohorts, the army and the police, can successfully attack those among us – decent Christians – who stand opposed to them. We can *not* let this happen!'

Prince's disciples were gazing up at him with rapt expressions on their young, unformed faces. Indeed, some worshipped him so much that they had even asked him if they could dye their hair blond like his. He had, of course, granted permission and now he was seeing clones of himself. Somehow this seemed right and fitting.

'Violence begets violence, evil must be fought with evil, and I send you to the iniquitous souks of Babylon to punish the fornicators for their sins. Think of yourselves as angels of mercy, inaugurating the fall of that evil city, thus setting the righteous free from hellish dominion. Remind yourselves again, as you release the poison, of the words of Revelation, which we have all been so assiduously studying ... *And a mighty angel took up a stone like a great millstone, and cast it unto the sea, saying, "Thus with violence shall that great city Babylon be thrown down, and shall be found no more at all ..."* Think of yourselves, then, as throwing that great stone into the sea to wreak havoc on Babylon. This is a mission for God.'

Prince studied each of them in turn, letting his green eyes bore into them until they could meet his gaze no longer and modestly lowered their own. When he was satisfied that they would all do as they were told, he smiled and nodded thoughtfully.

'You all have your maps of the Underground with you. You know exactly where and when to release the poison and make your escape. God go with you. God bless you. The van awaits you outside. I will pray as you leave.'

When Prince clasped his hands under his chin and bowed his head, his disciples did the same. However, Prince kept his head lowered and murmured a prayer to himself as each of the disciples picked up an innocent-looking cardboard box or carton and left the room. Only when the last of them had left the Portakabin did Prince follow them out. By this time, they were clambering up into the rear of the umarked grey-painted transit van that would take them to London. Standing there in the lifting darkness, just before first light, Prince took in his sprawling community at a glance – the other Portakabins, the machine-gun crew in the watchtower, the old aircraft hangars and the airstrip, the gates and wired perimeter guarded by armed men, all weakly illuminated by the pale, mottled, sinking moon – then solemnly raised his right hand in benediction and kept it there until the van roared into life and drove out of the camp. When it was gone, Prince lowered his hand again and smiled slightly, dementedly.

'The Lord's will be done,' he said.

Satisfied that all would go according to plan, he crossed the clearing between the building he had just left and the linear rows of Portakabins used as accommodation and sleeping quarters. Having risen so early for this special occasion, unable to go back to sleep and with time on his hands, he decided to check out how the latest newcomers were faring, entangled in the snares of a kind of trap that they had not anticipated – and would certainly not be enjoying.

Prince always needed newcomers, justifying what he was doing by telling himself that he was engaged in the Lord's work and, at the same time, saving otherwise helpless young people from self-destruction. So he had made it his standard ploy, when rescuing them from drug-addicted prostitution or beggary, to seduce them into visiting his 'non-denominational religious community' by promising to help them with their drug addiction without actually making them go cold turkey – in other words, by giving them more of the drug they craved whilst trying to wean them off it gradually, painlessly. With that desperation common to all drug addicts, they invariably agreed to come with him. They did so, the hypocrites, because deep down they believed that they could exploit his religious philanthropy by taking all the drugs they could get for free and then leaving when the drug supply was cut off.

Initially they *all* thought this, self-deluded as they were. However, the reality was that once a newcomer was in the community and had been allocated a room and given a 'holding' fix, Prince locked them in, gave them no more drugs at all for a while and let them endure all the horrors and unspeakable torments of cold-turkey withdrawal. Only in the final, worst stages, when the newcomers were out of their minds with the craving, did Prince offer a little of the necessary drug in return for their considered attention when he, Prince, preached to them. At this stage, when the newcomers were confusing how much better they were feeling (because of the drugs) with Prince's inspiring monologues, they were more open to suggestion and could therefore more easily be mentally and emotionally enslaved by him. Prince had just done this to the recent batch of newcomers and now he wanted to see the effects his 'treatment' was having, particularly on the most resistant one, that teenage whore Chloe.

Entering the Portakabin in which the three newcomers had been given their separate rooms (which they had thought was a blessing when it was, in fact, a curse), he checked the rooms one at a time by opening the viewing hole in each locked door and glancing in.

In the first room, one of the two male adolescents, Mark Sayers, was sleeping soundly. The newcomer with least resistance to Prince's psychological warfare, truly not very bright and therefore highly susceptible, he had shown himself to be practically converted already, believing all that Prince had told him, indeed already almost worshipping Prince, and so Prince had rewarded him with just enough smack to keep him pacified until the following morning.

In the second room, the other male adolescent, Jim Bleakly, was stretched out on his steel-framed bed, naked, a dreamy smile on his face, having finally broken down after a lot of pitiful tears and tantrums. Literally falling to his knees after two days of ever-weakening resistance interspersed with cold-turkey sweats and terrifying hallucinations, he had begged Prince to let him remain in the community under any conditions. Rewarded with the first of his constantly decreasing doses of injected heroin, he was now on a blissful high.

In the third room, however, the girl, Chloe, still wearing her hooker's outfit of skintight miniskirt, cotton jumper, black leather boots and blue ski jacket, was sitting upright on her bed, sniffling miserably, wiping her runny nose, and sobbing out of dark-ringed big brown eyes that were filled with despair. Chloe had been the most stubborn of the three. From the moment she heard Prince turning the key in the door, locking her into the room, she had realized what he was doing and had hammered on the door with her fists, screaming to be let out. When Prince had refused to open the door, talking to her through the viewing hole, explaining that she had to do without her skag for a few days, no matter how painful the process, she had screamed abuse at him and then proceeded to demolish her spartan room, smashing up what little furniture was in it.

Chloe had not been fed. There was a toilet in the room, a sink with hot and cold running water, and a single towel. She had been told to drink the water when she was thirsty – which, given her craving for smack, she was more often than not. That water was all she'd had for the past three days.

Like Jim in the adjoining room, Chloe had suffered the sweats and hallucinations of cold turkey, but with moments of lucidity in between. It was those moments that Prince had exploited by talking constantly, hypnotically to her, trying to break down her resistance and impress upon her fevered consciousness, her troubled emotions, the need to accept his wisdom, his religious insight, and embrace the healing beliefs of his community. She had shown great resistance, first screaming abuse, then sobbing, when not actually begging for a fix and saying, though he knew her to be lying at that stage, that she would do anything – *anything* – to get it. Of course, he knew what she meant – that for a fix she would let him fuck her – but he no longer wanted *just* her body; now he wanted her mind as well. He wanted none of her lies, no sly manipulations, no exchanges of sex for drugs, no pretended agreements; what he *did* want was her total compliance, the collapse of independent thought, her absolute reliance upon him, with or without the smack. He wanted her to be like the others, devoted to him, enslaved by him. Now, when he saw the state of her, he knew that the time was ripe.

'Chloe?' he said through the open viewing grill. 'How are you doing?'

She glanced up, her big brown eyes startled. 'What?'

'How are you doing?' he repeated.

'You know how I'm doing. You can *see* how I'm doing. Oh, God, Prince, I feel awful!'

'That will soon pass, Chloe.'

'I need a fix. Oh, Christ, *please*!'

'I'd help you if I thought it was wise, Chloe, but I don't think you're ready yet. You have to *want* help, Chloe, *really* want it, and not just pretend because you need a fix. If I was convinced that you really wanted to be cured and then, perhaps, stay here in the community – well, if I was really convinced of that, I'd let you withdraw more gradually, with some help up front. But I'm not convinced, Chloe.'

'I *do* want to stay here, Prince. Really, *I do*! I don't want to go back to being what I was, living off the streets. I don't want to be dependent any more. I want to belong somewhere – like you people belong here – and I want to have friends that I can talk to, not friends who're drug addicts like me.'

'Are you sure of that, Chloe?'

'Oh, God, yes! Help me out, just temporarily, Prince. I feel like hell now. I'm sick. God, I feel like I'm dying.'

'I'm coming in, Chloe.'

He opened the door and entered, being careful, aware that she might attack him. When she remained sitting on the mattress, he knew that she was coming around to his way of thinking. Pleased, he withdrew a disposable syringe and a brown glass phial from his pocket, stood the overturned bedside table back on its legs, then took the protective sheath off the needle and plunged it through the self-sealing cap of the phial. Drawing back the plunger, he filled the syringe barrel with a clear solution of heroin in distilled water and offered the syringe wordlessly to Chloe. Practically sobbing with relief, she grabbed it, jabbed the needle into her forearm, arched her head back, closed her eyes and then sighed with relief.

'Ah, God!' she said. 'Jesus!'

'Don't blaspheme,' Prince reprimanded her, placing his hand on her shoulder and gently shaking her until she opened her eyes again. Now the pupils of her brown eyes were unnaturally dilated, relaxed by the heroin.

'Sorry, Prince. Thanks. I want to stay here. Really, I do. Just tell me what I'm supposed to do.'

'Just rest up for now,' Prince told her. 'Then, at nine o'clock, go to the canteen and have breakfast. When you've finished eating, return here and someone will eventually come for you. You'll be shown what to do.'

When he leaned forward to kiss the top of her head, she burst into tears.

'Ah, God,' she sobbed. 'I've been so bad. I've been awful. I can't bear to think of the things I've done and now I want to be better. I want to be good, Prince. I want to be loved and respected. I want to have friends. God, I'm so glad to be here!'

Prince squeezed her shoulder in a fatherly manner while saying, 'You'll be loved and respected here, I promise you, as long as you're good. You'll have friends here. You'll have a home here. This is where you belong, Chloe. Now lie back and rest.'

Chloe lay back on the bed. Prince placed his cooling hand on her fevered brow and gazed into her stoned eyes.

'Feel better?'

'Yes.'

'I'll see you later.'

'Yes, Prince. Thanks a million.'

'My pleasure,' Prince said.

He turned away and left the room, closing the door behind him but not locking it this time. Leaving the Portakabin, he crossed the clearing to his own place and entered to have a light, quick breakfast of cereal and orange juice. After making himself some herbal tea, he sat in front of the television set and tuned it into the station that would show the news at 9.00 a.m. He turned the sound off, then checked his wristwatch. It was just turning 8.25. Feeling calm, in control, he sat there sipping his tea, imagining the events as they were unfolding in Babylon.

Right now, his six disciples would already be in the various Underground stations they had been allocated and making their way down to the platforms. Prince checked his wristwatch again. It was now 8.30 a.m. precisely. Each of the disciples had been told to catch a train at their designated station at 8.25, go one stop only, then get out again. Right now, having travelled from Bond Street to Oxford Street, Daniel Richardson, nineteen years old, from Richmond, Surrey, was leaving a tube train in Oxford Street Station, releasing his poison gas by surreptitiously dropping his package on the carriage floor and tramping on it as he stepped out to break the two plastic capsules inside it. Another disciple, Angela Pilchard, eighteen years old and as pretty as a picture, from Fowey, Cornwall, was doing the same in Tottenham Court Road Station, having travelled there from Leicester Square. The other four disciples were doing exactly the same at this very moment in the Underground stations of Piccadilly Circus, Marble Arch, King's Cross and Waterloo.

In every case, with the plastic capsules inside each apparently innocuous lunch box or drinks carton trampled and quietly smashed, a colourless, odourless, deadly vapour was being released into the halted carriages. Even as Prince's disciples were riding the escalators away from the endangered areas and, eventually, out of the stations, the killing gas, invisible, without smell, was wafting out of the open carriages, on to the station platforms, and was also filling the carriages themselves as the doors closed and the trains moved on. When they reached the next station platforms and their doors opened, the lethal process was being repeated.

Prince checked his wristwatch. Five minutes had passed since the capsules had been broken. He could imagine what was happening all over the London Underground network even as he sat sipping his herbal tea.

Prince's disciples would already have left their designated

stations by the time the passengers in the contaminated trains started coughing. Within minutes, the same passengers – men, women and schoolchildren – would be retching and half-blind.

By this time the lethal invisible cloud that had escaped through the open carriage doors would have spread along the platforms of the various stations and started seeping up stairs and escalators, thus contaminating hundreds of other travellers. Within fifteen minutes, the various trains would have covered a great many stations all over the network and their doors, when opening to let out the gasping, sobbing, half-blind passengers, would be letting more vapour escape to contaminate even more stations.

Twenty minutes after the first capsules had been broken, nearly a dozen passengers were already dead from heart seizures, many more were suffering from fatal brain damage, and hundreds were bleeding from their noses and ears and helplessly evacuating their bowels, retching and vomiting, either in the trains or on the stairs and escalators as they frantically made their way out of the stations.

Prince first saw all this in his vivid imagination, then observed it in reality when, at precisely 9.00 a.m., the news came on TV and he turned the sound up. Speaking over on-the-spot pictures of the swarms of passengers stumbling – retching, vomiting, bleeding and sobbing – out of various Underground stations, a BBC newscaster, clearly distraught and disbelieving, was explaining that some kind of poisonous gas had been released into the Underground and had been carried on tube trains over much of the central part of the network. Learning of this, the authorities had stopped all further movement of trains. But the stations themselves were dangerously contaminated and hundreds of passengers had been affected by the poison, with some dead and many seriously ill. Right now, the stations were being evacuated by army medics wearing protective CBW suits with respirators. Meanwhile, however, the gas was spreading and the death toll was mounting.

Prince watched the news all morning, his pleasure increasing as events unfolded, as the number of fatalities rose to just under a hundred, the quantity of those seriously ill reached over three hundred, and so-called minor cases – most involving extreme discomfort and almost certainly carrying hidden, long-term side effects – were estimated to be in their thousands. By the time he switched the TV off, just before noon, when his six disciples were marching in to make their reports, the whole of the London Underground network had been closed down and the tragedy was being described officially as the worst terrorist atrocity ever to take place on British soil.

'Hallelujah!' Prince said.

# CHAPTER NINE

'That bastard,' Blackwell said, 'has just killed nearly a hundred people, brain-damaged others, made thousands more seriously ill and brought the London Underground to a halt. He's taken credit for it in this latest communication and it's clear that he doesn't intend stopping there. This is *serious*, Cusack!'

He and Cusack were having an urgent meeting in Blackwell's office in the 'Kremlin', the SAS Operations Planning and Intelligence cell located at Stirling Lines, Hereford. Both men were wearing their SAS uniforms, though neither wore his badged beret. They were facing each other across Blackwell's desk, which was piled high with papers.

'What's in the communication?' Cusack asked.

'Here. Read it.' Blackwell handed over the letter that had been mailed to William Hargreaves, Commissioner for the Metropolitan Police.

'When did Hargreaves receive it?' Cusack asked as he checked the envelope.

'In this morning's mail.'

'Posted from Glasgow, Scotland,' Cusack said, studying the postmark on the envelope, 'and sent the day before yesterday, probably a few hours after the nerve gas was released into the Underground.'

'Correct. Not that there's much likelihood of finding our man in Glasgow. Obviously the letter was only *mailed* from there, just as the last one was deliberately mailed from Paris. Here, read the damned thing.'

Aware that his commanding officer was in an unusually agitated condition, Cusack removed the letter from the envelope, unfolded it and noticed immediately that it was on the computer-generated letterhead of the British Millennialist Movement. It was undated and had been printed out on an ink-jet printer. Prince had, however, signed it with an ornate signature that suggested he was a flamboyantly self-regarding character. Cusack read the letter.

To whom it may concern:

As war between us has already been declared, this communication is our formal declaration that the British Millennialist Movement was responsible for the CLEANSING OPERATION undertaken on March 3, 2003 in the London Underground and that it is the second aggressive action in our campaign of righteous terrorism designed to defeat the ANTICHRIST by destroying his disciples, notably the QUEEN OF BABYLON, the members of her so-called ROYAL FAMILY, and their secret cohorts in the CIVIL SERVICE, the POLICE FORCE, all INTELLIGENCE ORGANIZATIONS and the ARMED SERVICES, particularly your paid assassins, the SAS. This is war without quarter. Let it therefore be noted that similar aggressive actions will be undertaken by us in the near future and that we will not stop, OR BE STOPPED, until such times as Buckingham Palace is either in ruins or occupied by us – with your so-called Royal Family, in truth members of THE ILLUMINATI, terminated and your SATANIC PARLIAMENT stripped of its authority. Doomsday, your Day of Judgement, is at hand. You have hereby been warned. Yours sincerely,
*Prince*.

Cusack folded the letter neatly, replaced it in its envelope and handed it back to his grim-faced CO.

'He's fond of his capital letters, isn't he?' he said sardonically.

'Yes,' Blackwell replied without a smile. 'And as we know from past experience, that over-abundance of capital letters invariably indicates extreme political or religious fanaticism. So clearly this madman means what he says and will set few limitations upon his actions. In short, if he wants to occupy Buckingham Palace, he'll try to do just that and if he fails, he'll try to turn it into ruins. Either way, the bastard has to be stopped. So what's been happening, Sergeant?'

'We're working on it,' Cusack replied cagily.

'What does that mean?' Blackwell asked, not prepared for evasions. 'Have you come up with anything on him yet?'

'Enough to be getting on with,' Cusack told him. 'Scotland Yard has managed to match all the number plates found in the debris of the Whitehall explosion to their original vehicles, so now we know who last owned the truck used for the bombing. Guy named Thomas Simmonds. Thirty-five years old but never married. Owned a small dairy farm just outside Calne in Wiltshire. According to neighbours, he drank a lot and got into fist fights when drunk.'

'Like you,' Blackwell said.

Cusack was not amused. 'Our Simmonds was a racist with a particular hatred of Jews and Blacks. More interestingly, he was a member of a local gun club, liked collecting weapons, often illegally, and talked a lot, when drunk, about how he was going to sell his farm and join one of those right-wing racist organizations that these days are holed up in armed camps all over the country. When the police checked his house, they did indeed find a formidable stash of illegal weapons, including a sixty-millimetre anti-tank rocket launcher. He also had a computer and was heavily into the World Wide Web.'

'Does that have relevance?'

'Yes, boss. Even before the bombing, Simmonds was viewed by the local police as a potential racist troublemaker with violent leanings. He was therefore placed under police surveillance that included the intercepting of his cellular phone calls and the monitoring of his Internet browsing. At the end of the first year of this electronic surveillance, the police had a pretty good record of just who he was calling, both by phone and when surfing the Net.'

'Which means?'

'That we have a list of most of the people he was talking to by phone last year and can narrow it down to those he called the most and was still in touch with right up to the Whitehall bombing. When the police have finished reducing that list to a select few, they'll investigate those people with particular reference to their political, religious or racial beliefs and also find out if they belong to any radical organizations. They'll also check just what those people were doing on the day of the bombing. By those means, they might be able to identify this so-called Prince.'

'What about Simmonds's Internet browsing?'

'It was almost totally concentrated on visits to the websites of the many paramilitary-style right-wing racist and religious movements now proliferating all over the country. As you know, boss, most of those movements like to give advice and information about the purchase of weapons and the making of home-made bombs, so clearly he was surfing for that. However, his browsing confirms that he was indeed growing keen on the idea of actually joining one of those movements and was surfing to find the one most suitable to his needs. We're still sifting through the information taken off his computer records – at least, Scotland Yard is – and we're hoping to find out if he did in fact join one of the movements. If he did – and if that movement turns out to be the British Millennialist Movement – the connection between Simmonds and Prince will be proven.'

'Far be it from me to dim your enthusiasm, Cusack, but identifying this Prince isn't necessarily going to help us find him. If, as we believe, he's holed up somewhere in the countryside, in one of those armed camps, we won't necessarily know which one it is. I mean, those bastards don't put placards up outside their camps announcing themselves by giving the real name of their organization. Also, as you surely know, the police now make a point of giving such places a wide berth unless they have absolutely no choice: there are just too many of them to deal with, half of the members would be willing to die rather than surrender, and since most of them are ostensibly solid, honest citizens, the aftermath of any assault on a camp could be a legal nightmare. Which is exactly why, in this case, our otherwise excellent Commissioner for the Metropolitan Police wants to hand the actual attack over to the SAS.'

Blackwell's frustration was clear from his sarcasm, but Cusack was willing to wear it because he knew just how important this assignment was to him. In the past few years, the SAS had received strong criticism from politicians and the media, with more than one opponent demanding that it be disbanded, particularly as it had recently been used as an urban police force rather than as an army regiment reserved for special operations overseas. Blackwell was under increasing pressure to prove that the regiment still had a legitimate reason to exist and Operation Millennium, the neutralizing of Prince, was therefore of crucial importance. The thought that Prince might actually target the Royal Family would be giving him sleepless nights. Cusack had deep respect for his CO and sympathized with his plight.

'If we can identify Prince, we can track him down,' Cusack said, 'and we may be able to do that through the list of men that Simmonds talked to most often on his cellular phone. By that time, however, we might already have learned from our own Internet surfing exactly what the British Millennialist Movement is and where it's located.'

'Forgive my ignorance, but I don't see how that's possible.'

'I'm not too hot on it myself, boss, but from what my computer buffs tell me, the more serious websites use magic cookies to track visitors.'

'What?'

'Magic cookies . . . Little bits of code that enable websites to track anonymous browsers who visit them. In other words, when a browser first visits a particular website, he doesn't usually give his name or any other kind of identification because, though he wants to get in there, he may not necessarily want them to get back to him.'

'He wants to remain anonymous,' Blackwell said.

'Correct. So the website, wanting to identify the anonymous visitor, drops a magic cookie into the basket of the browser and then uses it instead of a name – like tagging a bird, say. The website can then track the magic cookie, that particular code, to obtain information on the browser.'

'How come?'

'Well, when the browser goes elsewhere, the website can track him by using the magic cookie and learn what his interests are by noting where else he browses and the kind of purchase he most often makes through the Internet. Then, the next time the same browser visits the original website, the one now clandestinely tracking him, the site will present him with an ad that he can't resist – say, an ad for a particular kind of modem, or for an on-line publisher or brokerage firm, a travel agency, maybe even just a restaurant – and finally, when the browser responds, he'll innocently give the website the information they request: his address or credit card details. It's as simple as that.'

'Sounds dodgy to me,' Blackwell said.

'Many people find it offensive,' Cusack replied, 'but despite that, it's now used by a lot of major on-line companies as a way of watching consumers without their consent. So magic cookies, good or bad, can be used to track down details of web surfers who think they're browsing anonymously.'

'I'm still not sure how this would help us find Prince or his British Millennialist Movement. I mean, assuming that the movement is always looking for new members, surely *they*'d be the ones to use magic cookies to track down, then draw in, the visitors to their own website.'

Respectful of Blackwell's perception, despite his computer

ignorance, Cusack smiled and said, 'Correct, boss. Beyond any shadow of doubt, the paramilitary movements, always looking for new recruits, will have magic cookies installed in their websites. However, if I personally use the Internet to visit the website of every known paramilitary movement – deliberately doing so as an anonymous browser – I can, in effect, let myself be tracked by them and, eventually, be approached by them as a potential new recruit, thereby finding out just who they are and where they're located. So, if one of those pseudonymous websites turns out to be Prince's British Millennialist Movement, I'll be able to track them all the way back to their real-time location.'

'Pardon?'

Cusack smiled again. 'Real time – any time not spent on-line. The real world as distinct from cyberspace. Their on-line location is cyberspace; their real-time location is somewhere right here on earth.'

'And, hopefully, in England.'

'You can bet on it, boss.'

Blackwell sighed. 'No wonder the regiment is in trouble. We're living in the past. Technologically Neanderthal, in fact.'

'I'm afraid that's true, boss.'

Blackwell leaned back in his chair and gazed at the ceiling, a man deep in thought. He sighed again, like one profoundly weary, then lowered his gaze.

'So what if we find him?' he asked, referring to Prince.

'Straightforward QRF assault on his hideaway,' Cusack replied. 'Given what he's already told us about his plans, there's no other way. Wherever he is, he won't come out with his hands up.'

'Damned right, he won't,' Blackwell said. 'On the other hand, that could give us more grief, politically speaking. I mean, imagine the headlines. The SAS slaughtering English citizens engaged in their legitimate right to express their opinions and defend their own values, albeit somewhat extreme. We're now like America, Sergeant Cusack, where certain highly organized groups of deranged individuals can insist on the right to defend themselves against so-called assassins sanctioned by the state. That's what's got us into trouble these past few years and it could do so again.'

'True enough, boss, but in this case we have something strong going for us.'

'Oh, yes?'

'Yes, boss.'

'Stop winding me up, Sergeant. What is it?'

'The extraordinary nature of the threat, boss. The threat of direct physical action against the Royal Family. In this particular instance, we're going up against people who're threatening either to destroy or occupy Buckingham Palace, neutralize the Royal Family, possibly with extreme prejudice, and then bring down the whole British government. This is no bunch of hopeful bank robbers; it's big-league time, boss. This bunch are grandstanders.'

'Mmmm,' Blackwell responded, looking slightly more hopeful. 'Yes, Sergeant, I see. I'd almost forgotten that.'

'What I'm saying, boss, is that we do what we normally wouldn't even consider: we *announce* the intentions of the enemy and thus emphasize just how important this mission is.'

'Brilliant, Sergeant, except for one thing. The Royal Family would never permit that.'

'So?'

'I am all ears.'

This was what Cusack had been waiting for. Already intent on leaking the fact that an SAS QRF squad, headed by himself, had been assigned the task of neutralizing the individual responsible for what was already being called the 'Whitehall Atrocity', as well as for the devastating gassing of the London Underground system, he needed to cover himself by having his CO sanction a similar leak: in this case, the serious threat posed by Prince to the Royal Family and the British government. When, as must inevitably happen, the source of the first leak – Cusack – was uncovered, he could defend himself by pointing out the necessity of the second leak, which would lend moral sanction to the first. Since his CO, Lieutenant Colonel Blackwell, would be responsible for that second leak, Cusack could argue his own case and get away with it. The morality of this situation was highly dubious, but Cusack had no choice in the matter. He was skating on thin ice with this mission, and he had to protect himself somehow. His respect for his CO, which was genuine, was not the issue here; the successful completion of the mission, however it was conducted, was all that mattered for now.

'We *leak* it,' Cusack said boldly. 'We let the country know the sheer extent of the threat – their intent to extinguish the Royal Family *and* the government – and then our so-called ruthlessness in dealing with that threat becomes both morally and politically acceptable. Such a leak would work, boss.'

Blackwell stared steadily at Cusack, wondering where he was coming from, knowing his penchant for trouble but also respecting him as a soldier, despite the man's personal problems, and clearly trying to ascertain just how far he could trust his judgement. Cusack, deliberately holding Blackwell's gaze, knew just what he was thinking and understood his concern. He himself had doubts about what he was proposing, but nothing else had so far struck him as being better. The regimental motto was 'Who dares wins', and he was going to stand by it.

'Could this leak get back to the regiment?' Blackwell asked, after a lengthy, thoughtful silence.

'No,' Cusack said. 'The SAS has become a virtual cult on the Internet. Hackers, who can penetrate the computer security of the most secret military establishments, are hacking into our mainframes and spreading formerly confidential information about us all over the World Wide Web.'

'Which explains our present difficulties,' Blackwell said, looking aggrieved. 'It's the hackers who've pre-empted us time after time, letting the whole damned world know what we're planning, despite our own attempts to work covertly. So what you're saying, I assume, is that even if we do the leaking ourselves, those leaks will be widely assumed to be the postings of hackers.'

'Right,' Cusack said. 'We simply throw our hands up in the air and deny all knowledge.'

'Or, even better,' Blackwell said, 'we use the leak to complain, as we've done in the past, about the lack of official control over the World Wide Web. Certainly, we wouldn't be alone in making *that* particular complaint.'

'Sounds good to me, boss.'

Blackwell picked up a ballpoint pen to tap it repeatedly, distractedly, against the edge of his desk. Eventually, he stopped tapping and said, 'What about your QRF team? Have you selected the men yet?'

'Yes, boss, I have. Sergeant Lewis and I picked them together.'

'So who are they, Sergeant?' When Cusack slid a piece of paper across the desk, Blackwell picked it up, studied it with pursed lips, then handed it back and nodded affirmatively. 'That looks like a pretty strong team.'

'The crème de la crème, boss.'

'They'd better be,' Blackwell said.

# CHAPTER TEN

Prince could hear the sound of gunshots even from where he was walking around the perimeter fence, exercising in the crisp air of a sunny April morning while also checking that his armed guards were doing their duty. The gunfire was coming from the shooting range inside one of the old aircraft hangars, where young men and women were being taught how to 'defend' themselves in the event of an attack – though they would most likely be used as aggressors against the forces of the Antichrist who were, in Prince's view, all those connected with the Royal Family or the government.

His armed camp was, in fact, preparing for war – though few in it knew that – just as many similar camps across the new Britain were doing.

As usual when taking his morning exercise, Prince wore his flowing, plain white kaftan, which he felt lent him a biblical appearance, though he was sensible enough to be wearing beneath it warmer modern clothing, including the regulation army-style pants and woollen pullover. Nevertheless, with his long golden-blond hair and white kaftan, he knew that he looked rather Christ-like and that this was all to the good. He was therefore not surprised when he passed one of his armed perimeter-fence guards and the young man, wearing the same military-style clothing and bearing an AK47 Kalashnikov assault rifle, automatically bowed his head in respect. Indeed, Prince would have been mortally offended and very angry had the young man forgotten to do so.

Nodding and smiling beatifically at the guard, raising his right hand in a sign of benediction, Prince moved on, occasionally glancing beyond the barbed-wire perimeter fence to the rolling green landscape of Wiltshire, now sublime in an early-morning mist. Indeed, it looked so beautiful here that it was hard to believe just how violently divided the country had become, what darkness lurked beneath the calm surface. Right now, all over the land, camps just like this one would be coming to life, with Millennialist fanatics preparing to spend yet another day in lecturing their young about government conspiracies, the iniquities of the established Church, the corruption of the police, the evils of the defence forces, the possibility of alien intervention in the affairs of humanity, and, most important of all, the ongoing need to go to war against the Antichrist.

*We have our friends in the United States to thank for that,* Prince thought as he turned away from the barbed-wire perimeter, from the sight of those lush green fields, and headed towards the old aircraft hangars, where the guns were still firing. *They lit the beacon that we follow.*

Indeed, as he approached the first rust-red aircraft hangar, listening fondly to the sound of gunshots, he accepted the fact that those weapons would not be firing had he and others just as enlightened not opened their hearts and minds to the teachings of their brethren in the United States. God bless the World Wide Web for that.

It was through the web that he, Prince, had first come to know about his American friends and had subsequently learned all that he knew now. It was through his American friends that he had received coherent explanations for many of the things that had been troubling him: the Jews, the Blacks and swarthies (as he now called them), the Nazis, UFOs, the Illuminati, Freemasonry, AIDS, government conspiracies and, most important of all, the coming of the Antichrist. More than anything else, however, he had learned from his American friends how best to defeat his growing feelings of impotence in an increasingly complex, threatening world.

Instead of standing by and looking on helplessly as the Jews conspired to take control of world economics, as the American and British governments, with the aid, respectively, of the CIA and MI5, conspired to aid the Jews, Blacks, swarthies and other ethnic subversives, as the Royal Family – secret Freemasons, thus members of the Illuminati – conspired behind closed doors to bring about the coming of the Antichrist . . . Yes, instead of letting all this happen and feeling increasingly impotent because of it, he had been shown the way by his American friends. Indeed, it was they, more than anyone else, who had given him the courage to do what he believed all true Englishmen should do: take up weapons against those who would conspire to take over their institutions and their traditions – their whole country, in fact. This he had done. His American friends had encouraged him. Now, as he entered the aircraft hangar and saw a row of young men and women, all lying belly down on the ground of the indoor firing range in order to train with deadly weapons, he felt proud of himself.

The weapons roared. The young people were firing at pop-up cardboard cut-out figures with painted-on rifles and balaclava helmets – cardboard enemies based on a hated real enemy: the SAS Quick Reaction Force. Instantly, however, upon seeing Prince enter the hangar, the weapons instructor, Ben Cole, a middle-aged racist former police sergeant from Clapham, respectfully bowed his head and ordered the young people lying on their bellies to do the same. In order to do this, they had to lower their weapons to the ground and raise themselves to their knees. Once in that position, they all inclined their heads submissively, then looked up with worshipful eyes as Prince, Christ-like in his white robes, again raised his right hand in benediction.

'God bless all of you,' he said, his voice theatrically resonant. 'Please continue your training.'

With that, he left the hangar and made his way across the airstrip to reach his own Portakabin. En route, he glanced up at the old air traffic control tower, now a watchtower with a machine-gun crew, and reflected on how much like America England had become during these past few years, with movements such as his own, armed to the teeth and prepared to fight, being deliberately ignored by the police. This was because the authorities feared bloody mayhem of the kind that had occurred in Waco, Texas, a good few years ago, when the US government's attack against the Branch Davidian cult compound, which resulted in the deaths of eighty-two American citizens, was widely compared by the Millennarians to the Nazis going into Warsaw.

Word was bound to have filtered out that Prince's own compound was armed to the teeth but, until he used the weapons aggressively, the local police would most likely avoid the place. This was Prince's strength, enabling him to build up his army quietly until he had chosen the time of his personal Judgement Day. He was probably perfectly safe until then.

Once inside his Portakabin, he made his own breakfast, as befitted a humble man, then sat at his desk for his daily input of information in preparation for the class he was conducting an hour later, after his students, mainly newcomers, had eaten in the canteen. Some of the information came from imported American Millennarian books, such as the apocalyptic *Behold a Pale Horse* by William Cooper, head of the Oklahoma Patriots' militia, and *Scarlet and the Beast* by the 'evangelical' John Daniel; some came from his restless surfing of the World Wide Web, with particular emphasis on electronic billboards such as 'rec.pyrotechnics' that offered advice on paramilitary activities and supplies; and the rest came from cassette tapes purchased over the Internet from the notorious Radio Free World and outfits like Christian Harvester Tapes. These pre-recorded cassettes, many taken off widely broadcast radio programmes, were crammed with esoteric 'teachings' about UFOs, the Luciferian machinations of rival groups, and all kinds of government, black militarist, Jewish and Muslim conspiracies designed to take over an increasingly threatened white Christian world.

Having completed his reading, Prince spoke into the intercom on his desk, informing two of his closest aides and personal bodyguards, Dennis Welsh and Clive Jones, that he was ready to be escorted to his class. The two men entered shortly after: both in their late teens, both with dyed blond hair, both wearing jungle-green combat clothing, with handguns holstered at the waist. They gazed at Prince with blind, brainwashed adulation.

'Good morning, gentlemen,' he said, giving a gentle smile as he picked a hand-bound book off his desk. 'How are you two this morning?'

'Fine, sir,' Welsh said.

'Me too, sir,' Jones said.

'Slept soundly?' Both men nodded. 'Had breakfast?' Both men nodded again. 'Good. Let's get going.'

Carrying the hand-bound book, which looked like an historical tome, though it contained only his own notes, Prince let his bodyguards escort him back across the compound, to the Portakabin used as a classroom. Dennis Welsh entered first, Prince fell in behind him and Clive Jones brought up the rear, his hand resting lightly on his pistol. They advanced past the rows of steel-framed chairs placed in front of a raised platform on which were a large blackboard and a lectern stolen from a local church. As usual, all the chairs were taken. Some had been occupied by newcomers, including Chloe, Jim Bleakly and Mark Sayers, but others had been occupied by the already converted, who simply couldn't get enough of Prince and his sacred words.

Pleased by the turnout, Prince strode on to the raised platform, rested the book on the lectern, waited until his bodyguards had taken up positions on either side of him, then took a deep breath and prepared to give his lecture – or sermon.

He actually began by smiling beatifically and asking, 'How are you all?'

'Fine!' the members of his class – or congregation – sang out simultaneously.

'Slept soundly?'

They all smiled and nodded affirmatively.

'Had breakfast?'

They all smiled and nodded affirmatively again.

'Good. Then let us begin.' He opened the hand-bound book on the table, studied it as if it were the Bible, then turned around to face the blackboard behind him. Two sentences were written in Prince's eloquent hand on it: *'God is love'* and *'The enemy is the Antichrist'*. Prince picked up a pointer and tapped the first sentence, positioning himself so that the class could see his face.

'We all know what this sentence means,' he said. 'God is love and we are here to worship God and, as I am one of God's servants, you must worship Him through me. I am not, however, God, and should not be treated as if I were, but your respect for and subservience to me will be noted by Him. I am here as your guiding light, as your channel to Him, and I am here to instruct you in how to prepare to face His enemy, whom we know as the Antichrist.' He tapped the second sentence with his pointer, once, twice, a third time, saying, 'Yes, the enemy *is* the Antichrist and we're engaged in the war against him and must not be defeated.'

Putting the pointer down, he turned around to face them fully once more, letting them see his clear, green-eyed, saintly gaze. He then spoke, his words ringing out dramatically against their reverential silence.

'What is the Antichrist and where do we find him? The Antichrist represents the forces of darkness and we find him in our very midst, in the city of Babylon, behind the façade of a palace in which resides a so-called Royal Family that is actually in the vile hands of the Illuminati, whose origins lie in the ancient Brotherhood of the Snake and whose aims are a Luciferian totalitarian state from which the Christian and the righteous shall be banished.' Having spoken in one lengthy rush of words, he now paused for emphasis, then thundered, as if assailing the very heavens, *'We cannot permit this!'*

'No!' his disciples called out in reply. 'The Lord be praised! *No!'*

'Indeed, no!' Prince rejoined. 'Have we not seen from the words in the Bible, though they may be couched in ambiguity and their true meaning only revealed to the righteous, we white Christians, that there is a global government conspiracy to destroy white Christianity and replace it with the satanic beliefs of the Illuminati, with their lust for an occult New World Order?'

'Yes,' his disciples cried out in response. *'Yes!'*

'And have we not seen through the lies and distortions of the puke-making media and sinful rewriters of history to the inner truth of what is really going on?'

'Tell us, Prince! Tell us!'

'Everywhere the new oligarchies are trying to take control – the *evil*archies of a satanic order fronted by our so-called leaders. In the case of America, this conspiracy is headed by an evil President and his generals; in our own country, by the so-called Royal Family and their mouthpiece, a degenerate Prime Minister. And how carefully, how insidiously, they've tried to conceal the knowledge that Freemasonry is but a branch of the secret Illuminati, that the birthplace of Freemasonry is right here in England, that modern Babylon is London and our presiding Queen is the Queen of Babylon, the patroness of English Freemasonry, that her children are known to have constantly taken part in Masonic rites, and that the Antichrist must therefore come from London. All this they have tried to cover up. But now the truth has come out. The global government conspiracy, which includes America and our own country, that Luciferian pact, has been designed to silence those seeking truth and wisdom. But this book –' and here he waved his hand-bound book of personal notes '– contains the word of the Lord and tells us exactly what we must do . . . So what *must* we do?'

'Tell us, Prince! Tell us!'

'We must prepare ourselves for the coming of the Antichrist, prepare to fight the good fight, prepare to take up arms if necessary, to defend our right to our own faith, our white Christian faith, which is not bound by the hypocrisies of the established Church, not corrupted by the hedonism of the Blacks and the swarthies, not yet tainted by the financial machinations of the global Jewish conspiracy. We must also be prepared for another kind of fight: that unavoidably bloody fight against the state's sanctioned death squads, including the police force, but particularly the SAS and its Quick Reaction Force, the notorious QRF, which we know to be as secret as the Masons, with its own obscene rituals. We must be prepared to stand by our beliefs and fight to the bitter end to protect them. *This is what we are here for!*'

So Prince went on and on, talking persuasively, even hypnotically, and thus making the incoherent seem perfectly logical. As he continued, his voice rising and falling, here beseeching, there threatening, always passionate and convincing, he was often carried away by his own stirring rhetoric, but at other times he carefully surveyed his audience to judge their reactions. Most of them were entranced, their power of logical thought drowned in emotion, hanging on to every word he said and questioning nothing. However, when *he* asked a question, always purely rhetorical, they responded with shouts and squeals, with the waving of their hands, each fighting for his personal attention, some of them almost springing up from their chairs, all flushed and wide-eyed. It was like an evangelical meeting, underpinned by the same emotions and, since those emotions were always running high, Prince was deeply satisfied.

Only Chloe responded differently, and he found this intriguing. This young lady had suffered all the torments of an enforced, almost cold-turkey withdrawal from drug addiction, followed by a less painful, more gradual withdrawal with ever-decreasing amounts of heroin being administered, followed by a change to methadone and, finally, when she felt that she could deal with it, a complete giving up of both drugs.

The gratitude Chloe had felt at being rescued from the horrors of drug addiction had been the basis for her increasing emotional dependence upon Prince, as he had always known it would be. Eventually, as her addiction to the drugs decreased and her reliance on him increased, he was able to make her believe that she would have no life worth living outside his community and could only be truly happy within it, surrounded by friends of her own age and motivated by what the community could teach her. As it had with all the others, so this seduction had worked with Chloe: soon she became a 'convert', an active member of the community, attending classes, helping in the kitchen and canteen, working in the craft shop that she had previously disdained, learning to fire weapons, and even going into the local towns with other converts to sell the craft goods they'd made.

Nevertheless, though now devoted to Prince, viewing him as a father figure and saturating herself in his particular bizarre mixture of Millennialist religion and politics, Chloe did not actually *worship* him as the others did, did not view him as God's personal messenger, and certainly did not become ecstatic, as the others did, when he gave his lectures or sermons. Almost certainly she would be willing to do most things he asked of her, but there remained a withholding, a native scepticism, a stubborn refusal to give up her all. This was something Prince would have to watch out for. He would, perhaps, have to test her.

At the end of this particular sermon, Prince did what he always did to test the devotion of his flock: he had his two bodyguards remove the sandals from his feet, each guard handling a separate foot. Then he sat on the chair placed right beside the lectern, in the middle of the platform, pushing his feet forward and inviting everyone in the room to kiss them. They all did so willingly, lining up like schoolchildren, the first kissing his right foot, the second the left, the third the right, the fourth the left and so on. When Chloe's turn eventually came, she did exactly the same, just as she had done many times before. Pleased, Prince stroked the back of her head and then said, 'Come and see me.'

'When?'

'In five minutes,' he told her.

Five minutes later, when Prince was back in the study of his personal Portakabin, Chloe knocked on the door and he bade her enter. Like most of the others in the compound, she had forsaken her old clothing and was now wearing the regulation army-style slacks and woollen pullover, with her feet in flat shoes. The dark rings had disappeared from under her large brown eyes and her formerly gaunt looks were now fuller. Nevertheless, though looking healthy, she seemed a lot older than her age and, Prince realized, she radiated the kind of mature sexuality that could only have sprung from her shameful experiences on the street. This part of her nature, he thought, could come in useful, so he wanted to check her out.

'Sit down,' he said, indicating the chair at the other side of his desk. He waited until she was seated, then said, 'So how are you coping, Chloe?'

'Fine,' she said. 'I think you must know that. I'm feeling healthier every day. I'm also feeling a lot more relaxed. I'm so glad I came here.'

'You appear to get on with the others.'

'Yeah, I do. I think they're really nice. I often think they're the first real friends I've had. Nobody's ever helped me like this before, and that's something I can't forget.'

'Now that you're off drugs and feeling healthy, do you ever contemplate returning home?'

'No, I don't want to go back home.'

'You don't want to see your parents even for a short time?'

'No!' Chloe said emphatically, as if frightened that he would actually *send* her back. 'They wouldn't understand what we're doing here. They'd think it was some kind of cult – you know, one of those dangerous sects – and nothing that I could say would change their minds. If I went to see them for even a short visit, to let them know I was okay, they might not let me come back here.'

'And you don't think you could live with them again?'

'I want to stay here with my friends. I don't want to go home.'

Convinced by her attitude that she was telling the truth, aware that she was his, if not yet entirely so, he tried to ascertain just how far she had come with him by asking, 'So you want to stay on because you've now got friends here and because we've managed to get you off drugs?'

'Yes,' Chloe said. 'That's right.'

'Do you believe in what we're doing here, Chloe? Do you understand why *I'm* here?'

'I think I understand most of what I'm told, but some of it I'm still not too sure of . . . The Illuminati and the Royal Family . . . Yeah, I'm willing to buy that; I mean, I hate the Royal Family and think they're really weird . . . As for the cops . . . well, they're scumbags – at least, the ones who harassed me were – so I'm pretty sure a lot of them are Freemasons, just like you said . . . But this thing about maybe having to shoot people . . . well, I'm not too sure about that. I mean, it doesn't seem Christian, like.'

'That will only happen,' Prince said smoothly, 'if we have to *defend* ourselves. Like any man would have the right to defend his home against thugs, his wife and daughters from rapists, his valuables from thieves; like the English had to defend themselves against the Germans; like the Christians of old sometimes had to take up arms to defend themselves against the Muslims. If we're threatened with violence – as we might be – we'll *have* to defend ourselves. And violence can only be defeated with violence. That's a hard fact of life, my child.'

Chloe nodded her understanding, still looking a little doubtful but clearly trying to accept what she was hearing. 'Yeah,' she said, 'I guess you're right. I mean, if it's going to be for the good of the whole community, then I guess I'd do what was asked of me . . . even pick up a gun. Yeah, I guess I'd do that.'

'Good,' Prince said. 'That's heartening.' He glanced at his

wristwatch, raised his eyebrows in feigned surprise, and said, 'Oh, dear, I didn't realize the time, and we've both got our work to do. Well, I'm glad we've had this little talk, Chloe, and happy to see that you seem to be doing well. Keep up the good work; come and see me any time you have doubts.'

'Yeah, I will,' Chloe said, pushing her chair back and standing up, preparing to leave. 'And thanks for everything, Prince.'

'Your salvation is my pleasure,' he responded, smiling sweetly and indicating with a wave that she could leave the building. 'Have a good day, my dear.'

Chloe returned his smile, then turned around and left the office. Satisfied, Prince turned to his computer, accessed the Internet and started surfing to browse the websites of other Millennialist movements and to check any electronic billboards containing valuable information on weapons, explosives, home-made bombs or the supposedly covert activities of the Metropolitan Police and the hated SAS. To his surprise, he found on a certain notorious billboard a message concerning himself and his movement.

According to this anonymous posting, it was rumoured that a covert SAS operation had been recently initiated to identify and locate the person who had claimed responsibility for the Whitehall Atrocity and the gassing of the London Underground. The posting claimed that this man had called himself 'Prince', and it named his organization as the hitherto unknown British Millennialist Movement.

The leader of this SAS mission, code-named Operation Millennium, the posting went on, was Sergeant Leonard 'Lenny' Cusack of the regiment's 'reprehensible' Quick Reaction Force, already revered and/or reviled as the man responsible for many previous 'atrocities' against other Millennialist movements.

Prince sat back and stared steadily, silently at his glowing monitor, hardly believing what he saw there but certainly thrilled to be seeing it.

For, indeed, he knew Lenny Cusack.

# CHAPTER ELEVEN

The Killing House could be worse than the real thing. Cusack and his QRF team, officially being trained by Sergeant Jack Lewis, were on a CRW exercise in the CQB (close-quarter battle) House, or 'Killing House', of the Counter-Revolutionary Warfare Wing in Stirling Lines in Hereford. There, wearing their all-black CRW overalls with Armourshield's GPV-24 body armour and SF-10 respirator masks, they had to make their way through the six 'killing rooms' of the mock-up house, each room different from the other, firing double taps from their regulation Browning 9mm High Power handguns or short bursts from their Heckler & Koch MP5 sub-machine guns, at various pop-up 'figure-eleven' targets. They were also armed with Brocks Pyrotechnics MX5 'flash-bang' stun grenades and had to use these, even more dangerously, in various unexpected situations recreated in any one of the six rooms.

The CQB House was dubbed the 'Killing House' for two good reasons. First, its purpose was to train men to kill at close quarters. Second, real ammunition was always used – and more than one SAS man had been killed accidentally while training with it.

As he made his own way through the Killing House, trying

to see through the smoke of the stun grenades already used by the men up ahead, Cusack felt a contradictory mixture of high tension and boredom. The tension came from the common fear that he would score an 'own goal' (accidentally shoot one of his own men) while using live ammunition; the boredom came from the fact that before these exercises in the Killing House he and the same band of men had already been repeatedly retrained to enter captured buildings by a variety of means, including abseiling with ropes from the roof, sometimes firing their Brownings with one hand as they clung to the roof with the other. The Killing House training was, however, an essential preparation for what they would meet in a hostage-rescue operation (as had been the case with Joshua and as could be the same with Prince), and would sharpen their skills at distinguishing instantly between terrorist and hostage.

This was done with the aid of pictures on the walls and with wooden dummies, the figure-eleven targets, that were moved from place to place or that popped out abruptly from behind artificial walls or up from the lower frames of windows. As an indication of the changing times, the figure-eleven targets, which had formerly been made to look like Soviet troops, were now dummy terrorists wearing anoraks and balaclava helmets.

The first trick was to learn to hit the 'terrorists' quickly and accurately; the second, more important trick was to avoid hitting a 'hostage' when there were only mere seconds to distinguish between the two.

Training in the Killing House was claustrophobic and nerve-racking, with the constant fear of scoring an 'own goal' always preying on the mind, particularly in those confined spaces, in the smoke and confusion. Cusack, however, while certainly feeling that tension, was also experiencing a distinct ennui. The changing nature of SAS work, which had moved from conventional warfare to Counter-Revolutionary Warfare (CRW) and CT (Counter-Terrorist) work, meant that most of his supposedly free time since Millennium Year had been spent on similar training overseas, learning an even wider variety of hostage-rescue skills of the kind required for dealing with Millennialist terrorists.

In fact, during the past two years alone Cusack had trained with West Germany's GSG-9 border police, France's Groupement d'Intervention de la Gendarmerie Nationale (GIGN) paramilitary units, the Bizondere Bystand Eenheid (BBE) counter-terrorist arm of the Royal Netherlands Marine Corps, Italy's Nucleo Operativo Centrale di Sicurezza (NOCS), Spain's Grupo Especial de Operaciones (GEO), and the US 1st Special Forces Operational Detachment, created specially for CRW operations.

That overseas training had placed a special emphasis on physical stamina, endurance and marksmanship, including indoor firing practice with live ammunition in other kinds of Killing Houses such as mock-up aircraft, ships and public streets, abseiling and parachuting on to rooftops, parked aircraft and boats, hostage rescue in a variety of circumstances (with crossover training in mountaineering, skiing and scuba-diving) and the handling of CS gas canisters and stun grenades. So right now, as he moved through the SAS Killing House one more time, Cusack was feeling thoroughly sick of it all, even as tension paradoxically tightened his stomach muscles.

Nevertheless, following the men in front, keeping ahead of the men behind him, trying to avoid scoring an own goal or becoming the victim of one, he made his way through the semi-darkness, kicking open doors, hurling flash-bangs into the rooms, dropping to one knee to fire his MP5 sub-machine gun, and eventually emerging from the swirling smoke and CS gas of the grenades to the welcome exit at the far end of the building.

Stepping through the exit into the fading light of this late afternoon in April, he removed his respirator from his face, took deep breaths of the fresh air, saw the green fields of Hereford beyond the camp's Nissen huts and then, right in front of him, Jack Lewis with four of his six chosen men, his *crème de la crème.* Having just emerged from the Killing House, they too were gratefully breathing the fresh air.

'Shit,' Corporal Chris Mapley, slim and black-haired, said as he rubbed his stinging brown eyes with a cordite-stained index finger, 'am I glad *that*'s over! I *hate* that fucking place.'

'Me too,' said Trooper Irwin Radnor, not as slim as Mapley but a good six inches taller, with auburn hair and long-lashed grey eyes. 'I think it's the pits.'

'Even worse than a sickener,' agreed Trooper Benjamin Wiley, hair red, eyes bright green, standing nearly six feet tall, referring to one of the toughest route marches that an SAS recruit would be called upon to perform during the Test Week of his brutal four weeks of Selection Training. The 'sickener' was so called because it was murderously difficult and most recruits failed it. 'I'd swap the Killing House for a sickener any day and that's a fact, man.'

'Not me,' Trooper Norman Carter said. He was of medium height, all muscle and bone, with a thick head of auburn hair and a piercing, aggressive blue gaze – not a man to mix with. 'I mean, I didn't mind the sickeners – they didn't bother me that much – but I really *enjoy* the Killing House. At least it's not fucking boring.'

'The man's crazy!' Radnor exclaimed.

In less than a minute, the remaining two men, Troopers Bill Stubbs and Mel Grant, emerged from the concrete block of the Killing House, Grant slamming the heavy steel door behind him. They both lowered their sub-machine guns to the side, removed their respirators, took deep gulps of fresh air, and blinked repeatedly, letting their watery eyes adjust to the light, which seemed a lot brighter than it actually was after the semi-darkness inside.

Bill Stubbs, who was built like a bantam cock and moved like one, practically vibrating with restless energy, forever running his fingers through his remaining hair to stroke his bald dome, glanced about him, first at the green fields beyond the perimeter fence, then at Sergeants Cusack and Lewis, and finally at the other four of the eight-man team who had got out of the Killing House ahead of him and Grant.

'So you no-hopers got through without scoring an own goal,' he said. 'You fuckin' amaze me!'

Mel Grant, fair-haired, not quite as thin on top as Stubbs, but certainly sharing his battered, bulldog features, grinned broadly at his friend's comment, revealing two missing front teeth. He and Stubbs were London East Enders who stuck closely together.

'I'm amazed you didn't get lost in there,' Irwin Radnor retorted. 'I mean, normally you come out the *front* door, saying, "Where the fuck am I?"'

'Ho, ho,' Stubbs said. 'Our Golders Green representative has spoken and left us speechless with wonder. Trust the Jews to be clever.'

'He's about as clever as a paratrooper stepping out of an aeroplane without his 'chute,' Mel Grant said. 'As clever as my arse over the bog, producing nothing but hot air.'

'The East Enders are true comedians,' Wiley said. 'They'd have their audience cramming the doorways – all fighting to get out of the fucking theatre.'

Sergeant Lewis glared at them. 'Why don't you bunch of pansies shut your mouths and make your way to the briefing room? Or should I RTU the lot of you right now?' he added, good-naturedly threatening to return them to their original units.

'Hold on,' Cusack said. 'You can forget the briefing room. I've got to get back home, so we can give today's Chinese Parliament a miss and catch up tomorrow.' By 'Chinese Parliament' he was referring to an informal meeting between the leader of a QRF team and his men, in which everyone was free to suggest ideas, irrespective of their rank or position in the team. 'Just gather around for a moment,' he added, 'and let me say a few words.'

As the six men gathered around him and Sergeant Lewis, Cusack realized how much younger they were than him and his best friend. Indeed, they were all too young to have fought in Operation Desert Storm in 1991, as he and Lewis had done, but they were certainly the *crème de la crème* of the regiment in the sense that they had all taken part in at least half a dozen operations mounted against the growing number of 'private armies' scattered throughout the country-side and masquerading as Millennialist movements. Like their American counterparts, the Millennarians or Patriots, most of the British groups were armed to the teeth and more than willing to defend themselves. More importantly, they were also ready, willing and able to engage in unprovoked attacks against any individual or group that they deemed to be 'the enemy', which in effect meant any individual or group that criticized them or otherwise displeased them. These six young men (the oldest, Bill Stubbs, being only in his late twenties) were, therefore, highly trained and widely experienced in exactly the kind of assault that would have to be undertaken should Prince's British Millennialist Move-ment turn out, as Cusack suspected it would, to be located in an armed camp somewhere in the countryside. Neverthe-less, Cusack still had something to tell them.

'Okay,' he said, 'I know you were simply swapping the customary bullshit there, but I also know that it was based on your weariness at having to repeat the same old training tactics, both in the open and in the Killing House. This, alas, will have to continue for a little bit longer.' Moans and groans rose from all concerned. 'It will, however, soon end.' Cheers and applause came from all six men. 'Yes, we've decided that the people we're going up against might be even more advanced than we presently are in both weapons and surveillance equipment. For this reason, you'll soon be taken off this routine training and introduced to an entirely new form of warfare in which none of you are experienced at all. By this I mean that, while your past battle experience and present skills will still be required, you'll be supplementing them with a whole new branch of technology that you'll have to learn quickly. I can't tell you what this is right now – it remains confidential – and I won't be training you myself, but when the time comes to take it on, which should be in a week or so, Sergeant Lewis here will be familiar with it and he's the one who'll train you. All I ask, then, is that you show a little more patience until that day comes. Any questions?'

'Yeah,' Corporal Mapley said. 'Just what kind of mission is this, boss? A proper war, or a CT operation? Can you tell us that yet?'

'No.'

'So when *can* you tell us?' Corporal Wiley asked.

'As soon as we know where the target is and how we can hit it.'

'You *don't* know what the target is?' Trooper Carter asked.

'No.'

'Shit!' Bill Stubbs exclaimed.

'We know generally what we're after,' Cusack tried to explain, 'but we still need to identify certain persons and, perhaps, locate the organization they head. We're working on that right now.'

'How close are you?' Trooper Radnor asked.

'So-so,' Cusack said.

'But either way,' Trooper Grant said, 'whether you're close or still far away, we're going to get off this conveyor belt and do something entirely new in no more than a week or so?'

'That's a promise,' Cusack said.

'Great,' Corporal Mapley said. 'At least that's better than nothing.'

After a short silence, Sergeant Lewis said, 'Any more questions?'

All the men shook their heads.

'Okay, men,' Cusack said. 'Dismissed.'

The six men reacted with big grins or mutual back-slapping, then they marched away from the looming concrete structure of the Killing House. When they had disappeared around some Nissen huts across a clearing, heading back to the Spider for some well-earned R&R (rest and relaxation), Sergeant Lewis, still holding his MP5 in his right hand, turned to Cusack.

'So what's happening, pal? I mean, why are you rushing home?'

'Let's get back to the Spider,' Cusack replied. 'I have to change clothes. We'll talk on the way.' He held his own MP5 level with his right hip as he and Lewis walked towards the Nissen huts, beyond which lay the more open public part of the camp. The sun was going down over Hereford and casting great shadows on the greenery beyond the perimeter. Cusack continued, 'An hour ago, I received a call on my mobile from William Hargreaves, Commissioner for the Metropolitan Police. Hargreaves thinks he can now identify the man responsible for both the Whitehall Atrocity and the poisoning of the London Underground system – the man who calls himself Prince.'

Lewis gave a low whistle. They were now walking through the shadows of the Nissen huts, with the rest of the camp coming into view. Troop trucks and jeeps were still on the move and SAS troopers could be seen all over the place, engaged in their various activities as the lights of the buildings came on, one after the other, to combat the descending darkness of the coming evening.

'That's good news,' Lewis said.

'Let's hope so,' Cusack said, 'because we want to neutralize this bastard before he does something else.'

'If they can really identify him, that's great,' Lewis said. 'But do they know where he is?'

'Hargreaves was being cautious over the phone, but I suspect that if, as he claims, they can identify him, they must surely know where he hangs out.'

'Where he *lives*,' Lewis corrected him. 'That isn't necessarily the same as where he hangs out.'

'True enough,' Cusack said. 'But finding out who he is and where he lives – or, at least, where he last lived – puts us right on his track. Besides, since he might actually come for me, I'd be happier knowing something about him. If you know what a man looks like, if you know his habits, you can at least plan ahead.'

'What makes you think he might come for you? Because you still think he might be the same man who broke into your house that dreadful night?'

'Yes, I think he might be the same man; and, if he is, he certainly won't have forgotten me and will want to come back, sooner or later, to complete my so-called punishment by putting my lights out. So that's one reason why I think he might come back – *if* he's the same man.'

'And if he isn't?'

'I recently leaked the news, on the Internet, that we're engaged in this mission and that I'm in charge of the QRF team involved. I posted it on an electronic billboard that specializes in pouring shit on the regiment. I worded it to make it seem like a leak from a Millennialist who hates the SAS and is hacking into our computer systems to spread confidential info about us and get us into trouble. I'm hoping that if our Prince sees that posting, he'll come gunning for me.'

'Cute,' Lewis said. 'So what happens if he comes gunning for you when you're all alone there?'

'I never sleep,' Cusack joked. In fact, since moving out of the Spider and back into his Redhill house, which he had taken off the market, he had indeed suffered many sleepless nights, being haunted by the almost palpable presence of his dead wife Mary and his daughter Jennifer in every room in the place. 'All joking aside, though,' he added, 'if the bastard, whoever he is, comes gunning for me, I'll be waiting for him.'

'You'd better be,' Lewis said.

They had reached the Spider and both entered the building, glad to get in from the cold of the descending darkness. This building, the sleeping quarters, did indeed resemble a spider, having eight 'legs', the dormitory areas, running off its central section. Though he had formally moved off the base, Cusack had retained a room in the same 'leg' that Lewis and the other members of the QRF team lived in. Being QRF NCOs, Lewis and Cusack each had their own room, one located right next to the other.

Once in his room, Cusack placed his weapons, hand grenades and ammunition in his steel locker, which could only be opened when a certain combination was punched in, then stripped off his CRW outfit and his underclothes to hang them up in the closet. After putting on a dressing gown, he went to the washroom for his ablutions and found Lewis already there, stark naked and huge, taking a shower with the other men of the team. A lot of traditional bullshit was traded between the men as they showered and dried themselves, then shaved and cleaned their teeth, but most of them were on their way back to their dormitories by the time Cusack and Lewis had finished. When eventually the latter pair, also dry, clean and feeling invigorated, were walking back to their leg in the Spider, Lewis, a man with a thirst for living, said, 'Fancy a quick pint in the Sports and Social before you go home?'

Though Cusack would have dearly loved a drink in the bar of the SAS barracks, he checked his wristwatch and said, 'Sorry, I can't. I've got to meet the Police Commissioner at five-thirty and that leaves me no time for shite and shinola.'

Lewis stopped at the door of his room. 'Too bad,' he said. 'I'm going to hang on a good one. But I'll see you tomorrow and, despite what I knock back, I'll be up fresh and early. I'm fucking *dying* to know what the Met found out.'

'So am I,' Cusack replied, 'so I'd better get going.'

Cusack entered his own room, dressed in civilian clothing, locked up and then left the Spider. Finding his Peugeot 106 (he didn't need anything bigger these days) where he had left it in the car park, he drove off the base and began the short journey to his home in Redhill, not far from Hereford and convenient for the train to London.

As he drove through the deepening darkness, watching the stars come out, the moon rising in the sky, he felt his invigorated mood fading away and being replaced with the tension that always increased the closer he came to home. As invariably happened, he could not make this journey without thinking of Mary making exactly the same journey, often with Jennifer in the car, and this in turn made him think of what had been happening to them, the brutal rape and murder, while he had been back in Stirling Lines, preparing to have his shower before coming home. Such thoughts, which were enough to break the strongest man, were certainly threatening to break him.

Cusack pulled up in front of his own house: a three-bedroom semi-detached property, only twenty years old, with a small front garden and a larger garden out the back. The house was in darkness. There were no welcoming lights. Cusack turned the ignition off, applied the handbrake, slipped out of the car, glanced up and down the street, always wary of potential aggressors, then locked the vehicle and walked along the garden path until he reached the front door. He took a deep breath, trying to reduce his tension, then turned the key in the lock and entered the unlit house.

When he turned on the light inside, he found Hargreaves waiting there.

# CHAPTER TWELVE

Prince had got to know Lenny Cusack as he had got to know a lot of people: by observing them from a safe distance and then invading their homes either to terminate them violently or, if he felt particularly venomous, to destroy them slowly by killing their loved ones first. He had decided some time back to begin a 'righteous war' against his hated enemy, the SAS, by first emotionally torturing and then murdering one of their more valuable men.

Prince had already come to loathe and resent SAS Sergeant Cusack before he had even seen him, because Cusack had been identified on the Internet on several radical websites and electronic billboards that specialized in finding and releasing confidential information about the regiment as the leading light of the SAS QRF, responsible for the deaths of so many 'heroic fighters' in the various Millennialist movements. Prince had therefore decided to make Cusack his first victim in his righteous war.

He found Cusack in the simplest way possible: by hacking into British Telecom's computer system and searching for his name in their list of ex-directory subscribers for the Hereford area. Being married, Cusack lived off the base in nearby Redhill and the ex-directory details included his address.

With those details to hand, Prince went to Hereford by car, booked into a room in a local pub, and then drove to Cusack's home in Redhill, timing his trip to ensure that he arrived outside the semi-detached house just before 5.00 p.m. He then waited for Cusack to come home. In fact, Cusack did not come home that evening or, indeed, any other evening for another four days (obviously off somewhere with some fellow assassins). But he turned up on the fifth evening, arriving home in a red Ford Cortina.

Supremely patient when he wanted something badly enough, Prince continued to observe Cusack's house for the next five days, making a point of being there every morning, when Cusack left to go to Stirling Lines, and every evening, when Cusack left Stirling Lines to return home. Prince followed him both ways, checking everything he did. When Cusack stopped off at one of the Hereford pubs for a drink with friends before going home, Prince followed him in and studied him carefully from a distance until Cusack's features were deeply imprinted on his memory.

During the day, when Cusack was at work with the regiment, Prince passed the time by observing the movements of Cusack's wife and 15-year-old daughter, observing that the woman drove her daughter to school every morning approximately an hour after Cusack had left for Stirling Lines and picked her up at four, approximately two hours before Cusack returned home when he was working normally.

Prince wanted to deliver the maximum shock to Cusack's system, the full horror, as it were, so he timed everything immaculately and was totally ruthless in the execution of his plan.

After five days of observation, when Prince was certain that Cusack was back in Hereford for a while, not away slaughtering God-fearing white Christian Millennialists on behalf of his satanic government, he decided to act. Calling his second-in-command, Tony Pearson, at the compound in Wiltshire, Prince arranged for two of his most fanatical followers, Andy Pitt and Ian Grant, both in their early twenties, to be sent to join him in Hereford. They were to come in a transit van with false registration plates and a painted advertisement for a fake plumbing company on its bodywork.

Pitt and Grant arrived in the early afternoon of the following day, which was a Monday. Just before 4.00 p.m. that afternoon, Prince was picked up in the van and driven by Pitt, with Grant in the rear, to Cusack's semi-detached house in Redhill. All three men were wearing overalls. They parked by the pavement, directly facing the front gate, knowing that Cusack's wife would park in her own drive.

Cusack's wife arrived back just after 4.00 p.m. and parked, as anticipated, in the driveway on the unattached side of the semi-detached house. Neither she nor her daughter took any notice of the plumbing van parked in the street. Prince knew that the most dangerous part of the operation would be preventing the woman and her daughter from screaming before they were silenced and then gagged, so he gave them no time to settle down. Instead, he immediately led his two men up the front path, all of them carrying plumber's toolboxes, and rang the doorbell.

Pitt and Grant had already been briefed. The instant Cusack's wife opened the front door, Prince pushed her back inside, spun her around, clamped one arm around her waist and slapped his free hand over her mouth to silence what would have been an automatic scream. The 15-year-old daughter, with shoulder-length auburn hair, pale, unblemished skin and the angelic appearance of the barely nubile, was still in the hallway, just about to hang up her overcoat, mere inches from her mother. She glanced around in bewilderment just as Pitt and Grant rushed in, the latter slamming the front door closed behind him.

Before the daughter could make a sound, Pitt grabbed her exactly as Prince had grabbed the mother, also slapping a hand over her mouth to silence her. As quick as lightning, while both women were still struggling, silenced, in the grip of their captors, Grant removed a roll of extra-wide masking tape from a pocket in his overalls, pulled out a long stretch of it, then nodded at Prince. The instant Prince removed his hand from the woman's face, Grant slapped the tape over her mouth, then wrapped it around her head a few times and pulled it tight. When he slashed the end off with a knife, Prince forced the struggling, silenced woman up the stairs and Grant went to work immediately on the daughter.

Prince checked both bedrooms and knew immediately, from the double bed and mixture of clothing, which one was used by Cusack and his wife. Wanting Cusack to find his wife on their marital bed, he pushed her into that room and on to the bed. In under a minute, Grant and Pitt had brought the terrified daughter up the stairs and thrown her on to the single bed in her own bedroom. Being above such things, not wishing to soil his hands, Prince let the other two get on with it, only insisting that they take their time about it, causing maximum damage, before putting the victims out of their misery.

Thirty minutes was long enough. The rapes took place between brutal beatings and dreadful handiwork with knives. Then, in a final act of perverse mercy, the women were killed, their throats cut, their bodies left on the blood-soaked beds for Cusack to find. Prince and his men then walked casually out of the house, again carrying toolboxes, piled back into the 'plumbing' van and drove at normal speed out of Hereford, knowing that the corpses would not be discovered for at least another hour, when Cusack would return home from Stirling Lines. At a lonely spot halfway between Hereford and Wiltshire, under cover of darkness, they transferred from the van, which had been stolen, to a Honda Accord that was waiting for them with a driver from the compound. They were all back in the compound before midnight, and Prince slept like a baby.

He awoke the next day to read about the double murder in the newspapers and to see sensationalist reconstructions on television. Naturally, there was no photo of the grieving husband and father, because Cusack was in the highly secret SAS and could not be reproduced photographically without a black band imprinted over most of his face. Nevertheless, since Prince now knew what he looked like, this was no great loss as far as he was concerned.

Now, as he drove from Wiltshire to Redhill for the first time since that apocalyptic event nearly a year ago, Prince wanted someone else to be able to recognize Cusack. Sitting beside him, glancing out at the sunlit fields, Chloe was a picture of health, cheeks full, lips lush, brown eyes clear, slim and attractive in skintight blue denims, tightly belted at the waist, and a tucked-in, open-necked shirt with a silk scarf hanging loose from around her neck. All in all, she was indeed strikingly attractive, even if she looked a bit older than her true age – slightly jaded, world-weary. In fact, she could have been in her early twenties. That was why Prince had picked her.

'We'll soon be there,' he said. 'Nice area, isn't it?'

'Yeah, really nice. So are you going to tell me before we get there just what we're going there for?'

'There's someone I want you to see,' Prince said. 'A man. You won't be talking to him. I just want you to know what he looks like for future reference.'

'Why?'

'I'll tell you when the time comes.'

'Why not tell me now?'

'I have my reasons,' Prince said.

'Okay,' Chloe responded, shrugging.

Glancing sideways at her as they approached the outskirts of Hereford, Prince caught her smiling at him and noted the reverential light in her eyes. She had been more resistant than the others, more suspicious of his intentions, but the agonies of her gradual retreat from drug dependency, combined with his constant encouragement and softly spoken, almost mesmerizing propaganda, attacking the outside world and extolling the virtues of his own community as she was suffering her withdrawal pangs, had finally put her on his side. Even then, when she had conquered her junk habit and committed herself to the community, a residual suspicion and mistrust had remained. This, however, had been broken down over the past fortnight with a highly concentrated series of indoctrination sessions run by his very best people, experts in the psychological manipulation of individuals.

Thus, shortly after conquering her drug addiction, just as she was beginning to feel at ease, Chloe abruptly found herself cut off from Prince who for a whole week simply refused to see her. At the end of that week, during which she was suffering emotional pain and bewilderment, wondering what she had done to offend Prince, who had rescued her from hell, she was ordered to attend a 'soul cleansing' in one of the Portakabins. When she arrived there, at seven on a Saturday morning, before she'd had breakfast, she found only two instructors, a man and a woman – no other newcomers – waiting for her.

As soon as Chloe walked in, the woman locked the door behind her and pocketed the key. Then, for the next three nightmarish, bewildering days, a steady stream of paired instructors relentlessly harangued her about her vices and weaknesses, never letting her out, only giving her a break when she needed to use the Portakabin's toilet or wanted something to eat. Even then, she still wasn't allowed to go out to the canteen and was given only light snacks of dry bread and cheese, washed down with plain water.

Chloe's instructors deliberately exhausted her by depriving her of sleep. They constantly harangued her about her moral worthlessness and the need to 'void' herself of all vanity and give herself totally to the community in general and to Prince in particular.

Initially she was defiant, screaming to be let out. But gradually, after twenty-four hours without sleep, with each pair of instructors being replaced every couple of hours by a fresh pair – always a man and a woman – Chloe began to break down, alternately screaming abuse and sobbing, then, invariably, begging tearfully to see Prince. He was looming ever larger in her consciousness as her one means of escape – her salvation.

In fact, Prince kept popping in and out, always arriving when Chloe was at her weakest, weeping and pleading to see him. And each time he made a point of consoling and soothing her, raising her spirits while softly, hypnotically talking to her about the need for this soul cleansing, carefully reminding her *en passant* of how desperately unhappy and self-destructive she had been in the outside world, of how useless her parents had been when she was growing up, and of how they would undoubtedly try to drag her back home against her will if they found out where she was – with him, the one person in the whole wide world who had shown her the way to peace and contentment. Then, having gently, persistently impressed these facts upon her, when she was numbly nodding agreement, he would get up and, despite her tearful entreaties, leave her alone once more with her tormenting instructors.

The instant Prince walked out the door, they would start all over again.

This went on for three days, with Prince coming and going, never failing to console her, never failing to whisper dire warnings about the outside world in general and her parents in particular. At the end of this time she believed fully in her own worthlessness, believed everything that Prince had told her, and could think of him only as her true salvation and guiding light.

At this stage, when she confessed her feelings to Prince, he ordered the instructors out of the Portakabin. Wearing only his white robes, he knelt on the floor beside her to cup her tearful face in his hands.

'Do you love me, Chloe?'

'You know I do.'

'And, through me, your God?'

'Yes.'

'Do you trust me fully, Chloe, as God's messenger, as your channel to Him?'

'I've never doubted you, Prince.'

'And do you know who the enemy is, Chloe, the Luciferian

enemy who would attempt to destroy us? Do you know that enemy, Chloe?'

'I know the enemy, Prince.'

'Is not the enemy the Queen of Babylon, the Patroness of Freemasonry, satanic child of the Illuminati, and her cohorts in government, the police and the army, particularly the SAS, which has been tasked with destroying us, as we have seen on the Internet? Is this not – are *they* not – the enemy, Chloe?'

'Yes, Prince, they are.'

'Will you do anything to defeat them, Chloe?'

'You don't have to ask, Prince.'

'And as I've been tasked by God to defeat them, Chloe, will you do anything – *anything* – that I ask?'

'Yes, anything. *Anything*!'

'Let me see it, Chloe. Show me. Prove how much you love me, Chloe. The body is the temple of the spirit and should be worshipped accordingly. So touch my body, Chloe. Touch me as I touch you. Lie beside me and let us give to each other as we would give to the Lord. Let us join our bodies together and make ourselves as one, a single temple, united in His sight. Be quiet, Chloe. There, there, close your eyes. Ah, yes! Lord have mercy!'

After that, Chloe was his, proud to serve as his mistress, always eager to please, always wanting his protection. Now she would do anything for him, which was just what he wanted.

Glancing sideways at her again as they left Hereford behind, approaching Redhill, as evening descended, Prince saw the spaced-out passivity that they all had in the end, a look revealing that she had lost her own will and become a mere instrument for others. The person playing that instrument was himself – and he was an expert.

'Here we are,' he said when they were driving along a lamplit street in Redhill, passing between rows of neat semi-detached houses with small gardens out front. About halfway along the street, he pulled into the kerb, switched the ignition off and applied the handbrake. He stared steadily, obliquely across the lamplit road at a semi-detached house farther along.

'See that black wrought-iron gate,' he said, 'six houses up from the one directly opposite the car?'

'Yes,' Chloe said after counting the houses off, moving her lips soundlessly, settling her gaze on the gate.

'That's where the man lives,' Prince said. 'The man I want you to be able to recognize.'

'What's his name?'

'You don't need to know that just yet.'

'I understand,' Chloe said.

Prince checked his wristwatch. It was just after 5.30 p.m. 'We might have to wait a bit,' he said. 'I think he'll be home about six-thirty. I'm going to rest my eyes now, so let me know if anyone comes along.'

'Yes, Prince, I will.'

'Good,' Prince said.

Closing his eyes, he let his thoughts drift here and there, but invariably they came back to what had happened in that house along the street just under a year ago. He recalled the blood and the pain, the humiliation and the torment, the final act of mercy – the killings – and he felt not a flicker of guilt, because the Lord had ordained it all. The SAS were satanic, the outriders of the Apocalypse, the bearers of destruction on behalf of the Queen of Babylon and her disciples, the dark angels of Lucifer. He, Prince, had a mission here – only one of many – and this particular mission was merely part of his campaign to purge the country of the enemies of the white Christian Millennialists. He had started with Cusack's family, punishing Cusack through them, and would soon put Cusack himself down for good, though not without inflicting further suffering. After that, he would engage in a righteous war against the whole of the SAS.

'There's someone coming,' Chloe said.

Opening his eyes, Prince checked his wristwatch and saw that it had just turned 6.00 p.m. Focusing on the other side of the road, he saw a man approaching Cusack's house. The man was not Cusack. He was silver-haired and wore a pinstriped suit, with shirt and tie and immaculately polished black shoes. As the man approached the front gate of Cusack's house, illuminated by a street light, Prince was startled to recognize the much-photographed William Hargreaves, Commissioner for the Metropolitan Police.

Looking back along the street, Prince saw a parked black Mercedes-Benz that had not been there before. No doubt it was chauffeur-driven. Hargreaves opened the black wrought-iron gate and walked up the garden path. He withdrew a key from his pocket, inserted it into the front-door lock of Cusack's house, let himself in and closed the door behind him.

'Well, well,' Prince murmured.

'Was that him?' Chloe asked.

'No,' Prince said. 'That's someone else I know, but it's not the man we want. But that man should be home soon. Let's just wait and see.'

They waited for another thirty-five minutes. During that time, the man inside Cusack's house did not show himself at any of the windows. Cusack finally arrived home at 6.35 p.m.

'That's him,' Prince said. 'Can you see him clearly?'

'Yes,' Chloe said, 'I can see him.'

'Clearly enough to recognize him the next time you see him?'

'Yes,' Chloe said. 'No problem.'

'Excellent,' Prince said.

Cusack turned up the garden path and entered his house, closing the door behind him. Prince continued to gaze across the road at the familiar semi-detached house.

'Can we go now?' Chloe asked.

'No,' Prince said. 'That other man should be leaving eventually, but I want to see just how long he remains in there. That will tell me a lot.'

'Anything you say, Prince.'

William Hargreaves was in Cusack's house a long time, a

good two hours, but finally emerged. Cusack stood in the doorway to wave him goodbye. Hargreaves walked along the garden path, closed the black wrought-iron gate behind him, and turned right to walk back the way he had come. Cusack closed the front door. Hargreaves walked along the street until he reached the parked Mercedes-Benz. He clambered into the back and closed the door as the vehicle's ignition was turned on. The Mercedes passed Prince's parked Honda and continued to the end of the street, then turned the corner and vanished. Prince had observed it in his rear-view mirror until it was out of sight. Now he smiled thinly and drove off.

'Well, well,' he said as he drove past Cusack's house. 'That little visit certainly told me a lot. Life is full of surprises.'

He drove back to Wiltshire.

# CHAPTER THIRTEEN

Shocked to find William Hargreaves in the living room, Cusack just stared at him for a moment. Hargreaves, who was sitting in an armchair facing the front door, an A4-size brown manila envelope on his lap, smiled in his tentative, kindly way.

'Sorry to have surprised you this way,' he said.

'How did you get in?' Cusack asked, advancing into the room, still disturbed by the sight of Hargreaves, whom he normally liked and respected. He removed his jacket to sling it over the nearest chair, which was by the fireplace, facing Hargreaves's chair.

'With a key,' Hargreaves replied. 'A special police key that will open just about any kind of lock.'

'I'm not sure I like that,' Cusack said, turning to the front window to check whether any passers-by were looking in. There weren't any.

Hargreaves sighed and nodded gravely. 'It's the sorry task of the policeman to be forced to do things that he himself may not approve of. I mean, I don't particularly approve of phone tapping, but we have to do it occasionally.'

Cusack smiled, relaxing. 'Yes, I guess so.' He went into the kitchen, removed a bottle of Jameson's from the Welsh dresser, adroitly picked up two glasses with the fingers of his free hand, then returned to the living room.

'Drink?' he said, setting the glasses on the table under the front window.

'Irish whiskey. How nice.'

'Does that mean "Yes"?'

'It certainly does.'

'Drinking on duty,' Cusack said.

'I'm sure you won't tell.'

Cusack poured the drinks and handed one to Hargreaves, then took the chair facing him. Both men raised their glasses in the air, said 'Cheers' simultaneously, then took a sip and lowered the glasses to their laps.

'So what have you found out?' Cusack asked.

'Can I just ask first,' Hargreaves rejoined, 'if those leaks we discussed previously were made?'

'Yes,' Cusack said. 'I leaked anonymously into the Internet, choosing an electronic bulletin board that specializes in hate mail about the SAS and hackers' information about the regiment's activities, the more confidential the better. I stated, masquerading as this anonymous poster, that according to confidential reports uncovered by a hacker the SAS had been called upon to form a special QRF team headed by Sergeant Lenny Cusack to locate and terminate Prince and his British Millennialist Movement. I haven't had a response so far, but I'm pretty sure that Prince will take notice and get back to me sooner or later – one way or the other.'

'Be very careful,' Hargreaves warned him.

'I will,' Cusack said.

Hargreaves took another sip of his whiskey, then lowered the glass again to his lap, resting it on top of the brown A4 manila envelope. 'I note that the media have been discussing the possibility that the perpetrator of the Whitehall Atrocity and the London Underground gassing may be planning to attack Buckingham Palace and the Royal Family in an attempt to get rid of them altogether. This frightening possibility was first raised by a report in *The Times*, written by journalist

Walter Adams and based, so he claimed, on leaked information from a protected source. The story was then picked up and widely discussed by other newspapers and radio and TV programmes. Can I take it that this was your second leak?'

'I *can* state categorically that it didn't come from me,' Cusack replied, poker-faced.

'But it *did* come from the SAS?' Hargreaves queried.

'I can't confirm or deny that.'

Hargreaves smiled, placed his unfinished glass of whiskey on the floor beside his chair, then opened the envelope on his lap. 'Well, I can only say that the very possibility of a direct threat to the Royal Family has caused a sensation and certainly gained a great deal of public support for SAS intervention in the affairs of Prince and his movement.'

'I'm glad to hear *that*,' Cusack said. 'So, what have you got for me?'

Hargreaves removed some papers from the envelope and rested them on top of it. He did not even glance at the notes, instead staring steadily at Cusack as he began: 'We finally completed our analysis of Simmonds's monitored cellular phone calls to the people he called most often and reduced the original figure to the half-dozen who received the most calls. We reduced that figure even more by noting that, in the week leading up to the Whitehall Atrocity, Simmonds called just two people. Number one: Michael Crowley. Number two: Laurence Grover. Naturally, we checked out all our half-dozen, but we knew we were on to something when we profiled those last two.'

He glanced down at his notes for the first time. 'Michael Crowley isn't our man, though he's indirectly involved. He and Simmonds were old friends, going a long way back, in fact all the way back to school: they were both born in and grew up near Calne, Wiltshire. Both were bad boys at school, but nothing particularly wild – truancy and bullying most prominent – and neither benefited much from his education. They both left school without qualifications. Simmonds went straight to work for his father on the family farm, if such it can be called, raising chickens, a few pigs, a couple of milk cows, and inherited the farm when his parents died. He's never worked at anything else and he never married. Crowley never married either and it's possible, though we have no proof, that he and Simmonds had a homosexual relationship.

'Crowley was no more successful than his friend. After leaving school, he had a succession of different jobs but was a disaster at most of them, sacked every time, usually for taking too many sick days, for fighting with fellow employees and, most often, for the theft of company property. He and Simmonds kept in touch, drank in the same pubs, were known locally to be racist, were in the local shooting club and shared an exaggerated passion for weapons. Both men were on the Internet and communicated regularly with the most dubious kind of websites, notably those of the more fanatical racist and Millennialist movements. They were also keen on sites that offered information on explosives, armaments and home-made bombs.'

'You said he was indirectly involved,' Cusack interjected impatiently.

'Yes,' Cusack said, briefly raising his eyes from his report. 'For the past two years – about the longest time he'd ever held down one job – Crowley had been working for a local company that refines fuel oil and transports it in plastic drums of the kind used in the Whitehall Atrocity. Even more relevant is that the same company uses bottled hydrogen *and acetylene* in the production of its fuel oil. It therefore seems almost certain that Crowley, if not directly involved with the British Millennialist Movement, certainly supplied his good friend Simmonds with the fuel oil and acetylene that were added to Simmonds's own ammonium nitrate fertilizer to make the bomb that devastated Whitehall. He also supplied the plastic drums that contained the explosive.'

'Have you questioned Crowley about this?'

'That, alas, is no longer possible. Michael Crowley died, unexpectedly, of a heart attack two days after the Whitehall

Atrocity. He was found slumped in a chair at his kitchen table. Foul play was not suspected, so no autopsy was performed and the body was cremated on the instructions of his sole surviving relative, a widowed cousin.'

'What do you think?'

'*I* think it's very possible that Crowley was murdered to ensure that he never mentioned, either accidentally or otherwise, that he had supplied his friend Simmonds with those plastic drums and the fuel oil and acetylene.'

'And the other man?'

'We think he could be the man we're after,' Hargreaves said, then looked down once more at his report. 'Laurence Grover. Born Kilburn, west London, sixteenth of February 1969, to Alfred and Gwendoline Grover, the father a clerk with the Inland Revenue in Hendon, the mother a machine-stitcher in a garment factory in Camden. Both parents had a reputation for serious drinking and violent fighting. The boy, Laurence, was an only child and the family doctor was called to the Kilburn house quite a few times when the boy, reportedly, fell down the stairs or otherwise physically damaged himself. The doctor suspected abuse by the alcoholic parents – you know, drunk all the time and couldn't stand the sound of the kid crying – but he could prove nothing or, possibly, simply didn't want to be involved in legalities. Questions of abuse, however, returned when young Laurence was at secondary school, suffered lots of crying fits, was recommended for psychiatric treatment and, while refusing to make any overt statements, gave the distinct impression that sexual abuse was one of the reasons for the tears.'

'Here we go again,' Cusack said, familiar with the psychological profile of the kind of people he had been asked to neutralize in the past five or six years – now already known as the 'Millennium Years'. Invariably, they were the dis-enfranchised: sexually abused as children, poorly educated, easily victimized and therefore themselves adroit at victimizing, flotsam recycled endlessly in God's squalid master plan. Cusack, who had once believed in God, now knew more than he had ever wanted to know about the deity's 'mysterious ways'. But certainly, for good or ill, he understood what Hargreaves was talking about.

Hargreaves sighed and nodded. These days it was all he seemed to be capable of doing. 'Yes, Sergeant Cusack, the same old sorry story. Child abuse and rejection in the last decades of the twentieth century. Perfect fodder, therefore, for any Millennialist freak working the turf. Come, lost child, be saved! Find meaning in the midst of your desolation. The Millennium is the beginning of the New Age when poor, broken men will be made whole. Join us and be saved . . . I'm sure you know what I'm talking about, Sergeant.'

'I do,' Cusack said. 'God knows, I do. So what else is in that report?'

'School record a disaster, with everything you can imagine under the circumstances. Written up repeatedly in school records as – naturally – a loner. Also a bully. Always picked on students even more obviously outcast than himself: Jews, Indians, Pakistanis, Irish. In short, anyone *not* like himself.'

'Sounds familiar.'

'Exactly. And all building up to the Millennium when God, who is, of course, Christian *and* white –'

'Of course,' Cusack interjected sardonically.

'– would return to earth to bring about Judgement Day and inaugurate Christianity –'

'*White* Christianity,' Cusack interjected again.

' –as the New World Order.'

'I follow,' Cusack said. 'So our Laurence Grover –'

'Blond-haired and blue-eyed.'

'Really?'

'Really. Blond-haired and blue-eyed, exploited by his own parents, therefore trusting no human beings and seeking refuge in a – doubtless – blond-haired, blue-eyed, *white* Christian God.'

'Thus hating all Jews and ethnics.'

'Very good, Sergeant Cusack.'

'So?'

Hargreaves sighed again. 'Our blond-haired, blue-eyed Christian joined the British Army in 1987, when he was eighteen years old, served as a regular soldier for two years, gaining an exemplary record and being promoted to corporal, then transferred to 22 SAS in 1989. In August 1990 he was flown out to Saudi Arabia with other members of D Squadron to take part in covert work relating to Operation Desert Storm.'

'Oh, shit!' Cusack exclaimed softly.

'Quite,' Hargreaves said. 'You didn't interact personally with him because you didn't go to Iraq until January 1991, by which time Grover was already operating behind enemy lines, travelling all over the place in Pink Panther Land Rovers and Light Strike Vehicles, collecting intelligence about Iraqi command centres, bunkers and nuclear, biological and chemical weapons, as well as the movement of men, aircraft, armour and food supplies. Did you know him at all when he was with the regiment?'

'No. You can't possibly know all the men in a regiment, even one as relatively small as the SAS.'

'By all reports, he was brilliant. Unfortunately, he was also racist and possibly mad. Shortly after the real war started, in January 1991, senior British staff officers in the Gulf received a report from the field stating that, in at least three or four instances, large numbers of Iraqi soldiers who had surrendered to Grover had been executed by him. He had made them dig long trenches, then lined them up facing their own graves and shot them in the back with his MP5 sub-machine gun.'

'Shit!' Cusack exclaimed softly again. 'I heard rumours about that when I was out there. I just couldn't believe them.'

'Understandably so. Alas, the rumours were true. Naturally, when this report came in, Grover was pulled out of Iraq, flown straight back to Stirling Lines, returned to his original unit, court-martialled and then dishonourably discharged.'

'Quite rightly,' Cusack said.

'According to these records,' Hargreaves went on, 'during his court martial Grover passionately defended his own actions in a way that made it perfectly clear that he was a rabid racist. Upon being told that he was being dishonourably discharged, he hurled a mouthful of abuse at the presiding army officers and vowed that he would have his revenge.'

'With his hatred focused, in particular, on the SAS.'

'Correct,' Hargreaves said.

'And then? Back in Civvie Street?'

'A loose cannon,' Hargreaves said. 'Moved back in with his parents for a while – obviously they couldn't abuse him any more and he had to live somewhere – and then got himself a place of his own, still more or less on his home turf but Cricklewood instead of Kilburn; just up the road, as it were. He soon became known to the local police as a combination of confidence trickster and evangelical Bible thumper. Conned more than one old-age pensioner, always female, into signing her savings and pension over to him – taken to court quite a few times by outraged relatives – and used the money to buy a local shop that he gutted and converted into a small meeting hall that could hold up to fifty people at a time. Advertised himself in local newspapers as a, quote, Christian counsellor, unquote, and invited those with serious emotional problems to come and see him for guidance. Life being what it is, particularly for the growing numbers of unemployed, he received a lot of visitors and soon had a fairly impressive following, most seduced by his gift of the gab and exploitation of the coming Millennium Year, which he sold to them as the year of the Second Coming. Six months later, with business booming, Grover registered his business as the Second Coming Movement.'

'The same movement that was later spreading racist-based Millennialist propaganda through the Internet.'

'That connection wasn't made by the police,' Hargreaves said. 'Why should it have been? I can only tell you that because of Grover's reputation as a religious confidence trickster – admittedly one who appeared to believe his own delusional, dangerously racist fantasies – he was placed under police surveillance and was seen, through that observation, to be involved with various other religious and occult fringe groups, all as obsessed as he was with the forthcoming Millennium. Then, in the year 2000, just before the Second Coming Movement started to spread its propaganda through the Internet, he sold his Cricklewood premises – which effectively put an end to the police surveillance.'

'You lost track of him?'

'More or less. With his so-called mission closed, the police lost interest in him. They knew where he lived – in a flat above an Indian restaurant in Cricklewood – and though they kept their eyes on that place for a while, they came up with nothing that caused them concern. Crowley had signed on the dole, appeared to be unemployed, and spent more time away from home than in it. Since none of this was against the law, they simply closed the file on him.'

'Not connecting him to the Second Coming Movement on the Internet.'

'The local police, if I may say so, would not have been investigating crank organizations on the Internet. I *can* confirm, on the other hand, that the British Millennialist Movement began advertising on the Internet within weeks of Grover closing down his Second Coming Movement in Cricklewood.'

'Does Grover still live in the flat in Cricklewood?'

'He still *owns* it. However, once we had obtained this other information we asked locally about him and found out that he hasn't been seen there for months. While no one can say *exactly* when he was last seen, he seems to have disappeared at approximately the same time as the Whitehall Atrocity. Indeed, the last person to have seen him, at least according to those we interviewed, was the woman serving in an Irish pub that he frequented. She remembered him especially because he was religious and never drank alcohol. The last time she saw him – the same day as the Whitehall Atrocity – he was joined by a friend and they left the pub shortly after noon. She never saw either of them again.'

'If they left that pub shortly after noon, they could have been in Whitehall at the time of the bombing.'

'Exactly,' Hargreaves said.

'So the friend who joined him may have been Simmonds.'

'Almost certainly,' Hargreaves said. 'We've been able to confirm from photos taken by anti-speeding cameras located on the M4 that the truck used for the Whitehall Atrocity, the one owned by Thomas Simmonds, was travelling east along the motorway shortly after eleven that morning. This makes it pretty certain that it was travelling from Calne to London. Given normal traffic conditions on the North Circular Road for that day and time, the truck could certainly have stopped at Cricklewood long enough to pick up a passenger and still have been in Whitehall by the time that bomb went off.'

'So you believe that Simmonds loaded the truck with explosives and rigged the bomb in his farm in Calne, left that morning to drive to London, travelling on the M4, stopped long enough to pick Prince up in that pub in Cricklewood, and then drove on to Whitehall.'

'Exactly.'

'Yet only Simmonds was killed in the bomb blast. How come?'

Hargreaves shrugged. 'Grover – or Prince – was taking no chances. Simmonds, being a heavy drinker and a gossip, would always have been a threat to him. So he killed Simmonds and left him there in the truck, assuming, correctly, that he'd be blown to pieces in the explosion and also assuming, incorrectly, that we would not be able to identify him. That was his only mistake.'

'By which time,' Cusack said, trying to fit all this together, 'the Second Coming Movement had dropped off the Internet and the British Millennialist Movement had come on-line.'

'Yes,' Hargreaves said.

'But we still don't have proof that Simmonds and Grover,

or the British Millennialist Movement, were connected.'

'Yes, we do,' Hargreaves said, sounding pleased with himself. 'We finally completed our sifting-through of Simmonds's computer e-mail, all of which he'd copied and filed on both his hard disk and his back-up diskettes. From this we can confirm that he *was* in regular contact with the British Millennialist Movement and, indeed, had recently joined it. He was communicating with someone only addressed, and signing himself, as "P".'

'Prince!'

'Exactly.'

'So can't you track down the location of the British Millennialist Movement from the e-mails?'

'No. Naturally, the e-mails Simmonds sent and received led us to the servers, but that didn't help as all of the outgoing e-mail destination addresses and incoming senders were Internet cafés. With that kind of system you can send e-mails anywhere in the world without actually using your own computer. In theory, Prince *could* send e-mails to anyone from anywhere in the world and it'd be impossible for us to track him down – because any investigation into the origin of those individual e-mails would always turn up a different source. Unless Prince wants to receive a reply – and so far, apart from his contacts with Simmonds, he hasn't – he'll just use a different cybercafé every time he wants to send another message, thus sinking ever deeper into the tangled web of cyberspace. In other words, by using different Internet cafés instead of his own computer – and as long as he doesn't actually pick up return e-mail at those cafés – he's virtually guaranteed his anonymity.'

'So what you're telling me, in effect,' Cusack said, feeling frustrated, 'is that our so-called "Prince" is actually Laurence Grover, that he's an old SAS hand who now has good reason to hate the regiment, that he's the head of the British Millennialist Movement, responsible, certainly, for the Whitehall atrocity, and that he has a flat in Cricklewood, north-west London, though he's rarely seen there.'

'Correct. Though I hasten to add that he's unlikely, after the recent atrocities, to be seen there again.'

'Have you been out there?'

'No. We've gone as far as we can go. From this point out, you'll have to go it alone, without official sanction. I can only tell you that Laurence Grover is almost certainly the man behind the Whitehall Atrocity – him and his dead friend Simmonds – that he's probably also responsible for the London Underground massacre, and that he *could* be the man known as Prince. That's for you to find out.'

'Thanks a million,' Cusack said.

'My pleasure,' said Hargreaves. He stood up and placed his report on the chair where he had been sitting. 'You'll find a photograph of Crowley in there,' he said, then walked to the front door. Cusack stood up as well and followed his friend to the door. Hargreaves opened the door, then paused and turned back to face Cusack. 'If we're talking about Prince,' he said, 'then he has to be the Prince of Darkness who came to this house. This man has a grudge against the SAS and you're his first regiment victim.'

'I'll make sure I'm the last,' Cusack said.

'I hope so,' Hargreaves said.

He left the house. Cusack watched him walk down the path and turn right at the gate. Then Cusack slammed the door shut and went back across the room to sift through the report and find the photograph of Grover, or Prince. The photo showed a man who was blond-haired and handsome, with a steady, slightly wide-eyed gaze. Cusack tried to remember if he had seen him with the regiment, but doubted that he had. He studied the photo a long time, trying to gauge what kind of man this was, but only succeeded in reawakening his hatred over what the monster had done – right here, in this very house. This bastard was Prince, all right.

A car started up outside and moved off along the street, passing the house, but Cusack thought nothing of it.

'Where are you, you bastard?' he said aloud. Then he put the photo of Prince back on the chair and poured himself another stiff drink. He would need it to help him sleep.

He was just falling asleep, a few hours later, when the telephone rang.

# CHAPTER FOURTEEN

'Sergeant Cusack?'

'Yes.'

'Did I interrupt your sleep, Sergeant?'

'Who is this?'

'A former visitor. I've been in your house before. Attending to your beloved wife and daughter. Would you like me to describe the house, Sergeant?'

'No,' Cusack said.

Prince smiled. He could hear the shock and revulsion in Cusack's voice even over the cellphone. Having drafted Chloe off, Prince was driving in his car, miles away from his camp, and was using his mobile to ensure that his call could not be traced if Cusack's phone happened to be tapped, which it probably was. Prince was driving expertly, at high speed, with one hand while holding the phone in the other. He was racing along a deserted, moonlit road on Salisbury Plain.

'I'm Prince,' he said. Cusack did not respond. 'I've seen on the Internet that you're trying to find me, so I thought I'd best find you first.'

'Oh, really?' Cusack said, obviously trying with all his might to sound calm, though his breathing was harsh.

'Yes, really,' Prince responded. 'Had a nice little chat with

Police Commissioner Hargreaves, did you? Making plans with him, were you? Well, I'd think those plans through carefully if I were you, because I have my own plans.' Dead silence at the other end of the line. 'Are you still there, Sergeant Cusack?'

'Yes,' Cusack said.

The odd resonance of that single word was enough to reveal to Prince just how desperately Sergeant Cusack was trying to keep control of himself. Hearing it in the give-away quivering of that single word coming down the phone line, Prince understood, with the instincts of the psychopath, just what Cusack was feeling: revulsion, anger, disbelief and the shaming lust for revenge. His emotions would be in conflict right now and this knowledge made Prince feel good.

'I broke into your house once before,' Prince said, 'and here I am, doing it again, more or less. This must anger you, Cusack.'

'Go fuck yourself,' Cusack said, not raising his voice, speaking instead in a flat, careful monotone. 'I'm going to find you and kill you.'

'Vengeance is mine, saith the Lord. You should not take it upon yourself, Sergeant. To do so is a sin.'

'You with your clean hands.'

Prince smiled again, amused by Cusack's sarcasm, feeling that he was actually there in Cusack's house which, of course, he knew well. Perhaps Cusack, who had clearly been sleeping, was sitting up right now in the very bed where his wife had been raped and killed. But Prince sensed that if he asked that question he would be going too far. Cusack might slam the phone down.

'My hands are clean,' Prince said. 'My hands perform the Lord's work. I'm engaged in a righteous war against the forces of darkness, against the Satanists and other sinners, against the disciples of the Antichrist and those who do their bidding. This is my God-given mission.'

'The Whitehall bombing?'

'Yes.'

'The London Underground atrocity?'

'I refuse to accept the word "atrocity" as a description of that action. It was a cleansing operation, no more and no less.'

'You killed and maimed hundreds of innocent people and made many more ill for life. What kind of "cleansing" is that?'

'As you well know, there are no innocents in a war – and I'm fighting a war.'

'Like the soldiers you butchered in Iraq when you were with the regiment. They surrendered; you slaughtered them.'

'All Muslims, Sergeant Cusack. The children of Satan. I struck down the enemies of the Lord and was punished, instead of being rewarded, for it. This was my proof, if proof was still needed, that the British Army, which defends the Queen of Babylon, is in the hands of the Satanists. You're part of that army, Sergeant Cusack, and so you have to be punished.'

'You've already punished me,' Cusack said.

'That was just the beginning. It was meant to cause you pain and distress, but it wasn't the whole of it. The rest – the best – is yet to come. And it won't be long now.'

'What are you planning?'

'Wouldn't you like to know! But I'm a man who takes pleasure in surprises, so you'll have to wait, Sergeant.'

'How long will I have to wait?'

'Not too long now. Never stop looking over your shoulder. And sleep lightly at nights.'

Cusack didn't respond immediately. He was clearly deep in thought. He would be thinking of what had happened to his wife and daughter – and that, as far as Prince was concerned, was all to the good. Cusack's punishment was to suffer extreme pain before being put down. Price viewed this as justice.

'Why do you call yourself "Prince"?' Cusack asked after a lengthy silence, subtly trying to take the initiative. 'Are you the Prince of Darkness?'

'The Prince of *Light*, Sergeant. *Illuminating* the darkness. Casting light into the lairs of the Luciferians, exposing the filth of their existence and then cleaning them out. I represent the righteous wrath of the Lord and I cannot be stopped. *You* won't stop me, Sergeant.'

'I might,' Cusack said. 'You're only human, after all. Like me, you're a creature of flesh and blood and that makes you vulnerable. You might make a mistake.'

'I don't make mistakes, Sergeant.'

'You made a couple of mistakes in Iraq and were dishonourably discharged.'

Prince faltered at that, but soon rallied, though he had to be careful now. 'Are you trying to anger me, Sergeant?'

'I'm simply stating a fact.'

'I made no mistakes in Iraq; I simply did what I believed to be the right thing. I cut down the satanic enemies of the Lord and did so with pride. That my superior officers, other Satanists, the Queen of Babylon's paid assassins, then punished me for my virtue can only be another source of pride to me. I can hold my head high.'

'I hope you're holding your fucking head high when I blow it apart with a well-aimed double tap.'

Prince chuckled. 'Very good, Sergeant Cusack. I admire a man of spirit. Unfortunately, you'll go down before I do, despite your skills as a soldier.'

'I'm coming to get you, Prince.'

'You and your QRF team – your fellow Satanists and assassins. What's it like to be an execution squad for the offspring of Lucifer?'

'Why ask me?' Cusack said. 'You should know. You were once one of us – one of the SAS. Is that what we were then?'

'Of course,' Prince replied. 'I just didn't know it at the time. I was innocent about certain matters until the Lord came and spoke to me. I didn't know that the Queen of England was really the Queen of Babylon; that she and her Royal Family were the offspring of Freemasonry, children of the Illuminati; and that her army and police were engaged in the subtle, insidious extermination of white Christian values. Innocent of all this, I went to Iraq, a young man with Christian ideals, believing that in killing Muslim Satanists I was doing the right thing. Instead, I was punished, humiliated, cast out, and this showed me the error of my ways. I was, however, saved when the Lord came and spoke to me, letting me know the true way. It was through the Lord that I learned that I had no need to be ashamed of what I had done in Iraq, that I had done the right thing, only to be punished by secret Satanists, that those Satanists were merely part of a larger conspiracy involving the Queen of Babylon, her so-called Royal Family, and the politicians, the Freemasons, who served them. In learning this, I was being shown the right path, which is the path that I'm taking right now. The Lord's will be done.'

'What happened to the Second Coming?' Cusack said, not sounding impressed. 'Did He disappoint you?'

'Your sarcasm is heavy-handed,' Prince said, determined not to sound angry.

'Well, did He or did He not? What happened when the year 2000 came? Did He put in an appearance, as anticipated by the Second Coming Movement, or did He let you down?'

Prince turned hot with rage, felt the urge to scream abuse, his grip tightening on the cellphone, wanting to strangle something, perhaps Cusack, but unable to do so. Eventually, realizing that Cusack had managed to make him lose his temper, he calmed down and paid attention to his steering, which, at this speed, driving with one hand, required concentration.

'That blasphemy has been noted,' he said, 'and will be punished in due course.'

'Is that why the Second Coming Movement disappeared,' Cusack retaliated, ignoring the threat, taking the initiative again, 'and re-emerged as the British Millennialist Movement? I mean, did the members of the Second Coming Movement desert the sinking ship when, during Millennium Year, there was no Second Coming?'

'When I get you, before I actually kill you, I'll make you suffer for that impertinence. Perhaps wash your mouth out with sulphuric acid, purify it with burning.'

'That's not an answer,' Cusack said. 'Did you not truly expect a Second Coming? And did He not disappoint you?'

Prince was silent for a moment, appalled by the blasphemy, again fighting to keep himself under control and not betray his potentially murderous rage. 'The Lord works in mysterious ways,' he said, his voice level, 'and if He did not come, He had His reasons. The Lord requires no defence.'

'But the Second Coming Movement is dead and buried?'

'Yes,' Prince confessed, 'it is. It's given way to the British Millennialist Movement – much larger and more far-reaching in its aspirations.'

'Which are largely to do with violence,' Cusack said.

'Cleansing actions,' Prince sternly corrected him. 'The extermination of secret Satanists everywhere and the cleansing of all forms of moral squalor, including the filth spread by the Jews and Muslims.'

'You're fucking mad,' Cusack said.

Now Prince really had to fight to control himself, realizing that, even though he had initiated this call, Sergeant Cusack was starting to lead the conversation – and, worse, lead it in directions that he, Prince, did not want it to go. This Sergeant Lenny Cusack, whether suffering pain or not (compelled, as he was, to talk to the man who had supervised the butchery of his wife and daughter), was a clever, experienced man. Accepting this, Prince forced himself to stay calm and sound like a reasonable human being.

'Madness is in the eye of the beholder,' he said, 'though the common, ignorant man is inclined to attribute it to those actually displaying uncommon courage. So I'll treat your comment with the contempt it deserves and move on to other things.'

'It's your phone bill,' Cusack said.

Prince closed his eyes, took a deep breath, then opened his eyes again. His car was racing through the moonlit night as if driving itself. 'I note from the Internet that the SAS has formed a special QRF team just to get little old me.'

'True,' Cusack said.

'That QRF team is, of course, headed by Sergeant Lenny Cusack, already notorious for his ruthless assassination of the leaders of other Millennialist movements.'

'My pleasure,' Cusack said.

'You'll burn in hell, Sergeant Cusack, for those words and I'm the man who'll put you there.'

'You think so?'

'Yes, I do.'

'I don't think you'll pull it off,' Cusack said. 'I don't think you're that good.'

'Yes, I am,' Prince responded, knowing that Cusack was taunting him. 'I'm not your commonplace Millennialist, after all. Unlike the others, I'm a former member of the SAS, which means I know how you operate. So whatever you try, Cusack, I'll be one step ahead of you, perhaps circling around you, coming up on you from behind. Whichever way you turn, I'll be there first, prepared to do what I have to do.'

'You're grandstanding,' Cusack said.

'You think you can beat me, Cusack?' By now Prince was really fighting to control himself. 'Well, you're deluding yourself. The devil can't strike the hand of God and I'm God's clenched fist. I'm here to crush the sinners, to hammer them into the ground, and I'll pulverize you at my leisure, once I've dealt with your men. A QRF team? What does that mean to me? Believe me, I'll squash them like bugs and leave you defenceless.'

'Why bother me with this horseshit?' Cusack said. 'Why not just come and get me?'

Prince sucked in his breath and let it out with a sigh, hoping that Cusack hadn't heard him. 'Because that would be too easy. I want to make an example of you. I want the world to know that it can't risk the wrath of Prince, and you'll serve to get that message across for me. You're going to die, Cusack, but not until I'm ready – and I won't be ready until you've been humiliated ... you *and* the SAS. That humiliation will be brutal and public, so be prepared, Sergeant. This is one war you're going to lose. This is the last war you'll wage on earth.'

A lingering silence ensued, making Prince uneasy. Then eventually Cusack said, 'Is that it?'

'Yes,' Prince said. 'That's it.'

'You know something?' Cusack said with clear, heavy sarcasm. 'It's pretty late and I'm tired of being bored. I think I'll have to hang up now.'

'You're going back to bed?' Prince asked quickly, before he could stop himself.

'Right,' Cusack confirmed, 'I'm going back to bed.'

'So what bed are you lying in?' Prince said, though earlier he had determined not to raise this subject in case Cusack slammed his phone down. Now, with his repressed rage finally breaking loose, he could not resist the impulse. 'Your wife's or your daughter's?'

Cusack didn't hang up. But he was silent for a long time and Prince tried to imagine what he was feeling: the vivid recollection of horror, a resurgence of shocking grief, whole cataracts of pain replacing normal human feelings, the racing heart, the shaking hands, a bottomless pit of dread opening up at his feet, rage and hatred for the man who had reminded him of his loss welling inside him like a black plague. Yes, Cusack would be suffering the fires of hell and it was Prince who had placed him there. So Prince waited . . . waiting for the phone to drop but hearing only slow, heavy, anguished breathing . . . until Cusack spoke again.

'How are your parents?' Cusack asked.

It was Prince who slammed his phone down.

# CHAPTER FIFTEEN

Even thirty hours later, when Cusack was supervising a Long Drag over the Brecon Beacons with Jack Lewis, both wearing full battle kit under rubber ponchos, shielding themselves from the driving rain and waiting for the first of their QRF team to arrive at the final RV, or rendezvous point, of the lengthy, arduous hike, the mere recollection of his conversation with Prince still made him feel shaky.

'Part of it, of course,' Cusack tried explaining to Lewis as they sat side by side on a rock outcropping at the foot of the mountain range, whipped by the wind, drenched in rain, 'was being jerked out of sleep; the other part was what he actually said, how he verbally toyed with me. He was pretty damned clever. First, he waited until the early hours of the morning, when he knew that I'd be asleep; then he launched into his spiel by informing me that he'd been in my house before "attending", as he mockingly put it, to my wife and daughter. He even volunteered to describe the house.'

'The evil bastard,' Lewis said as he smoked a cigarette, shielding it with his inverted hand, and kept his eyes fixed on the towering green and brown mountain slopes, waiting for the first of their six-strong QRF team to appear in the distance. 'He knew just what he was doing.'

Cusack nodded agreement and glanced over the wind-lashed, rainswept slopes, distracting himself briefly from thoughts of Prince by thinking instead of what his QRF team were going through right now. The Long Drag, a forced march of exceptional length and difficulty, was usually undertaken by new recruits in the dead of winter, when these steep hills were often covered with snow. This one, in late April, was taking place in weather only marginally less vile, with high winds, rain and mist. For those engaged in the Long Drag, the hike over those hills in that dreadful weather, with each man forced to hump a brick-filled bergen rucksack weighing twenty-five kilos, would be a brutal, exhausting experience.

In fact, the six members of the QRF team had been dragged out of their beds before dawn, without prior warning, been given M-16 assault rifles (used only for exercises these days) and bergens filled with bricks, and had then had to almost run to the four-ton Bedford truck that was waiting for them in the pre-dawn darkness of Hereford. Driven to South Wales and deposited behind another Bedford truck, this one empty, at the foot of the towering Brecon Beacons, they were con-fronted by Cusack and Lewis – who had gone on ahead in a jeep – and informed that the Long Drag would be a twenty-four-hour hike over the mountain range, from one trig point to another. Any man who failed to complete the course in that time would be dropped from the QRF team. To make the hike more difficult, they would not be told where it was to end until they had actually *reached* the end. Only one RV was marked on their maps: once they reached it, they would have to exchange their map for another that they would get from the DS (member of Directing Staff) waiting for them. This new map would also show just one RV . . . and so it would go on – and on – around the whole gruelling course. The DS team had arrived earlier in the first Bedford truck and were already in position along the route before the men began their hike.

Cusack had, of course, designed this system to ensure that the men hiking would never know in advance just how far they had to go between one RV and the next; therefore, they could never relax or feel too encouraged. It was a deliberate form of psychological torture that could break a man more brutally than the actual physical hardships of the march. Yet, according to calls made by Sergeant Lewis to the DS men at the other RVs, no member of the QRF team had so far dropped out. This was proof, if any were needed, that those six men were top-class.

'It was a bit unnerving, I'll admit,' Cusack said, referring again to Prince, 'to realize that that bastard had been watching the house even as I was inside discussing him with the Police Commissioner.'

'Fucking right,' Lewis replied. '*I'd* find that pretty creepy.'

'I even heard a car start up and move off shortly after Hargreaves left,' Cusack went on, finding it hard to shake that evening – and the subsequent phone call from Prince – out of his mind. 'I mean another car. One that started up a little way along the street – certainly parked close enough for observation of the house – and slowed down noticeably as it passed, then kept going and gradually went out of earshot.'

'Could have been anyone,' Lewis said.

'Could have been, but I'm convinced it was him driving off after seeing the Police Commissioner leave.'

'So he drove himself home – or back to his camp or wherever – then made that early morning phone call. Could the call not be traced?'

'No,' Cusack said. 'He made it with a cellular phone while driving all over the place. We kept losing the signal and, of course, each time we found it again, it was coming from somewhere else. The bastard really *is* clever.'

Gazing across the fields, squinting against the falling rain, Cusack saw the first of the QRF team appearing over the brow of a hill, stooped under the weight of his brick-filled rucksack and still carrying his M-16 in the raised position. Though the distance was too great to make out the man's features, he assumed that it must be Corporal Mapley, who had been the first to leave. The six men had been sent out, one after the other, at thirty-minute intervals, their route having been carefully devised to ensure that they would have to hike all through the day and the pitch-black night.

Between them, Cusack and Lewis had deliberately checked the weather reports to ensure, in the absence of snow, that the men would at least be faced with high winds and heavy rain. As the six men would have soon found out, the route had been selected to take them up ever steeper, higher hills where, in some places, the gradients would have been so nearly vertical that it would seem they were climbing a sheer cliff face. In other places, they had been deliberately forced to climb over dangerous ravines and loose gravel that would slip beneath their boots and frequently make them slide backwards, losing precious time from their tight twenty-four-hour schedule. Even worse, when dawn finally broke, the mist and constant rain would have reduced visibility, thus making the hike still more dangerous, even after first light.

Now, on the morning of the second day, the wind was still howling over the hills, sweeping the rain across the advancing men, threatening to throw them off balance and send them tumbling downhill, with the additional threat of bruised limbs or broken bones. Nevertheless, they kept advancing, appearing one after the other, the distance between each of them considerable, all bent under the weight of their brick-filled rucksacks, holding their M-16s across the chest in the required, though muscle-tormenting manner as they toiled up and down the high hills, heading for this final RV. Respecting them for what they were achieving, Cusack smiled at the sight of them.

'They look good,' he said. 'They're bearing up well. How have they been doing otherwise?'

'Fine,' Jack said. 'They're the best of the best. A few complaints about the repetitive training, but those stopped when I put them on to special training with our new weapons. Most of them were amazed and intrigued by what they were working with. Now they all want to try them out in a real action. So they're raring to go.'

'You think those new weapons will do the trick?'

'If they don't, nothing will . . . So what else did that insane bastard say on the phone?'

'Well,' Cusack sighed, 'basically, he was phoning to let me know that he'd seen that leak about us on the Internet and to say that he's going to get us before we get him. And, of course, having once been in the SAS himself, not to mention being right off the wall, he's convinced he can do it.'

'Just how crazy do you think he is?'

'Certainly crazy with hatred and paranoia,' Cusack said. 'He hates the regiment not only because he was RTU'd then dishonourably discharged from the army, but also because he now believes we're a sanctioned execution squad working for those he deems to be the offspring of Lucifer. He deduced that from the fact that he was court-martialled and dishonourably discharged for the killing of those Iraqi soldiers who, being Muslim, were clearly satanic. Ergo, he was punished by other secret Satanists, the Freemasons of the army, the Queen of Babylon's evil minions. Now that charge embraces the whole SAS and the QRF in particular. To him, we're all Satan's disciples.'

'Christ!' Jack exclaimed softly, automatically, neither intending nor registering the irony of his own comment. 'And, of course, he wants you especially because you've been responsible for the deaths of other well-known Millennialist movement leaders.'

'Correct,' Cusack said.

Jack gave a low whistle, thinking about what he had heard, but still keeping his gaze on that long line of men in the rainswept distance, the furthest away still minute, though the first one, coming close, was indeed now clearly discernible as Corporal Mapley. 'So did you pick up any clues as to his intentions?'

'Yes. I clearly recall him saying that he would pulverize me at his leisure, once he had dealt with my men. Which strongly suggests that he intends picking off the individual members of the QRF team before getting to me. He said he would squash them like bugs and leave me defenceless.'

Sergeant Lewis snorted with contempt. 'Some hope!' he exclaimed. 'Just because the bastard was once in the regiment, it doesn't mean he can do that. No way! He's not *that* good! Not as good as those men over there, marching towards us. *He*'s the one who'll be squashed like a bug. We'll turn him into minced meat.'

'I'm not so sure,' Cusack said.

He and Lewis stood up together as Corporal Chris Mapley, also draped in a rubber poncho, hunched under his heavy rucksack and absolutely drenched, covered the last few metres to stop right in front of them. He wiped the rain from his brown eyes and gave them a cocky grin.

'First out and first home,' he said. 'How does that grab you?'

Sergeant Lewis, who was soft on no man, checked his wristwatch. 'You made it with fifteen minutes to go. I'd put that down to pure luck.'

'*I*'d put it down to tenacity. Credit where it's due, boss.'

Lewis grinned. 'You did all right. Go back down to the truck and warm yourself up with your flask of tea. You can smoke if you want to.'

'I want to,' Mapley said.

In fact, as Mapley made his way down the slope to the trucks parked at the bottom, only thirty metres below, the heavy rain started to lighten up. By the time the next man, Trooper Radnor, arrived, the rain had stopped altogether.

'This *is* the final RV, isn't it?' Radnor said, removing his beret, shaking the rain off it, running his fingers through his auburn hair and gazing down at Cusack and Lewis. 'I mean, it isn't a trick?'

He was referring to the fact that some Long Drags included so-called 'sickeners', meaning that, when the hikers arrived at what they had been promised was the final RV, they were told that there was actually one more to go. For new recruits to the regiment, this was often the foul blow that broke their spirit and made them give in, thus failing the selection course. It was a nasty, effective ploy.

'No, it isn't a trick,' Cusack said. 'You're not here for Selection Training; you're just here for a little toughening up. The truck's just down the hill.'

'Fucking great,' Radnor said. 'I can't wait to sit down and close my eyes.'

Shortly after Radnor had made his way down the hill, Troopers Wiley and Carter came in together, the former having caught up with the latter.

'Are we home and dry?' Wiley asked, blinking his eyes and looking even taller than his six feet where he stood beside the medium-height Carter, both drenched and shivering.

'Home but hardly dry,' Sergeant Lewis said. 'But go down the hill and dry out in the truck. We've no complaints in this instance.'

'Thank Christ for that,' Wiley said.

Troopers Stubbs and Grant, the two inseparable East Enders, came in last, but only because they had been the last to be moved out, one half an hour after the other. Either Stubbs had deliberately slowed down to let his friend catch up or Grant had marched like hell to catch up with him. Either way, it didn't matter to Cusack, as they had made it in good time.

'You call that an exercise?' Bill Stubbs said pugnaciously, glancing from Cusack to Lewis. 'It was a piece of piss, that was.'

His friend Mel Grant grinned broadly, exposing his missing front teeth. 'So easy, we were practically asleep,' he said. 'A bunch of old-age pensioners could have done that hike, it was such a duck-walk.'

'You want to go back the way you came?' Sergeant Lewis challenged them.

'No, Sarge!' they sang out simultaneously.

'Then go down that hill and get in the truck while I'm still feeling good-natured.'

'Yes, boss!' both men chimed.

Cusack waited until both men were on their way down the hill, then he nodded at Lewis and they, too, started making their way back towards the trucks and jeep parked by the side of the narrow road that snaked across the lower slopes of the mountain range and led back to Hereford. Though the rain had now stopped, the green and brown fields were dark and desolate under low, leaden clouds. It was a landscape for bad dreams.

'He was just trying to rattle you,' Sergeant Lewis said, abruptly referring back to Cusack's telephone conversation with Prince. 'The guy's a psycho and that's why he made the call – just to put you on edge. That's why the fucker said he'd been in the house before, reminding you of what he'd done there. He surely must be one hard, evil bastard.'

'Yes,' Cusack responded, 'he was certainly trying to do that and for a while he almost succeeded. But I think I got through to him in the same way he was trying to get to me – not nice, but effective.'

'How come?'

'Well, he opened his conversation with that reference to what he'd done in my house. Then, when I didn't bite, he talked about other things, trying to sound like a reasonable man. In the end, however, when I started to get sarcastic and threatened to put the phone down, he really struck hard by asking me what bed I was sleeping in – my wife's or my daughter's.'

'Oh, fuck,' Lewis said. 'That's pure evil. That must have chopped you in two.'

'Almost,' Cusack said. 'I nearly slammed the phone down. Then I realized that he'd lost control of himself and was trying his damnedest to really hurt me.'

'You weren't wrong there, mate.'

'So I *didn't* slam the phone down. I didn't bite at all. I waited for a moment, let him sweat for a little, then I asked him how his parents were and *he* cut *me* off. I knew, then, that I'd managed to make him lose control and that he wasn't as self-possessed as he wanted to seem. Our Prince is a man with a burning fuse and he could explode at any moment, without reason or rhyme. That's his weakness. Our strength. He only thinks straight when he's calm, but he can be easily wound up. I wound him up with a question about his parents and in that sense I defeated him. That's why he slammed the phone down.'

'He's still sensitive about the child abuse?' Lewis asked.

'Yes,' Cusack said. 'At least enough to let me see that he isn't as strong, as invulnerable, as he appears to be. He didn't want me to know that.'

'Good,' Sergeant Lewis said with satisfaction. 'Let's hope he sweats over it.'

They had just reached the track at the bottom of the hill and four of the QRF team were already in one of the trucks, waiting to be driven back to Hereford. Bill Stubbs and Mel Grant, however, were still standing side by side on the path, both smoking cigarettes and trading badinage with the other four while the DSs came down off the mountains from the individual RVs of the Long Drag. The DSs would be driven back to Hereford in the other truck while Cusack and Lewis went back in the jeep.

'Look at 'em,' Stubbs said to Grant, as both turned their battered bulldog faces towards the truck containing the other members of the QRF team. 'So fuckin' soft, they have to get their fat arses on a seat the instant they come off the Long Drag. Four Girl Guides we've got there.'

'Just listen to that dumb cunt,' Corporal Mapley responded tartly. 'Another mindless East Ender farting hot air. If he's so fucking energetic after coming off that mountain, how come he looks at least twice his age?'

'Right,' Wiley said. 'He'll be flat on his back in his bunk in the Spider when we're still living it up in the Sports and Social. Him *and* his mad mate!'

'You hear that, mate?' Grant said to Stubbs. 'Those geriatrics think that by staggering breathlessly across a mountain range – the one *we* practically ran across – they're also capable of lifting pints of bitter without breaking their arms. If they actually make it from their bunks to the bar, I'll be fucking amazed. They'll be lying there paralysed.'

'If we're paralysed, it'll be due to the shock of your insane conversation,' Radnor said. 'So please spare us by shutting up.'

'Shut up, the fucking lot of you,' Sergeant Lewis said, seeing the last of the DSs clambering up into the second truck. 'And you two,' he added, turning to Stubbs and Grant, 'put out those fags and get your arses up in that vehicle with the other no-hopers.'

'Yes, boss!' both men chimed.

As Stubbs and Grant clambered up into the QRF truck, Cusack and Lewis made their way to the jeep that was parked a good distance along the road. Knowing that the drivers of the two trucks would wait until they had left and then follow them back to Stirling Lines in Hereford, Lewis turned on the ignition as soon as Cusack had slipped into the seat beside him. Lewis made a tight U-turn and headed back the way he had come the day before, passing the two parked trucks.

As he passed them, one of the trucks exploded.

Cusack heard the explosion as a detonation inside his head, instantly deafening him. Then he was hammered by the blast, swept by a wave of heat, and felt the jeep rocking as Lewis swerved off the road and braked to a shuddering halt. Thrown forward into the windscreen, Cusack cracked his forehead against a steel bar, but he jerked upright and glanced back over his shoulder as his hearing returned, bringing with it the subsiding roar of the explosion and the screaming of men in dreadful pain.

He saw one of the two trucks as a brilliant ball of fire, a phosphorescent inferno, within which the skeletal metal framework of the rear of the truck, bent out of all recognition, was clearly outlined for just a few seconds, though it seemed a lot longer, before billowing, oily black smoke obscured it and the men screaming inside it. Some were burning to death in there, but others were stumbling out of the inferno, either smouldering or covered entirely in flames, making insane, animalistic sounds and beating at their own burning limbs even as they collapsed.

Another, smaller explosion followed the first one – the petrol tank blowing up – and more yellow flames spewed out of the others erratically, nightmarishly illuminating the horrific scene and casting pale, wavering striations through the thickening smoke.

Cusack saw it all in seconds: a tableau of pain and death, quivering silhouettes in the flames, smaller explosions, louder screams, metal shrieking as it bent and broke, the air filled with the stench of burning – burning materials, burning flesh. Then he saw men spilling out of the untouched truck and wondered who had survived. He was shocked beyond measure, mercifully numbed by disbelief, but knew instantly, as soon as Sergeant Lewis spoke, sounding unnaturally, eerily calm, exactly who had committed this atrocity.

'A UCBT,' said Lewis.

*Of course,* Cusack thought. *Naturally.*

Prince had been in the SAS.

# CHAPTER SIXTEEN

*UCBT: an Under-Car Booby Trap.* Yes, Prince knew all the acronyms used by the SAS and all the filthy tricks that they got up to, so he'd given them a taste of their own medicine, though unfortunately he had picked the wrong truck, killing the DSs instead of the assassins of Cusack's QRF team. Nevertheless, as he sat in his Portakabin in the compound in Wiltshire, watching the news on television, listening to a newscaster talking about an 'unsubstantiated report' concerning the deaths of six SAS soldiers in what 'appeared' to have been 'a training accident' in the Brecon Beacons, he took his pleasure from the knowledge that he had struck his former regiment a bad blow – so bad, in fact, that they were trying to keep the truth of the matter secret.

They would not succeed. Prince had already arranged for the full details to be released on the Internet. Those details would soon get back from the Web to the media and then the whole world would know that Prince had struck again.

It had been so easy to do. Knowing that Cusack's QRF team would be undergoing special training related to their designated task, Prince had returned to Hereford with a group of his young followers and placed both Cusack's house and the entrance to the SAS base under surveillance, using a combination of unmarked vans, binoculars, and STG laser surveillance equipment. They had only been doing this for a couple of days, with instructions to call Prince at his Hereford hotel the instant anything unusual occurred, when one of his teams observed a truck containing six SAS men leaving Stirling Lines. This vehicle was followed by Cusack and his friend, Sergeant Jack Lewis, in a jeep; that in turn was followed by a second truck containing another six men, the last lot humping bergens and M-16 rifles.

Experienced in the ways of the regiment, Prince had deduced immediately that the men were being taken on a training exercise, probably a hike, almost certainly in the customary Brecon Beacons. Convinced of this, he had followed them in an unmarked van driven by one of his young followers, taking the route that he knew from personal experience the SAS would have taken. Once in the Brecon Beacons he had stuck to the old route, back roads over the looming hills, hardly more than dirt tracks. Eventually he saw the SAS trucks far ahead, parked, with Cusack's empty jeep, by the side of the road with nobody guarding them in this desolate spot known widely to be used by the SAS and therefore avoided by the locals.

Surveying the area with binoculars, Prince had seen the SAS men hiking in a long, snaking line across the wind-blown, rainswept mountain range, making their way from trig point to trig point as night fell. He waited until the last of them was out of sight, then advanced alone, on foot, under cover of darkness, with a home-made Semtex bomb in a satchel slung across his shoulder, approaching the parked trucks and jeep. While he would have dearly loved to have blown up Cusack's vehicle with him in it, he was saving him for last, for further torment, so he attached his bomb to the underside of one of the trucks, picking it at random, and wired its initiator to the vehicle's ignition system. When the truck's ignition was turned on, the bomb would explode.

Prince was too smart to wait around for that to happen. Once the UCBT was in place, he made his way back to the van still waiting for him and instructed the driver to take him back to his hotel in Hereford. He checked out of the hotel that same morning and returned with his followers to the compound in Wiltshire, where he waited for the early evening news. Now, watching the television, he knew that the bomb had indeed exploded, killing the six DSs in the booby-trapped truck. Prince was slightly disappointed that he had picked the wrong truck, but not too much so. He had still managed to kill six SAS men, and Sergeant Cusack would pay for it.

This was something he very much wanted, he realized as he turned the TV off and picked up the intercom to call Chloe. Indeed, every time he thought back to his phone conversation with Cusack, he burned up with childish shame at the recollection of how he had lost control when the sergeant mentioned his, Prince's, parents. 'How are your parents?' he had asked, knowing full well what he was doing, pushing a blade into Prince's soul and then twisting it viciously. Prince burned still. Because Cusack knew. What else was that remark but a nasty reminder of what Prince had suffered in his childhood and, indeed, was still suffering even now? For some experiences – yes, *some* experiences – were never truly cast off. They remained there, like acid in the stomach, like a tumour in the brain, to cause constant pain and nightmare. Cusack must have known that.

*How are your parents?*

Prince gulped and almost sobbed, his pure thoughts becoming cloudy, overlaid with shadowy forms and elongated shadows as those two, Satan's curse upon him, made their way staggering up the stairs. He had always seen the shadows first, though perhaps only in imagination, the tormenting phantoms of his fear. But *they* had certainly advanced into his room, both drunk and determined – and all too real. What's a beating here and there? Any child can take a beating. But what few children can take, what Prince had to take and swallow, is the pain and humiliation of the abuse that only adults can dish out. Even now – dear God, no! – he could hardly bear to think about it, and preferred to block it out of his thoughts, dwelling instead upon more positive matters. Like paying pain back with pain, humiliation with humiliation, torment with torment, compensating for the sins of the father (and, in his case, the mother too) with actions that spoke louder than words and made him feel less destroyed. There was a need to rise above life's teeming squalor, and God would show him the way.

'Chloe?' he said into the intercom, his voice calm, mellow, seductive. 'Is that you, my child?'

'Yes, Prince, it's me.'

'I need you, Chloe. Please come right away.'

He turned the intercom off and lay back on the bed, staring at the blank TV screen hanging down from the ceiling. Wearing only his white robe, no clothes beneath it this time, he could feel every pore in his skin and that impatient stirring. The hungers of the flesh, indeed. The lust that gave life and took it. He was training Chloe to encourage lust in others and then use it against them. She was certainly a good pupil, believing everything he told her, stretching herself out below him or arching backwards above him, her thighs a soft vice, her fingers like feathers, desperately trying to make them both as one in the eyes of the Lord. She was good in his bed (better than Lorna) but now he needed her elsewhere.

Waiting for Chloe to arrive, he wondered what, precisely, Cusack and Sir William Hargreaves, the Commissioner for the Metropolitan Police, had been talking about that evening in the former man's house. Obviously they had been talking about their troublesome Prince, but what, precisely, had they said? Clearly, if Hargreaves was involved, a serious investigation was under way; equally serious, if Hargreaves had come up with anything he would have passed it on to Cusack. That information would almost certainly have included details of Prince's previous existence as Laurence Grover and, most likely, his Cricklewood address. Well-nigh inevitably, then, the flat would have been searched, either by the police or by Cusack, perhaps by both, and it would now be under constant surveillance, so Prince could not go back there. This knowledge made him resentful since now, even if he just tried to sell the flat, the police would be on to him. He simply had to forget that he had ever owned it – and this was a bitter blow, financially and otherwise. He felt that the flat had been stolen from him – and he blamed that on Cusack.

Someone knocked on the door of his Portakabin.

'Come in!' he called out.

The front door opened and closed, someone padded towards his room, then Chloe appeared in the bedroom doorway. She was dressed in the community's standard-issue jungle-green overalls, belted at the waist, and flat shoes, with her auburn hair pinned up on her head, above the large, romantic brown eyes and full, experienced lips. Even in that sexless outfit, even with her hair pinned up primly, she had a distinct, unavoidably carnal appearance that made her seem older than her years. When she walked up to the bed to gaze upon him, Prince rose, despite himself, to the occasion.

'You look beautiful,' he said.

'Thank you,' Chloe responded.

'You were sent here by the Lord to bring me comfort and save me from temptation. Let me satisfy my lust that I might not dwell unhealthily upon temptation. Please lie beside me, Chloe.'

'Yes, Prince,' Chloe said.

She rarely said much these days. That was all to the good, when she let her hair down and lay beside him and he turned in towards her and she fondled him and he fondled her and they moved together as one. 'Ah, God!' he gasped as his belly slapped upon her belly. 'The Lord be praised!' he cried out when he almost came and had to control himself. He did so, breathing deeply, then started again, this time rolling her on to her belly to do to her what his father had done to him while his mother looked on. Chloe took it as he had taken it, though without the tears and shame, and he groaned aloud as he strove manfully upon her, visualizing her as a boy, the tight buttocks, the ridged spine, that pale, exposed neck, and then he shuddered and cried out, 'Ah, God!' and spilled himself into her. He lay upon her, breathing deeply, for a long time, but eventually, with the sigh of a contented cat, he rolled off her to lie peacefully beside her, his gaze fixed on the ceiling.

'Was that good?' Chloe finally asked him, sounding anxious, always wanting to please these days.

'Yes, dear, it was excellent. My mind has been purged of temptation and for that I have you to thank.'

'My pleasure,' Chloe said. 'Want me to go now?'

'No,' Prince replied, gratified to note again that Chloe really didn't talk much these days, and seemed content to serve the community in general by serving him in particular. Since giving up drugs and eating regularly instead, since attending PE classes every day and listening to the daily lectures on the need to protect 'white' Christianity by fighting the Forces of Darkness, including the Royal Family, the police, the hated SAS, the Blacks, swarthies and Jews – yes, since immersing herself in all of that she had become a lot calmer, indeed almost beatific. She now lived with her horizons greatly reduced, no farther away, as it were, than the perimeter fence of the compound, beyond which lay the world she now feared and no longer wanted. She belonged here now, thought of it as her home, and was willing to do anything to defend it. She was a real success story.

'I mean, yes,' Prince said, correcting himself. 'But I only want you to go back to your room and put on some street clothes. When you've done that, meet me by the motor pool. We're going out for the day, Chloe.'

'Oh? Where to?'

'Hereford.'

'We're going back to that house?'

'No, dear. We're going to a funeral and I simply don't want to go alone.'

'Whose funeral?'

'Never mind.'

'What kind of clothes should I wear? Something black and formal?'

'No, dear. This is going to be a very public funeral, so we

both have to look like normal people, like locals, who're just attending the funeral because they've read about it in the papers. There'll be a lot of that kind about and we'll just merge with the crowd, so wear simple, casual clothes – say, jeans, shirt, jacket and flat-heeled shoes. I'll be at the motor pool in thirty minutes.'

'Okay,' Chloe said.

Thirty-five minutes later, Prince and Chloe were wearing almost exactly the same kind of clothing – blue jeans, open-necked shirts and jackets – though Prince's long, golden-blond hair was still hanging down to his shoulders and Chloe's hair was again pinned up on her head.

'You look very attractive,' Prince said.

'You look handsome,' Chloe told him.

Prince did the driving and he took the scenic route: along the A4 to Chippenham, through Malmesbury to Cirencester, from there to Gloucester and Ross-on-Wye, then along the A49 to Kingsthorne and Hereford. He had always loved this journey and he talked non-stop en route, enthusiastically pointing out the pretty villages with thatched-roof cottages, the white-fenced dairy farms, the fine old pubs and market squares, the green hills and winding rivers, telling her that this was the *real* England, the England of *This England* magazine, the kind of England that was gradually being eroded by Royalist traitors, Luciferian schemers and foreigners of all kinds.

'This is the kind of England I was brought up in,' he said, fantasizing wildly because he was in a good mood and believing it simply because he was saying it. 'In a little village near Calne, in a thatched-roof cottage with gardens front and rear. Our milk was delivered every day to our doorstep. We had a village store that sold only English produce and I was educated in the village school and attended the village church, located on the edge of the village green. No foreigners there, dear! All English, and proud of it. No question *there* about delaying our education in order to let subliterate immigrants catch up. No school politics. Just pure education. We were taught to be proud of our heritage and I grew up proud to be English.'

'It must have been a nice childhood,' Chloe said distractedly. 'Growing up in the countryside and all.'

'Yes,' Prince responded, enjoying his little fantasy, 'it was an *idyllic* childhood. All my school chums were English, all white; there were no gangs of blacks to beat you up when you were going to and from school. No dirty old men or serial killers to worry about. My mum ran the village post office, my dad sold farm produce, and I spent my free time fishing, collecting tadpoles and playing games like hide-and-seek in orchards with the other kids. There weren't any problems at all – and do you know why, Chloe?' He was far too excited to wait for a reply. 'No immigrants, Chloe! No blacks or swarthies! English neighbours, English education, English religion and English customs. We were all one big happy family because we were all in agreement. That's the way of life we started to lose when we let in the immigrants. Those were the Garden of Eden days.'

'You must have been a happy child,' Chloe said.

'Yes, I was,' Prince lied blatantly, temporarily forgetting the elongated shadows moving eerily up the stairwell, breathing heavily, obscenely, in that two-up, two-down house in a backstreet in Kilburn, London where he had really been born and bred, his parents alcoholic city dwellers, his childhood a living nightmare. 'I was as happy as any child has the right to be. Happy and content. Because I grew up in the England you see around you and I'm proud of my heritage. They can't take that away from me.'

His ebullient mood was dampened slightly, temporarily, when they passed through the picturesque market town of Ross-on-Wye, on the last leg of the journey to Hereford. Thinking of the funeral that he was about to attend, of how it had come about, somehow made him think of what he had really come from, what had led him to this point, and his resentment came bubbling out accordingly.

'Of course, they're trying,' he said. 'You can see it

everywhere, elsewhere. They're trying to destroy our heritage, our culture, our faith, by flooding the country, particularly the cities, with every kind of immigrant – Indian, Pakistani, Greek, Turkish, Chinese, African, Caribbean, Abyssinian and Jew – all of whom have imported their satanic religions along with their vile customs and beliefs. Then, of course, you have the Irish – they're everywhere you look – and the less overt but more pernicious influence of American culture. It's a deliberate, worldwide conspiracy and it has to be stopped.'

Indeed, even just thinking about it reminded Prince of why he had left the city to live in the countryside. In Wiltshire the faces were mostly white and the air was still clean.

'This is what we have to get rid of,' he explained to Chloe as he drove past green meadows stretching out to the river Wye and saw Hereford Cathedral rising in the distance. 'We have to get the ethnics out, destroy their temples and mosques, burn their obscene religious books, ban their children from our schools, give their jobs to our own kind, prevent them from spreading the moral filth of their weird traditions and in general make England what it used to be before they took over. Ethnic cleansing's the only way to stop the rot and that's what we're about. God has chosen us for this great task, my dear, and His light will guide us.'

His mood lightened again when he reached the outskirts of Hereford and turned into the road that led to St Martin's Church. Even before reaching the church, he saw the many vehicles parked outside it, including the vans of national TV and radio stations. Parking well away from them, his car out of sight, Prince disembarked with Chloe and walked with her to the cemetery, guided there by the flow of people around it.

Located behind the church, the SAS regimental plot was divided from the rest of the cemetery by six yew trees and a low loose-stone memorial wall lined with plaques inscribed with the details of the SAS men buried there. The six new graves in the plot were presently surrounded by bereaved, weeping relatives, men, women and children, as well as a lot of uniformed SAS troopers, NCOs and officers, some of whom were about to fire a rifle salute. It was, indeed, a public burial with a mass of onlookers, most attracted by media reports of the atrocity. Those onlookers included the representatives of the media, including TV cameramen and radio commentators who, along with the other spectators, were pressing against the low memorial wall.

However, as the crowd almost certainly also included plain-clothed 'Green Slime' – members of the SAS Intelligence Corps – who would be looking out for suspicious persons in the throng, Prince decided to put a safe distance between himself and the graveyard.

Finding a good position at the rear of the crowd beside Chloe in an area where the ground was conveniently raised, whilst still ensuring that his face could not be seen from the cemetery, Prince looked beyond that sea of bobbing heads to where the military funeral was taking place. The six men in the guard of honour had already aimed their rifles at the sky and they fired a salute over the new graves, abruptly breaking the silence, even as Prince caught sight of Sergeant Cusack. Wearing his full SAS uniform with beige beret and winged-dagger badge, he was standing to attention beside his commanding officer, Lieutenant Colonel Blackwell. Both men looked sombre.

'That's the man we saw before,' Chloe whispered to Prince, 'when we were watching that house in Redhill.'

'Correct,' Prince replied. 'Now, please be quiet and show some respect. This is a solemn occasion, dear.'

Chloe remained obediently silent throughout the rest of the ceremony, allowing Prince to observe his quarry at length. Clearly, from the barely suppressed grief in his face, Cusack had been devastated by the deaths and was in a bad way. This was all to the good.

Also present at the funeral, Prince noted, were the six members of Cusack's QRF team, the ones who should have been killed by Prince's bomb. Prince knew who they were because he had studied them on the video film that his surveillance team had taken as they were being driven out of Stirling Lines in an open-topped troop truck that fateful early morning, just three days ago. Now, since he knew them, as it were, individually, he could do something about them.

Nevertheless, his main interest was still Sergeant Cusack, with whom he had already spoken and to whom he intended speaking again. Observing Cusack, his quarry, Prince could see that he was suffering, was still in a state of shock, and was almost certainly feeling guilty over the deaths of his six comrades. His guilt was his weakness, his breaking point, if used correctly, and Prince intended to do just that with the help of young Chloe.

Eventually, with the sermon delivered, the rifle salute completed and flowers laid on the six new graves, the funeral service ended, the people around the graves began to disperse to the waiting cars, and the spectators, including Prince and Chloe, started drifting away. Not wishing to be recognized by Cusack, who would almost certainly know him by now from police photographs, Prince turned away from the cemetery and hurried back to his car with Chloe by his side. He waited until Chloe was strapped in beside him before turning his head to stare steadily, hypnotically, at her.

'I think it's time you moved to Hereford,' he said.

'Anything you say, Prince.'

Prince nodded his approval, turned the ignition on, then drove away from St Martin's Church, heading back to Wiltshire.

# CHAPTER SEVENTEEN

Standing in the regimental plot of St Martin's Church in the shadow of the yew trees, near the low memorial wall that now held back a mass of onlookers as well as TV cameramen and radio commentators with microphones, Cusack was more grief-stricken than he cared to acknowledge and also filled with an all-consuming guilt. He attempted to distract himself from the sight of the weeping wives, mothers, sisters and children, from the wet-eyed, tight-lipped fathers and brothers, by focusing on the spire of Hereford Cathedral, soaring high in the distance, sharply outlined against a clear blue sky, but his attention was inexorably drawn back to those six new white tombstones, each of which had inscribed upon it the individual's number, rank, name, an acknowledgement that he was a member of 22 SAS, the date of his death and his age when he died. When the rifle salute was fired, Cusack actually winced, which was a fair indication of his emotional state. By the end of the ceremony, he felt as if he was suffocating.

This was the worst blow to the regiment in years, and Cusack carried the weight of it. He was almost relieved, therefore, when, after the funeral, his commanding officer, Lieutenant Colonel Blackwell, looking handsome in his full dress uniform with beige beret and winged-dagger badge, his chest covered in medals, indicated that he would like Cusack to accompany him back to Stirling Lines for a drink in the Paludrine Club. Nodding his agreement, Cusack fell in beside him and they made their way out of the graveyard, following sobbing relatives and the dispersing crowd of onlookers, some drawn here out of genuine respect for the dead, others out of ghoulish curiosity, while the TV cameramen and sound men humped their gear back on to their trucks and radio commentators rushed back to their cars. It was a media circus.

'This is the most exposure we've had since the Princes Gate Siege,' Blackwell said. 'And that was way back in 1980.'

'Not good, boss,' Cusack replied.

'Not good at all,' Blackwell agreed.

The short drive to Stirling Lines took no time at all and soon they were in the Paludrine Club, the bar on the base, having an informal, boozy wake with other SAS men who had attended the funeral but were not joining the grieving relatives in their homes. The social logistics of burying six men at the same time had been considerable, with some bereaved relatives insisting on returning for the wake to their own homes, located either in the married quarters or off the base, and others preferring to drown their sorrows in the bar. As the commanding officer of 22 SAS, Lieutenant Colonel Blackwell made a point of initially having a few drinks with the bereaved present and chatting with some of the other men, particularly the closest friends of those who had been killed. But eventually, when the others were deeply engaged with one another, their tongues loosened by the drink, he took Cusack aside for a private talk. Cusack sensed that the conversation would not be pleasant, but it was better than nothing.

'How do you feel?' Blackwell asked him by way of a gentle opener.

'I'm okay,' Cusack lied.

'Bullshit, Sergeant. You were in a drunken fist fight last night in a pub in Hereford. That wasn't a good sign.'

'Some cunt was making jokes about those six we buried and I guess I just couldn't take it. Okay, so I landed one on him. So what? He deserved it.'

'A civilian.'

'More reason to down the bastard.'

'Are you blaming yourself for what happened, Sergeant?'

'Who else can I blame? That UCBT was placed under the truck when we were all up in the mountains. Prince, the bastard, must have followed us all the way out there, waited until we'd hiked up into the mountains, leaving the trucks behind, then planted his booby trap and lit out again. I was in charge and I left the trucks unattended, so obviously I'm the one who's to blame. It was irresponsible of me.'

'No, it wasn't,' Blackwell said. 'That was the last thing we were expecting. That bastard must have been monitoring the movements of our men in and out of the base; then he picked just the right time to follow us. Not your fault at all.'

'I should have thought about it,' Cusack insisted.

'*I* should have thought of it,' Blackwell said, 'but thinking about it wouldn't have helped us too much. Prince could only have monitored our movements by placing this base under surveillance and that's something we can do little about since the public pass by every day. Besides, that kind of surveillance can be conducted from a safe distance with hi-tech, long-distance equipment.'

'Which Prince certainly has,' Cusack interjected, 'having made a bloody fortune by conning money out of his so-called disciples. Peddle religion and get rich!'

Blackwell grinned and nodded. 'Yes, right. Anyway, to continue . . . With regard to your leaving the trucks unattended out in the training area of the Brecon Beacons – well, we've been doing that for years and what you did was no different.'

'So Prince could still be watching the base?'

'Well, I think that if he tried it once, he won't attempt it a second time because he knows we'll be specifically searching for a surveillance van – which, indeed, we're doing right now. Despite the protestations of the public about so-called infringements of their freedom of movement, I've placed the whole area around the base under *our* surveillance and any vehicle that parks within a mile of the place gets a good going-over. I'm pretty sure he'll have moved on by now but I'm taking no chances.'

'Good move, boss, but it may have come too late.'

'What does that mean, Sergeant?'

'If he had us under surveillance with hi-tech equipment, he's likely to have videotape footage of us, taken as we left the base to go on that ill-fated outing. We were in open-topped trucks, so his cameras could have picked us out individually. Given that, he can probably physically identify the six surviving troopers, my QRF team, plus me and PC2, Sergeant Jack Lewis, who were in the jeep.'

'Yes, I thought about that. He could only identify *you* before; now he has all of the team. This is going to become pretty hairy, Sergeant, if you don't get to him soon.'

'That's my fear,' Cusack admitted. 'Particularly because he told me during that phone call that he plans to neutralize my team members before settling with me. If he can identify them, if he now has video footage of them, he can track them down easily.'

'Damn it, Lenny,' Blackwell said, dropping the formality of rank. 'I'm so pleased to be drinking right now. In fact, right now, I could do with another.'

'Let me get it,' Cusack said. He went to the bar, which was crowded with NCO friends, including Jack Lewis, all there to mourn the six who had failed to beat the clock – the men who had died. They were mourning them by getting as pissed as newts and deliberately not mentioning their names.

'I see you're deep in conversation with the CO,' Jack Lewis said, brushing the red hair from his forehead, his green eyes bloodshot. 'I bet he's not in a good mood.'

'Neither am I,' Cusack said, waiting for his drinks to come.

'The clock stops for no one,' Lewis said, 'and already it's so far in the past, I can't even remember it.'

'Fuck off,' Cusack said, though he was grinning when he

said it. After chatting amiably to Jack for another minute or so, he received his drinks and returned to Blackwell.

'Thanks,' Blackwell said, taking his drink. He glanced across the crowded room, at the men drinking and smoking, determined to drown their sorrows, and said, as if continuing a conversation that he'd been having with himself in his head, 'And, of course, to make matters worse, we can no longer keep the ghastly truth secret.'

'What truth?'

'That the six men didn't get blown up in a training accident.'

Cusack shook his head from side to side. "Fraid not,' he said, referring, as was Blackwell, to the fact that Prince had already sent an open letter to the press, claiming responsibility for the bombing and promising more atrocities in the future. In the same letter, he had called the SAS the Angels of Death and Lucifer's Children, supporting those descriptions with his assertion that the SAS were the Royal Family's official executioners and that the regiment was ruled by Freemasonry and backed by a secret group of Illuminati. The British Millennialist Movement, he had added, was proud to have made this latest contribution – the death of six covert SAS assassins – to the fight against the Forces of Darkness and was calling on similar movements to rally to their cause, with the downfall of the Royal Family and the British government as their ultimate aim. 'That press release?' Cusack added.

'Yes?' Blackwell responded.

'Similar shit was released through the World Wide Web, so it's all over the globe now.'

'Oh, God,' Blackwell groaned. He looked like a man who wanted to go to bed and pull the sheets up over his head. Taking another sip of his drink, he said, 'If we don't track that bastard down soon, we're going to be in real trouble.'

'I'm doing my best to catch him,' Cusack said, 'but he's a slippery eel.'

'So what's on the agenda?'

'If I can't get to him, I might be able to bring him to me,'

Cusack said. 'I mean, I don't think he's as controlled as he tries to seem – I think he's potentially explosive – so I'm going to try goading him into losing control and, perhaps, revealing himself by coming for me, maybe at my home, without taking his customary precautions.'

'How do you plan to do that?'

'When we talked on the phone, when he rang me at my home, I goaded him about his parents, his sexual abusers, and he cut me off. He was actually goading *me* at first, wanting *me* to slam my phone down, but *he* was the one who weakened in the end, quickly too. So I think his strings *can* be easily pulled and I'm going to try my best to pull 'em.'

'How?' Blackwell repeated.

'I think he's going to call me again,' Cusack said, 'to boast about this latest atrocity and see how I respond. I think this bastard's going to try tormenting me and that's just what I'll use. Instead of him goading me, I'll goad him into coming to get me. He just might break and do it.'

'Then I'd better arrange to have your house and car fixed up by the Special Services Division.'

'That won't please the neighbours,' Cusack said. 'It'll make them all paranoid.'

'Fuck the neighbours,' Blackwell replied. 'If they don't want to face the heat, they shouldn't live beside SAS men. Anyway, I'll have the job done today. This afternoon, in fact.'

'I'll be home,' Cusack said.

Blackwell glanced around the crowded, smoky bar, at the men drinking to drown their sorrow over six dead comrades and laughing loudly to hide their pain and rage. Obviously disturbed to be reminded of the mass funeral, he turned back to Cusack, waving his empty glass in front of his face. 'I need one more,' he said. 'Just one more and then I'll go back to work, arranging for your protection. Do you mind?'

'No, boss, I don't mind.'

Cusack took the empty glass from his CO and crossed the room to the bar, again stopping beside Jack Lewis. Cusack ordered his drinks.

'Still talking to the CO, I see,' Lewis said, turning his crimson-eyed gaze upon Cusack.

'Right,' Cusack said. 'We have a lot to talk about.'

'Any progress on that bastard Prince?' Lewis asked.

'Not much at all.'

'We want to pin that fucker down good and proper. Find him quick and put his lights out before he does us more damage.'

'That's exactly what the CO said, but it doesn't help much. You got any ideas, Jack?'

'Right now I've got only one idea and that's to drink my way into oblivion and forget this whole business.'

'We can forget it when it's finished,' Cusack said, 'and not until then. But have a couple for me.'

'You're going home soon?' Lewis asked, looking surprised.

'The Special Services Division,' Cusack said. 'The CO is having me fixed up and I've got to be there this afternoon.'

Lewis raised his eyebrows. 'Oh, really? He must be pretty concerned.'

'He has his reasons,' Cusack said.

'You're expecting a visit from that bastard or his friends?'

'I'm hoping – just hoping.'

'Rather you than me,' Lewis said.

The barman brought the drinks. Cusack paid and returned to the CO, where he was still standing alone in a corner. They touched glasses and drank.

'You went to Prince's flat, didn't you?' Blackwell said. 'That place in Cricklewood, London.'

'Yes,' Cusack confessed.

'Without the help of the police?' Blackwell asked, looking anxious. 'Without a search warrant?'

Cusack shrugged. 'The police have done all they can or are willing to do and passed the job on to us. They don't want to be connected in any way any more, so they wouldn't come up with a search warrant. I had to go in alone.'

'Jesus!' Blackwell exclaimed softly, thinking of the legal complications if Cusack had been caught in that flat. 'How did you get in? You smashed the lock?'

'No. With a set of special police keys, given to me, off the record, by our esteemed Commissioner for the Metropolitan Police.'

Blackwell smiled. 'That baby-faced, sweet-smiling, clever bastard. Okay, so you let yourself in . . . ?'

'Yes. He'd moved most of his stuff out, but he'd obviously left in a hurry and one plastic shopping bag of printed PR material and old letters had been left inadvertently behind a chair. It contained enough information for me to be able to confirm that the Second Coming Movement did indeed close down in January 2001 – when it was obvious that Millennium Year had produced no Second Coming as promised by the movement – and that it resurfaced a few weeks later as the more formal-sounding British Millennialist Movement. This movement, as you know, avoids all mention of a Second Coming and instead cleverly uses the present worldwide interest in conspiracy theories to suck in the same breed of post-Millennium truth-seekers – the flower children of the year 2003. Unfortunately, though all of this was confirmed by the papers I found there, the only address on the publicity sheets was Prince's home address.'

'The actual flat you were standing in.'

'Exactly.'

'So you still don't know where the British Millennialist Movement is physically located.'

'No.'

'So until you find out, your only option is still to bring him out into the open.'

'Correct,' Cusack said.

'Does Prince still own that flat?'

'Yes, but he's bound to know that it'll be under constant surveillance, so it's highly unlikely that he'll return there in the foreseeable future.'

'When did he buy it?'

'About eight years ago. When he was still living with his parents in Kilburn. Unfortunately, that'll be the only address on the deeds, and unless he tries to rent or sell the flat, the deeds will be no help in tracing him.'

'Any contacts?'

'His parents are dead and we don't know of any close relatives.'

'His parents died when the house burned down,' Blackwell said. 'At least, as far as I recall from the police reports.'

'Your recollection's correct, boss. They were both killed in their sleep when the house in Kilburn burned down. Prince – then known, of course, by his real name of Laurence Grover – was eating in a nearby café at the time. Apparently the fire broke out just after he'd left the house. The police investigators concluded that the fire was started accidentally by the father when he fell into a drunken stupor – his wife was in the same condition – with a lit cigarette still in his hand. Forensics concluded from the pattern of the blaze that the fire had started from Mr Grover's side of the bed, travelled across the room, then, once it had taken hold properly, had swept through the whole house. Both victims would have choked to death in the smoke before being incinerated. At the time it was believed that there were no suspicious circumstances. But now, given what we know of Laurence Grover, or Prince, and given that those people were killed by fire a mere month after lending their son the money for the hefty deposit on the flat in Cricklewood, I think it's safe to assume that it was their son who set the house on fire.'

'As vengeance for the sex abuse and also to ensure that he didn't have to pay them back the money that he'd borrowed for the flat.'

'That's my bet, my scenario,' Cusack said. 'His father and mother are both in a drunken stupor in their bed. Their son, who knows from personal experience that a bomb won't waken them when they're in that condition, enters the room, sets fire to the bedclothes with a lit cigarette – probably drenching them first with the same alcohol that his parents were drinking – then slips out of the house and hurries across the road to the nearest café.'

'Sounds plausible,' Blackwell said.

'It is,' Cusack said. 'A fire started that way would take some time to spread, so Prince, as Laurence Grover, would probably have been in the café a good half-hour before the neighbours smelled the smoke or saw the flames. It's no accident, therefore, that his story about being in the café was believed. It was perfectly true, after all. So my bet is that Prince killed his own parents and now we've no one left, no known relative, who could give us a clue as to where he might be now.'

'And, as you've just said, as long as he doesn't try to sell or rent his flat – so long as he just leaves it sitting there, empty – it's of no help to us.'

'None at all, I'm afraid.'

Blackwell finished his drink and placed the empty glass on the table beside him. 'I'd better get back,' he said.

'Right.'

'You'd better get back as well, Sergeant. I'll have the SSD there this afternoon and they'll need you to be present.'

'Can't it wait till tomorrow?' Cusack asked on an impulse, suddenly feeling the need for another drink.

Blackwell stared steadily at him. 'No, it can't,' he said. 'I want this over and done with. I haven't forgotten that drunken fist fight, the one you had last night, and I know that it won't take too much to send you back to that old routine. Besides, if you're not careful, you'll find yourself being sent for an LFT,' he added, using the abbreviation for a liver function test and grinning to lighten the load. 'Now, we don't want that, do we?'

'No, boss, we don't.'

'Then you head straight home and wait for the SSD, Sergeant Cusack, while I go to my office. Come on, walk me out.'

'Anything you say, boss.'

Ignoring Cusack's sarcasm, Blackwell went around the noisy, smoky club, saying farewell and shaking hands as he made his way gradually to the exit. When he left, Cusack left as well and stood beside him just outside, glancing around at the Nissen huts and brick buildings of Stirling Lines in the bleak light of the afternoon.

Blackwell turned to face him. 'I'll have them there by seventeen hundred hours, Sergeant.'

'I'll be there,' Cusack replied.

'Make sure of it,' Blackwell said firmly. Then he smiled and marched off, heading for his office in the regimental headquarters where the Kremlin – the SAS intelligence section – was also located. Right now, the spooks were trying to track down Prince, but they weren't getting far. No wonder Blackwell was anxious.

Cusack picked his car up at the motor pool, where he had left it before being driven to St Martin's Church by Jack Lewis, and drove back to his house in Redhill, less than ten minutes' drive from the base. Arriving there just after 4.00 p.m., he parked the car in the driveway and went into the house to make himself a strong cup of coffee.

As usual, the instant Cusack entered the house he felt the oppressive weight of all his memories, prompted by the unnerving feeling that Mary and Jennifer were still alive and simply being quiet in one of the other rooms, either downstairs or upstairs. This feeling of being haunted by his dead loved ones was only increased by his recollection of the funeral he had attended earlier, so instead of making a coffee, he poured himself a stiff whisky which he drank while slumped in an armchair in front of the TV. He was waiting for the news but he was too early for it, and he was on to his second large whisky when the front doorbell rang.

Cusack quickly finished off his drink, then went to open the front door. Three men in overalls were standing outside, all burdened with rolls of cable, toolboxes, and cardboard cartons containing lights and other electrical appliances.

'Steve Ransom,' one of the men said, grinning broadly and flashing an SSD identity card. 'Home Office, Special Services Division. We've come to make you secure.'

Cusack sighed and nodded. 'Come in.'

Over the next couple of hours, the three men covered the

whole house, downstairs and upstairs, fitting various security devices, including alarms in every room, security lighting front and rear, a video entry system and even a bombproof mailbox. The more security devices they put in, the less secure Cusack felt. Now he wouldn't be able to forget for a second that his life was in danger.

'You got lights in that garage?' Steve Ransom asked him three hours later, when the house had been fully secured.

'Yes,' Cusack said.

'If you run the car into the garage, we'll attach a UCBT Detector.'

Cusack sighed again. 'Right.'

When he switched the garage light on and drove the car in, the three SSD men followed him and went to work. As they were working, making a good bit of noise, Cusack saw that some of his neighbours had come out to watch with concerned expressions on their faces. The SAS was always reluctant to install this kind of security because it could not be done covertly and it actually made neighbours, those who were not military people themselves, nervous; made them wonder what kind of trouble could be coming their way. Not that any of Cusack's neighbours actually complained: they just looked on, then eventually went back inside to worry quietly about assassins and mad bombers – which was, in this particular case, a justifiable concern, had they but known it. Cusack sympathized with them.

Nevertheless, in under an hour, with no interruptions, the SSD team had fitted the car with an elaborate alarm system. Eight electronic detectors, designed to detect any suspicious metal object placed underneath the car, were fitted at various points on the vehicle. A strong magnet with a mercury tilt switch that would detect the slightest movement was also fitted underneath. An LED control panel with flashing red, green and orange lights was fitted to the dashboard and could, as Steve Ransom explained, be automatically armed and disarmed by simply turning the car's ignition on or off.

'When you first open the door,' he continued, 'all three

lights will come on. When the red and green lights are flashing, the system's on standby and won't arm until the final door or the boot lid is closed. Once all the doors are closed, all three lights will flash for twenty seconds, then a single constant green light will come on to indicate that the system's working and armed.'

'And if no lights come on?' Cusack asked.

'Then you'll know that something's wrong with the system.' Grinning, Ransom held up a device that looked like a high-powered torch in a compact metal case. Removing the device from its case, he pulled out an extendable handle with a small mirror attached to its lower end. 'That's when you use this mirror,' he began.

'I know,' Cusack interjected wearily, taking the device and its case from Ransom. 'I use it to check under the car. I walk around all sides of the car, holding the mirror pointing upwards down near ground level to ensure that no bomb's been attached underneath.'

'Right,' Ransom said, still grinning. 'I forgot. In your line of work, you'd have needed this kind of protection before, wouldn't you?'

'Yep,' Cusack said. 'But tell me if there's anything that's changed since I last had this done.'

'Well,' Ransom said, looking more serious now, 'they're being updated all the time, so I'd better take you through it, even at the risk of telling you what you already know.'

'You do that,' Cusack said.

Ransom rolled the driver's window down and indicated that Cusack should lower his head and check the new LED display on the dashboard. 'Before entering the vehicle,' Ransom explained, 'you check if the single green light's still on, indicating that the system's armed and working properly. If, instead of the green alone, you have an amber light as well, it means that one of the vehicle's doors, or the boot lid, has been tampered with. Another indication of danger is a single red light with a flashing green light. This is an indication that the magnetic alarm's been activated, that a bomb's probably been attached to the underneath of the vehicle, and that it'll go off if you open the door.'

'But if it's only the green light, I'm okay.'

'You've got it, Sarge.'

'Anything else?'

'No, that's it.'

'You guys want to come in for a drink?'

'Not while we're on duty.'

'You work late.'

'We blame your CO for that. He was pretty insistent on us doing it today, even though it was mid-afternoon. So! We're off now. The best of luck, Sarge.'

'Thanks,' Cusack said.

He watched the three men drive away in their unmarked van. Then he set the alarm on his car, turned the garage light out, locked the doors and went back inside the house. He locked the front door, checked the back doors, then set the alarm on his new household security system. Aware of what this action signified, reminded that he was in danger, he poured himself another stiff drink and took it into the downstairs bedroom, the guest room, which was where he always slept these days. He downed the drink quickly – too quickly – and fell asleep almost instantly.

He had no dreams that night.

# CHAPTER EIGHTEEN

Prince sat like a spider at the centre of its web, though his personal snare was the World Wide Web. He was in his study in the Portakabin in his strongly defended Wiltshire compound – more strongly, more openly fortified every day, with all of his disciples now accepting that their righteous 'war' was inevitable – surfing the Net as a lurker and as a poster, certainly as a hacker, keeping in touch with his fellow cyber-terrorists and group-mind fundamentalists worldwide through their newsgroups, chat groups, bulletin boards and mailing lists. But, most enthusiastically of all, he hacked into mainframes to insert malignant viruses where he wanted to cause damage or steal confidential, usually dangerous information.

Prince lived for power and he had learned what true power was when he first got into the Net in a really big way, discovering that it came naturally to him. Starting as a simple 'phone phreaker', stealing phone time from telephone companies by generating tones that enabled him to bypass the billing system or charge someone else's account, he progressed to breaking into the main computers that controlled phone calls for miles around. Once in, he eavesdropped on phone calls, misdirected them, planted obscene or threatening messages on answering services, and linked calls together in a daisy chain that allowed a lengthy transnational conference to take place between him and his overseas cyberterrorists without costing any of the participants a single penny. Then came the Internet. As a thrasher, he learned to insert worms into threads to cause maximum disruption to chat groups, and soon progressed to more skilful pastimes, such as hacking into the e-mail and websites of rival organizations or the military and police, to leave threatening messages or replace the original pages of the websites with pages of his own. He had even done this to the websites of Scotland Yard and Buckingham Palace.

Prince had, of course, heard about the legendary American hackers like Agent Steal and Dark Dante and Condor, who at various times broke into telephone switching-system centres to take control of phone calls, worked as computer 'bounty hunters' for the FBI, tracking down other hackers for the agency, and siphoned hundreds of thousands of dollars out of major banks, transferring them to anonymous accounts in other banks. They also broke into NORAD, the North American Air Defence Command, the very heart of America's early-warning system, and even formed on-line espionage services, selling stolen trade and government secrets – anything from designs for new toys to plans for cruise missiles – to anyone willing to pay.

For a while those hackers had been Prince's heroes, but they had all been caught eventually, either to be imprisoned or blackmailed into working for their potential jailers, the intelligence agents who had caught them. Prince had then despised them for letting that happen to them and had gone on to nurture his own skills, applying them first for the running of his Second Coming Movement, then, when that business collapsed, for the building up of his British Millennialist Movement through the Internet. This work included selecting new recruits, keeping in touch with similar movements worldwide but particularly in the US, electronically stealing from banks some of the finance required for the administration of the organization, and obtaining weapons and explosives for the protection of the compound. Now, he felt that he was a web wizard and, in truth, he wasn't too far wrong.

He did, however, want to boast about it. And who better to talk to than the man many of his fellow Millennialists feared most: SAS Sergeant Leonard 'Lenny' Cusack? Given the extensive surveillance he had conducted on Cusack and the rest of his QRF team, including the hi-tech long-distance observation that had produced videotape of them entering and leaving Stirling Lines and their own homes, Prince had most of the details of them that he required and had, indeed, entered those details into his upgraded Dell 310 computer system, with its helpful 640MB hard disk. He was, in fact, preparing for a campaign of computerized harassment against all the members of the team, wishing to terrorize them before terminating them. But right now, just past the midnight hour, when Cusack would doubtless be either in bed or preparing to go to bed, almost certainly sleeping downstairs to avoid the bedrooms of his slaughtered wife and daughter, Prince thought it a good idea to interrupt him and give him a hard time. As Cusack's personal details were now in Prince's computer, the terrorist was able to phone the SAS man simply by clicking on his phone number. Someone picked the phone up at the other end.

'Yes?' Cusack said, sounding wary.

'Good morning, Sergeant Cusack. This is Prince. The man you're failing so dismally to find. How are you, Cusack?'

'I'm fine,' Cusack said, speaking carefully.

'Were you asleep?'

'No, I was reading.'

'Reading what?'

'Today's papers,' Cusack said.

'I'm disappointed. I thought you might have chosen something more elevating – perhaps Aristotle or Descartes in the old Penguin paperback editions.'

'Sorry to disappoint you,' Cusack said, 'but it was just the newspapers.'

'Looking for something about me, were you?'

'No. I just wanted something to read before going to bed.'

'Can't sleep, is that it? Too much on your mind?'

'You might say that.'

'*Me* on your mind, is it?'

'No point in denying it.'

'How romantic.'

'Not quite,' Cusack said.

'So what were you thinking as you were distracting yourself by trying to read the newspapers?'

'I'll keep my thoughts to myself, thanks.'

'Thinking of the six SAS men killed out on the Brecon Beacons? Thinking of how much you hate me for that?'

'Yes,' Cusack said.

'Hate is a redundant emotion,' Prince said, 'that simply keeps us from sleeping at night while getting us nowhere. Think of those six men as casualties of war, and you won't hate me so much.'

'Go fuck yourself,' Cusack said.

'Come, come, Cusack, don't be crude. Don't let your anger make you foul-mouthed; you're too decent for that.'

'What makes you think I'm decent?'

'I could see it in your face at the funeral of those six men. I was one of the onlookers, my friend, one of the public, the ghouls. You looked quite distraught.'

Cusack didn't reply immediately, and Prince sensed that he was trying to control his anger, his disbelief, his shock. Eventually, after a lengthy silence, Cusack said, 'I hope you enjoyed it.'

'I did,' Prince said. 'I was truly, deeply moved.' He waited for the anger that he had hoped to unleash this time. When it failed to materialize, he sighed and said, 'So what else were you thinking?'

Again, Cusack did not reply immediately and Prince sensed that he was choosing his words carefully. Eventually he said, 'I was wondering where you were hiding out and contemplating what I'm going to do to you when I finally find you.'

'If you ever do.'

'I'll find you,' Cusack said. 'And when I do, you can count off the seconds because that's all you'll have left.'

'You're trying to antagonize me,' Prince said, knowing this to be true. 'You want me to lose my temper like I did the last time, but I'm not about to fall for it this time. You're going to put my lights out if you find me? Well, finding me won't be easy; and even if you *did* find me, my friend, getting at me would be even more difficult.'

'You can't be *that* well defended,' Cusack said.

'Oh, I'm well defended all right,' Prince said, realizing in the back of his mind that he was probably saying too much but unable to stop himself from boasting. 'I'm as well defended as an SAS troop in a sangar – or in an armed camp.'

'Well, you'd know all about that, having been with the regiment.'

'Yes, indeed. Which is why I know how you operate and why I can make your life difficult.'

'Is that what your place is like?' Cusack asked. 'Like an armed camp?'

'Yes,' Prince boasted. 'Like a lot of the fortified camps that have sprung up all over the country in the past few years – the ones so carefully ignored by the police, who can't risk a bloodbath, particularly with people only trying to protect their chosen way of life: a *religious* way of life, Cusack.'

'Not a charitable religion,' Cusack said, still trying to needle him. 'Not a forgiving religion. A religion of hatred, based on paranoid conspiracy theories and racism and other forms of intolerance. That's not really the English way, is it? More like the American Patriot or Millennarian Movement – or the Oklahoma Citizens' Militia. No, it's just not the English way.'

'I'm as English as you are,' Prince said, almost snapping, growing hot under the collar on the instant.

'You might be English by birth –' Cusack began.

'I am!' Prince snapped.

' –but that doesn't mean you're living your life the English way. You know? Decency. Tolerance. Seems to me you're slavishly following the Americans, mostly racist Americans, in the way you're living your life. That's hardly inspiring.'

Prince was just about to scream a mouthful of abuse when he realized that Cusack had managed to wind him up and that he had to control himself. So he took a deep breath, controlled himself and said, 'I don't "slavishly follow" anyone. But I don't mind admitting that I see eye to eye with our American friends and that I learned a lot from them.'

'Such as?'

'Such as not letting my country be taken over and corrupted by Blacks, swarthies and Jews. Such as not letting a secret cabal of Freemasons and Illuminati run the country while hiding behind the Royal Family. Such as not letting an equally secret police force and military establishment covertly take over our lives. Such as protecting myself and those who follow me with arms obtained from other fighters for freedom – our white Christian brethren. Yes, we're very well armed indeed, Cusack, and I'm proud to say so. Carrying arms for one's defence is a basic right long respected by the Americans and too long denied to we English. Through the glories of the World Wide Web, however, with the help of other white Christian freedom fighters, I've been able to rectify that situation. My compound is a fortress.'

'So how did you finance it?' Cusack asked. 'From what I've read about you in intelligence reports, you didn't really have all that much money. Not even from all those people you robbed when running your so-called Second Coming Movement.'

'You're trying to anger me again,' Prince said, feeling his blood starting to boil with rage but refusing to let Cusack know it this time. 'But I'm not going to bite.'

'I'm just finding it hard to believe,' Cusack responded with quiet insistence, 'that you could finance that kind of defence. Where did the money come from?'

'Easy,' Prince boasted. 'Any hacker worth his salt knows that most banks had viruses and back-door programmes covertly inserted into their computer systems years ago.

Why, even the Bank of England recently reported that it had found a sniffer programme – used to search out passwords and codes and transmit them back to the hacker – in its central computer. So, being aware of this, I simply broke through the security systems of a number of British banks, hacked into their electronic vaults and siphoned out money to accounts held anonymously in the banks of other European countries. That money was used to renovate my extensive property, now my compound, and obtain the arms – also purchased through the Internet – required to defend it. And, of course, as banks are notoriously reluctant to discuss computer theft, now costing them untold millions, the police weren't even notified about the money *I* stole from them.'

'Very clever,' Cusack said. 'But I'm still not convinced that it could be done. It sounds like good old bullshit to me, though, I have to admit, I'm fairly ignorant about computers.'

'You shouldn't be, Cusack, because in the end that's how I'm going to defeat you, your pitiful QRF, the rest of the SAS and, eventually, the police force and the government itself. What we're engaged in is cyberwar, and you're out of your depth there.'

'What does that mean?' Cusack asked.

Prince was dying to talk about it, to let Cusack see how clever he was, and so the words just spilled helplessly out of him. 'These days, everything – communications, commerce, transport, electricity, gas, even the defence of the nation – is done through computers, and all of these computers are linked together by telephone lines. What does this mean, Cusack?'

'I don't know. You tell me.'

'It means, for instance, that an American farmer innocently digging a hole to bury his dead horse cuts through a crucial fibre-optic cable and accidentally shuts down four of the Federal Aviation Administration's thirty main air traffic control centres for over five hours. It means, for instance, that by taking out one simple cable in the grounds of an unprotected building near the site of the Great Library of

Alexandria, Egypt – using, let's say, a small, home-made Semtex bomb – the whole of the 23,600-mile FLAG cable that crosses the South Pacific, Asia, the Middle East and the North Atlantic to provide four continents with broad-bandwidth fibre-optic communication could be put out of action, thus causing havoc to global communications. It means, for instance, that when a Bank of America employee accidentally shuts off power to the on-line unit in his data-processing centre, the bank's ATM system crashes and takes two hours to reboot, putting 1,500-odd ATMs in Northern California out of action. In other words, Cusack, the more dependent the world becomes on computerized technology, the more vulnerable it becomes to remote attack in a cyberwar.'

'The kind of war you're planning to wage.'

'Exactly,' Prince said.

'You and your brethren overseas.'

'Exactly,' Prince repeated. 'We're spread all over the globe now, from Europe to the United States, from Australia to Greenland, from Hong Kong to Dubai, so we're able to hack into any nation's information infrastructure and wage cyberwar on its government. Money? By hacking into banks, as I've already said, but also by hacking into the social welfare system, we've been able to siphon off hundreds of thousands of pounds and transfer them to our own anonymous accounts. Our fellow cyber-terrorists – though naturally I prefer to call them freedom fighters – particularly our brethren in America, share access codes to corporate computers with us, thus enabling us to wreak havoc on – and siphon funds off – the capitalist system.'

'I didn't know you were a socialist,' Cusack said.

'I believe in the brotherhood of man,' Prince informed him, 'and that capitalism is an international conspiracy designed to keep mankind divided into the haves and have-nots. I believe that it's the duty of all Christians to defeat that conspiracy.'

'*White* Christians,' Cusack said drily.

'The Jews are part of the international financial conspiracy.

The Blacks and swarthies come from degenerate, decadent races that can never be saved. So, yes, I believe in white Christianity and I'm not ashamed to say it. Most Millennialists believe the same and they're prepared to fight to the bitter end to uphold those beliefs. You want to know our plans, Cusack?'

'I can't wait,' Cusack said.

'Sarcasm, Cusack, sticks and stones. Well, let me tell you anyway, since knowing about my plans won't help you to stop them. Because we're vegetarians, we're planning to access remotely the process-control systems of the manufacturers of meat-based foods to change the levels of iron supplement, thus seriously damaging the health of those who purchase that food and eat it. Because we believe that pharmaceuticals are an unnatural method for curing illnesses, we plan to alter remotely the formulas of medication at pharmaceutical manufacturers, which will lead to an unaccountable loss of life and bring the production of pharmaceuticals to a halt. Because we're socialists, we plan to destabilize the capitalist system by disrupting the banks, the international financial transactions and the stock exchanges by hacking into their mainframes and critically altering their data. Also because we're socialists, we plan to gain control of the air-conditioning systems of financially corrupt multinationals and remotely raise the temperature of their premises to the point where their computers will crash and their systems fail. Because we're anti-government and wish to destroy whole countries' infrastructures in order to start afresh, we plan to bring down whole telephone networks by swamping them with computer-generated automatic calls; to attack air traffic control systems and rail lines, thus causing aircraft to collide in mid-air and trains to crash; to disrupt the national defence system with worm attacks on computerized battle plans, on military telephone systems, and on radio and TV news or propaganda transmissions; and, finally, to launch, where necessary, against selected blood types, such as the Jews, the Blacks and the swarthies, genetic, biological and chemical war, also by remote control. Why, we even plan to change the pressure in gas lines, thus causing valve failures, which will lead to detonation and conflagration. Talking of which . . .'

'Yes?' Cusack said, obviously gritting his teeth and preparing to say something inflammatory.

'Simply as an example, as it were . . .'

'Yes?' Cusack said again, obviously sensing that he was about to hear something awful and unable to wait patiently for it.

'That young member of your QRF team, the Jewboy, Trooper Irwin Radnor . . .'

'You bastard!'

Prince chuckled. 'I believe he's gone to London for the weekend and should be, right now, sleeping in his terraced house in Golders Green with his nice Jewish parents and equally Jewish brother and sister. Well, unfortunately for him – for all of them – the mainframe computer controlling the gas in that area has been hacked into and the gas pressure is about to be remotely altered to a dangerous degree. So . . .'

But Prince could say no more because Cusack had slammed his phone down and was obviously, desperately, about to attempt the impossible: to somehow warn them in Golders Green.

Prince sat back in his chair and smiled at his glowing computer screen, imagining what Cusack was frantically doing that very second.

*Too late*, Prince thought.

# CHAPTER NINETEEN

*Too late.* Cusack *had* been too late. Now he was drinking heavily – a dangerous sign – and watching the devastation on his television set as he waited for his CO, Lieutenant Colonel Blackwell, to arrive. Blackwell had, of course, seen the same newsflash, broadcast within a hour of an horrendous gas explosion that was still being widely viewed as an accident. Slumped in his armchair, watching the newsreel footage of burning, collapsing houses, the dead and badly burned (some of whom would wish, Cusack thought, once they regained consciousness, that they had died instead) being carried out of smouldering ruins on stretchers and driven away in ambulances. According to the latest estimates, an area of about two square miles had been devastated by the explosion, with whole streets destroyed and hundreds burned alive, suffocated in smoke, crushed by the collapsing walls and floors, or badly burned. The cause of the explosion was believed to have been a fault in the mainline ducts, possibly due to unnatural pressure of gas leading to bursting pipes. Prince, or the British Millennialist Movement, had not taken credit for it so far.

Cusack had tried to warn them, but of course he had been too late. First – after slamming the phone down on Prince – he had tried calling Radnor at home and had received what had sounded like a dead line. He had known, then, beyond any shadow of doubt, that the explosion promised by Prince had already taken place and that Radnor and his family were victims of it. Knowing this, but unable emotionally to accept it, he had phoned the Transco emergency number, only to be informed, by someone sounding hysterical, that a serious explosion had already occurred in Golders Green and that representatives of British Gas were on the way to the scene of the 'incident'.

Hearing that crap, Cusack had instantly switched on his TV set, then rung Blackwell at his home in the married quarters at Stirling Lines. When Cusack had informed Blackwell about the explosion – and, more particularly, about Prince's part in it – Blackwell had insisted on coming over to Cusack's house to talk with him. When Cusack had volunteered to drive to Stirling Lines instead, Blackwell had said tersely, 'No, not here. I'll come to your place.'

Hanging up, Cusack, even though it was now well after midnight, had poured himself a stiff whisky and planted himself down in front of his television set. Sure enough, as he had anticipated, a newsflash about the explosion had come on, accompanied by newsreel footage of the carnage. Waiting for Blackwell to arrive, Cusack couldn't take his eyes off the TV screen, though he managed to keep pouring more whiskies for himself. Luckily, Blackwell turned up thirty minutes later, thus preventing Cusack from drinking himself into a stupor. In fact, when he heard his front doorbell ringing, Cusack was already on his third large glass of whisky.

'I think this house is under surveillance,' were the first words he uttered, which he did without thinking.

'Not being eyeballed any longer,' Blackwell responded tartly as he practically pushed his way past Cusack to get inside. 'That shit's coming in through cyberspace.'

'At Stirling Lines?' Cusack asked as he closed the front door behind his commanding officer.

'Yes,' Blackwell said. 'So we have to talk right now. Have you been drinking?'

'Yes,' Cusack confessed.

'I can smell it on your breath,' Blackwell said. 'Is it whisky?'

'Yes.'

'At this time in the morning?'

'Yes.'

'Okay, let's share one.'

Blackwell, who knew the house well, went straight into the living room and took the chair that Cusack had been sitting in, angled obliquely from the TV set. Cusack, after pouring them both drinks, took the chair beside him, though he turned it until he was facing in Blackwell's direction. Cusack had turned the sound down on the TV, but the flickering light, sending striations through the semi-darkness, never left them alone, relentlessly sending out ghostly, soundless images of the disaster in Golders Green. They both drank as they talked.

'I came here,' Blackwell said, 'instead of asking you to Stirling Lines, because that bastard is hacking into our computer system, sending mocking messages through our e-mail and also replacing our web page – the one we use to give the public nominal access to us – with his own foul out-pourings. Until we caught it, our web page was advertising that bloody British Millennialist Movement and all they support. We've just corrected it, of course, but for how long? He'll hack in and redesign it the instant his sniffers find our new security codes. That swine is an expert.'

'Did you understand what I was telling you over the phone?' Cusack asked.

'Yes. The Golders Green gas explosion. It's being blamed on those now running British Gas – commercial companies largely despised by the citizenry – but, as I gather from you, Prince was actually the one behind it.'

'Yes,' Cusack said.

'Remote interference with the computer controlling the flow of gas to that area.'

'Yes,' Cusack repeated. 'So what have you heard from Golders Green?'

'Nothing good,' Blackwell said. 'Trooper Radnor and all of his family were at the epicentre of the blast and none of them survived – which was, perhaps, lucky for them, given the state of some of the other burns victims.'

'But the media still think it was an accident?'

'Yes,' Blackwell said. 'And, of course, it will *seem* like an accident – an inexplicable rise in pressure – to the British Gas investigators unless Prince decides to tell them otherwise. Do you think he will?'

'Yes,' Cusack said. 'He'll deliberately wait until British Gas has declared it an unavoidable accident, then he'll step in, via the Internet and, possibly, a hacker's telephone call, with the news that it was his own cyber-terrorist act. Apart from striking terror into the community, this will considerably damage the public's trust in the efficiency of British Gas. So, yes, he'll take credit for the atrocity, but only when it suits him.'

'Which will be soon.'

'Soon enough.'

Blackwell sighed, shook his head from side to side, then had another sip of his whisky and looked up again.

'We've got to find this bastard,' he said. 'We've just *got* to find him. But we're no closer to him now than we were at the beginning. Isn't that true?'

'Yes, boss, I'm afraid it is.'

'What about your Net surfing? Did you get any of those magic-cookie responses you were talking about?'

'Yes, quite a few, in fact. Most of the Millennialist websites I visited anonymously did, as I'd thought they would, track me with a magic cookie every time I browsed elsewhere. Naturally, I was deliberately browsing at websites that downloaded info or sold printed booklets on bomb-making, explosives, telephone phreaking, hacking and other forms of Internet subversion. I knew that they'd dropped magic cookies into my basket and were tracking me with them because each time I returned to those original sites, they'd inserted ads for the kind of items that I'd made it seem I was after. So I purchased certain items from them, buying electronically, using my credit card and thus giving them my details, including my phone number and mailing address. Once I did that, most of them came back to me, telling me more about their organizations, including their motivation and aims, and, more importantly, their addresses right here on earth as distinct from in cyberspace. None of them, however, turned out to be Prince's elusive British Millennialist Movement. I'm still waiting to hear from them.'

'But they *do* have websites that spew out their propaganda.'

'Yes, boss, but Prince has been using telephone phreaking to access international phone lines at no cost, and using servers all over the world. He's never used any single server more than once, and thus he's kept his movement's physical location virtually untraceable. So although I can get into Prince's various websites, I won't be able to track his movement back to their location until the movement actually contacts me and gives me its address – in other words, until it tries to recruit me.'

'Which so far it hasn't done.'

'Unfortunately, no.'

'Though Prince is personally contacting you by telephone, to tease and torment you.'

'Right.'

'So he must know that you've been browsing on his websites.'

'No, he doesn't. I repeat: my browsing was done anonymously and only those sites that tracked me with a magic cookie found out my details. Prince's movement hasn't so far given me a reason to break my browser's anonymity, so neither the movement, nor Prince, knows the identity of this particular anonymous browser. Prince is only calling me because he learned all about me from his first surveillance of Stirling Lines, when he wanted to track his first SAS victim, me, from the base to his home, and because he then came to my house to . . .' But Cusack still couldn't bear to recall it, let alone mention it. 'Well, because of that and because he now wants to finish the job with me personally. Right now, he's just teasing me, trying to goad me, torment me, but he's boastful and starting to let a few things slip.'

'Such as?'

'Well, he *has* confirmed that his movement is located in some kind of large compound, and that it's heavily armed.'

'Then we might eventually find it. Scotland Yard's presently investigating every Millennialist movement in the EU, but given that there are now literally hundreds of them – in England, Scotland and Wales, in Northern Ireland and the Republic of Ireland, and in nearly every European country – they have a hell of a job on their hands and it could take a long time. Also, as you know, since many of those groups are claiming to be purely religious and are protecting themselves with the new legislation brought in during Millennium Year, giving so-called bona fide religious groups not only total tax exemption, as they always had in America, but also the right to run their own communities and defend themselves with weapons – again, just like in America – the police are reluctant to visit those sites personally without an invitation – and, naturally, they never get invited. This means that they have to investigate covertly and that takes a lot longer.'

'If we take much longer to find Prince,' Cusack said, 'he'll use that time to carry out what he's planning – and what he's planning, according to what he told me, doesn't bear thinking about.'

'Oh?' Blackwell responded. He glanced at the television screen which, though silent, was still showing newsreel footage of the ghastly aftermath of the Golders Green explosion. Then he returned his disturbed gaze to Cusack. 'So what's the lunatic planning?'

Cusack repeated what Prince had told him during that last phone conversation, then added, even as Blackwell was looking shell-shocked: 'And those plans have received the backing – and the support – of most of the other Millennialist groups, both here and in Europe. What we're faced with, in effect, is an all-out, no-holds-barred cyberwar against the whole of the EU . . . And Prince is already working to rev it up. So we don't have too much time left.'

'It doesn't sound like it,' Blackwell said. He sipped at his whisky, glanced at the silent TV screen – the smouldering, still burning and collapsing houses of Golders Green; the weeping or dazed survivors; the dead and badly burned being carted off to the waiting ambulances – then said, his mind on two subjects at once: 'If he's making all those phone calls, why can't we just tap your phone and trace him through it and send the cops in to nab him?'

'Because he's phone-phreaking to access phone lines and illegally use other people's accounts. Even if we trace the call and go to the source, we'll only land ourselves with an embarrassing situation: breaking into the home of someone who's just had their phone line used illegally. We certainly won't find the caller.'

'Damn!' Blackwell exclaimed softly. He glanced again at the TV screen and saw the start of what was obviously a newsflash. Instantly, he was on his feet to cross the room and turn up the volume. Against a massively enlarged grainy photo of burning houses, a newscaster was informing the nation that an organization called the British Millennialist Movement, headed by the notorious 'Prince', had just informed the authorities, by phone, fax and e-mail, that it was responsible for the carnage at Golders Green. Since the same organization had also claimed responsibility for the Whitehall Atrocity and the London Underground Massacre (as they were now termed by the media) the authorities were inclined to believe them.

'Shit!' Cusack exclaimed.

Blackwell turned the sound down again and turned back to Cusack. 'So,' he said. 'Prince has let the cat out of the bag and now we're in trouble – with Whitehall, with the army, and with the media. Why haven't we found him yet? They'll all want to know. The regiment, which is already under pressure, will be called upon to deliver the goods and deliver them quickly. What the hell do we tell them?'

'I don't know,' Cusack admitted. 'I'm at my wits' end.'

'That's no help.'

'I know it's no help, but it's all I can say. Until I can find some way to fix Prince and his organization to a specific, physical location, I'm . . . well, frankly, boss, I'm fucked.'

Blackwell's look was grim. 'We're about to have another SAS funeral and we can't keep it quiet.'

'I know that,' Cusack said.

'Two funerals in one week. Seven men dead. This is unprecedented.'

'I know that as well, boss.'

'The phone calls,' Blackwell said, obviously grabbing at straws. 'As long as he keeps making the phone calls, he might make a slip.'

'A slip of the tongue,' Cusack clarified. 'Yes, I'm depending on that.'

'It's not enough, Sergeant. That could take too long as well. Depending on Prince having a slip of the tongue, or on you receiving a magic-cookie response to your web browsing, it could take more time than we can afford. From what you've told me, this . . . *person* . . . this. . . *maniac* . . .' Blackwell's head was obviously racing. 'This *psychopath* could cause murderous havoc throughout the whole of Europe before we could find him. So we've *got* to do more than sit back and, as it were, wait for him to find you, either through a magic-cookie response to your browsing or by having a slip of the tongue. We *have* to think of a more proactive approach.'

Cusack knew that he was right, but he was too weary to think about it, too shocked by what had happened, too filled with a sense of defeat and, possibly, despair, to take a clear view of the problem. He loathed himself for this, seeing his weaknesses magnified, aware that Prince had cleverly engineered his demoralization with those insidious phone calls. He was being defeated by Prince, humiliated and shamed by him, even as he sat here, in his own house, the very house that Prince had entered, truly like a Prince of Darkness, to cause bloody mayhem. Just recalling it made Cusack tremble, turned his throat dry; but then, when his rage welled up to protect him, his head cleared just enough to let him glimpse something he had missed.

'Yes,' he said. 'There *might* be another way.'

'I'll listen to anything,' Blackwell responded. 'Just spit it out, Sergeant.'

'Sir William Hargreaves,' Cusack said.

'You have my full attention.'

'The Metropolitan Police and various intelligence services often make deals with convicted hackers, offering reduced sentences if the hackers work for them, usually by tracking down other hackers who've been causing trouble to the government, national security, British intelligence or the police force itself. In other words, William Hargreaves, our venerable Police Commissioner, is bound to know some exceptionally talented hackers, and that person might be able to tell us how to track Prince, or his British Millennialist Movement, through the labyrinth of cyberspace. Could you ask him about that?'

'I could and I certainly will,' Blackwell said. 'That's a damned good idea. Are you drunk, Sergeant Cusack?'

'Yes,' Cusack admitted, 'I'm drunk.'

'It's still a good idea,' Blackwell said, 'and I'll certainly pursue it. But for now, since we can do nothing about Trooper Radnor, the poor soul, I think it's best that I make my way home and that you go to bed.'

'Right, boss. I agree.'

Cusack walked his CO to the door. Once there, before proceeding to his car, Blackwell said, 'Be very careful about that drinking, Sergeant Cusack. It got you into trouble before and it could do so again.'

'I'll be careful,' Cusack said.

But he wasn't careful. When he had seen Blackwell drive off, he went straight back to his living room, poured himself another stiff one and drank it while watching the early-morning TV news programmes, skipping restlessly from one channel to the next, saturating himself in the full horror of the explosion in Golders Green. The more he saw, the more despairing he became, the more guilty he felt, thinking of Trooper Irwin Radnor, the seventh dead in a few days, and blaming himself for the fact that those deaths had occurred and that Prince, who had caused them, was still well ahead of the game. More frustrating, more tormenting, was the knowledge that Prince, as he had stated on the phone, was intent on causing even more grief and that, if he succeeded, the damage would be far more widespread than Cusack or anyone else could previously have possibly imagined. It was clear to him now that the Royal Family, which up to now he'd imagined to be Prince's biggest target, were no more than small fry, and that far bigger fish had been envisaged for Prince's net. Prince was going to cast that net as far and as wide as he possibly could and he would, beyond any shadow of doubt, destroy anyone, or anything, caught in it. Just give him the match and the whole of Europe would go up in flames. Prince was ready and willing.

Cusack fell asleep in his chair, in front of the glowing, silent television screen, purveying its ghastly newsreel footage of the Golders Green conflagration – the burning, collapsing houses, the dead and burned victims on the stretchers, the grieving relatives, the smoke-filled sky – and had dreadful dreams about it, the same scenes magnified, rendered even more nightmarish. He jerked awake in the early hours of the morning, groaning in protest.

On the 9.00 a.m. news it was announced again that the British Millennialist Movement had claimed responsibility for the explosion.

The rest of Cusack's day was another sort of nightmare, a subjective eternity of grief and guilt, as more news came in and as the death toll steadily mounted and as incoming calls – from Jack Lewis, from the other five members of Cusack's QRF team, from Lieutenant Colonel Blackwell, every one of them sounding shell-shocked – reminded him of just how real, how absolutely fucking dreadful, Prince's latest atrocity was. By lunchtime – and it took another eternity to arrive – he had let the guilt sweep him away into another dimension.

He was, in fact, in hell, when, after another morning of solitary drinking, his presence not being required at Stirling Lines, he decided to continue his self-intoxication in a pub in Hereford, one normally frequented in the evenings by the SAS. This being lunchtime, there was no one else there from the regiment and, indeed, the pub had only a couple of customers. One of them was, however, an attractive young woman with auburn hair, beatific brown eyes and a wonderful figure. Wearing a discreet black dress, the hemline just below the knees, her long legs emphasized by sheer black stockings and high heels, she was sitting on a stool at the bar, almost shoulder to shoulder with him. When he nodded at her automatically, not thinking, as he ordered his first drink, she gave him a warm smile.

If Cusack was ready for anything in the world, he was ready for that smile.

It had been a long time.

# CHAPTER TWENTY

Chloe had moved into the area just under a week ago, but she felt that she had been here twenty years. Financed by Prince, she was staying in a detached cottage on the outskirts of Bishopstone, just six miles west of Hereford. The location had been carefully chosen by Prince because it was isolated enough to make Chloe completely private while, at the same time, being close enough to Hereford to make daily trips there no trouble at all, particularly since Prince had given her a ten-year-old but well-maintained red Volkswagen Golf. He had also given her a cellular telephone.

The first week had seemed like twenty years because it was the first time since Chloe had been picked up by Prince five months ago at King's Cross Station that she had been completely on her own, and it had made her feel oddly disorientated. Indeed, she was now so used to the rigorous daily activities of Prince's Millennialist community, to the companionship of the other members, the constant round of lectures, the daily PE classes, the seemingly endless duties – work in the kitchen, the laundry rooms, the stores and the living quarters – and was also now so used to bedding down and awakening in the company of others in a ten-bed dormitory, that the abrupt transition to total privacy and long, empty days had come as a shock to her. Luckily, the cottage contained a television set and, when not out and walking about, she spent a long time in front of it.

It was, in fact, the television that had just led to her first faint misgivings about what she was doing. Like a lot of her new companions, most of whom were former teenage drug addicts, Chloe was in thrall to Prince for having cured her of her addiction and put some meaning into her life. Unable to fully forget her time as a whore, her nightmarish street-walking, that final, degrading beating in an alleyway near King's Cross Station, she viewed her new way of life, her new disciplines, her health, as being heaven-sent and was secretly terrified of the thought of somehow losing it. Thus, even though what she had just seen on TV had planted a seed of doubt in her mind, she chose to ignore it while she got on with what Prince had sent her here to do: seduce SAS Sergeant Lenny Cusack and then, once involved with him, report his every movement back to Prince via the cellular phone.

For this purpose, she had moved into the cottage and let it be known to any Bishopstone locals with whom she had contact – the owners and customers of the bar restaurant, where she sometimes ate, and local shopkeepers, all of whom assumed that she was older than her eighteen years, thinking her to be somewhere in her mid-twenties – that she had recently been divorced after a short, disastrous marriage and had come here for a month or so to sort herself out. She had made a point, therefore, of going out every day, usually driving to Hereford to walk around the tourist sites on her own. Every day, however, she had also made a point of being in Hereford both at lunchtime and in the evenings, when she would trawl the pubs recommended by Prince as being those most frequented by off-duty SAS men from Stirling Lines. She did so in the expectation of sooner or later seeing Sergeant Cusack – and at last, after a fruitless week, he had just walked into this pub where she was, as usual, perched on a seat by the bar.

As the bar was short, it was inevitable that Cusack, when he approached it to order his drink, would be standing close to her. Cusack looked distracted and hardly noticed her at first. Then, when he had ordered a double whisky, he turned his head to glance at her.

Chloe knew her men. She knew more about men than many women twice her age, and she had learned it all from bitter experience. She knew about the shy ones, the guilty ones, the lustful and the lovelorn, about the straight and the bent. This one, she saw instantly, was sleepless and anxious, veiled pain in his green-blue eyes, with the look of an essentially decent man who was out on a limb. He also looked like a man who had not had a woman in a long time. Chloe wasn't too sure just how she could tell that, but when she had made that assessment of a trick in the past, she had nearly always been correct. Of course, in this instance, she had been told by Prince that Cusack's wife and daughter had been murdered by persons unknown just over a year ago, so she had also assumed, rightly or wrongly, that he hadn't yet taken up with another woman. Nevertheless, for whatever reason, she was convinced that this man needed comfort, sexual and otherwise. She could use that against him.

Chloe gave him a smile.

Cusack gazed at her for a time, blindly at first, a man in a daze, then he gradually focused upon her and, seeing her smile, automatically smiled back.

'Hi,' he said as mechanically as he had smiled, then turned back to the bar. Chloe deliberately said nothing and merely sipped at her iced tonic water, letting the uncomfortable silence build, as it usually did between male and female customers when they were strangers and this close at a bar. Eventually, when Cusack's drink had been brought to him, he raised it in the air, as if toasting Chloe, then smiled again and said, 'Cheers.'

Chloe returned his smile and raised her own glass. 'Cheers.' They drank and she put her glass back on the counter. Cusack held on to his – almost desperately, Chloe thought. She said nothing, waiting for him to speak, which he did, eventually.

'I haven't seen you around here before,' he said, his voice hoarse from too much drinking. 'Just passing through?'

She shifted slightly on her stool until she was facing him. He was now leaning sideways against the counter, propped up on one elbow, facing her. 'Not exactly,' she said. 'I mean, I'm staying here for at least a couple of weeks; maybe a month or so. No definite plans as yet. Just thought I'd get away from home to clear my head and work out my future.' She shrugged. 'I don't know why I picked here. I just drove out of London, took the A40, stopping at scenic places en route, and passed through here on my way to Ross-on-Wye. I saw this cute little cottage up for rent just outside Bishopstone and took it on an impulse. That was a week ago. So! Here I am still.'

'Am I allowed to ask why you have to clear your head? If it's too personal to discuss, just tell me so. I mean, I'm only making casual conversation; I don't mean to pry.'

Chloe smiled and nodded. 'I'm sure you don't. My name's Chloe, by the way.'

'Lenny.' After a slight hesitation, he held out his hand and Chloe shook it. She knew from that slight hesitation that he'd never been a ladies' man. This one was sincere. 'Lenny Cusack,' he added. 'So why the need for head-clearing? If, I repeat, it's not too personal.'

Chloe shrugged and crossed her legs. She had deliberately chosen to wear a discreetly attractive black dress with a neckline low enough to show her swanlike neck but not the tops of her breasts, and a hemline that fell to just below the knees, *except* when she crossed her legs. She had good legs, she knew, and right now they were sheathed in sheer black stockings, with her feet in moderately high heels. She wanted to look neither overtly sexy nor too conservative, but softly, undeniably, feminine. His gaze fell instinctively on her crossing legs, then was instantly raised again. He looked slightly embarrassed, surprised, as if silently reprimanding himself for that moment of weakness. He also looked as if he desperately needed sleep, and that could help her as well.

'The usual,' she said. 'A failed marriage. I married too young and too quickly, so it didn't work out. We're separated and the divorce is coming through. We were only married three years.'

'Any children?'

'No.'

'That was lucky.'

'Yes.'

'So when did you get married?' Cusack asked. 'I mean, you still look pretty young to me. Certainly too young to be getting divorced.'

'I'll take that as a compliment. Actually, I'm twenty-three,' she lied, adding five years to her true age, confident that, while attractive to men, she certainly looked, due to her past experience, more mature (yes, all right, *older*) than she was. 'I got married when I was twenty, which isn't really *that* young.'

'It is, these days,' Cusack said. 'But I guess it's none of my business.'

'And you?'

'Not much different from you, actually – just a good bit older. Married at nineteen, had one daughter, now a teenager ... Well ...' He hesitated again, looking ravaged on the instant, his gaze shifting rapidly, out of focus. Then he finished off his drink in one gulp and ordered another. 'Sorry,' he said, turning to Chloe. 'What about you? Can I buy you another?'

'Well ...' Chloe's hesitation was deliberate, suggesting nervousness at accepting a drink from a strange man.

'It's okay,' he said. 'You've no need ... I mean, really, I don't mean anything by it. It's just ... nice to have a chat and so on. Please, it's my pleasure.'

'Well ...' She shrugged again, crossed and uncrossed her legs, baring her knees and svelte calves and a touch of thigh, then gave him a smile. 'Thanks. It's just tonic with ice. I'm not big on alcohol.'

'Don't start,' Cusack said. He ordered two more drinks, his whisky and her tonic water, saying nothing more until they had arrived. They touched glasses before drinking.

'What are your wife and daughter like?' Chloe asked eventually, breaking what had been a lengthy silence. 'I mean, do they look alike? Are they –'

'They're both dead,' Cusack said abruptly, almost curtly, then took another stiff pull on his drink and wiped his lips with the back of his hand. He glanced at Chloe, then just as quickly looked away, as if embarrassed again. 'An accident . . . well, no. Why lie about it? A gang of men broke into our house and . . .' He shrugged, as if bereft of words. 'Murdered them both. It happened just over a year ago.'

'Oh, God, I'm sorry,' Chloe said, meaning it, truly feeling sorry for him, the naked pain in his face, even though Prince had, of course, told her about the murder. Despite her reason for being here, despite her own subterfuge, she couldn't fail to feel sympathetic when she saw his face. The pain was naked and he was fighting to conceal it, though he wasn't succeeding. 'Truly,' Chloe added, reaching out to lay her hand on his forearm, doing what she had come here to do and, at the same time, responding instinctively to his grief. Confused, she quickly withdrew her hand and said, 'Sorry, I didn't mean to . . .'

'That's okay.' He gave a slight, hesitant smile and covered his embarrassment by taking another drink. Then he put his glass back on the counter, though his hand did not leave it. When he glanced around the almost empty pub, Chloe followed his wandering gaze.

'Quiet today,' she said.

Cusack checked his wristwatch. 'It'll start filling up about one. We're just that little bit early.'

'Don't make me feel guilty,' Chloe said. 'A woman sitting all alone in a pub just after noon. I'll be the talk of the town.'

Cusack smiled at that, nodding in the direction of her glass.

'You don't drink.' He held his own glass up in front of his face. 'I'm the one they should talk about. A man standing all alone in a pub just after noon. *I'*ll be the talk of the town – not that I give a damn.' He had another defiant sip of his large whisky and then lowered the glass back to the counter, though he still held on to it.

'You live here?' Chloe asked him, though in fact she knew exactly where he lived.

'Nearby,' he replied. 'In Redhill.'

'What do you do?'

'I'm in the army,' he said. 'SAS. Our camp, Stirling Lines, is out in Redhill, so I'm close to my work.'

'You're not working today?'

'No, I have the day off.'

'I'm surprised you don't live in the camp. I mean, since your wife and daughter are no longer – Oh, God!' She reached out once more to lay her hand on his lower arm, on his wrist, and give it a light, sympathetic squeeze. 'I'm *so* sorry. I didn't mean to . . . Damn it, it just kind of slipped out. I mean . . . Oh, God, I'm a fool!'

'No, you're not. It's okay. It's kind of hard to avoid the subject, isn't it? *C'est la vie!*' He drank from his raised glass, finishing it off, then nodded to the barman for another. 'And you?'

Chloe indicated that her own glass was still nearly full. 'No, I'm fine, thanks.'

Again they were silent until the drinks came, but this time it was Chloe who gazed around the bar, as if lost for words, but actually giving him the chance to look at her more fully, to take in her youth and beauty, her fine skin and svelte figure. She knew that he was looking at her, she could *feel* it, and she turned back in time to catch him at it.

Instantly, his eyes flicked away and he covered his embarrassment by having another sip of his drink. She could tell from his embarrassment, which came easily to him, that already he wanted more than just her body: he wanted to lose himself in her. He wanted her to help him to forget and ease the pain of his suffering. This was a decent, tormented man and she sensed that when she finally betrayed him, which was why she was there, she would feel bad about it. Nevertheless, she was doing it for Prince and that was all she could think about. Without Prince, she was nothing.

'What's it like in the SAS?' she asked him.

'It has its moments,' he said.

'I mean, I've read a lot about it in the papers. They make you guys seem like supermen.'

'Is that what I seem like to you?'

Chloe smiled and rested her chin in her hands, her elbow propped up on the counter, bringing her face closer to his, looking directly at him. 'No,' she said. 'You don't look like a superman. You just look like a very nice man who could do with some sleep. You look like you've been up half the night. You look very tired.'

'I *am* tired.'

'*Have* you been up half the night?'

'Yes.'

'Thinking about . . . ?'

'No. Not my wife and daughter. A few days back, six of my friends, all men from the regiment, were killed in a bomb explosion. Yesterday – or early this morning, to be exact, just after midnight – another SAS man, one of my own troopers, was killed with an awful lot of other people, civilians, in that gas explosion in Golders Green, London.' He shrugged. 'It's been a pretty bad week, but last night, or rather, this morning, was the worst. So, yes, I've been up half the night.' He waved his glass to and fro in front of his face. 'And I've been drinking too much. I don't want to attend another funeral. Not this week. Not any week.'

Watching him as he raised his glass to his lips and took another stiff drink, trying to deaden his pain, Chloe felt the return of the doubt that had struck her when she had first seen the Golders Green carnage on the television set in her rented cottage. Every bit as shocking to her as the carnage had been this morning's late announcement that Prince had claimed responsibility for the outrage.

Like all of her comrades in the compound, Chloe now believed everything she had been told by Prince and his chosen teachers and was convinced that she would be justified in using any means, including violence, to defend those beliefs. Indeed, Prince had personally talked to her so often, so relentlessly, so hypnotically, that now she could barely separate his thoughts from her own, had become increasingly reluctant to think for herself, and accepted totally his assertion that the community was under threat from the 'Establishment' and would, sooner or later, have to repulse a full-scale attack from the Establishment's paid assassins, the SAS. While Chloe still believed this and had no cause to doubt it, the awesome destruction at Golders Green, the killing and maiming of so many innocent civilians in order to terminate a single SAS soldier, had seriously shocked her, placed doubts in her mind, and made her question the justification for it.

Disturbed to find herself thinking that way, Chloe was even more disturbed to realize, as she talked to this SAS sergeant, Lenny Cusack, that she was more sympathetic to him than she had thought she would be, and was having doubts about her purpose in being here. Frightened by these thoughts, also fearful of failing Prince and being rejected by him, she cast them out of her mind and resolved to see through to its completion what she had started: the seduction of Cusack.

'It sounds like a *hellish* few days,' she said. 'No wonder you're looking so tired and having trouble sleeping. Is that why you're drinking so early today?'

'Yes,' Cusack said bluntly.

Chloe removed her hand from her chin, glanced at her wristwatch, then looked up again, smiling ruefully, like someone who felt that they should leave but was reluctant to do so. 'Well,' she said, 'if I sit here much longer I might end up drinking whisky like you. I think I'd better go walkabout.'

'Is that how you pass the time?' he asked, clearly not caring to be left on his own and so trying to keep the conversation going.

'Yes. More or less.'

'Where do you walk?'

Chloe shrugged. 'Oh, here, there and everywhere. Around High Town. Along the near bank of the Wye to the Waterworks Museum. Along the far bank at Bishop's Meadow, from Wye Bridge to the Victoria Footbridge and Castle Green. Around the pool. Back along St Owen's Street to High Town, where I do the tourist sites with a little map. I also drive a lot – Ross-on-Wye and so on. A cup of tea here, a sandwich there; sometimes – obviously – a visit to a pub. Actually, I know the place pretty well now. It's nothing very exciting, that's for sure, but it helps me get through the day.'

'Do you *ever* drink?' Cusack asked her.

She smiled and nodded. 'Oh, yes. I just avoid it at lunchtimes. I like wine with my meals and I certainly won't say no to the odd whisky. It's just too early right now. Anyway, I think I'd better hit the road again. It was nice meeting you, Lenny.'

She slipped off the high stool, deliberately letting the hem of the dress ride up her thighs as she did so, then tugged it back down and slung her bag over her shoulder. Because Cusack was still leaning sideways against the counter, she was standing close to him, practically touching him. He pushed himself away from the bar, straightening up, placing himself directly in front of her and looking down at her. His green-blue eyes were bloodshot and his expression was deadly serious, almost desolate. He certainly had the look of a haunted soul.

'Well,' he said, sighing, 'yes, it was nice meeting you, too.'

'Thanks,' Chloe said, making no move to leave, as if undecided, wanting him to say something else, waiting for him to do so. It was obvious that he *wanted* to say something but didn't know how to say it.

'Maybe,' he managed after a while, 'we'll meet again somewhere. It's a pretty small town.'

'Yes,' Chloe said, 'maybe. That would be nice.' She smiled and shrugged forlornly. 'So!'

Cusack shrugged as well. 'So.'

Sighing loudly, melodramatically, Chloe turned away, started towards the exit, then stopped and walked back up to him. 'Listen,' she said, groping about in her shoulder bag and pulling out a small notebook and ballpoint pen. 'I don't want to seem forward or anything – I don't want to compromise you – but I don't know a soul around here and . . . Well, you seem like a nice guy and . . .' She tapered off as if embarrassed, then hastily scribbled in the notebook, tore the page out and thrust it at him. 'My phone number,' she said as she put the notebook and pen back into her shoulder bag. 'If you feel like a drink or a cooked meal or even just a chat . . . well, give me a call.' She smiled again and rolled her eyes, as if scarcely able to believe that she was doing this. 'Oh, God, I feel like such a bloody fool. Goodbye, Lenny Cusack. Nice to meet you. *Goodbye!*'

Before he could respond, she hurried out of the pub and darted down the nearest side street, making sure that *if* he followed her out he wouldn't immediately find her. The more disappointed he was, the more frustrated he would be and the more he would think about her and want to see her again. She was depending on that.

Nevertheless, as she drove back to the cottage in Bishopstone, passing orchards and pasturelands, Tudor houses and smallholdings, all resplendent in the afternoon sunshine, she felt deeply depressed and realized that she was still having doubts about what she was doing. She tried to rationalize the doubts away by convincing herself that she was merely displaying what Prince would define as despicable feminine weakness, letting herself be swayed by misplaced sympathy for her intended victim, by maternal and, possibly, sexual feelings for a man who was clearly decent and in genuine pain. She could not let this happen and *would* not let it happen, because that would, indeed, be a sign of weakness even worse than self-doubt.

There was one thing, however, about which she had no uncertainty at all. As she pulled up in front of her rented cottage in Bishopstone, preparing to wait for the phone to ring, she knew beyond any shadow of doubt that Cusack would call.

In fact, he called her that evening.

# CHAPTER TWENTY-ONE

Prince was ecstatic with the feedback he was receiving from Chloe via the cellular phone. The first call had come the afternoon after she had first met Cusack, and it was everything he had hoped for.

'I met Cusack earlier today, just before lunchtime, in a Hereford pub – the one you recommended that I visit – and we talked for half an hour or so.'

'Excellent,' Prince said. 'So how was he?'

'He looked pretty unhappy and told me that he'd been up most of the night. He was upset, I gather, about the deaths of those six SAS men on the Brecon Beacons and that other one who died in the Golders Green explosion. He was drinking an awful lot of whisky, particularly for that time of the day. He was still drinking whisky when I left.'

'Did you get close to him?'

'Yes. I came on to him strongly and think I've succeeded in attracting him. He definitely needs someone in his life right now and I think I can manage to be that person. I'm pretty sure he wanted to ask me if we could meet again, but he didn't manage to do it, so I took the initiative and gave him my phone number before I left the pub. I think he'll call me real soon.'

'Good girl,' Prince said.

He had told her to call him instantly after any meeting with Cusack, and she called him the following morning at 8.30.

'I'm calling from the cottage. Cusack spent the night here. He phoned yesterday evening, sounding drunk and emotional, and asked me if he could come over. I said he could and he came. When he got here, it was clear that he'd kept on drinking all afternoon after we'd talked and was in a very depressed state. I tried to get him to eat something, but he just wanted another drink, so I poured him a couple. He said he was frightened to go to bed at home. He was convinced he'd have nightmares. He just wanted to sit up and talk. So we talked.'

'About what?' Prince asked.

'I sat beside him on the sofa. He drank everything I poured and I kept moving closer to him and eventually I was holding and squeezing his hand, being sympathetic, like. He said he wanted to get out of the SAS. He said he'd had enough. He said the recent deaths were more than he could bear, but unfortunately he had a job to finish first. I asked him what job. He said he couldn't discuss it. He asked if he could kiss me and I let him and then we went to bed and made love.'

'You had sex?' Prince asked, wanting to be precise.

'Yeah. I mean, that's what I meant. I mean, we had sex, but I think that for him it was something more than that.'

'He was emotionally involved.'

'Yeah, Prince, right. He was desperately emotional – it was more than just sex . . . He wanted to *hold* me, you know? He wanted to cuddle and be embraced. He wanted to stroke me and smell my hair and . . . and press his cheeks to my breasts, listening to my heartbeat . . . Yeah, pretty emotional. He slept okay after that.'

'Slept till when?' Prince asked, wanting every last detail.

'He didn't wake up till this morning. He was kind of shame-faced but nice – a bit embarrassed but sweet with it. He said something like, "Don't tell me what I did. I don't remember too much of it." So I said, "Yes, you do," and he smiled and said, "Maybe". But he was late for work, he explained, and would have to go straight back to the base. Which he did, still being in his uniform. But before he left, he said he'd give me another call. Then he rushed out and drove off.'

'Perfect,' Prince said.

Chloe called him back two days later, just before midnight. 'Cusack didn't call or come round last night, but he called me at lunchtime today from Stirling Lines and asked if it'd be all right to drop in at the end of his working day. I said I missed him already and wanted to see him again. So he came around about seven this evening, apologized for not contacting me the day after he'd spent the night with me, and said it was because he'd had doubts about us. Thought maybe I'd be angry about him and me going to bed together. Said something like, "I wouldn't have done it if I hadn't been drunk, though I certainly wanted to do it, so please don't feel insulted." He kept talking like that while looking guilty and confused and I realized he was really pretty nervous. When he kissed me, which he did after a lot of talking, I smelled whisky on his breath and sussed that he'd dropped into the pub on the way to see me.'

'Quite,' Prince said. 'He'd finish his normal day at Stirling Lines at about 5.30 p.m., so he obviously dropped in for a couple before driving on to Bishopstone. Obviously guilty and nervous about his little interaction with you. Obviously wanting it, but also frightened by it. This is beautiful. Perfect.'

'Yeah,' Chloe replied. 'Right.'

'And?'

'We went to bed again . . . then he went home.'

'What?'

'Well, we went to bed and made love –'

'Had sex.'

'Right . . . But again, it was very emotional – I mean, *he* was very emotional – though when it was over, he insisted on going home and sleeping in his own bed. Not his own bed, he said, not really – the bed in the guest room. He said he couldn't sleep in his marital bed any more because of the murders. Couldn't sleep in his daughter's bed for the same reason. Both those rooms, he said, were kept exactly as they'd been before his wife and daughter were murdered. So now he sleeps downstairs in the guest room, though he doesn't sleep well.'

'So he went home earlier this evening?'

'Yeah, he went home. Said he'd drop by tomorrow.'

'He's involved. You've involved him.'

Chloe sighed. 'Yes, Prince.'

'And did he say anything worth hearing before he left? Anything about his SAS work?'

'He only repeated that he wanted to get out, wanted to leave for good. Said he had to go to the funeral of that young trooper killed in the Golders Green explosion and couldn't bear the thought of it, though he was certainly going. Said he had to get this shit off his back or else he'd go mad.'

'What shit?'

'He didn't say. I assume he meant the killings . . . The six in the Brecon Beacons, then the kid in Golders Green. My impression is that they were somehow tied together, though he didn't say how. He just said that he couldn't sleep for thinking about them. He seemed right on the edge when he left. I mean, he seemed really strung out.'

'But you think he meant it when he said that he'd call again?'

'Oh, yeah, he meant it. I mean, he wants me, he needs me, right now, so he'll come back for more.'

'Make sure he does.'

Chloe called back two days later. 'Cusack came to see me again yesterday evening. He'd just come back from the funeral of the young SAS kid and he went all the way to London for it. It took place in Golders Green crematorium. Not an SAS funeral.'

'Trooper Radnor was Jewish,' Prince explained.

'Right. So though he hadn't wanted to go, Cusack went to London with his CO, representing the regiment, and attended the funeral there, then came back the same day. Cusack had been drinking again when he got here – some drinks at the wake, then some more in a pub in Hereford before he got here.'

'He's hitting the sauce a lot,' Prince observed, feeling good about it.

'Yeah ... Well, he was particularly upset about that last death and talked a good bit about it, saying that he felt guilty about the explosion 'cause it was connected with a job he was working on.'

'What job? Did you ask him that?'

'Yeah. I asked him, but he said he couldn't discuss it. I reminded him that, according to the news on TV and in the papers, Prince and the British Millennialist Movement had claimed responsibility for the Golders Green explosion, so if his job had anything to do with the explosion, it also had to involve Prince and his movement. When I said that, he admitted it was true – that he was after you – then he added that he felt guilty about the deaths of all those men 'cause he wasn't getting anywhere, couldn't find out where you were, and was worried about what you'd do in the future if he didn't catch you soon.'

Prince chuckled. 'Wonderful!'

'We made love after that and –'

'You fucked,' Prince corrected her.

'Yeah, we fucked. When we'd finished, he said he loved me, then he fell asleep with me in his arms. He went straight from here to Stirling Lines this morning and that's where he is now.'

'Did he actually say he loved you?'

'Yeah.'

'That's a hook and a half to pull him in by. Don't let him go, Chloe.'

In fact, it was Cusack who wouldn't let Chloe go. She called Prince the following morning to say that Cusack had turned up the previous evening, dropping in after his normal working day at Stirling Lines.

'I made him dinner and then he drank too much again and became emotional about his murdered wife and daughter.

Said he'd loved them a lot and felt that he was betraying their memory by getting involved with me. I told him this was nonsense, that they'd been dead over a year, that he was a normal man with normal feelings that had to be satisfied, that he shouldn't feel guilty. "I still feel guilty," he said. "I feel it's not right, somehow." So I took him to bed and it was all very emotional –'

'You fucked again,' Prince interjected impatiently.

'Yeah, we fucked again. But it was more than just sex, it was really emotional, lots of feeling, kinda . . . *deep* . . . and then he talked a lot, just lying there, holding me, smelling my hair, stroking me, telling me about his wife and daughter, about the kind of life they'd had together; about how he'd loved the SAS until his wife and daughter were killed and how, since then, he'd wanted to kill all the men he was sent out to track down – because he wanted revenge. That's why he wants to leave the regiment, leave the army altogether –'

'Self-hatred?'

'Yeah. Because he feels that he's let his hatred dominate his life and turn him into someone who's no better than the men he wants to kill. "Men like Prince," he said. "The so-called Prince that I'm trying to find."'

Prince chuckled again.

'He also said,' Chloe continued, 'that he often felt that you were his other half – the darker, more violent half he was trying to suppress. "I'm hunting my own reflection," he said, "and maybe I'm frightened of finding it." Despite that, he's determined to find you. He made that perfectly clear.'

'You're gaining his confidence, Chloe. Keep up the good work.'

Chloe sighed. 'Yes, Prince.'

She didn't call for three days and Prince began to grow anxious. But eventually, on a Monday morning, she called back. 'Cusack took me away for the weekend,' she explained. 'He said he wanted to drive for a couple of days, to go somewhere different, to clear his head and sort out his thoughts.'

'This sounds promising,' Prince said.

'We didn't go far. Initially we just drove around this area, around places he knew, not new places. But then we went farther afield, like a couple of sightseers, spending Friday and Saturday evening in two different hotels, one in Oxford, the other in Trowbridge.'

'*Where?*'

'Trowbridge.'

'That's close,' Prince said. 'Continue.'

'Like I said, at first we drove around places he already knew, a kind of nostalgia tour, places where he'd been with his wife and daughter, and he talked a lot about them, sounding calmer than before, as if he was finally facing up to, and accepting, their deaths. Then he drove us around the Brecon Beacons, pointing out various places where he'd done his Long Drags and Sickeners during SAS training and, finally, exactly where those six Directing Staff guys were blown up by a bomb. He still blamed himself for that. Said he shouldn't have left the trucks unguarded, though they'd always done that in the Brecon Beacons because that area, an SAS training ground, was so isolated. Still, he insisted on blaming himself for the deaths of those men.'

'Good,' Prince said. 'Excellent.'

'Then we went travelling. All the way back through Hereford and Worcester to Warwickshire and Stratford-upon-Avon. Had a pub lunch there, then took the scenic route, down to Shipston on Stour, Moreton-in-Marsh, then Chipping Norton and on to Oxford. He hadn't been to any of those places and he just wanted to see them, to see something different, and he talked a lot about all the things he hadn't done because of the SAS. Said he wanted to get out of the SAS and do something different. We spent the night in a pub just outside Oxford and made love again.'

'You had sex,' Prince corrected her.

Chloe sighed. 'Yes, we had sex. He wasn't as upset as he had been, but he was still emotional.'

'Maybe imagining he was fucking his wife,' Prince said brutally.

Chloe said softly, 'Yes, Prince, maybe that.'

Prince had to prompt her into continuing. 'Well,' he said impatiently. 'What next?'

'We drove on the next morning, Saturday morning, down through Oxfordshire and Berkshire, across Salisbury Plain, stopping at Stonehenge, then back up through Wiltshire, stopping for lunch at a pub in Hungerford.'

'That seems gruesomely fitting,' Prince said.

'Oh? Why?'

'A long time ago a lot of people were shot there by a crazed local.'

'I didn't know that,' Chloe replied. 'Cusack didn't mention it.'

'It was just a passing comment,' Prince said testily. 'So you had lunch in Hungerford.'

'Yeah.'

'And then?'

'Well . . .'

'Yes?' Prince prompted her again.

'After lunch he drove to Marlborough and Calne. He drove more slowly than usual, looking around him a lot, as if looking for something specific. Eventually, he stopped at a small farm just outside Calne and, though it clearly wasn't being used any more – I mean, the fields were empty and the house had a "For Sale" sign on it – he spent a long time walking around the property and studying the landscape on all sides.'

'Trying to get a fix on something,' Prince speculated.

'Yeah, I think so.'

'Did you ask him what he was doing?'

'Yeah. He just said it had to do with his work, with the man he was looking for. When I asked if the man he was looking for had lived there, he said, "No, the guy who lived here is dead. That's why this place is up for sale. But him and the man I'm looking for were friends and I thought I might get a clue here."'

'The home of Tom Simmonds,' Prince explained. 'The man

who drove the truck that contained the explosives used in the Whitehall bombing.'

'Oh,' Chloe said. 'Cusack didn't mention that.'

'No, he wouldn't. So did he pick up any clues?'

'Not really. But he kept looking at the landscape on all sides of the property, then he said something like, "It could be in this area. You could hide a whole army in this area. I don't think he's too far away." That's all he said. Then we got back into the car and he drove around the whole area, stopping every now and then to ask locals if they knew of any large group, or community, of outsiders living near them.'

'He *is* getting close,' Prince said. 'He's virtually on our doorstep.'

'Yes,' Chloe said. 'I think so.'

'So where else did Sherlock Holmes drive?' Prince asked.

'He just kept driving around the same area, in ever-widening circles, as far north as Malmesbury, as far south as Trowbridge, west to the outskirts of Bristol, east as far as Burbage.'

'Thankfully not far enough,' Prince said. 'And he kept asking locals about large groups, or communities, of outsiders?'

'Yeah.'

'And they all said, "No"?'

'Yeah.'

'Which they wouldn't have done if he'd travelled farther south to this area. Almost certainly, had he done so, some blabbermouth would have said, "Yes". Well, well, that government-sponsored assassin is on to us.'

'Maybe,' Chloe said.

'Why *maybe*?'

'Because I think it was just a hunch. Just a sudden thought that came to him when we were driving back through Wiltshire and ended up in Hungerford and he realized that the road ran straight from there to Calne, where . . . What's his name?'

'Tom Simmonds.'

'Right . . . where Tom Simmonds had lived. So Cusack

drove there on an impulse, suddenly making a connection between Simmonds and you, between the location of Simmonds's farm and your place, and deducing that you might be located in that area too. But then, after driving around that area all afternoon, asking everyone we met about large groups of strangers, he received enough negative answers to convince him that he had to be wrong. I mean, he apologized for wasting our whole afternoon that way. "I just had this crazy notion," he said, "that the gang I'm looking for might be in this area. I guess I was wrong." Then he drove us to a hotel he knew, just outside Trowbridge, and we spent the second night there.'

'That must have soured love's young dream for you a bit,' Prince said sarcastically, 'being so close to home, as it were.'

'Yeah,' Chloe said, 'it did.'

'So what about Sunday? He didn't drive around this area as well, did he?'

'No. By Sunday, he'd given up on that idea and he wasn't looking for anything. We just headed back here, enjoying the scenery, taking our time, stopping for another lingering lunch in a pub outside Gloucester. Then we drove back to my place, arriving here about six in the evening.'

'So how did Cusack seem then?'

'He seemed a lot more relaxed. We watched a movie on TV and he had a couple of whiskies, but that was all. When the movie was over, he asked if he could spend the night again and go straight to Stirling Lines from my place – he'd left his uniform here on Friday afternoon. So naturally I said, "Yes" and we went to bed and made love –'

'You prostituted yourself again, even if not for money,' Prince insisted icily.

Chloe sighed. 'Yes, Prince, I suppose I did.'

'Had he anything more to say?'

'Yes. He talked a lot after we made . . . after we . . . *fucked*. He said, "I think I'm in love with you, though it may be too soon to say. I only know that I haven't felt like this since I first met my wife, when I was a young man in love, and even though I loved her throughout our marriage, it wasn't quite like this." He went on to explain – I think he was trying to be as honest as possible, I think that's in his nature – that although he'd loved his wife, their relationship had changed as the marriage progressed, becoming less sensual, more familiar, based on mutual trust and respect, a shared love for their daughter, rather than on passion. He said that what he felt for me was more passionate, more intense, and that he thought of me every moment, night and day, which was something he'd not felt for his wife, even when they were young.'

'That poor, self-deluding bastard,' Prince said. 'You have him in the palm of your hand. So when did he leave your place?'

'This morning. He went straight to Stirling Lines. He asked if he could come back this evening and of course I said "Yes".'

'Good girl,' Prince said. 'But please remember this. This man is first and foremost a highly effective killing machine, not an angel of mercy; don't let his passion for you blind you to the fact that he's our enemy and is out to destroy us. No matter how nice he may sometimes seem – and may, indeed, actually *be* – he's a member of the SAS, head of their murderous QRF, and his sole function at the moment is to track down our community and destroy it. He's a paid assassin, Chloe, a man who does what he's told to do, and as his orders come from above, from the highest echelons of the Establishment – an Establishment ruled, as we now know, by a degenerate Royal Family backed by Freemasonry and the Illuminati, representatives of the Antichrist – as his orders come from there, it's our task – our *Christian duty* – not to let him blind us, as only Lucifer can and always could, with his superficial decency and charm.

'Think of Lucifer, dear Chloe, the seductively smiling face of evil, that sly creature who appears to offer only good things when what he actually offers is venomous. Sergeant Cusack may well be a decent man. I have no argument with that, Chloe. But it's always the decent men – men who seek moral guidance – who commit the most evil acts because they're so easily persuaded, so ready to believe, that what they're doing is *righteous* and, therefore, beyond reproach. So beware of him, Chloe. Beware of your own feelings. I can sense, from the way you've been talking about him, that you do have feelings for him. Your softer instincts have betrayed you. Just keep in mind that Sergeant Cusack, decent though he may seem, has lost everything in life but his work – and that work is the SAS. So what's the SAS? A murder machine for the government! And who does the government most wish to kill? You and me, Chloe! Our community! Our compound! Our beliefs! They wish to kill everyone who opposes them and the SAS, particularly its Quick Reaction Force, is their chosen instrument. Sergeant Cusack, no matter how decent he may seem, heads the QRF. Could you possibly feel affection for this man, Chloe?'

Chloe paused, obviously thinking about it, then sighed and said, 'No.'

'Then don't pretend that you can,' Prince said. 'Reserve your feelings for your friends, for your brethren in the movement, and think only of the preservation of the community and of all it means to you. Do you understand, Chloe?'

'Yes, Prince, I understand.'

'God bless you, my child. The Lord be with you. Stick like glue to Cusack and report back to me every time you see him. I need to know everything he does, when he does it, where he goes. I need to know his movements more precisely than he knows them himself. Can you give me this, Chloe?'

'Yes, Prince,' Chloe replied.

'And please remember that when I pull you out of there you must leave immediately, with no hesitation.'

Chloe briefly delayed replying, then said, 'Yes, Prince.'

'Keep calling,' Prince said.

Switching off his cellular phone, he sat back in his chair to study the glowing computer screen in front of him. He tried to put himself into Cusack's shoes, into his mind, his feelings, and thought with pleasure of the guilt and confusion that the

SAS man must now be feeling. Cusack, the fool, thought that he was in love with Chloe, thought that Chloe, actually eighteen, was twenty-three years of age, thought that she, this supposed 23-year-old, could help him forget what he was going through. What would Cusack do when he found out that he'd been set up and ruthlessly used by the woman he thought he loved?

*We'll soon find out*, Prince thought.

He would, he also realized, *have* to find out soon because it was clear, from the way she was speaking, that Chloe, if not exactly in love with Cusack, was feeling dangerously sympathetic towards him. That foolishness could certainly impair her judgement at the wrong time. Women were unpredictable at best, totally irrational at their worst; and if Chloe was feeling emotional about Cusack, she could blow the whole thing.

One had to be very careful. Indeed, he, Prince, also had to be very careful and ensure that he made no more little slips of the tongue when impatience got the better of him. Like using words such as 'fuck' and 'bastard' to ardent believers like Chloe, who viewed him as a religious figurehead, God's mouthpiece, no less, and would wonder where such language was coming from.

Prince *knew* where it was coming from. Prince's father had groaned 'Fuck, fuck' when buggering his only son. His mother, whose only child was in fact certainly not her husband's biological offspring, rather the random accident of a careless night with another man, had called Prince a 'bastard' every time she got so drunk that she could hardly stand and so had, instead, sat on the edge of the bed, holding him down while her husband had his way with him. Life was truly a charnel house, the domain of the devil, and Prince, despite his own frequent falls from grace, needed God for that very reason. God was his rod and staff, his guiding light, and he truly believed in Him. There were those who would never understand this because of what Prince was doing. But Prince knew that what he was doing *was* the right thing, his ordained task, despite his occasional lapses, his frustrated outbursts – which God would surely forgive.

Nevertheless, he would have to be more careful when speaking to Chloe, giving her no cause to doubt him. At the same time, he had to move things along before Cusack, who was presently Chloe's victim, turned her head with thoughts of love and compassion. That could lead to disaster.

It would be best, then, to accelerate matters, to cause maximum disruption to Cusack and his QRF team, then pull Chloe out of the Hereford area, with its freedom, its temptations, and bring her back to the disciplines of the community.

The affair between Cusack and Chloe would be short-lived and, with luck, would bring Cusack only heartbreak. This was what Prince was after.

It was time, he realized, for some more remote harassment: phone phreaking and e-mail intervention and computer hacking conducted by a master. He, Prince, was that master.

Satisfied with his thoughts, he manipulated the computer's mouse on his workbench and watched the dance of the cursor.

Prince wreaked havoc with ease.

# CHAPTER TWENTY-TWO

Cusack was unhappy. He couldn't stop thinking about that trip he'd made with Chloe, going outward in ever-widening circles from Tom Simmonds's farm near Calne, not really knowing why he was doing so, just impelled by some instinct that told him he was in the right area, near the centre of Prince's web. Yet he'd felt, as he was driving, that he was circumnavigating his own mind, spiralling about his own thoughts, his own confusion and fear, looking for his own reflection in a dark glass, though fearful of finding it. It had been an impulsive action, springing out of his subconscious, and though he hadn't found anything, though no sign of Prince had materialized, he was still convinced that his instincts had been sound and that he should have gone farther.

Cusack was also unhappy because he was involved with Chloe – was in love with her, or simply loved her, these being two distinct issues. He felt guilty about it, convinced, as he was, that it was too soon after his personal tragedy for him to be involved with someone else – a much younger woman, at that – and that he was somehow betraying the memory of his wife and daughter. On the other hand, he *was* involved, wanting Chloe desperately, perhaps needing her to fill the dreadful void that the loss of Mary and Jennifer had left within him.

He wanted to live again, to be a normal human being. But he knew that this was not going to happen until he found Prince. That bastard was responsible for the devastation of Cusack's life, and only when Cusack had taken him out would he sleep soundly again. Perhaps this, in its brutal simplicity, explained why Cusack had made that impulsive trip with Chloe, driving around, desperately hoping to find Prince or, as he increasingly imagined it, his own dark reflection. He was still convinced, though he hadn't picked up Prince's trail, that he was on the right track.

Since then, of course, a mere five days ago, his whole world had been turned upside down, and now Lieutenant Colonel Blackwell had called an extraordinary Chinese Parliament to deal with all that had been happening and, worse, to deal with the remaining members of the QRF team, who had their own reasons to be unhappy. Cusack wasn't looking forward to this meeting, but he couldn't avoid it.

In the normal run of events, a Chinese Parliament was an informal meeting held by the commanding officer of an SAS patrol, troop or squadron to discuss the plan of action before an assault or operation. But this particular meeting had been convened at a late hour in Blackwell's office in the Kremlin – the SAS Planning and Intelligence Cell at Stirling Lines – to discuss the havoc that had been wreaked over the past five days by a phone-phreaker and hacker who was either Prince himself or a member of his British Millennialist Movement. Attending the meeting, apart from Cusack and Blackwell, were Sergeant Jack Lewis and the rest of the QRF team. It was evident to Cusack, as soon as he entered Blackwell's office, that his CO, normally so self-contained, was battling to control an inner fury.

'You're late,' he said curtly to Cusack, who was the last to arrive.

'Sorry about that, boss,' Cusack replied, taking the vacant chair between Jack Lewis and Corporal Benjamin Wiley. 'I wasn't home when my answerphone recorded your message.'

He had, in fact, been at Chloe's place – a fact that made him feel even more guilty.

'You actually *received* the message, did you?'

'Of course, boss. What do you mean?'

'Because no one else living off the base received the message. Their answering machines were tampered with.'

'Tampered with?'

'Phone-phreaked. Someone phreaked their way into the phone lines, blocked all incoming calls, and replaced the original – the owner's – response with their own.'

Though every member of the QRF team had his own room in the Spider – the barracks at Stirling Lines – where he could keep his kit and weapons, only three of them were single and actually lived there: Sergeant Jack Lewis, a twice-divorced playboy, and Troopers Bill Stubbs and Mel Grant. The others, including Cusack, lived off the base and were obliged to have answering machines to receive urgent messages in their absence. Clearly, Cusack's was the only one of those machines not to have been tampered with.

'So what did the replacement message say?' he asked.

Blackwell read from his notebook. ' "You have just made contact with the British Millennialist Movement. If you're calling this number, you must be a Son of Satan and should have been put down at birth. Don't ring back, filth." ' He looked up again, his grey gaze smouldering with that suppressed fury. 'Obviously a message from Prince,' he said. 'Like all the other messages he's been sending the past week, either by phone-phreaking or by hacking into e-mail. This man is causing chaos.'

Cusack knew what he meant. For the past week, Prince had been relentlessly hacking into the computer system right here at Stirling Lines, leaving his own messages, usually mocking or obscene, on the SAS website and replacing them almost as soon as they were erased by the SAS computer operators. More frustratingly, he had been hacking in to remotely change computerized documentation, including requisition and shipping details for equipment and the personal details of SAS members, thus causing equipment not actually ordered to be sent to the base, weapons and explosives to be sent out from the base to the wrong locations, and even troopers to be sent false orders, erroneously posting them in or out of the regiment. Twice during that week the whole base had been placed on alert after the Green Slime (Intelligence) had received false e-mail alarms about imminent terrorist attacks. Twice the air-conditioning and central-heating systems had been remotely interfered with, thus damaging the base's computer systems, causing food supplies to rot, bringing about near-accidents in the kitchens and chaos in the water supply, and in general creating great discomfort for the SAS men living in the Spider. E-mail messages from the British Millennialist Movement had appeared on just about every computer screen on the base, leading to administrative chaos and enormous frustration. Now, it seems, Prince had phone-phreaked the personal phones and answering machines of every member of the QRF team who was living off the base – all of them, that is, except Cusack. He had to wonder why.

Glancing uneasily at the men seated on both sides of him, Cusack asked, 'So how did you all know about this meeting?'

'Certainly not by phone,' Blackwell sharply informed him. 'Receiving no response from them, I sent messengers personally to their homes to tell them about it. All of them received the exact same message – and it wasn't the first.'

'No,' Corporal Chris Mapley said, stroking back his jet-black hair and turning his intense, brown-eyed stare on Cusack. 'That bastard has been tormenting me – *and* my family – all week by fucking up our answering machine and also with e-mails so obscene that I've had to keep my kids away from the computer. He even sent a death threat to my wife when I was here on the base. She's in a right state, I can tell you.'

'Same here,' Trooper Wiley said. 'I don't have a computer, but my answering machine's been tampered with and callers were receiving that message the boss just read out instead of what I had on it. That message must have been on my answering machine most of the week, because I didn't even think to check it until the CO sent his man around to tell me about this meeting. When I checked, I found that message instead of my own and realized why my social life – as well as things to do with the general running of the household – had been going bloody haywire. I could kill that bastard. I really could. I mean, what are we waiting for?'

'We're waiting until we find him,' Jack Lewis said, 'and we haven't found him yet.' He turned his gaze upon Cusack. 'So what's happening, Lenny?'

'What's happening,' Cusack said, feeling defensive and hating himself, 'is that I'm trying to find him and not getting very far. I mean, this guy lives out there, somewhere in cyberspace, and that's somewhere we haven't been.'

'Right,' Trooper Carter said, shifting his well-muscled mass on his chair and looking every bit as intense as he always did. 'The SAS has been to Africa and Asia and the Falkland Islands and Iraq, but we haven't yet been in cyberspace. I'm beginning to feel like Neanderthal man. I'm starting to feel old before my time.'

'You dumb cunt,' Trooper Stubbs said, quivering like a bantam cock about to fight, his scarred bulldog face turning red. 'The regiment's been to all those places, but *you* haven't, you under-aged git, so feel old in your own time.'

'Right,' Trooper Grant said, looking every bit as pugnacious as his mate Stubbs, both of them from the East End – the rough end – of London. 'Let's stop whimpering about what the regiment did before and decide what to do *now*. I wouldn't know a computer from my arsehole – and, believe me, I've never seen *that* – but if cyberspace is where we've got to go, then let's get up and *go*. I mean, excuse my language, boss –' here he turned to Lieutenant Colonel Blackwell '– but we've been wanking around for weeks now, doing retraining after retraining, practising with these new, so-called secret weapons, and what's it all for? Are we gonna move against this bastard or not? I mean, he can't be *invisible!*'

This being a Chinese Parliament, where everyone had their say and did not bow to rank, there was little that Blackwell could do about this outburst except respond with: 'I understand your frustration, Trooper Grant, and it's one of the reasons we're here now. Unfortunately, this isn't a normal assignment, so you'll have to be patient. What we're dealing with now is something we haven't had to deal with before, so we are, you might say, in deep waters. As we all now recognize, we're dealing with a man who dwells in cyberspace and we've no experience of that. We *are* dealing with an invisible man.'

'Excuse me, boss,' Jack Lewis said, running his fingers through his hair and letting his breath out as if his lungs were giant bellows, 'but I don't think there's any such thing. There's no one so invisible that we can't find him. We *can* find him. We have to.'

'Fucking right,' Chris Mapley said. 'That fucker's tormenting me *and* my family, so he has to be found. I mean, he's flesh and blood, right?'

'Right!' Stubbs exclaimed. 'He eats and drinks like the rest of us, his shit smells just like ours, so there must be a way to sniff him out. Why the fuck are we blocked here?'

'Cyberspace,' Ben Wiley said. 'He rarely moves in the physical world. He just sits there, a fucking spider in his web, playing with his computer. We exist in real time – time not spent on the web – while he lives by his fucking mouse and cursor, running rings around us with his hacking. He's operating in a place we've never been and that gives him the edge. That bastard's shredding us daily.'

'Too bloody true,' Grant said. 'He phone-phreaks and hacks us to ribbons –'

'Good joke,' Stubbs interjected sardonically.

'– while we sit here, wondering where he's coming from, why this hacker is killing us. I have to tell you – and I hate to admit it – but I feel absolutely bloody humiliated. We're being shat upon, right?'

'Right,' Bill Stubbs said.

'So what do we do?' Jack Lewis said. 'You guys living off the base are being phone-phreaked while we guys here, on the base, are being invaded by this cunt and his computer. Do we wear this? How *long* do we wear this before we can move? Sorry, Lenny, please tell me.'

Lewis had turned to Cusack, his best friend, probably thinking *Who Dares Wins*, the regimental motto. Cusack, though loving him as a friend, also felt like strangling him. He knew that Lewis, *because* he was his best friend, would push as hard as he could. This was the SAS way.

'We don't *wear* it,' Cusack responded. 'We simply have to live with it. We're still trying to track Prince down – we're not sitting on our arses – and until we do –'

'*If* you do,' Lewis cut in.

'*Until* we do, we'll just have to be patient and take what he dishes out.'

'What?' Trooper Carter said aggressively. 'Take what he dishes out? That may be easy for you to say, Sarge, but I'm sitting there with my wife and two kids and *they*'re being tormented. That bastard, when he phone-phreaks or breaks into e-mail, has no regard for sex or age or personal privacy. He just wants to cause damage. By damaging my family, he's damaging me and that's what he's after. So no, thanks, I won't take it – not at all. We don't find him? Fuck it! Let's drop it. Give me an RTU and let's say bye-bye. I'll leave the SAS happily.'

'You don't mean that,' Stubbs said.

'Yes, I do,' Carter replied.

'No, you don't,' Grant said. 'You're just saying it 'cause you're frustrated and angry. You worked your arse off to get into the regiment and you won't leave for this. That's a fuckin' joke, Carter.'

'Fuck *you*,' Carter said.

'Order, order,' Cusack said. 'We don't need this kind of abuse. A Chinese Parliament is one thing – you can all say what you want, so long as it's reasonable – but a bullshit session won't get us anywhere and that's what you're starting. We're here to solve a very serious problem, so let's *keep* it serious.'

'Thank you, Sergeant, for those helpful words,' Lieutenant Colonel Blackwell said sardonically. 'But to get back to Prince, our phone-phreaker and hacker, can I ask at least one leading question?'

'Sure, boss,' Cusack said.

'If he's phone-phreaked the others living off-base,' Blackwell said bluntly, 'then why hasn't he also phone-phreaked you?'

Cusack felt a shiver go down his spine. Everything about Prince sent a shudder down his backbone, but this time the chill went even deeper. He could feel it, but he didn't know why and that made it even worse. He sensed that something bad was coming.

'Well,' he said carefully, 'he probably hasn't interfered with my answering machine because, as you know, he often makes personal calls to me, trying to wind me up.'

'He leaves messages on your answer machine?'

'No,' Cusack said. 'Oddly enough, he's never done that. So far, he's always caught me when I'm at home.'

'*Caught* you at home?' Blackwell asked.

'What's that, boss?'

'Surely,' Blackwell said, 'if he's always caught you at home, it must mean that he always knows *when* you're home. Which means, in turn, that he has you under observation.'

Cusack nodded. 'Right. But we've both – you and I - suspected that for some time, boss. Certainly ever since that call he made to me shortly after Hargreaves left my place. Prince made it clear then that he'd seen Hargreaves entering and leaving my house. It's also obvious – though I hate to remind us all of this tragedy – that he'd had Stirling Lines under surveillance long enough to know about the movements of troopers in and out of the base and to ascertain just when we were going to the Brecon Beacons. He knew enough about our movements to be able to follow us there and then plant a bomb under one of our trucks. Finally, having killed those six men, he knew enough to be able to attend their funeral as a member of the public. So, yes, he had Stirling Lines in general and me in particular under long-term surveillance. But what's the conclusion, boss?'

'The conclusion,' Blackwell said, 'is that we don't know how the hell he's doing his present surveillance – the kind of surveillance that enables him to know exactly when you'll be home.'

'I'm not sure that I –'

'As you know, Sergeant,' Blackwell interjected, '*we*'ve also placed you under observation – or, to be more precise, placed your *street* under observation – and so far we've seen nothing suspicious there.'

'Such as?' Jack Lewis asked, clearly bemused.

'No parked vehicles or loitering individuals,' Blackwell clarified.

'So how the hell is he doing it?' Lewis asked. 'He can't actually *observe* you with phone-phreaking or computer hacking,' he added, turning to Cusack, 'so how does he know when you're home?'

Cusack sighed, feeling at a loss. Feeling helpless. Impotent. 'I don't know,' he confessed.

A long silence ensued and to Cusack, feeling worse every second, it was an eternity. He knew what his men wanted because he knew what they were like: they were SAS, after all, believing that 'Who dares wins'. They were men who lived with inner tensions that always had to find a release in fast action: find a target and go for it. Now they were being toyed with, tormented, and it was driving them crazy.

'Seems to me,' Jack Lewis said, 'that this Prince is a lot brighter than we thought and, being covert, living deep, he has tentacles everywhere. I mean, we're keeping Lenny's street under surveillance and nothing's ever turned up – yet Prince always rings when Lenny's at home. That means Prince has eyes elsewhere.'

'Where?' Corporal Mapley asked.

Everyone looked at Cusack. 'How the fuck would I know?' he said. 'Prince's tentacles *are* everywhere. He gets into our telephones, into our answering machines, into our computers and our e-mail, so it's pretty obvious that he can handle modern technology. We already know he's not sitting outside my house, observing me with obsolete surveillance equipment, so clearly he's capable of *anything*. I don't know. Don't ask me.'

'We're asking you,' Lieutenant Colonel Blackwell said, sounding calm, though his eyes were smouldering with suppressed frustration and rage, 'because you're the head of a QRF team that has nothing to go for. We're asking you because Prince is *after* you and so you're all we've got to snare him with. So what have *you* got?'

Cusack, feeling like hell on earth, slumped deep in his chair.

'Nothing,' he said.

Another long silence descended. Eventually, with a sigh that sounded like a sermon, Blackwell said, 'We *do* have something.'

'What?' Cusack asked.

Blackwell didn't answer his question. Instead, he removed his gaze from Cusack and let it take in the men sitting around him, one by one, gaining their undivided attention before he spoke to them.

'This hasn't been a satisfactory meeting,' he said, 'though it may at least have vented a few frustrations. Please believe me, gentlemen, when I say that I understand those frustrations, but unfortunately there isn't a damned thing I can do about them until we manage to track down this . . . this *individual* called Prince. In the meantime, no matter how difficult it may be, please try to be patient, *please* keep retraining, and be assured that you're not wasting your time because our day *will* come. Thank you, gentlemen. We'll meet again in a few days. Sergeant Cusack, please stay here.'

'That's it?' Bill Stubbs said, running his fingers through his remaining hair to stroke his bald dome, looking as pugnacious as ever. '*That*'s what we came here to talk about?'

'That's it,' Lieutenant Colonel Blackwell said.

'No offence meant, boss,' Stubbs's friend Trooper Grant said, 'but that isn't much to take back to the Spider or the Sports and Social.'

'I can't help you,' Blackwell said. 'You take back what you've been given. I promise, the minute anything comes up you'll be the first to know. Until then, however, what can I say except goodnight and sleep tight?'

'Aye, aye, aye!' Stubbs exclaimed histrionically, breaking the sombre mood, raising a few laughs and allowing everyone – except Cusack – to leave the room in a reasonably calm frame of mind. Cusack, having no choice, sat on, being crushed by an unending silence that Blackwell eventually, feeling merciful, decided to break.

'We *do* have something,' he repeated.

'What?'

'William Hargreaves has found a wizard hacker and he's bringing him here five days from now – when he gets him released.'

'Released from where?' Cusack asked.

'Pentonville Prison.'

Cusack grinned. 'Fucking wonderful.'

# CHAPTER TWENTY-THREE

Chloe was shocked by the call. The phone rang at 8.30 a.m., just after Cusack, who practically lived with her now, had gone off for his routine day's duty at Stirling Lines. Still stupefied from sleep, languorous from waking-up sex with Cusack, not quite together, as she rarely was in the mornings, Chloe automatically put the phone to her ear, yawned and said, 'Yes?'

'It's me, Chloe. Prince.'

Instantly Chloe felt a slight lurching of the heart, a dryness in her throat of the kind that she had experienced recently each time Prince had called her. She hadn't yet worked out the reasons for it, but she sensed that it was to do with her changing attitude to Cusack. Now, though she was still in thrall to Prince, she was finding that the sound of his voice made her uneasy, as it was doing right now.

'Oh,' she said. 'Hi, Prince.'

'You sound distracted, Chloe.'

'It's early in the morning.'

'Ah, yes, you're not good in the morning.'

'No,' Chloe said.

'I take it that Cusack isn't there; that he's gone off to Stirling Lines?'

'Yes.'

Prince chuckled. 'Almost like married life, isn't it? I mean, he practically lives there.'

'Practically,' Chloe said. 'I thought that was what you wanted.'

'Oh, it was. Yes, indeed! It was *exactly* what I wanted, my dear, and you did very well.'

'*Was?*' Chloe said with a sinking heart, sensing what was coming and surprised to find herself so concerned by it.

'Yes, *was*. It all ends today. I'm pulling you out of there, Chloe, with immediate effect.'

This time, Chloe felt a sharp shock, like a blow to the midriff, leaving her winded and slightly dizzy. Despite her every effort to treat Cusack as just a job of work, an enemy to be destroyed, some part of her had been withdrawing, refusing to go on with it, surrendering to emotions that she was not supposed to feel. She had grown guiltier, more confused and increasingly uneasy with each passing day. Now the thought of abruptly leaving Cusack, of not seeing him again, of leaving him betrayed and hurt and baffled, which was clearly Prince's intention, filled her with pain. She tried not to reveal that pain through the tone of her voice, but her words still betrayed her.

'With . . . with *immediate* effect?'

'I'm sure you heard me correctly, Chloe.'

'How immediate?'

'Your rent was paid a month in advance, so you just pack your suitcases, throw them into the car, drive into Hereford, drop the keys off with the estate agents, then drive on to Wiltshire. Any problem with that, Chloe?'

'Well, no . . . I mean . . . It just seems a bit . . .'

'Abrupt?'

'Well . . . yes.'

'I warned you about that, Chloe. I always said that when I finally pulled you out, I'd do it at short notice. What's the problem, apart from packing your suitcases? Are you saying that you feel the desperate need to say a personal goodbye to Cusack?'

'Well, no, not exactly. I'm just a bit surprised, that's all, and I thought . . .'

'Thought what? What's there to think about? I'm telling you to leave there this morning and drive straight back here. I should have thought that was pretty simple, Chloe. Unless, of course, you have your own reasons for wanting to stay on.'

Chloe heard the change in Prince's voice, that slight edge that could come into it when he started losing patience or was feeling frustrated. When that happened, he could say awful things, cruel, cutting things, and the thought that he was about to speak to her in that way filled her with dread.

'No, of course not,' she said, shocked to realize it was a lie, that she *did* have her reasons for staying on: her growing feelings for Cusack. She found it hard enough to admit that to herself, let alone to Prince.

'You're still sounding shocked, Chloe. Don't tell me you want to see him one last time before you light out of there.'

'No, no, I don't,' Chloe lied desperately. 'You just took me by surprise, that's all. Of course I'll do as you say, Prince.'

'Good. Make sure you do. I expect to see you back here by lunchtime.'

'I'll be there,' Chloe said.

She did as she was told, though her heart wasn't in it. A new fear of Prince began to grow insidiously within her. After switching her cellular phone off, she packed her things into two suitcases, placed them in the car, switched off everything in the house, and drove to the estate agent's in Hereford. There she explained that she had to return prematurely, unexpectedly, to London. Then she gave the key back, left the office, and drove out of Hereford.

An almost irresistible impulse made Chloe want to drive to the SAS base, Stirling Lines, just to look at the gate and imagine Cusack coming out of it. But she managed to resist the impulse and instead kept driving, taking the A49 to Ross-on-Wye, then continuing along the A40 to Gloucester. While bypassing the town and heading south, through Upton St Leonards and Nailsworth, she could not stop thinking obsessively of Cusack, of the hurt and bafflement he would experience when he realized that she had gone without even leaving a note. The thought made her feel sick.

Though she had tried to avoid the issue, denying the truth to herself, Chloe now had to accept that she had grown too close to Cusack, was emotionally involved with him, possibly even in love with him, and that this was a betrayal of everything she had come to believe in as far as Prince and the other members of his community were concerned. She was a member of that community and had come to depend upon it, looking on it as her extended family, with Prince as the father figure and even, in a more religious sense, the godhead.

Eventually, of course, Chloe had been totally mesmerized by Prince, turned inside out by him, emptied of all her former beliefs and filled instead by the message of his relentless preaching – an overwhelming, often confusing mixture of fundamentalist Christianity, radical politics, esoteric philosophy and mysticism – while also surrendering her pride, at Prince's urging (he preached that pride was a vice) by serving him, sexually and otherwise, without question or doubt. She had done all he'd asked of her, all the community required of her, believing everything she had learned since being rescued by him, being cocooned and conditioned by his crusade, even going so far as to use her whore's talents to entrap one of the enemy – Sergeant Lenny Cusack. Only then had doubt crept in, the first hints of uneasiness, thoughts that rose up like question marks when she looked into Cusack's eyes. She had seen herself twice reflected in his eyes and had been disturbed by the sight.

Chloe drove at a steady, careful speed down through Malmesbury, bypassing Chippenham and going on to Trowbridge through a landscape filled with churches and the ruins of ancient castles, starkly beautiful against a blue sky, in lush green fields pock-marked with megalithic traces. As she travelled, she finally accepted that, even as she was betraying Cusack by doing what Prince demanded of her, she was betraying Prince by hiding from him her growing feelings of love for the man she was supposed to be setting up.

Profoundly confused by this knowledge, also deeply disturbed by it, Chloe felt that all she had gained over the past few months had been lost, that her emotional state, always fragile, was turning dangerously frail again, and that deceiving Cusack and returning to Prince was going to cause her great damage. Nevertheless, despite her personal misgivings, she had already surrendered too much of herself to Prince to feel whole without him. For this reason, if for no other, she was going back to him.

*I'm only eighteen years old*, Chloe thought, filling up with self-pity. *I shouldn't have to deal with this. Cusack would understand the problem . . . But he thinks I'm twenty-three.*

That thought made it worse for her. Chloe wondered what Cusack would think if he knew that she was really only eighteen years old – only three years older than the daughter who had been so brutally murdered. Cusack, she suspected, would be shocked and thus would reject her immediately. Surely this knowledge was justification enough for returning to Prince.

She just didn't want to.

Now, as she drove across the western edge of Salisbury Plain, feeling eerily haunted in its undulating, almost treeless fields, a landscape of dreams or, more likely, nightmares, Chloe felt crushed by her own confusion. She was tormented by guilt, increasingly aware of the fact that she was betraying not one man but two, and that one of those men, Cusack, she almost certainly loved, while the other one, Prince, whom she had formerly revered, now filled her with unaccountable terror. She felt that she was being torn in two, both in heart and mind.

*Oh, fuck,* she thought, *I just want to die. I don't want any part of this. I'd rather be back on drugs.*

She passed through Longbridge and Deverill, crossed the A303, then turned south-east until she came to the small town of Hindon. There she turned east, following the signs to Salisbury, but stopping long before she reached that city.

About five miles from the confluence of the rivers Wylye and Nadder, in an area of rolling, grassy hills, no village or even house within sight, she turned off the narrow road into the old flying school that was now the large barbed-wire compound of the community known as the British Millennialist Movement. After showing her identification to the guards at the gates, she was allowed to drive on in.

As Chloe drove to the motor pool, passing the erstwhile air traffic control tower, rows of Portakabins and Nissen huts, all spread out around the airstrip, and fields of mown grass surrounded by rolling hills, she grew increasingly fearful at the thought of seeing Prince and wondered why this was so. Indeed, for the first time since coming here, she found herself wondering just what kind of man he really was. Thinking of one of the phone conversations she'd had with him about Cusack, she recalled the shock she had felt when he had repeatedly used the words 'fuck' and 'bastard' – hardly the language of a truly religious man. She also recalled the shock she had felt only this morning when she had heard the icy cold sarcasm in his voice. His tone had again given her doubts about what kind of man he was.

Once in the motor pool, Chloe parked the car, signed the attendant's book confirming that she had returned the borrowed vehicle, then removed the suitcases from the boot and carried them to the Portakabin that she shared as a dormitory with nine other girls approximately her own age, all former drug addicts, all present disciples, all in awe of Prince . . . just as she had once been. None of them were in the Portakabin. Right now, she knew, they would be scattered around the compound, performing their daily duties, which were numerous and filled an eighteen-hour day. Only now, after her few weeks in the cottage near Hereford, alone except when Cusack came to visit, did she realize just how little freedom anyone actually had here in the community; how totally subservient to Prince they all were. This place was less free than an open prison: it was guarded by stony-faced young men armed with sub-machine guns and pistols. For the first time since she had been here, Chloe wondered what would happen if she tried to walk through the main gates without a signed note from Prince giving permission. She didn't think she would get very far.

*Yes,* Chloe thought, *it's a prison. I was just too blind to see it. All of us here, all of the so-called converts, the disciples, have been brainwashed by Prince. He did a good job on us.*

Having been instructed by Prince to come and see him the instant she returned, Chloe placed the suitcases on the bed and reluctantly left the Portakabin. As she crossed a broad strip of closely mown lawn, under a darkening sky, heading for Prince's Portakabin, she experienced a deepening dread of a kind she hadn't known since her arrival here. It was a dread of being questioned by him, of having to meet his pale green fathomless gaze with its unblinking, mesmeric quality, of having to bend to his will once more and do what he demanded. She didn't want to do that any more, and yet she knew that she would.

*I'm too weak to refuse him,* she thought. *I've come too far to turn back.*

Aware of this, she climbed the steps of his Portakabin and pressed the buzzer with a sinking heart. His voice emerged from the intercom fixed to the side of the door.

'Yes?'

'It's Chloe. I'm back.'

'Oh, good,' Prince said. 'Come in.'

When she heard the door click, she pushed it open and entered. Prince was not in the living room, but she heard the sound of the television set in the bedroom.

'I'm in here,' he called out.

Though despairing even more at the realization that he was in bed, Chloe walked through to the bedroom, thinking, as she did so, of how big his Portakabin was, much bigger than all the others, more luxurious as well, not spartan like the accommodation of his disciples, not as humble as he insisted that theirs should be. Filing this fact away in the hard disk of her brain, she entered the bedroom to find that Prince was, indeed, stretched out on the bed, lying on the quilt, wearing a white robe, his legs outspread and his golden-blond hair tumbling down around his shoulders to frame his gaunt, pale, handsome face and steady green gaze.

He had been watching the television set hanging down from the ceiling, angled over the bed, but he switched it off when Chloe entered. She stopped at the end of the bed, looking down at him, not knowing what to say. He raised his right hand, waved her towards him, then lowered the hand to his side. Chloe walked around the bed and stopped when she was standing beside him, a little in front of him. He looked up at her, not smiling, unblinking, his inexpressiveness frightening.

'So you came back,' he said.

The remark instantly chilled Chloe, convincing her that something bad was coming, though she didn't know what. 'Yes,' she said. 'Of course I did. You *knew* I would, Prince.'

'No, Chloe, I *didn't* know. In fact, I had serious doubts about it. It was the way you were talking on the phone that gave me those doubts. Now why would that be?'

The tone of his voice made her think of a cold blade scraping over her warm skin. It had an abrasive edge.

'I don't know what you're talking about,' she said. 'You asked me to leave immediately and that's just what I did. I said I would and I did.'

'You said you would after some hesitation, Chloe. I heard that hesitation in your voice, so please explain it, my dear.'

'I'd just got out of bed,' Chloe lied, 'and I was still half asleep. That's all you heard. Me half asleep and trying to take in what you were telling me. I mean, it *was* pretty early.'

'Eight-thirty in the morning is pretty early for you, is it?'

'Yes, it is,' Chloe said.

'But Cusack had gone by then, so you must have been up a good bit earlier, making him coffee, giving him cornflakes or whatever. You know? The good little housewife. Which means you must have been out of bed a good while before I called. Is that not the truth, Chloe?'

'Okay, Prince, I got out of bed earlier. About forty-five minutes earlier – with Cusack. So what? I'm really not good in the mornings and I wasn't expecting your call, so when it came it made me more vague than normal.'

Prince's green gaze remained steady, unblinking, penetrating, making Chloe feel that she was being raped. It was a pretty weird feeling. 'But you always knew that sooner or later I'd call,' he said, still sounding as cold as ice. 'To tell you to move out immediately. So why the surprise?'

Chloe sighed, trying to look exasperated, though she felt clammy with dread. 'I was just surprised that you phoned me so early and that I had to leave right away, practically on the instant. I mean, I always knew that when you told me to move out, I'd have to do it immediately, but I didn't expect it to be *that* quick.'

'So what's your definition of "immediately"?'

Chloe shrugged and spread her hands in the air as if actually bewildered by the question. 'A day, at least. Maybe the *same* day, but a day at least. You know? Six or eight hours to pack up and go – not as quick as you asked.'

'Not as quick as I asked,' Prince said, slyly mocking her grammar. 'I'm sorry if that gave you a problem, Chloe. So what *was* the problem?'

Chloe sighed again – once more trying to look as if she was exasperated when in fact she was terrified. 'There wasn't a problem. I told you . . . I was just surprised, is all.'

'Just surprised, is all,' Prince echoed, again mocking her lack of proper grammar. Then he sat up straighter in the bed to stare more closely, more intently, at her, making her blood run cold. 'Dear Chloe,' he said, 'are we not talking, in reality, about a little case of sudden, unexpected, divided loyalties?'

Chloe was convinced that she was sweating, though in fact she felt icy cold. 'What do you mean?'

'What I mean, dear Chloe, is that you sounded like a woman distraught at the thought of leaving her man – that man being Sergeant Lenny Cusack. Was that not the case, Chloe?'

'No!' Chloe said, shocked to hear the note of panic in her own voice.

'No?'

'No!'

'You didn't, during the few weeks you were with Cusack, being fucked by him – sorry, making love to him – find yourself becoming emotionally attached to him? Perhaps feeling actual love for him?'

'No!' Chloe lied.

'It would have been so easy, Chloe.'

'It didn't happen,' Chloe kept lying.

'So did you feel, Chloe, after your few weeks living alone in Hereford, in your own little thatched-roof cottage, with your private life and your adoring man, that you could have a better life outside our community than you're having inside it? It wasn't that, Chloe, was it?'

'No!' Chloe lied again.

'Well, I'm glad to hear that, Chloe,' Prince said softly, maliciously, almost hypnotically, somehow drawing her down through her own fear into his dark, deceptively safe web. 'Because, if it was otherwise, I'd have to remind you of how dreadful your life was before you came here . . . Worthless parents, you poor thing. A life of boredom in a provincial town. No past that you could look back on fondly and no future at all. Then the Big City, Chloe, the Big Smoke, London, and the drug addiction and the whoring to pay for it . . . That, in its bitter essence, is the pitiful life that you had before you came here.'

'I know that,' Chloe said, feeling faint to be reminded of it, even as her dread of Prince was overcome by a different kind of dread altogether: the fear of being cast out of here and returning to what she had been. On the other hand, she thought, if she had managed to remain with Cusack, they could have helped each other to . . .

'Did you think Cusack would change your life?' Prince asked, as if reading her mind. 'Did you think, in your little thatched-roof cottage, in your privacy, in your warm bed, that

Cusack would somehow *enhance* your life and, perhaps, liberate you from what you'd suddenly started imagining were the restrictions of life here in our little community? Was that it, Chloe?'

'No!' Chloe said, feeling as if she was choking.

'Are you sure, Chloe?'

'Yes, yes, I'm sure!'

'Do you want to remain here, Chloe, cured of your drug addiction, with lots of friends your own age, all believing what you believe, all working for the same cause, with none of the doubts and insecurities that would plague you outside?'

'Yes, Prince, I do!'

'And do you still believe, Chloe, all that you've learned here? Do you know who the true enemy is, Chloe, and would you do anything asked of you to defeat that enemy?'

'Yes, Prince! Yes! Yes!'

'So, do you believe, Chloe, do you now remember, that Sergeant Cusack, whom you may have felt was a decent man, is, despite his superficial decency, a hired assassin for the British government and, through them, for the Royal Family, which makes him a tool of Freemasonry and the Illuminati – a son of Satan, in other words?'

'Yes!' Chloe gasped. 'Yes!'

'So if you wish to give of your love, Chloe – and I'm sure that you do – who should you give it to? Sergeant Cusack or me?'

'I . . .'

'Yes, Chloe?'

'To you.'

'No, Chloe, to God.'

'Yes, of course, Prince, to God. But . . .'

'To love God, you must give your love to me, approaching Him through me. Is this true or not, Chloe?'

'Yes, Prince, of course.'

'Do you trust me, Chloe?'

'Yes!'

'You haven't been corrupted by Cusack?'

'No!'

'Then love me, Chloe. Show me that you love me, love the Lord, not Cusack, and let me know that I won't have to cast you back out to that world which always treated you so badly, so indifferently, without pity, with vileness. Show me by becoming one with me in the eyes of the Lord. Join your flesh to mine, Chloe. Do so without shame.'

'I . . .' But Chloe couldn't say any more, being trapped by her terror of the world she had recently come from, feeling safe only right now, *this instant*, and unable, or unwilling to think beyond it. 'I . . .'

'Take your clothes off,' Prince said softly, soothingly, seductively, patting the area of quilt by his right hip, 'then lie down beside me. Let me see that you have no shame or fear. Let me feel your love, Chloe.'

Feeling weak, slightly unreal, as helpless as a child, Chloe stripped off her clothes and then stretched out on the bed beside Prince. He turned in towards her. She turned in towards him. He told her what to do. She did what she was told. She served him, gave him pleasure, rendered homage, sighed and moaned, and all the time, in her dread and despair, she was yearning for Cusack.

# CHAPTER TWENTY-FOUR

'He's planted a sniffer programme somewhere in your computer network,' Jake Bailey told Cusack and Lieutenant Colonel Blackwell as he checked the files in the main computer of the SAS Information Warfare Centre in the 'Kremlin' at Stirling Lines. There were twelve other computers in the large room, lined along the four walls, all manned by SAS operatives, but Bailey, nicknamed 'Black Stealth' and renowned as the best hacker in Britain, could do things that no normal computer operator could.

Though only twenty years old, Black Stealth had been given a two-year prison sentence for phone-phreaking and hacking his way into the most strongly defended national defence computer systems to leave taunting messages for the operators to read. Though Black Stealth was serving his time in Pentonville prison, which these days was bursting at the seams with similar criminal hackers, William Hargreaves had promised him a reduced sentence if he succeeded in tracking down the hacker, Prince, who had been causing havoc at Stirling Lines for the past week or so. Agreeing, he had been brought from Pentonville to this top-secret area of the Kremlin and was now enthusiastically settling into his task. Long-haired, bright-eyed and nimble-fingered, he was enjoying himself.

'A sniffer programme?' Blackwell asked.

'Yeah. The sniffer records the first 128 keystrokes of people gaining legitimate access – the people your computer network normally interacts with. Those keystrokes hold the password and log-in information for your system and the sniffer transmits them back to the hacker. That's how your hacker, Prince, is getting into your system any time he wants. That's why you can't keep him out.'

'How can you tell there's a sniffer programme in the system?' Cusack asked.

Black Stealth pointed to some of the files shown on the glowing computer monitor. 'Those,' he said, highlighting a number of file names, one after the other, 'are unfamiliar file names. Now, most computer code writers have their own idiosyncrasies that are as distinctive as handwriting and an expert, such as myself, can spot 'em a mile off. In this case, I noticed straight away that those files didn't have military-style names, not like the others, so I opened 'em and found they were sniffer files. This hacker, this Prince guy, has been reading your e-mails and copying anything he wants ever since he put those files into your system – and that's a long time. What this means, in effect, is that he has access to your most confidential information, knows what you're doing or planning to do, and can change anything in your files by simply hitting his keyboard. Which explains how he's managed to cause all that chaos on this base – by changing orders and so on. You might as well invite him into this control room and tell him to help himself. I mean, this guy's in your bed.'

Cusack was still feeling awful and finding it difficult to concentrate. He had been feeling awful since that evening, five days ago, when he had gone to see Chloe and found, to his surprise, that she wasn't at the cottage. Surprise because he had told her before leaving that morning that he would be coming back in the evening, as usual, after his normal day on the SAS base. His surprise had turned to concern when he had spent the whole evening sitting in his car, parked outside the cottage, and Chloe had still not returned. His concern had turned to bafflement and despair when, after spending a sleepless night in his own home, then an uneasy day at Stirling Lines, he had gone back to the cottage only to find that Chloe still wasn't there. His bafflement and despair had turned into dreadful pain and humiliation when, that same evening, he had gone to his own home to find a devastating e-mail on his computer screen.

chloe is mine, cusack. she's left hereford for good and now she's with me again, telling me everything that you two did together.
she's been spying on you, cusack, every day of your relationship, and reporting every detail back to me.
chloe is only 18. you were fucking a girl who's only three years older than your dead daughter.
shame on you, cusack.
goodnight. have sweet dreams.
prince.

Worse was to come. The following morning, when he reported to Stirling Lines, he was called in to see the CO, who showed him an e-mail that had turned up on every computer screen in the Kremlin.

to lieutenant colonel blackwell.
for the past couple of weeks your esteemed sergeant lenny cusack has been fucking one of my 18-year-old disciples and the girl has been reporting back to me.
everything he told her, she told me.
i recommend you keep your eye on sergeant cusack. he's a very bad boy.
yours helpfully, prince.

Blackwell had been furious and Cusack had been devastated, not only because of his betrayal by Chloe but because just about everyone in the Kremlin would have read the e-mail. Though Blackwell, when he calmed down, was kind enough to concede that Cusack had been ruthlessly set up, with no way of knowing about Chloe's relationship to Prince, he had bluntly pointed out that Cusack's affair had placed the whole regiment in jeopardy and would seriously undermine his credibility as leader of the QRF. It was Blackwell's belief that the damage done to Cusack's reputation would only be rectified if Prince was located and neutralized in a matter of days. For this reason, he was giving Cusack two weeks and no more to complete his task. If Cusack failed, Blackwell would have him replaced as head of the QRF.

Deeply shocked to hear this, though understanding the need for it, Cusack had, over the next four days, been tormented even more by thoughts of Prince's e-mail to him – particularly that comment about Chloe being only three years older than his beloved daughter, Jennifer – and by Chloe's manipulation and betrayal of him. Worse than the humiliation of knowing that so many of his comrades had read the second e-mail, worse than the shock of learning that Chloe was only eighteen years old, worse than the shame of knowing that he had endangered his comrades by engaging in the affair – worse than all of that was the pain he had experienced every time he thought of Chloe, in his arms, in her bed, of being resurrected as a human being by her, given back the will to live, renewed as a whole man. To think of what she had given him while betraying him was almost unbearable.

'It amazes me,' Blackwell was saying, 'it just absolutely amazes me, that an outsider could get so easily into our confidential records and change them at will.'

'Don't be too amazed,' Black Stealth said as he continued to search through the computer system. 'According to an official US Directorate of Defence report, which I obtained by hacking, there are over 250,000 hacker attacks per year on the US defence establishment's computers. You think that's bad? Well, given that only one in every 150 attacks is actually detected, you can imagine what the real figures are – in the millions!'

'That's terrifying,' Blackwell said.

'It's pretty exciting,' Black Stealth responded happily, shamelessly. 'Those hackers have obtained and corrupted sensitive information, stolen and destroyed data and software, and installed unwanted files and so-called 'back doors' that get around system protection, allowing the hackers unlimited access in the future. They've shut down and crashed entire systems and networks right across the board, adversely affecting everything from weapons maintenance to finance and personnel management.'

Blackwell gave a low whistle of appreciation.

'And that's only the *routine* hackers,' Black Stealth said proudly. 'The *real* operators, guys like me, can plant all sorts of time- or logic-based programmes that can be activated at any time in the future when a specific set of instructions is run on the system. We call them "bombs". They can just hide in there, unseen, for years, then be activated at any given moment to infect, or even destroy, the entire system. Pretty neat, eh?'

'That's why you ended up in Pentonville Prison,' Cusack said. 'Too neat for your own good.'

Black Stealth grinned. 'Yeah.' His fingers were still flying over the keyboard and his eyes were glued to the screen. Files were flashing on and off there with dazzling speed.

'So what are you doing about Prince's sniffers?' Cusack asked him. 'Are you trying to block him?'

'No. The opposite. If you slam a door in your hacker's face, he'll know instantly and go away. That way you lose him until he comes back unnoticed again. So, no, that's not what I'm doing. What I'm doing, instead, is rearranging your system so that the hacker can still get in but his movements will be restricted and we can watch what he's doing as he's doing it. This gives us a chance of tracing him back to his home computer.' He hit a final key with a flourish, then straightened up in his chair to stare at Blackwell and Cusack with a big, cheesy grin on his face. '*Voilà*! I've just blocked all the doors but one, so now we can watch him.'

'How long will all this take?' Blackwell asked him.

Black Stealth shrugged and spread his hands in the air. 'That depends upon when he returns and how much stealing he does. Could take hours; could take days.'

'You're on an eight-hour day,' Blackwell said, 'but you only have two weeks.'

'That should be enough,' Black Stealth said.

Blackwell nodded to Cusack. 'You'll deal directly with Sergeant Cusack here,' he said. 'You have the number of his cellular phone. Please keep him informed.'

'Right,' Black Stealth said, then swung around in his chair and enthusiastically went back to his keyboard.

'Let's get out of here,' Blackwell said.

He led Cusack out of the busy Information Warfare Centre and headed back to his operations office, located in the same anonymous building.

'So what do you think, boss?' Cusack asked as they walked side by side though the network of the Kremlin's recently repainted corridors. The walls were a featureless, dreary lime green that had encouraged more sour jokes about the Green Slime, the SAS intelligence officers who worked in this building.

'About what?'

'About the chances of our bright young convict, Black Stealth, tracking Prince down.'

'I haven't a clue, Sergeant, but it's the last chance we've got. Time is running out for both of us. If we don't locate Prince some time during the next fortnight, you're going to be out of a job. My own situation's not much better. The pressure is on from all sides from those who want an excuse to disband the SAS as an irrelevance in the modern age. Our inability to find the mastermind behind the Whitehall Atrocity and the London Underground Massacre has been widely publicized by those whose interests it suits. Now, of course, it's also been broadcast far and wide that Prince and his British

Millennialist Society are dedicated to the destruction of the Royal Family and the overthrow of the British government. I now have frequent nightmares about turning on the morning news and learning that Buckingham Palace has just been bombed. And, God knows, Prince would do it. So, given all that as well, we're both in dangerous waters and that hacker, Black Stealth, whether criminal or not, is our only remaining hope for salvation.'

'God, this business has really changed these past few years,' Cusack said, thinking back to the more conventional war he had fought in the Gulf, though even that was considered in its time to be the first of the truly hi-tech wars. 'I mean, you listen to that kid, that so-called Black Stealth, and you feel like a Neanderthal man.'

Blackwell chuckled while nodding his agreement. 'I won't argue with that,' he said, stopping when he reached the door of his office. 'So,' he said, 'why don't you avoid home, use your room in the Spider instead, and have a good rest-up until you hear from our bright young friend?'

'Well, I . . .' Cusack was ashamed to realize that despite all that was happening, he actually wanted to go home, not only to nurse his wounds in private but also because he was desperately, pitifully hoping that Chloe still might contact him. Of course, since that e-mail from Prince, the likelihood of Chloe contacting him was minuscule; nevertheless, in his aching need and hurt, that's what he was hoping.

'*Don't* go home,' Blackwell said, as if reading Cusack's mind. 'You'll only brood about what's happened, blame yourself even more, and probably try to drink yourself to sleep, which would be the wrong thing right now. So stay here on the base, use the Spider, and try to keep off the booze. Who knows? Black Stealth might find our man for us and then you'll feel better. Until then, try to stay sane.'

'Okay, boss, I will.'

'Make sure you do,' Blackwell said as he went into his office.

Reluctantly, Cusack made his way to his room in the

Spider, fighting the urge to go to the bar for a beer or two. Managing to resist temptation, he stretched out fully clothed on his bed. He was convinced that he wouldn't be able to sleep, but in fact he did, though he awakened in the early hours of the morning, feeling worse than ever. The rest of the night was sleepless and he spent most of the subsequent day acting as a temporary DS (member of the Directing Staff), putting a bunch of new recruits through their paces on the firing range, using conventional weapons. That evening, growing impatient to hear from Black Stealth, he was convinced he wouldn't sleep and succumbed to the temptation of a couple of beers in the Sports and Social with Jack Lewis. He kept it down to two drinks, however, and when eventually he rolled into bed, he slept like a log – slept so deeply, in fact, that he was only awakened late the next morning by an urgent phone call from Black Stealth.

'I think you'd better get over here,' Black Stealth said. 'I've got some good news for you.'

Cusack was there in ten minutes. 'What's happening?' he asked as soon as he hurried into the busy Information Warfare Centre in the Kremlin and stopped at Black Stealth's workspace, his computer glowing and humming with promise.

'Well,' Black Stealth replied cheerfully, 'he's entering by the one door I've left him and I'm quietly pursuing him. The first part was easy. Knowing that he'd be using a number of routes to get into your system, I checked 'em out and found that most of the penetrations were coming through a couple of US Internet providers, one in Washington DC, the other in New York, both set up by the notorious Legion of the Apocalypse, a hacker group responsible for countless intrusions over the past ten years, with many of its members serving time for computer crimes.'

'And?' Cusack asked impatiently.

'Well, that's where the chase became . . . well, just a little bit more difficult.'

'I'm listening.'

'First, I tried following your hacker's, Prince's, activities through keyboard monitoring. That's kinda like a wiretap 'cause it records the keys that are typed when the intruder enters the system. Unfortunately, it's only effective if the system's being attacked and right now Prince isn't doing that – he's just lurking and watching.'

'So?'

'So then I tried to trace the phone calls he was making to send down his modem commands, but that was even less effective 'cause Prince has been phone-phreaking to access international phone lines at no cost and routing his calls through phone networks and Internet sites all over the world. Like, today he lands in Europe, tomorrow in the United States, the next day in Australia, the next in China – and so on. So he's leaving a pretty confusing trail that would be next to impossible to track in the time we're permitted. This guy is real clever, right?'

'Right,' Cusack said impatiently. 'So what's the *good* news?'

'The good news is that I got lucky,' Black Stealth said with a lopsided grin. 'Prince made a false move. Like, he made an attack. In an attempt to launch from here to a site in the US – the Space Surveillance Center in Colorado Springs, no less – he exposed his code names for the first time: Data Flow and Dream Maker.'

'That helped?'

'Damned right. Being in the game, I've got a number of informer friends with lots of connections and a vast fund of knowledge about the players in cyberspace. These are guys who can cruise the Internet and search for information about illegal computer security breaches and hacking. So I asked them to track those two code names and eventually one of them came up with an e-mail exchange that he'd had with someone calling himself Dream Maker – one of the two names used by your hacker. This Dream Maker revealed that he'd set up his own electronic bulletin board where messages could be placed. Obviously not thinking for one second that anyone would connect the bulletin board with the 22 SAS break-ins, he left a phone number with a code that indicated he was based right here in the UK – the code number for Wiltshire.'

Instantly recalling his car trip around Wiltshire with Chloe, his relentless, distracted driving in ever-widening circles, convinced, as he was, that Prince was somewhere in the area, Cusack felt his heart racing with excitement. At the same time, though, he also felt a whiplash of pain, recalling how Chloe had betrayed him. He still couldn't believe it.

'So what happens now?' Cusack asked.

'What happens now is that you contact our mutual friend, William Hargreaves, your venerable Commissioner for the Metropolitan Police, hopefully my get-out-of-jail card, and ask him to trace this phone number to its source.'

'And when they find it?'

'They're to do nothing except monitor all calls until they can verify that the phone is being used for phreaking, which is, of course, illegal in this country, which is why I was in Pentonville. If that phone is being used for phreaking, we've probably got the right man.'

Excited, Cusack got in touch with William Hargreaves, passed on the number and sat back to wait. The following day, Hargreaves called to confirm that the telephone number had been traced to a former flying school near Salisbury, in Wiltshire, that it was listed as the number for one Andrew Pitt, a former member of the now defunct Second Coming Movement, believed to have been resurrected as the British Millennialist Movement, headed by Laurence Grover, alias Prince, and that the phone was definitely being used for phreaking. Hargreaves could also confirm that every time a phone-phreaking had been initiated from that number, there had been a simultaneous hacker incident at 22 SAS, Stirling Lines.

'Can I take that as proof?' Cusack asked.

'Not yet,' Hargreaves replied. 'This is all circumstantial at best, so we really would like some more evidence. Have your young friend Black Stealth watch and wait for another slip-up.

Prince is obviously growing more arrogant every day, so I think he *will* make another wrong move. Just watch and wait, Cusack.'

'Okay,' Cusack said.

His patience was rewarded. Over the next three days, Dream Maker used the doorway deliberately left open by Black Stealth to systematically read Stirling Lines's e-mails and copy files to himself. Black Stealth let him do so because that single doorway was only offering unclassified material souped up to make it seem confidential and, sometimes, top secret. On the fourth day, Dream Maker captured the user name and log-on password of a contractor used by the Kremlin for the supply and maintenance of their computers and software. Then he broke into the contractor's system, using an Internet Scanning Software attack, to degrade the information held there and cause future confusion within the regiment. The following day he did the same with another company contracted to supply the regiment confidentially with radio and surveillance equipment. Meanwhile, Black Stealth, when not watching and waiting, was keeping in touch with his cyberspace informers, asking them to track the code name Data Flow.

Like Dream Maker, Data Flow was using phone-phreaking and the same illegal Internet provider, the Legion of the Apocalypse, based in New York City, to dart from one continent to another, leaving a confusing international trail while initiating Internet Scanning Software attacks against a wide variety of military and top-secret research establishments. Gradually, after many such attacks, it became clear that when Data Flow was having difficulties in obtaining illegal access, he would log on to the New York Internet provider to exchange e-mails with, and be tutored by, Dream Maker. Clearly, then, Dream Maker and Data Flow were either closely connected or, just as likely, were two professional hackers operating from the same base and always prepared to help each other out.

Finally, on the fifth day, one of Black Stealth's informers

came back to say that Data Flow, like Dream Maker, had set up his own electronic bulletin board where messages could be placed, leaving a phone number with a code indicating that he, also, was based in Wiltshire. Though the actual number was different to the one for Dream Maker, Scotland Yard soon traced it back to the same address being used by Dream Maker.

'That's your proof,' William Hargreaves said to Cusack when he had relayed this information by phone. 'The man who's been phone-phreaking and hacking into Stirling Lines and the homes of some of your QRF team, the man signing himself "Prince", is responsible for Dream Maker and Data Flow, both of which were traced back to that old flying school near Salisbury. We've just run a remote check on that location and it's presently owned by a paramilitary-style Millennialist group formally calling themselves the White Christian Brothers. Though registered as a legitimate tax-free religious organization, the White Christian Brothers has to be Prince's British Millennialist Movement. You can run with it, Cusack.'

'I will,' Cusack said.

The assault on Prince's domain could be launched at last.

# CHAPTER TWENTY-FIVE

*From: <dataflow@prince.com>*

be warned. the watchers are being watched.
did you think i was so foolish that i would not know when i was
being tracked.
you bloody fools.
i am prince and i know just what i want and i will not be denied.
you left me an open door and let me walk in and thought that by
so doing you had trapped me but such was not the case. instead
i watched you as you watched me, tracking you with a magic
cookie even as you were on my trail. of course i knew that sooner
or later you would find me and i wasn't concerned.
confrontation, that first and final conflict, is what i am after.
you are sons of satan. filth representing the antichrist. you
protect the secret machinations of the royal family and the
government, the civil servants and the secret service, the
military-industrial complex, the worldwide jewish conspiracy,
the immigration policies that are destroying our society and
turning england into a modern sodom & gomorrah, london into
babylon. you will pay for your sins.
r u sending cusack to get me.
u r wasting your time.

*he will not get me because he will not dare to touch me and here are the reasons why.*

*five computerized bombs have been placed around london, all simultaneously transmitting their own numeric patterns, with each receiving the pattern of the others. If any one of those bombs stops transmitting to the others – which it will do if anyone attempts to defuse it or if i activate it from my computer – all the bombs will go off at the same time.*

*in other words, even if you find the bombs, you will not be able to touch a single one of them without detonating all the others.*

*those bombs are my protection.*

*if you launch an assault against the british Millennialist movement, against this compound in wiltshire, against me, i will set the bombs off.*

*as you dare not touch them, even if you find them, i can give you the approximate locations for each of the five bombs: (1) the city; (2) victoria station; (3) king's cross station; (4) duke of york's barracks, king's road, chelsea (5) the mall, near buckingham palace.*

*all of them are biological/chemical bombs and the wind will disperse their poisonous gases.*

*touch one and you detonate them all so don't bother to look for them.*

*r u still coming to find me, cusack.*

*no, i don't think so.*

*i sit on the right hand of god and i have his authority.*

*i have the power.*

*yours sincerely.*

*prince*

# CHAPTER TWENTY-SIX

'We're fucked!' Trooper Stubbs exploded, his pock-marked bulldog face livid. 'He's fucked us again. That bastard has us hands down.'

'Damned right,' his best friend, Trooper Grant, said. 'He's shot his wad all over us.'

'It sure seems like it,' Trooper Wiley said from where he was sitting, almost rubbing shoulders with Sergeant Jack Lewis. 'I mean, those bombs . . . Touch one and they all go *boom*! And that's *if* we find them.'

'Which we probably won't,' Trooper Carter said, 'since he's probably spent months hiding them, under cover of darkness, in the most obscure places, though almost certainly where they'll do the most damage.'

'Right,' Corporal Chris Mapley added, less agitated than the other two, though his dark eyes were glittering intensely. 'And just think of those locations. I mean, imagine that bomb detonating in the Mall with the wind blowing in the direction of Buckingham Palace. The Royal Family snuffed by chemically poisoned air. No way can we take that risk.'

'No way,' Jack Lewis agreed.

'Not to mention the targeting of the Duke of York's Barracks,' Carter said, running his fingers through his dishevelled hair. 'That's the supreme HQ of the Special Forces Group. Wipe that out and we're *all* done.'

'Shit and piss,' Grant summarized, looking as battered as Stubbs and sitting, as usual, beside him, two good old hard-hitting East End friends. 'We're in the toilet, all right. I feel like slitting my own throat.'

The QRF team, including Cusack and Lieutenant Colonel Blackwell, had gathered together in a briefing room in the Kremlin to discuss the latest, most frightening e-mail from Prince. They were doing so by way of an informal conversation, a Chinese Parliament, in which anyone could say what he wanted, irrespective of rank. Right now, wreathed in a cloud of cigarette smoke, they were doing just that, though all of them were feeling devastated by this latest setback to their plans. Having been informed by Cusack that the assault was being launched immediately, they had psyched themselves up for it – only to be dashed down again when the e-mail from Prince had arrived on the Kremlin's computer screens. Now, faced with an apparently insoluble dilemma, they had a lot to thrash out.

'There must be some way to defuse those bombs,' Corporal Mapley said.

'Yeah,' Stubbs replied. 'Just charge in there and shoot the hell out of his computers before shooting *him*.'

'Won't work,' Jack Lewis said. 'The kind of bombs he's using, those computerized bombs, will explode if the controller's computer system is turned off without his special coded instruction being keyed in first. So shoot out that system and you're going to take out half of London, all credit to you, mates.'

'They won't forgive us for that,' Blackwell said, referring to all those in positions of authority who were presently trying to have the SAS disbanded. 'We make one mistake from here on in and this regiment's finished. What do you think, Sergeant Cusack?'

'I think you're right, boss.'

'No, I meant what do you think we can do? I mean, how do we win this one?'

Still trying, none too successfully, to recover from the shock and humiliation inflicted upon him by Chloe, Cusack had been especially keen to launch the assault, exact his revenge on Prince, and, hopefully, regain some of his lost pride. Now, however, he felt humiliated yet again by the taunts Prince had deliberately sent to him personally (*r u sending cusack to get me . . . r u still coming to find me, cusack . . .*) on an open e-mail that everyone in the Kremlin could read. Clearly, Prince was a master of cruelty and those taunts had been included in the e-mail to humiliate Cusack further in front of his comrades. In this he had certainly succeeded and now Cusack felt a terrible rage that he had to fight to control.

'We'll get the bastard, all right. There's always a way to reach these scumbags. We just need time –'

'We've run out of time,' Blackwell said bluntly. 'We've gobbled up every second of our time. I can feel people breathing down my neck, so we have to come up with *something.*'

'Right,' Bill Stubbs said. 'I mean, we've been training for weeks with these new weapons – these fan-fucking-tastic weapons – excuse my language, boss – and now we're raring to go. I say we do it, one way or the other, even *if* we have to take some large chances. What choice have we got?'

'We *can't* take large chances,' Blackwell said firmly. 'If we make a mistake, we'll be finished for good, so that's *one* chance we can't take.'

'Okay,' Cusack said. 'I know, boss, *I know*, that I'm slow to make decisions, that I'm better in the field where I don't have time to think – that's my strength, as you've often told me – but let me just chance my arm here.'

'Go ahead, chance your arm,' Blackwell said.

'Right,' Cusack responded. 'What were we going to do before that e-mail arrived?' It was a rhetorical question and everyone stared steadily at him, waiting for him to answer it. 'We were going to make a more or less conventional assault with unconventional weapons. By which I mean that we were going to move in on Prince's compound under cover of darkness, using our new weapons to silently neutralize the guards, then rush into the centre of the compound, where Prince's Portakabin is located, and take that bastard out with no holds barred. So that's what we *were* going to do. What's that e-mail changed?'

'What the e-mail told us,' Lewis said, always calm, always in control, 'is that the minute Prince knows we're attacking, he's going to punch a code name or number into his fucking keyboard and set off those bombs. So that kind of attack is definitely *out*.'

'In other words,' Cusack said, 'we somehow have to reprogram Prince's computer system, to deactivate those bombs with the proper code name or number, before he even knows we're on the premises.'

'That sounds absolutely logical in theory,' Blackwell said sardonically. 'It also sounds impossible in practice.'

'Why?' Mapley asked. 'I mean, there *must* be a way, boss.'

Blackwell shook his head, indicating that there was no way, even as he spread some papers out on his desk and studied them without enthusiasm. 'Though the police are always reluctant to break into the defended compounds of the Millennialist movements, they *have* been surveying them from the air with UAVs –'

'What's that?' Bill Stubbs interjected.

'UAVs – Unmanned Aerial Vehicles. Remarkably small, low-cost, high-return intelligence gatherers, or pilotless spy planes, often looking like weather satellites and generally not much larger, that are fitted with video cameras, transmitters and sensors that can capture close-up images of anything on the ground from as high as 65,000 feet, irrespective of weather conditions, by night or by day, and transmit those images back to base, no matter how far away that base is.'

Ben Wiley gave a low whistle of appreciation. 'Sounds good,' he said.

'They *are* good,' Blackwell said. 'Anyway, to continue . . . By using UAVs, the police have been able to survey and photograph just about every compound in the country, so once they knew where Prince's place was located, they were able to send us the relevant surveillance data that had been picked up by the UAVs that flew over it on a regular basis ever since it was established. The UAVs took literally thousands of feet of videotape and hundreds of still photos over a period of thirteen months, and from those they could build up a comprehensive picture of exactly what was in the compound, where everyone lived and worked – this was nailed right down to every single individual, including Prince himself – how the compound was guarded and what kind of defensive surveillance they have, including radar and night-vision aids.'

'Sounds like we could walk right in,' Grant said.

'That's exactly what we *can't* do,' Blackwell retorted. 'The camp is surrounded by an electrified high-wire and the perimeter is patrolled night and day by armed guards, all of whom, as we know, are religious – or Millennialist – fanatics.'

'We could knock those guards out silently with our miniature MEMS,' Chris Mapley said, referring to the regiment's new insect-sized Micro-Electro-Mechanical Systems that could be filled with explosives, chemicals or gas, and be fired silently at, or flown silently to, the target, there to be set off by remote control.

'Which leaves all of the other fanatics,' Bill Stubbs said. 'His so-called fucking disciples. They're all armed as well, I'll bet my balls, if the other Millennialist groups we've tackled are anything to go by. So no way would that place remain silent once we were inside.'

'Correct,' Jack Lewis said.

'Which gets me back to my first point,' Blackwell said. 'We now know precisely where everything – and everyone – is located in that compound, which means we also know where Prince is: in a Portakabin slap-bang in the middle of the compound, surrounded by the other Portakabins, in good view of – by which I mean well protected by – the old air traffic control tower, now being used as a watchtower with a machine-gun crew and night-vision scopes.'

'We can take them out, no trouble,' Ben Wiley said as if he wanted to prove it.

'That's not the point,' Blackwell retorted abruptly. 'The point is twofold. Number one: assuming that Prince's computer is in his Portakabin, also used as his living quarters, we haven't a hope in hell of reaching that computer before he knows that we're inside the compound perimeter. Number two: more crucially, we don't know the code name or number that will deactivate the bombs before the computer system is shut down or destroyed.'

'Not necessarily so,' Cusack said, suddenly coming up with a long shot that frightened him even as he thought about it. 'Do we still have Black Stealth on the base?'

'Yes,' Blackwell said. 'He still has his room in the Spider and is, reportedly, enjoying himself in the Sports and Social until tomorrow morning, when he'll be transported under police protection back to Pentonville Prison to await his well-earned parole.'

'Can we keep him here for another few days, boss?'

'He'll be straining at the leash,' Blackwell replied, 'but we can possibly manage it. Why do you ask?'

'Because I think we can use him again.'

Everyone glanced at everyone else, some rolling their eyes. Then they all focused once more on Cusack with considerable, if rather sceptical, interest.

'How?' Blackwell asked.

'Well, boss ...' Cusack hesitated, wondering if he was doing right or wrong. Then he decided, because he was in such pain and could no longer bear it, to go all the way with this. 'If we can get Black Stealth to Prince's computer –'

'*If*!' Stubbs interjected.

'An inmate of Pentonville Prison,' his friend Grant, added. 'We're certainly taking on some wonderful helpers these days. And this regiment used to be *hard* to get into! Now all you have to do is go to prison. I must have made a mistake somewhere.'

'Your mistake was being born,' Norman Carter retorted, 'in

the East End of London. Most computer hackers have a better background, so don't complain *too* much.'

'Ha, ha,' Grant replied.

'Smart-arse,' Stubbs added.

'Shut up, the pair of you,' Lewis said, defending his own friend, Cusack. 'Okay, Sarge, continue.'

'Well, my theory is that if we can actually *get* Black Stealth to Prince's computer – before Prince can punch his bomb-detonating code into his keyboard – Black Stealth will be able to find the code that switches the bombs off without detonating them. I'm pretty sure he could do it.'

'You're saying we take a . . .' Chris Mapley was lost for words and had to start his sentence all over again. 'You say we take a . . . a *civilian* . . . with us for this assault?'

'Yes, Corporal, that's *exactly* what I'm saying.'

'A sentenced *criminal*,' Wiley emphasized, shaking his head from side to side in disbelief.

'Certainly not a professional *soldier*,' Stubbs said. 'I mean, I don't mind going in with a hard case, but I don't want to go into a potential firefight dragging an anchor. Ships get wrecked doing that.'

'We can carry him,' Cusack said. 'The important thing is that he could probably break that code, and that's what we need.'

'We *know* Black Stealth,' Blackwell said. 'He's as sharp as a whip. But he's hardly more than a smart kid who has no interest in anything other than playing with the Internet and breaking the law with great glee. You take him in there – thank God, I won't be with you – and he's liable to bolt for it as soon as he gets the chance, leaving you with nothing to do except fight on for no gains. If that happens – if he lights out and you're left with nothing but the long chance that Prince *won't* be at his computer – well, thank you, but we can call it a day. The SAS is all over.'

'I don't think he'll run,' Cusack said. 'I don't think he's that kind. He's the kind who can't resist a challenge and he won't get a better one.'

'Please explain that,' Lewis asked. 'I surely need that explained.'

Cusack wasn't offended. In fact, he knew it was their friendship that was making Jack sound so careful. Jack Lewis would not want to see Cusack go down into something so disastrous that neither he personally nor the regiment in general would ever recover from it. Friends like that were hard to find.

'What I'm saying,' Cusack responded, 'is that a sharp kid like Black Stealth, loving a challenge, not afraid to take chances, already thrilled by the scent of danger, will want to help finish what we made him start – the tracking and neutralizing of Prince, the only hacker in Great Britain who can equal him. Let's just tell him what we're doing, tell him exactly where we're going, tell him what his task is – finding Prince's code and neutralizing his computer system – and he simply won't be able to resist it. He'll go all the way with us – *all* the way – to be able to do that. He won't hide. He won't run. So I say bring him in.'

A lengthy silence followed this apparently positive speech – though Cusack was, in fact, feeling more desperate than positive, more frightened as his idea evolved. The silence was only broken when Lieutenant Colonel Blackwell coughed uneasily into his fist and asked, 'Any more comments?'

'A sentenced criminal!' was Grant's heated comment.

'Fucking Pentonville!' Stubbs added, just as heatedly.

'As you two come from the East End,' Wiley said sardonically, 'you've probably got more criminals in your family history than I've got fucking hairs on my well-thatched head. Why the hell should that bother us?'

'Right,' Carter said. 'From what I've heard, the guy's a fucking computer wizard and right now that's just what we need. Given that – and what Sergeant Cusack's said about him – I say let's take him in.'

Another lengthy silence ensued. Cusack decided not to break it because he, too, still needed time to think, to work out what he was planning, if it was right or wrong, good or bad, if he was fooling himself or not. He needed that time to think because he had his personal interest here, his pride, his pitiful vanity, his need to know the truth about matters that were too intimate to be discussed in this smoky, crowded room. This was, of course, the danger because it concerned not only what they were doing here together – all these old friends, his comrades in previous battles, his brothers – but also the damage that his love, or his foolishness, had created in the past few weeks. He needed to know if his faith in Chloe, in their love, had indeed been betrayed or if both of them had been victims of their individual grief: two shipwrecked souls needing a rock to cling to and finding it in each other, despite their conflicting interests in the matter. Without knowing that, he would feel like a fool for the rest of his life.

Unfortunately, because of that, as he instantly realized, he was risking the lives of his men and, in the long run, also threatening the continued existence of the regiment.

Contemplating that was more than he could bear.

Though *not* taking the risk, he realized, with a sinking heart, would be infinitely worse.

'So Trooper Carter,' Lieutenant Colonel Blackwell said eventually, 'thinks that we should take Black Stealth in. Are there any dissenters?'

There was another long, uneasy silence, until Jack Lewis broke it with: 'I'm not exactly dissenting, but I *do* have reservations. I mean, even if Black Stealth *can* break Prince's code, he can only do so if he gets access to that computer before Prince realizes we're inside his compound and activates the bombs with his keyboard. And since it's a virtual certainty that Prince keeps his computer in his Portakabin – where, according to our surveillance, he also lives – I'd say that gives us a problem.'

'The problem,' Cusack said, 'is getting Black Stealth to Prince's computer before Prince can press the keys that'll detonate those bombs.'

'And that's a problem for Einstein himself,' Wiley said.

'Not necessarily,' Cusack said. 'Let's look at it this way.' He had thought it through and knew that it was, at best, a calculated risk, something based on intuition rather than logic, which meant that it could be suicidal. But such was his conviction, his need to believe, that he was willing to take the risk. Perhaps he had to risk everything to prove something to himself, to confirm what it was he needed to know. If so, he *would* risk it. *It's a matter of faith*, he thought. 'We know from the surveillance photos that Prince lives and mainly works in his Portakabin. And we can safely assume that he keeps his own computer in the same place, yes?'

'Accepted,' Blackwell said.

'So the major problem isn't getting into the compound quietly, which almost certainly we *can* do, but getting into Prince's Portakabin quickly enough to ensure that he can't get to his keyboard before we do.'

'Which means you're fucked if he's already *at* his keyboard,' Jack Lewis said.

'He could be watching TV,' Grant added.

'Or be in bed,' Stubbs said. 'Having his cock sucked by one of his disciples. *That*'d certainly give you all the time you need to get to his bleedin' keyboard before he does.'

'True,' Mapley said. 'But what if he isn't in his bed, having his cock sucked or otherwise?'

'Or not watching TV?' Wiley said.

'We have to go in,' Carter said, 'on the assumption that he *will* be at his keyboard – because if we assume otherwise and we're wrong . . . well, let's face it, we're fucked. It's as simple as that.'

'I agree,' Jack Lewis said.

'The big question, then,' Lieutenant Colonel Blackwell said, looking directly at Cusack, 'is how do we get him away from his keyboard *before* we go in?'

'Exactly,' Cusack said.

'Another problem for Einstein,' Wiley said. 'Other dimensions and so forth.'

'Not necessarily,' Cusack said, growing more tense – and

also more determined – with each passing minute. 'I think we can do it.'

'Is that wishful thinking, or a positive plan of action?' Blackwell asked.

'I have a plan,' Cusack said.

# CHAPTER TWENTY-SEVEN

Prince prepared. He knew that, despite what he had said in his e-mail, the SAS *would* come and try to get him. They would come because they couldn't afford not to at least make the attempt, because they were in a corner and had to get out, because they couldn't ignore their own motto – 'Who dares wins' – and, in particular, because Sergeant Lenny Cusack, first betrayed and now humiliated, would push the rest of them into it. They would come. And Prince wanted them to come, because he wanted to explode his bombs and then to announce publicly that he had done so because of the attack on his compound by the SAS. He wanted the destruction of the Royal Family, the downfall of the British government, a whole New Order led by himself. But most of all he wanted revenge for having been cast out of the SAS and then dishonourably discharged from the army. So Prince prepared for the coming of the SAS.

Having called a mass meeting of all the members of the compound – all, that was, except those on guard duty on the watchtower and around the perimeter – he stood in front of them, wearing his white robes, his long golden-blond hair newly washed and shining, and said, 'Greetings, my children! I have brought you here to prepare you for the event that we all knew would come sooner or later – an assault on our compound by the satanic SAS, who are determined to put an end to our community. You have, of course, been well trained for this eventuality and will be suitably armed after this meeting and given your individual instructions. Right now, I merely wish to say that you must treat those who are coming here as agents of the Antichrist, as paid assassins for the degenerate British government and a Royal Family that acts as a front for the evils of Freemasonry and the diabolical machinations of the secret Illuminati, both of which, as we know, are behind the worldwide conspiracy to hand financial power over to the Jews and turn white Christians into second-class citizens in their own countries.'

Prince paused for dramatic effect, gazing down from his raised platform on all those upturned faces, those *young* faces, raised from the dust of dissolution, swept clean by brain-washing, eyes wide and jaws slack with the awe that they held him in, some smiling beatifically, others with their hair dyed golden-blond like his, wanting to be just like him, a twin or a clone. In truth, they could no longer think for themselves because their reprogramming had made them dependent upon him, dedicated to his cause, no matter what it might be, deeply fearful of all outsiders and suspicious of any system of beliefs not shared by the community. There was nothing that they would not do for him. And now he could test them.

'The men who are coming here,' he continued, 'will engage in an all-out fight and show no mercy to anyone. In the words of Isaiah: *Their feet run to evil, and they make haste to shed innocent blood.* Their aim is not only the death of your leader, myself, but the death of anyone who resists them and, ultimately, the annihilation of this whole compound and the loving community it harbours. I would urge you, therefore, to show no mercy to them, to fight them with all your might, to refuse to surrender even at the point of death and, if necessary, to kill yourselves rather than be taken captive. For, indeed, if you *do* surrender or are taken captive, you will undoubtedly be submitted to their so-called debriefing, which is actually brainwashing designed to erase your most deeply held beliefs – the white Christian beliefs of this community – and replace them with the vile and blasphemous teachings of the Antichrist. You will then become one of them and, turning away from the true God, sell your soul to the devil. *How art thou fallen from heaven, O Lucifer, son of the morning!*'

There was one face in his congregation that stood out from the others, being neither wide-eyed nor slack-jawed with awe, but, rather, gravely interested and slightly frightened. It was, of course, Chloe's face. Prince studied it with interest, aware that she had never been quite the same since returning from her sojourn in Hereford, since the abrupt termination of her affair with Cusack. He, Prince, having gauged her state of confusion after that trip, had managed to turn her around, to fill her with fear again – fear of anything outside the community – and to confirm her total dependency upon him and his organization. But he sensed that something had shifted in her thinking and that she hadn't fully come back to him. The fear that he saw in her face now was of a different kind altogether – it was fear of the forthcoming attack and, most likely, the fear of having a personal confrontation with Cusack during the conflict. He would therefore have a private session with her once this meeting had ended.

'Thus,' he concluded, 'I can only reiterate that there must be no surrender on our part, no submission to captivity, but, rather, a fight to the bitter end, even if that end also means your own. Yet victory *will* be ours because God is on our side, our strength is in our faith, and they have only satanic forces to guide them. Bear this in mind, my children: *The devil is come down unto you, having great wrath, because he knoweth that he hath but a short time.* Yes! A *short* time! Not eternity as we will have it. We will win because we are fighting a righteous war and they are no more than the legionnaires of filth, the disciples of Satan. So I say to you one last time: *No surrender*! God will be with you even in death – and no white Christian can ask for more.'

Prince lowered his head and muttered to himself, as if

offering a prayer. Then, when he had finished, he raised his head again and nodded emphatically. 'That is all I have to tell you, my children, except to add that I bless you. Now, please proceed to the armoury to collect your weapons and to be told what positions you will defend when the battle commences. And while you wait, bear these immortal words in mind: *Be sober, be vigilant; because your adversary the devil, as a roaring lion, walketh about, seeking whom he may devour.* Do not let the devil, the SAS, devour *you.* God go with you, my children.'

He jumped down from the platform, white robes whipping out behind him, and hurriedly made his way through the congregation, deliberately looking straight ahead and ignoring the hands that reached out to touch him. While his reverential disciples were still rising from their seats, flushed and tearful with emotion, he left the building, a converted Nissen hut, and then stood by the door, like a minister outside his church, to shake hands and embrace them one by one as they followed him out. When Chloe emerged, her gaze wide and fearful, Prince embraced her as well, but whispered in her ear, 'Go straight to my place,' before letting her go. She stepped back, now looking confused as well as fearful. Then she nodded and turned away to cross the old airstrip and walk on to his Portakabin, disappearing around one of the Nissen huts along the runway.

Satisfied, Prince continued to greet the others coming out. Eventually, when the last of them had left, he too made his way to his Portakabin, accompanied by his two fanatically devoted guards, Dennis Welsh and Clive Jones. Armed with Heckler & Koch MP5 sub-machine guns and with 9mm Glock-19 handguns holstered on the hip, they escorted Prince all the way to the steps of his Portakabin and took up positions on both sides of the steps as he went inside. Prince felt well protected.

Chloe was waiting inside, in the living room of the Portakabin, standing by one of the two black leather settees that framed a low, glass-topped coffee table. She was wearing the standard-issue jungle-green overalls that everyone in the community wore, but they were tight enough to show off her fine figure. When Prince entered, she nervously stroked her pinned-up auburn hair and her big brown eyes widened.

'Sit down, Chloe,' Prince said. 'Please. I didn't expect you to stand at attention while you were waiting for me.'

'I just felt like standing,' she said. 'No special reason.'

Prince nodded, smiling, thinking of the banality of her response, then sank languidly on to one of the settees. 'How do you feel, Chloe?'

'Okay,' she said.

'You still seem a little . . . unsettled . . . since returning from Hereford.'

'I'm okay,' she insisted.

'I hope so,' Prince said. 'I mean, I hope you're not secretly thinking fond thoughts of that man who's coming here to try to kill me.'

'No, I'm not.'

'Certainly not while you've been in my bed, I hope.'

'Not then. Not at all, Prince.'

*Liar,* Prince thought. *You've been thinking about Cusack every time you've come to my bed since returning from Hereford. You've been trying not to. I could sense that when we were fucking. But I could also sense that something else had shifted within you and subtly removed you from me. You're still mine, but now you harbour doubts.*

'Besides,' Chloe continued, 'you don't really know that he's coming here to kill you. You don't know that he's coming at all. From what you told me the other day, you've fixed those bombs to ensure that he can't touch you. Why, then, should he come?'

'Because he wants me so badly,' Prince said, 'that he'll convince himself he can pull it off somehow. Formerly unacceptable risks will become acceptable and that's always a bad mistake. He'll come to get me because he's now a driven man and you can't stop that kind. We *will* stop him, of course, when he gets here, but he's not to know that because the man is obsessed.'

'Why's he obsessed?' Chloe asked him.

'It's nothing you'd want to know about,' Prince replied. 'There are things about Cusack you don't know and don't need to know. Just believe me when I say that he's obsessed. Just leave it at that.'

'Why don't I need to know?' Chloe said. 'That makes the things I don't know about sound like bad things.'

'Think what you will,' Prince replied, fully aware that he had further confused her and planted a seed of doubt in her mind about Cusack. Yes, she would think the SAS man's unknown past held something so bad that he, Prince, was loath to reveal it to her. Now, whilst she doubted Prince, she would also doubt Cusack, wondering what his unknown sins were, what vices he had managed to hide from her. The poor girl was torn in two.

'You look frightened,' he said.

'Yes,' Chloe admitted, 'I am.'

'What frightens you, Chloe? Please tell me. Is it the thought of the coming fight with the SAS? The possibility of dying?'

'Yes, Prince, that's it.'

Prince nodded and smiled. 'That's understandable, my dear. We all fear death, if we're honest about it. But you've been trained to use a weapon and will be given one just like all the others. When the time comes, will you use it?'

'I'm not sure,' Chloe confessed. 'I'll try to, but I can't be certain. I've never fired a weapon at a man before and I don't know that I can.'

'If someone aims a weapon at you and you don't fire first, the weapon aimed at you will kill you, Chloe. So you'd better fire first.'

'They might not want to kill us. I might be asked to surrender.'

'They'll either kill you with a bullet – and that's what they're trained to do – or they'll take you prisoner and throw you into prison for a very long time. You know what prison's like, Chloe? Even a women's prison? It becomes your little portion of hell on earth, turning you into everyone's victim in more ways than one. Perverted sex, Chloe. Slow torture by the perverted. The screams of the demented at night and wardens with foul traits all around the clock. You'll die in there, Chloe, you'll waste away like a cancer victim, lose your mind and become a pitiful creature, prey for all comers. You're not the type for prison, Chloe, not strong enough for it. You won't be able to withstand the brutality, the sadism, the daily threats, and you'll find yourself wishing that you'd been killed by an SAS bullet. So if anyone asks you to surrender, Chloe, shoot yourself instead. Believe me, it's the best way.'

Chloe still looked frightened, but she also seemed doubtful, as if she couldn't fully accept what he was saying; as if she wondered why he was saying it. He knew exactly why he was saying it: to make her more frightened of surrender than of death; to make her fight to the bitter end. Right now, she was glancing distractedly about the room, her brown eyes filled with confusion. She did, however, eventually, boldly, return her gaze to him.

'Why didn't you say that to the others?' she asked him.

'Say *what* to the others?'

'All that stuff about prison.'

'The others have more faith than you, Chloe, and will do what they have to do because of that faith. Thus, I merely had to remind them of what they'll be up against – Freemasonry, the Illuminati, satanic forces – to make them see the light. They'd rather die for their beliefs than surrender, but you're not the same breed.'

'So what kind of breed am I?'

'The doubting kind, Chloe. The kind that doubt even themselves. The kind that lean heavily towards self-destruction if they're not wisely led. Confusion comes naturally to you; it's the source of your indecision. At base, you're more material than spiritual; thus you need different reference points. What could I say to the others, Chloe, that wasn't within their frame of reference? God and the devil, the SAS as Satanists, the threat of losing their minds by brainwashing, thus losing their souls. They can relate to all that, Chloe.'

'And me?'

'You need only the truth, Chloe. The bitter truth of reality. To know that we're viewed as criminals by those coming to destroy us and that if you surrender rather than die, they will throw you in prison. I gave the others what they needed to endure what is coming – and what they needed was the belief that they would gain more by dying than they would if they surrendered and lived: redemption and resurrection in heaven. You don't believe in that, Chloe. You've tried to, but you can't accept it. You do, however, because of your past experience, believe in hell right here on earth. For you, that would be prison, which is why I raised the subject. Believe me, Chloe, if you surrender to the SAS – if they don't shoot you first – you will end up in prison . . . and for a very long time, too. Think about this, my dear, when the SAS launch their assault, when the battle commences. The choice is between a quick, merciful death or years of hell on earth in a state prison. It's your choice and only you can make it.'

'I'm not sure I can do that,' Chloe said. 'It's too hard a choice for me.'

'You'll make it instinctively,' Prince said, confident that he had turned her in his direction. 'When the time comes, you won't have time to think about it, but you'll certainly choose.'

Chloe sighed. 'I guess so.' She glanced at him and just as quickly looked away, surveying the darkening room, which was luxurious by the standards of the others in the community, though even that was relative. 'So what now?' she asked eventually, reluctantly.

'Now you go to the armoury and collect your weapons – a sub-machine gun and a pistol – and return to your own room. Just try to behave as normally as possible until the attack comes.'

'When do you think it'll happen?' she asked.

Prince shrugged. 'Tonight. Tomorrow. Who knows? It will, however, be soon, because their time has run out.'

'Right.' Chloe sighed again – a sigh of despair. 'Okay, I'm

off.'

Prince stood up and took her by the shoulders to shake her gently. Then he kissed her on both cheeks.

'God go with you,' he said.

Chloe opened her mouth to retort, then shut it again. She smiled, took a deep breath, let it out slowly, then shook her head in resignation and walked to the door. The door opened, slammed shut and she was gone.

Prince smiled. 'She's all mine.'

Wanting to give her time to get away, he entered his study and checked his computer screen, which was located, conveniently, near his hi-tech surveillance systems that included CCTV. In this instance, however, his only interest was in checking the file that controlled the bombs that had been carefully planted under cover of darkness in five different locations in London. Satisfied that all was in order, he left the Portakabin and found his two personal bodyguards still keeping watch outside.

'I want to run a final check on our defences,' he told them. 'We'll start at the armoury.'

Both men nodded, neither saying a word, and fell in, one on either side of him, as he made his way from the Portakabin, across the airstrip, to the old corrugated-iron hangars and Nissen huts that had been turned into stores for food supplies, clothing, bedding, weapons, ammunition and explosives. The young man in charge of the armoury confirmed that every individual on the base had been allocated personal weapons and a specific defensive position to be taken up the instant the alarm was raised in the event of an SAS QRF attack.

Leaving the armoury, Prince walked a circuit of the whole perimeter, checking that the guards, all wearing their jungle-green overalls, were in position and that the Claymore mines, buried in a twelve-foot-wide area that ran like a deadly ribbon right around the perimeter, inwards from the fence (so placed as to explode when anyone broke through the fence and entered the compound), were properly covered and already primed to be remotely exploded. This was confirmed in every case.

'Isn't it wonderful what one can do in the new Britain?' Prince asked rhetorically, smiling benignly at his two handsome, blond-haired, stone-faced bodyguards. 'Why, we're just like America now!'

Both men smiled in response, though neither said a word. Prince, understanding that they were in awe of him, therefore understandably frightened of saying the wrong thing to him, led them away from the last guard post they'd visited, along the side of the old, now overgrown airstrip, until they reached the line of sangars (improvised circular walls of rock, in this case all manned by fanatically religious machine-gun crews) that formed a protective wall between the living accommodations, including Prince's Portakabin, and the perimeter fence running along the road that eventually led into the compound. The machine-gun crews were alert, their weapons cleaned and oiled, and so Prince, being satisfied, moved on.

'God be with you!' he called out to each sangar team as he moved on to the next.

'And with you, Prince!' they called back.

He checked the former air traffic control tower, which was now a watchtower manned by another machine-gun crew equipped with binoculars, night-vision aids and American Magnavox AN/PRC-68B transmitter/receivers that enabled them to communicate directly with Prince or any of his lieutenants. Standing at the base of the high building, he spoke to the head of the machine-gun crew through his own transmitter and received a quick, alert response. 'God be with you,' he said to the commander.

'And with you, Prince,' the commander replied through his transmitter/receiver.

Satisfied, Prince moved on again.

He checked everything – the booby-trapped motor pool, the booby-trapped canteen, the booby-trapped latrines, the wide variety of supply huts, all booby-trapped as well. Then he entered the various living accommodations to ensure that his disciples, including his hopeful twins and clones, the lost children of the Millennium, cooped together, ten to a Portakabin dormitory, all had their weapons close to hand and were willing to use them.

No problems on any count.

Finally, he entered the Portakabin – an unusually small one, rather like a bungalow – where Chloe, being one of his mistresses, known as a 'server', now lived alone to enable her to respond to his many phone calls, or, to be more precise, to visit him the instant he called for her to do so. Chloe was there all right, sitting in front of her TV set, watching an idiotic quiz show, but with a Browning 9mm High Power handgun holstered on her hip and a Heckler & Koch MP5 sub-machine gun leaning against her chair, ready to be grabbed when the time came. Prince studied her in silence, then smiled and left the Portakabin without saying another word.

Even Chloe might make it.

Still protected by his two blond-haired bodyguards, Prince returned to his own much grander Portakabin, left the bodyguards outside and entered to freshen up with a shower and energize himself with a light meal. Duly refreshed and invigorated, naked under a white towelling dressing gown, he thought of the conflict to come – a religious conflict, a *spiritual* conflict, the final battle between good and evil – and decided to relax as best he could before all hell broke loose.

Feeling in a religious mood, this being a religious war, Prince phoned his chief administrator, Lorna Peterson, and asked her to come and see him. Then he placed a personally edited cassette tape in his state-of-the-art Panasonic music centre. It was, in fact, a selection of the shorter tracks from a wide variety of great sacred music: Charpentier's *Te Deum Laudamus*, Vivaldi's *Domine Deus*, *Agnus Dei*, Handel's *Dettinger Te Deum*, Bach's *Matthäus-Passion*, Mozart's *Missa brevis, K.275*, Beethoven's *Missa Solemnis*, Cherubini's *Requiem*, Brahms' *Ein Deutsches Requiem* and so forth. It was therefore no accident that approximately twenty minutes later his cock was being sucked by the blonde, glacially beautiful

Lorna Peterson as he sat in his chair, legs helpfully wide apart, in front of his hi-tech surveillance systems, his CCTV, which covered the whole compound, and his upgraded Dell 310 computer system, double-checking the numeric patterns of his five precisely placed, absolutely deadly biochemical bombs while listening reverentially to Schubert's exquisite *Mass, D.452, Benedictus 1*.

Like Jesus Christ, he was prepared for anything.

# CHAPTER TWENTY-EIGHT

Cusack knew about the Claymore mines laid around the inner perimeter of Prince's compound. He knew about the watch-tower near the old runway, manned by a crew with a 5.54mm RPK-74 light machine-gun and night-vision aids. He knew about the sangars located between the compound's main entrance road and the Portakabins being used as living accommodation; and that those sangars were also manned by machine-gun crews. He knew about the people living in those accommodations, all Millennialist fanatics, and knew that most of them would be armed in preparation for an attack. He knew that Chloe had been moved from a large Portakabin used as an eight-person dormitory to a smaller one that she lived in alone, except when spending time in Prince's Portakabin. Cusack knew exactly where Prince's Portakabin was and had often watched, on the close-up infra-red videotapes taken by the UAVs, Chloe making her way from her own place to Prince's, invariably under cover of darkness, no doubt to be fucked by him.

Cusack also knew, despite his emotional pain, that his main task was somehow to get into Prince's Portakabin and get Black Stealth to Prince's keyboard before Prince could activate his bombs.

Cusack knew just how dangerous this mission was, how potentially catastrophic, because he knew what would happen if he failed and Prince activated his bombs: deadly biological and chemical poisons would be released in the Mall and would spread out to encompass Buckingham Palace and contaminate all those inside the building. Released in Victoria and King's Cross Stations, they would spread through the whole Underground system and kill or seriously harm thousands of innocent commuters. Released somewhere in the City they would kill or harm hundreds, possibly thousands more and bring the financial world to a standstill. And released in the King's Road, Chelsea, they would contaminate the HQ of the Special Forces Group, which included the offices of the Commander of the SAS, then spread out in all directions through the surrounding neighbourhood, eventually turning it into a dead zone. That, Cusack knew, was exactly what would happen if he failed with this particular mission.

He simply couldn't afford to fail.

While the members of the QRF team returned to their private wing in the Spider to prepare themselves for the mission, Cusack and Lieutenant Colonel Blackwell waited in the latter's office for the arrival of the 20-year-old former Pentonville prisoner, Jake 'Black Stealth' Bailey. When Black Stealth eventually arrived, wearing a blue denim shirt and trousers, a black windcheater jacket and black shoes, he was escorted in by two burly Regular Army MPs and had his wrists in handcuffs in preparation for his trip back to Pentonville, prior to receiving an early parole as thanks for what he had done here at Stirling Lines. At a nod from Blackwell, one of the MPs loosened the handcuffs to allow a delighted Black Stealth to grin broadly and rub his chafed wrists.

'Boy,' he said as the two MPs left the office, closing the door behind them, 'that sure feels a lot better. I *hate* wearing those damned things. So what's up, guys? Am I being released already? What's going on?'

'We want you to do another job for us,' Blackwell said.

Black Stealth raised his fine eyebrows in enquiry, glancing first at Cusack, then at Blackwell. '*What*?'

'You heard me. Another job.'

'Excuse me, but I thought we had a deal. At least, *I* had a deal with Commissioner Hargreaves and the deal was that I get my parole if I pulled off that one job. Which I did. Did I not?'

'Yes, you did,' Lieutenant Colonel Blackwell agreed, 'and we're truly grateful.'

'So I get my parole?'

'Yes,' Blackwell said. 'I don't think our present Commissioner's the kind of man to go back on his word.'

'That's it, guys,' Black Stealth said, 'I'm out of here. I've got nothing to gain by doing another job and I don't work for free.'

'We can't *force* you to do this job,' Cusack said, 'and we're not going to try, but we think it's a job that you might like.'

'Come again?'

'A job that you might find irresistible.'

Black Stealth's cocky grin widened as he glanced from Cusack to his CO, then back to Cusack again, mock disbelief on his sharp, amoral, youthful face. 'You've got to be kidding me,' he said. 'The only job that *I*'d find irresistible is the one that gives me irresistible profit, and you guys can't provide that. I mean, what are you offering? I've already got my fucking parole lined up, so what *else* can you give me?'

'We can't give you anything,' Blackwell said. 'In fact, we can't even take you on board officially. If you do the job, you'll get no credit for it. No credit. No payment. There's not a thing we can offer you.'

'Except –' Cusack began.

'What?' Black Stealth interjected.

'A real challenge,' Cusack said, completing his sentence. 'An *unusual* challenge.'

Black Stealth stared steadily, enquiringly at him, just the hint of a grin on his face. Then he said, '*Unusual*?'

Cusack nodded. 'That job you did for us? That other

hacker, Prince, that you tracked down for us?'

'Yeah? What about him?'

'He's the best damned hacker in the business,' Cusack said.

'No, he's not,' Black Stealth retorted instantly. '*I* am.'

'You think so?'

'I *know* so.'

Cusack shrugged. 'Well, let me put it another way. You may be the best hacker in the business, but Prince uses his lesser skills for numbers you just can't believe. His latest one is out of this world.'

'You're just trying to wind me up,' Black Stealth said. 'You're just trying to draw me in.'

'Well, I won't deny that,' Cusack said, knowing that he'd intrigued Black Stealth already. 'But do you want to hear just what that bastard is up to?'

'Yeah,' Black Stealth said. 'Why not? Do you mind if I pull up a chair?'

'Not at all,' Blackwell said, pointing to the free chair at the other side of his desk. Cusack was sitting right beside him, both of them behind the desk. When Black Stealth pulled the chair back and sat in it, Cusack told him in precise, clear detail about Prince's five computer-controlled bombs. When Cusack had finished talking, Black Stealth gave a low whistle of admiration.

'Oh, boy!' he exclaimed softly. 'You're right. That's some number he's pulling. Jesus Christ, just imagine it!'

'He could virtually wipe out London,' Cusack said.

'Damned right he could,' Black Stealth responded, his eyes bright with excitement – or envy. He leaned back, raised his arms above his head, clasped both hands together and stretched himself without getting out of the chair. Then he lowered his arms again. 'So you guys want me to break through his security systems, then find the file for those bombs and deactivate them?'

'Right,' Blackwell said.

'Can you do it?' Cusack asked.

'Can you shit?' Black Stealth rejoindered. 'Of *course* I can do it. There isn't a fucking system I can't hack into – not even Prince's. The question is, how do we get to it? And that's the *big* question, right?'

'Right,' Blackwell said.

'You're looking a little bit nervous there, Colonel. Just what the hell *is* this job – apart from what you've just told me? I mean, why are you nervous? Is there more to this little offer than meets the eye?'

Cusack gave him the details of Prince's well-defended compound and his plan for the assault. He summarized matters with: 'So the toughest job – the part where we have to be most careful – is somehow getting you to Prince's keyboard before he uses it himself. *That*'s the job, Mr Bailey.'

'Black Stealth,' Bailey corrected him.

'Sorry,' Cusack sighed. 'Black Stealth.'

Black Stealth stared steadily at him, with mounting incredulity, for what seemed like a long time, though in actual fact it only lasted a few seconds. Eventually, raising his eyebrows in histrionic mockery, he said, 'This time you've *got* to be fucking kidding me! Are you *really* trying to tell me that you expect me to go along with an SAS patrol, take part in an assault against a defended compound filled with fanatical armed Millennialists, and risk my balls in a firefight just to get to that lunatic's computer and hack into his system? Do you *really* think I'd do that?'

'It's a challenge,' Cusack repeated quietly, insistently. 'An *unusual* challenge. A *rare* kind of challenge. The kind that only comes once in a lifetime.'

'Fuck that,' Black Stealth retorted. 'You guys are asking me to risk my fucking life for no fucking return – no money, no credit for doing it. So why the hell *should* I do it?'

'Maybe to save the whole of London?' Cusack suggested. 'Because London, believe me, will be wiped off the map, will become a dead zone, not fit to live in, if Prince detonates his biochemical bombs. The whole city of London will be contaminated, almost certainly for years to come. London, with air not fit to breathe, will become a ghost town . . . But you, Black Stealth, could single-handedly prevent that.'

'Yeah, I could,' Black Stealth said, his eyes brightening at the thought, 'but since you guys can't use me officially, since I'd be an invisible man, I'd get no credit for it. So why the hell should I do it?'

Realizing what Black Stealth was about – pure rampant ego – Lieutenant Colonel Blackwell cleverly interjected: 'You wouldn't get *official* credit for it, that's true, but no way can this assault be kept secret, so the Internet is bound to pick up on it and spread the whole story worldwide. You'd get credit, all right. The best kind of credit that a hacker as renowned as you can get: credit on the Net. You'd be a hero of the Net for years to come. You'd be talked about endlessly. Think about it, Black Stealth.'

The young man thought about it, taking his time. He stretched himself again, flexed his fingers, yawned and sighed, studied the ceiling at great length and then offered a broad, cocky grin. 'Okay,' he said finally, condescendingly, 'I'm in. I mean, how can I resist it? Do I get to wear a uniform and put on camouflage make-up?'

'Yes,' Blackwell said.

'Do I get a weapon?'

'Can you handle one?'

'No.'

'Then you don't get a weapon.'

'Okay. When do we start?'

'Right now,' Cusack said, pushing his chair back and standing up to walk around the desk.

'Right *now*?'

'Yes, right now. Come with me, please.'

He led the visibly excited Black Stealth out of Blackwell's office, along a few anonymous corridors in the Kremlin – safe enough from prying eyes because every door was closed – then out of the building. Darkness was falling and the lights of Stirling Lines were coming on, one after the other, to illuminate the Nissen huts and brick buildings. Military trucks and jeeps were heading this way and that, their headlights beaming into the dark; and SAS troopers were visible everywhere, walking to and fro, many carrying weapons, most standing down for the day. Cusack led Black Stealth away from the Kremlin, walking slightly ahead of him.

'Where are we going?' Black Stealth asked.

'To the Spider.'

'The *what*?'

'The Spider. That's SAS slang for our sleeping quarters. The central section of the barracks, the accommodation, has eight dormitory wings running off it – like the legs of a spider. When the number of men in the regiment was greatly reduced last year, because of budgetary restrictions, the Quick Reaction Force was given their own wing and that's where we're going.'

'I'm going in with the QRF?' Black Stealth asked, looking amazed.

'That's right,' Cusack said.

'Oh, boy!' Black Stealth exclaimed, not trying to hide how thrilled he was. 'Just wait till *this* gets out on the Net. I'll be a fucking hero, all right.'

'If you survive,' Cusack said bluntly. 'Okay, we go in here.'

Entering the enormous barracks building, he led Black Stealth through another series of anonymous corridors, passing other SAS troopers, many almost naked, with towels slung around their necks and ablution bags in their fists, until they reached the central section, where the eight dormitory wings stretched out in all directions – like the legs of a spider, indeed. They entered one of those wings and came within seconds to a dormitory where six men were either wriggling into black CT suits, painting their faces with night camouflage, checking their weapons or packing their bergen rucksacks. Everyone was busy and the beds were cluttered with weapons and kit.

'The QRF team,' Cusack informed his young friend, then he raised his voice to address the men in the room. 'Your attention, please, gentlemen,' he said. 'I'd like to introduce you to a new, temporary member of our team – the young man I told you about – Jake Bailey, beter known as Black Stealth, which is how he prefers to be addressed.' There were some reluctant mumbled greetings, a few silently nodding heads, but before anyone could come out with a mouthful of bullshit, Cusack introduced Black Stealth to the members of the team, beginning with Sergeant Jack Lewis, continuing with Corporal Mapley, and finishing with Troopers Carter, Wiley, Stubbs and Grant.

'Hi!' Black Stealth said when Cusack had completed his introductions. 'Great to meet you all. I mean, I've read a lot about you guys on the Internet and I have to say, not bullshitting or anything, that you're really something. I'm thrilled to be joining you.'

They all stared at him in frozen silence, as if he was crazy. The silence was finally broken by Stubbs, who turned to Cusack and said, with his customary bluntness, 'So who has to look after him?'

'I do,' Cusack said.

'I can look after myself,' Black Stealth said, affronted.

'Not on this assault, you fucking can't,' Grant retorted. 'We'll have enough shit raining down upon us without having a . . . a *civilian* to look after.'

Cusack turned to the outraged Black Stealth before he could retort in kind and perhaps cause a riot. '*I* look after you,' he stressed. 'You stick close to me. You won't have a weapon, so you can't defend yourself: your priority is to get into Prince's command centre and disarm those bombs. Right now I have a plan, but it's a dangerously flexible plan, so nothing can be anticipated and we're going to have to play a lot of this by ear. So, like I said, you stick close to me. Don't let me out of your sight. It's my job to protect you until we both get into Prince's lair and to keep protecting you while you're disarming those bombs. Nothing matters except getting to that computer. When we get you there, you can use your specialist skills. Until then, you do nothing except let us use *our* specialist skills to keep you in one piece.'

Black Stealth shrugged. 'Anything you say, boss. That's what your men call you, isn't it?'

'Right,' Cusack said. 'Now let's get you fixed up.' The rest of the QRF team had already gone back to their preparations when Cusack walked Black Stealth to a bed at the far side of the main group, where two sets of kit had already been laid out for them. 'That's yours,' Cusack said, pointing to the kit on the left. 'We got your measurements from your Pentonville records, so they should fit perfectly.'

'What the fuck is it?' Black Stealth said, lifting up various items in the kit and studying them with a puzzled look on his face.

'It's a CT – counter-terrorist – outfit, including a GT Specialist Supplies suit, made from Nomex, which gives high body protection, with flame-barrier asbestos at the knees and elbows, to enable you to crawl over sharp objects or the hot surfaces of a burning building. The respirator mask is integral and is left dangling loose at the back of your neck; you only have to put it on if someone releases CS gas or uses a biological or chemical weapon. The gloves are fire gloves, which protect the hands and wrists while not impeding the use of weapons or other pieces of equipment. So that's what you're putting on.'

'Jesus, man, you make it sound like we're marching into hell. So what's *this* fucking number?' Black Stealth was holding up what looked like a bulky, thickly padded, sleeveless vest.

'A Dowty Armourshield GPV – General-Purpose Vest – incorporating lightweight Kevlar body armour, a trauma shield that can prevent serious injury from what would otherwise be a fatal bullet strike, and hard armour made from ceramic contoured plates, with a fragmentation vest and groin panel. It all looks heavy, but it's surprisingly light. Now please put everything on exactly as I do. If you have problems I'll help you.'

When both of them had wriggled into and zipped up their GPV outfits, which took a considerable time since Black Stealth hardly knew where to begin, they put on thick socks and Danner boots made from full-grain leather and cordura nylon, with Gore-Tex lining.

'I feel like Flash fucking Gordon,' Black Stealth said with undisguised pleasure.

'He travelled lighter,' Cusack retorted. 'Now let's camouflage you.'

He applied night camouflage, first to Black Stealth's face and hands, then to his own, using a cosmetic camouflage – 'cam' cream – that broke up the shape and outline of the features, then painting their foreheads, noses, cheekbones and chins – the so-called 'highlighted' areas of the face – with black stick camouflage.

'Now I feel like Geronimo,' Black Stealth said, studying his bizarrely striped face in a mirror.

'Why not? It's warpaint.'

Once fully dressed and camouflaged, Cusack started sorting out and checking his weapons and ammunition. His choice of conventional weapons included the standard MP5 sub-machine gun and Browning 9mm High Power handgun, the latter holstered at the hip. His unconventional weapons included two different Micro-Electro-Mechanical Systems (MEMS), one filled with normal explosive, the other with a gas that would render its victims unconscious for three or four hours without actually harming them. Both MEMS looked like, and were no larger than, ordinary bullets and could be fired from silenced conventional weapons. The MEMS were placed in small metal containers, then packed carefully into Cusack's bergen, along with his conventional hand grenades and spare ammunition. As this was an assault, not a patrol, no food was packed, though the bergen also contained a personal medical kit. Cusack attached his VHF/UHF Landmaster hand-held transceiver to his belt and he was all set to go.

'That's a walkie-talkie?' Black Stealth asked him.

'A bit more advanced than that,' Cusack said, 'but it serves the same purpose. Now, see that sergeant over there?' he added, pointing to Jack Lewis.

'Yeah.'

'He's my 2IC, my second-in-command, so if you happen to lose track of me – and I hope you don't – take your orders from him.'

'Right,' Black Stealth said.

'From now on, you stick to me like glue. Okay?'

'Okay,' Black Stealth said.

Cusack approached the rest of the men, with Black Stealth in tow. By now all of them were in their GPV and CT outfits, had camouflaged their faces and hands, and had humped their packed bergens on to their backs, with remarkably small computers attached to the bergens. All of them were carrying a variety of conventional weapons, mostly sub-machine guns and pistols, but they also had weird-looking helmets on their heads and miniature keyboards strapped to their forearms. Jack Lewis handed Cusack a similar helmet and keyboard.

'Your Head-Up Display control panel,' he said. 'And this,' he added, holding up a minicomputer of the kind that was strapped to the bergens of the other men, 'is the computer that controls them. We've trained and retrained with these items, pal, and now it's time to start using them. I never thought I'd see the day.'

Cusack strapped the miniature keyboard to his left fore-arm, then checked the helmet. One of the extraordinary new products of microtechnology, it incorporated a tiny laser sight/range finder/video camera and a VDU that were attached to the minicomputer. By pressing one of the buttons on his miniature keyboard, he could command a miniature UAV (Unmanned Aerial Vehicle), no larger than a bullet, to fly in any direction over the target area, at any altitude, including at almost ground level, and relay pictures of the scene back to the VDU in the Head-Up Display in his helmet. In short, without even moving from his position, even in the dead of night, he could view his distant, and now only hypothetically unseen, enemy.

'Very nice,' he said, putting on the helmet and adjusting it until it was comfortable.

'Turn your back to me,' Jack Lewis said, 'and I'll put this item on you.'

'Thanks.' Cusack turned around to let Lewis strap the computer to his bergen. When Lewis had done so and also plugged Cusack's helmet into the computer, Cusack turned back to face the others.

'All set, are we?' he asked.

'*I*'m all set,' Trooper Stubbs said, as pugnacious as ever. 'But I've got to admit that I don't feel comfortable with all this new shit. I mean, it's not *natural* soldiering, is it? I mean, it's not what we're used to.'

'You've had weeks to get used to it,' Cusack said, 'and now's your chance to try using it.'

'I'd rather use my MP5,' Corporal Ben Wiley said. 'That's what *I*'m used to.'

'Unfortunately for you,' Cusack said, 'the world moves on and we've got to move with it.'

'I like it,' Corporal Mapley said. 'I think it's bloody marvellous. The most exciting gear we've used in years. It's a real change at last. We're coming into the modern age.'

'I was born in the East End of London,' Trooper Grant said, 'and I prefer the old days. I *don't like* the modern age.'

'You're *frightened* of the modern age,' Trooper Carter told him, 'because anything hi-tech makes you shit bricks. I'm with Corporal Mapley on this one: I think this stuff is terrific and I can't wait to use it.'

'Any more valuable comments,' Cusack said, 'or can we move out now?'

'Let's move out,' Jack Lewis said.

They left shortly after that, making their way out of the Spider at 2100 hours, all bent under their packed bergens, humping their weapons and other kit and then marching through the lamplit twilight of the base to the motor pool. They did not take a troop truck, selecting instead an unmarked transit van that was just about big enough to hold them and their mass of equipment. The van came with a driver, Trooper Les Harper, and he drove them out of the main gates, then took the A49 to Gloucester. No one spoke in the back of the van. No one traded the traditional bullshit. They just sat there, hemmed in by weapons and equipment, each man with his own thoughts. The van had no windows. They couldn't see a damned thing. The journey wasn't all that long, a couple of hours at most, but to all of them it seemed like an eternity in which their thoughts slipped and slid.

Eventually, the van stopped. Trooper Harper opened the rear doors. 'This is the RV,' he said. 'You're about two miles from the compound. I'm going to stay here with the van until you return. Out you get – and good luck.'

All of them clambered out, weapons rattling, and found themselves in a narrow road that curved through moonlit, undulating countryside with not a house in sight. Cusack knew where they where, a couple of miles out of Hindon, equidistant between the Wylye and Nadder rivers, two miles west of Prince's compound.

Not saying a word, preferring to use hand signals, Cusack led his men away from the van, through a gate and across the first of many cultivated fields, their corn and grass wind-blown. They hiked in single file, knowing the enemy was up ahead, with Corporal Mapley out front on point and Trooper Wiley bringing up the rear, just as they would normally do in enemy territory. Eventually, just under forty minutes later, they saw the lights of the compound.

Corporal Mapley, still out front on point, silently raised and lowered his right hand, then dropped out of sight. Those behind him, including Cusack, did the same, disappearing into the shadows.

The wind moaned in its misery.

# CHAPTER TWENTY-NINE

Belly down and invisible in the grassy field, with Black Stealth belly down right behind him, unable even to see any of the other men who were, nevertheless, spread out in a semicircle behind them, listening, like himself and Black Stealth, to the wind's miserable moaning, Cusack studied the lights of the compound and judged it to be about two hundred metres away.

Some of the lights were about fifteen feet off the ground, being fixed to and illuminating the barbed-wire perimeter fence. Other lights, beyond the fence, placed at about the same height, were clearly beaming down from the upper reaches of the old Nissen huts and corrugated-iron aircraft hangars. Highest of all were the two searchlights beaming down in opposite directions from the old air traffic control tower, now the watchtower with its machine-gun crew: those lights were moving constantly to and fro in wide arcs, their beams meeting each other and then moving apart again, thus covering the whole of the compound and repeatedly illuminating the rows of Portakabins which were, Cusack knew, the living accommodations for the community. At this distance, in the moonlight, Cusack could not see much more than that, though he knew that armed guards were constantly patrolling the perimeter fence and that sangars with machine-gun crews had been placed between the main road and the Portakabins.

Needing to see more, Cusack reached behind him to remove from the side of his bergen the small tin can containing the bullet-sized remote-controlled UAV, an aerial micro-camera that would scan the compound for him while he remained where he was. After removing the UAV from its protective box, he placed it beside him on the ground, an arm's length away from his head. Covering his right eye with the Head-Up Display on his helmet, he pressed a couple of the buttons on the miniature keyboard strapped to his forearm and the UAV, propelled by minute whisper jets, spread its wings and lifted silently off the ground. Rippling like live muscles, the wings of the UAV were ribbed with minute sensors and actuators that maximized lift with every square millimetre of surface; now they enabled the UAV to rise higher, to a height of about thirty feet, where, after hovering silently for a few seconds, it glided off in the direction of the compound's perimeter fence.

The UAV was being remotely controlled by Cusack, who could see what the video camera was seeing as the images were relayed back to the VDU in his Head-Up Display. Cusack could make the UAV go anywhere he wanted, up or down, left or right, by using a variety of number combinations on his miniature keyboard. Right now, it was gliding at a height of about thirty feet towards the barbed-wire perimeter fence, now illuminated in the eerie green glow of the camera's night-vision optics. When the UAV, so small as to be invisible in the night, was directly above the fence, allowing Cusack to look directly down upon it, he moved it to the right and proceeded to make it glide around the whole perimeter, revealing one armed guard after another. As the camera came to a position above each individual guard, all of whom were wearing overalls and carrying MP5 sub-machine guns, Cusack relayed the guard's exact position back to a different member of the QRF by means of his hand-held Landmaster transceiver.

As each member of the QRF team, still unseen by Cusack, received the location of his intended victim, he rose out of the darkness and advanced at the half-crouch to that particular part of the perimeter fence. Once there, within range of the guard on the other side of the fence, he fell to his belly again, inserted a gas-filled MEMS, again no larger than a bullet, into the discharger attached to the barrel of his silenced MP5, and fired it on a trajectory calculated to make it fall, silently and still unseen, mere feet from where the guard was positioned. By punching a specific code into his miniature keyboard, the SAS trooper was able to explode the tiny MEMS, releasing the gas.

Cusack dispatched his men one by one and tracked them with the hovering UAV. Thus he was able to watch them, in the eerie green glow of the camera's night-vision optics, as they advanced to their given positions at the perimeter fence, dropped on to their bellies, and fired their MEMS. The minute MEMS exploded with a noise so slight as to be virtually silent, and in every case the guard standing near where the gas was released almost instantly became visibly drowsy, then groggy, staggered like a drunk for a moment, and finally dropped his weapon and sank unconscious to the ground. The gas was not poisonous, being designed to render its victim unconscious for a period of three to four hours.

Within an hour, close to midnight, every guard around the perimeter fence had been taken out with not a sound being made. The SAS men who had silenced them then advanced on the perimeter fence, still belly down, and proceeded to cut entrance holes in the barbed wire, using sharp pliers with rubber grips. When this was done, they remained where they were, unable to advance any farther because of the Claymore mines laid inside the fence, waiting for further instructions from their patrol commander. When the time was right, when Cusack gave the command, they would fire explosive MEMS into the minefield to explode the Claymores and clear a safe path for themselves.

With the guards neutralized, Cusack, the Patrol

Commander, could now advance into the compound. Rising to his feet, he indicated with a hand signal that Black Stealth should follow him, then advanced at the half-crouch, automatically weaving left to right, across that two hundred-odd metres of dark, grassy field until he reached the barbed-wire fence. Once there, he dropped again on to his belly, indicating that Black Stealth, close behind him, should do exactly the same. Black Stealth, now keen to see what was happening, did indeed drop to his belly, but then crawled forward until he was stretched out beside Cusack.

'What happens now?' he whispered.

'We're going in,' Cusack whispered back. 'All the way to those living accommodations, the Portakabins. That means we have to cross a lot of exposed ground. So keep your mouth shut, move as silently as possible, and do exactly what I do. Understood?'

'I'm your man.'

Cusack couldn't help smiling, though he kept himself well focused. After inching forward until he was up against the fence, he unclipped a small pair of shears from his webbed belt and cut an entrance hole in the barbed wire. The night was cold, but he was sweating. The wind continued to moan. Glancing left, he saw the main gate with guard boxes on either side and overhead floodlights illuminating the road. That road ran all the way past the stone-walled sangars and on to the first of the Portakabins. The sangars were visible from here only as low, dark walls; Cusack could not see either the machine-guns or the men who were manning them. Farther on, he could see the Portakabins, rectangular dark shapes, by the lights shining out of the windows and the moonlit, starry sky beyond them. The two searchlights on the watchtower kept sweeping across the compound, moving in opposite directions, completing half a circle, meeting and then moving back again, taking in the whole area and briefly lighting up the Portakabins. Cusack knew which Portakabin he wanted, and that was where he was heading.

'Okay,' he whispered. 'Let's go. Stick to me like glue.'

He pushed his MP5 through the jagged entrance hole, manoeuvred it to the side, out of his way, then wriggled cautiously forward, looking intently for the slightest irregularity in the grassy ground that might indicate where Claymore mines were buried. The laying of the Claymores, a few weeks back, had been filmed by a UAV's video camera during a routine surveillance flight, so Cusack knew that they were buried right around the perimeter in an area extending outwards from the fence for about twelve feet. He also knew, however, that the first line of Claymores began a good three feet away from the fence, to create a 'safe' path for the circulating perimeter guards. He knew, further, that the vast ring of Claymores ended a good six feet away from both sides of the main gate to allow the gate guards a safe area around their guard posts. Knowing this, his intention was to crawl no farther than two feet into the compound, then make his way along that 'safe' path until he reached the rear of the guardhouses at the main gate. From there, if he was careful, he could make his way along the rear of the guardhouses until, twelve feet farther on, he was beyond the ring of Claymores, safely inside the compound.

Having decided to do it, he inched forward – literally inch by painful inch – until half of his upper body was through the entrance hole that he had cut out of the barbed-wire fence. Once in that position, he bent himself sideways and wriggled around the entrance hole until his legs and feet were through. Then he stretched out, well within that three-feet-deep area, and took hold of his MP5 as he rose to his knees. Turning back, he indicated that Black Stealth should do the same. The kid did so, grinning like a schoolboy, probably not aware just how dangerous this was. When he started to wriggle all the way through, not twisting sideways away from the first line of buried Claymores, as Cusack had done, Cusack grabbed him by the shoulders and roughly jerked him sideways until he, too, was stretched out along the safe path, parallel to the barbed-wire fence. Placing the fingers of his free hand to his lips, indicating that Black Stealth was to remain absolutely silent, then waving his left hand in a forward, downward motion, indicating that Black Stealth was to follow him, Cusack advanced in a half-crouch, parallel to the barbed-wire fence, until he had reached the back of the first guardhouse. Once there, he froze.

It was a fairly normal kind of structure, like the average army guardhouse: a square-shaped, ten-feet-high pineboard box with a doorway and two windows, neither with window-panes. The window at the front overlooked the road and main gate, facing the guardhouse opposite; the one at the back, where Cusack and Black Stealth were kneeling, overlooked the Claymore-mined inner perimeter. The light from that window shone down over the safe area of the perimeter, a few feet in front of where Cusack and Black Stealth were kneeling. From his own position, just in front of Black Stealth, Cusack could see the back of one guard's head and hear the voice of another as he talked with his friend – something about his relationship with his parents, who did not under-stand him.

Cusack had no wish to neutralize the guards, as this would only alert the others in the guardhouse at the far side of the gate. His immediate aim was to get into the compound proper and make his way unseen to a particular Portakabin. When the time came, Troopers Stubbs and Grant would, if luck prevailed, take care of these guards and clear the main gate.

Glancing back over his shoulder, Cusack saw that Black Stealth was right there behind him, staring out over the compound with a keen, enquiring gaze and a grin of childish pleasure. Convinced now that the young man would go to the limit with him, driven by his rampant, amoral ego, Cusack used a hand signal to indicate that he was going to cross under the rear window of the guardhouse and that Black Stealth was to follow. Receiving Black Stealth's nod of acknowledgement, Cusack rose to the half-crouch position, holding his MP5 at the ready, then advanced along the rear of the guardhouse, his head just under the bottom of its window frame. He made his way to a point about ten feet beyond it, coming to rest at what he had to assume was the outer edge of the minefield, mere feet from the nearside of the main road that ran on to the fortified sangars and, beyond them, the Portakabins he wanted to reach. Glancing back over his shoulder, he saw Black Stealth doing the same. A bright kid who lived for excitement, Black Stealth made no mistakes and was kneeling on the grass beside Cusack a few seconds later. There, they both froze again.

Cusack carefully studied as much of the compound as he could see. From where he was kneeling, a mere ten or so feet out from the two guardhouses of the main gate, just out of range of the overhead lights, he could now see more clearly the stone sangars located strategically between his position – the entrance to the compound – and the Portakabins farther on. Behind the sangars, soaring high above them, on the edge of the old airfield runway, was the watchtower, with its alert machine-gun crew and those searchlights continually covering the whole area, moving back and forth ceaselessly.

'Fuck!' Cusack whispered, breaking his self-imposed silence.

'What?' Black Stealth whispered back.

'Shut up,' Cusack responded, annoyed with himself for his involuntary exclamation. 'Don't make a move that I don't make.'

'Say no more,' Black Stealth said.

Realizing that he had a young hothead on his hands, albeit one thankfully bright of mind and thrilled at the prospect of danger, Cusack rose again to the half-crouch position and advanced into the exposed ground that lay between him, the sangars and, ultimately, the Portakabins. Mindful that his QRF team (God bless Jack Lewis and those others belly down around the perimeter) was ready to leap to his defence at the press of a button on his Landmaster transceiver, he darted across the moonlit area, glancing left and right. He saw little movement in this midnight hour, in this well-disciplined establishment, except the occasional silhouetted figure going about some unknown community business, walking resolutely (*They're always so fucking resolute*, Cusack thought, recalling the other Millennialist compounds he had attacked in the past) from one starkly illuminated building to another.

Aware that there were eyes everywhere, that the methodically wandering searchlights could pick him and Black Stealth out at any moment and, also, that Prince was almost certain to have his own laser and CCTV surveillance systems scanning the compound, Cusack stayed in the half-crouch position until he had reached a point about fifty metres from the circular sangars: a flat, grassy area with no protection at all. This was a seriously bad moment.

'Fuck,' Cusack whispered.

'What?' Black Stealth responded.

'Get belly down,' Cusack whispered. 'I mean, as flat as you can manage. Try to make yourself invisible and crawl forward as far as you can go, staying close behind me. Say one word and I'll cut your throat.'

Black Stealth didn't reply. He didn't want his throat cut. Cusack jumped up and wove his way across the exposed ground, advancing parallel to the stone sangars where, for the first time, he could see the silhouetted outlines of the machine-gun crews and, more ominously, the upthrust barrels of the machine-guns themselves.

Cusack dropped again on to his belly and Black Stealth, still behind him, did the same. Taking a deep breath, Cusack studied the stone-walled sangars to ascertain that no one was looking in his direction. In fact, the machine-gun crews had their backs to him, though they could turn around at any moment. Beyond them, rising to the night sky, was the watchtower with its searchlights continually sweeping the whole area. To his right was a flat, open stretch of ground falling away to the mined area inside the perimeter fence. Straight ahead was the first row of Portakabins, including the one he wanted to enter. The Portakabins were about forty metres away. Light was shining from some of the windows, indicating that those inside were still awake. There was no one around outside. By and large, then, the community was asleep at this midnight hour.

Cusack lay there, breathing evenly. He watched the beam of the northern searchlight on the watchtower sweeping towards him, pressed his face to the ground just before it reached him and let it pass over him. Then, as it continued on its way, leaving him in darkness again, he rose quietly and advanced at the half-crouch across that final forty metres to the first row of Portakabins. Black Stealth did the same.

They crouched, side by side, beside the steps of the target structure. It was the smallest of the Portakabins and light was streaming out of the front window, indicating that the person inside was still awake. Cusack turned to Black Stealth and indicated with his index finger that they were about to go up the steps and try the front door. Black Stealth nodded his understanding. Cusack checked that the watchtower's searchlight beam was moving away from him again, not coming towards him. Then he moved swiftly, silently up the steps and stood in front of the door until Black Stealth had joined him.

Cusack took hold of the door handle and turned it gently. The handle turned. The door was not locked. Cusack opened the door a little, heard muted conversation, took a deep breath and peered inside.

The main room of the Portakabin was small and sparsely furnished: a wooden table with folding legs, a couple of matching chairs, a single settee, a couple of cheap mats on the wooden floor. A single cup and saucer were on the table, beside a pile of books and magazines. The television in the far corner was turned on with the volume down low, this being the source of the muted conversation. Someone was sitting in a chair, watching the television. An MP5 sub-machine gun was propped up against that person's chair. A door led into another room, presumably a bedroom, but that room was in darkness.

Holding his breath, Cusack opened the door further and stepped into the room. He advanced silently upon the person watching the television and pressed the barrel of his MP5 against the back of her head.

'Hi, Chloe,' he said.

Then he slapped his hand over her mouth to prevent her from screaming.

# CHAPTER THIRTY

'It's me,' he said. 'Cusack. Don't make a sound. I'm going to take my hand away from your mouth, but if you attempt to scream I'll have to kill you. Do you understand, Chloe?'

She had stiffened automatically, but she relaxed, at least a little, when she heard the sound of his voice. She nodded her head, the movement restricted by Cusack's grip on her face.

Cusack slowly, carefully, removed his hand: Chloe made no sound. He stepped around in front of her, keeping his MP5 trained on her, then leaned back to turn the television off. He straightened up, but kept his MP5 aimed at her. Black Stealth, standing behind Chloe's chair, did not say a word.

'How are you, Chloe?' Cusack asked.

'I'm okay, I guess. You don't have to point that thing at me. I'm not going anywhere.'

She was wearing the same kind of jungle-green overalls that the guards were wearing – that all the others here wore, as he had seen on the UAV videotapes – but she still looked damnably attractive and the sight of her brought a lump to his throat. Trying not to show the emotions he was feeling, he stepped forward, removed her MP5 from the side of the chair, handed it to Black Stealth, then moved around in front of her again.

'Stand up,' he said.

Chloe did as she was told. Cusack removed the Browning 9mm High Power handgun from the holster on Chloe's hip and handed that to Black Stealth as well.

'Sit down again,' he said to Chloe.

Chloe sat back in the chair and Cusack looked down at her, feeling inexpressibly sad as he gazed into her large, luminous brown eyes. He sighed and lowered his MP5 to his side, holding it in his right hand.

'We've come for Prince,' he said.

'He's expecting you,' she replied. 'He didn't know when you were coming, but he knew that you'd come.'

'He's armed the camp?'

'Yes.'

'He's in his Portakabin?'

'Yes.'

Cusack nodded and sighed again. Then he went down on one knee in front of Chloe and gazed steadily at her, still trying not to show his emotions, speaking quietly, precisely.

'Listen carefully to me, Chloe. I haven't come here alone. My men have surrounded the camp and they're going to launch an assault the instant I tell them. Before I give the order, however, I have to get to Prince's computer and let my young friend here –' he nodded in the direction of Black Stealth '– hack his way into Prince's system to deactivate five bombs that Prince has placed in various areas of London. I repeat, Chloe: five bombs. They're biological or chemical weapons that will kill and disable thousands of innocent people if they detonate. Did you know about them?'

'No,' Chloe said.

'You're still on Prince's side, are you?'

Chloe sighed and nodded. 'Yes.'

'So what about those five bombs, Chloe? How do you feel about that?'

She didn't answer for some time. Cusack thought she was going to cry. She put her hand up to her eyes as if to wipe tears away. But no tears had actually formed, so she lowered her hand again.

'I didn't know about them,' she said. 'I can't think . . . It sounds bad.'

'It *is* bad, Chloe. It's a lot more than just bad. It'll be a slaughter of unimaginable proportions, so we've got to prevent it – and you've got to help us. Will you do that, Chloe?'

She was having serious difficulty in meeting his intent stare. Her moist gaze roamed about the small room, then returned, lowered, to focus intently upon her clasped hands. 'I can't go against him,' she confessed. 'I don't know why, but I can't. He's kind of . . . taken me over. I . . . I just can't go against him.'

'You don't *have* to go against him,' Cusack said, recalling how she had gone against *him* by betraying him at Prince's command. 'You just have to find out if he's at his computer and, if he is, get him away from it long enough for us to get at it. That's all I ask, Chloe.'

She raised her face to look at him, finally met his gaze, then turned away. 'I don't know what you mean.'

'Call him, Chloe, and ask him to come over here. Say you need to see him.'

'He never comes over here. I always go over there, to him. If I asked him to come over here, he'd think it was pretty unusual.'

Cusack thought about that, wondering if it was true. Then he recalled that on the UAV videotapes he had only seen Chloe going to Prince's Portakabin; it had never been the other way around. She was telling the truth about this, at least.

'Okay,' he said. 'How about this? You call him and say you want to see him. If he tells you to come on over, we go with you. Presumably, if he does tell you to come over, he won't be at his computer. He'll be in his bedroom.'

Chloe sighed again. 'Yes.'

Cusack felt that his heart was breaking. He couldn't bear the thought of Chloe in Prince's bed, but he would have to go with it. 'So we go over with you,' he said, still speaking calmly, precisely, 'and when you enter his bedroom, we enter the Portakabin and take over from there.'

Chloe closed her eyes, then bit her lower lip. This time, a couple of tears did roll down her cheeks, but she wiped them away. Then she opened her eyes again and stared straight at Cusack. Her gaze was unreadable.

'You're going to kill him,' she said.

'Not unless he resists.'

'You're going to kill him anyway. I know you will. That's what you've come here to do.'

'That isn't true, Chloe. We've come here to stop the bombings. If Prince doesn't resist, we'll take him prisoner and he'll be slung in prison. But if we don't get at his computer, Chloe – and please remember this – thousands of people in London will die and even more will be made mortally ill.'

'How do I know you're telling the truth? Even Prince wouldn't . . . *do* that. I mean, he may be a Millennialist, against the government and the Royal Family, but he doesn't do *that* kind of thing. You're just trying to. . .'

'To fool you? No, I'm not. Prince, the man you revere, your religious leader, your guru, was the brains behind the Whitehall Atrocity and the London Underground Massacre. He'll set off those bombs, Chloe, believe me, unless you help us to stop him.'

He noticed that she was wringing the hands resting in her lap, that she seemed dreadfully confused, torn in two. Her mouth opened and closed soundlessly a few times, as if she was lost for words. She gazed down at her clasped hands again, then she sighed, in despair.

'All of that could be a lie as well,' she said. 'I don't believe Prince would –'

'It's not a lie, Chloe. You *know* what he can do. He used you as a whore to get at me, so he's hardly a saint. He –'

'Oh, God!' Chloe interjected, sounding as if she was choking, turning her eyes up to the ceiling, then looking down at her hands again.

'You can't deny that he did that, Chloe. And a man who can use you that way isn't a man to be trusted.'

'I –'

'Prince is no saint, Chloe,' Cusack said again. He knew that he had to push her. 'In fact, he's quite the opposite. He's a man who's already killed hundreds of people – in Whitehall, in the London Underground – and he certainly won't stop after killing a few thousand more when those bombs go off. This man, your religious leader, your guru, is a psychopath, Chloe. Please believe me, he *is*.'

'I –'

'He made you prostitute yourself. He made you do it to get at me. Would a truly religious man, even a Millennialist, ask you to do *that*?'

Chloe turned her head away, covering her face with her hands, sobbing silently and trying to hide it but trembling too much to do so. Cusack reached out, placed his hand on her shoulder and squeezed gently, just once. Then he withdrew his hand.

'I'm sorry, Chloe. *So* sorry. Please look at me, Chloe.'

She did so reluctantly, wiping fresh tears from her eyes, then dropped her hands back to her lap and lowered her head. She looked as if she was praying.

'Promise me you won't kill him.'

'I can't make that promise, Chloe. I'll *try* not to kill him, but if he resists me – or if he runs to his computer – I may not have a choice.'

'Then promise me you won't kill him if he doesn't do that. Make that promise, at least.'

'I promise,' Cusack said. 'If I can get what I want without killing him, I won't kill him, Chloe. I'll just take him prisoner. *Now* will you make that call for me?'

Chloe nodded. 'Yes.'

''Scuse me, boss,' Black Stealth said, speaking for the first time, using the SAS term of address, having picked it up originally on the Internet before he'd heard the QRF team using it. He was still holding on to Chloe's weapons. 'But even if she takes us over there, how will we know when she's gone into Prince's bedroom?'

'Good question,' Cusack said, compelled to admire his amoral young friend's intelligence. 'Chloe?'

She raised her head to look at him – *forcing* herself to look at him. 'Prince likes to play music when he fucks – he *always* plays music – so when you hear the music come on, you'll know we're in his bedroom.'

Cusack sensed that she had used the word 'fuck' to hurt him and she had certainly succeeded. Almost wincing, he managed to control himself and asked, 'What kind of music?'

'Religious music. Bach, Handel – that kind of stuff. He says it makes the sex spiritual.'

'Jesus Christ!' Black Stealth exclaimed.

Cusack ignored him. He glanced at Chloe's telephone. 'Are you willing to make that call right now?'

Chloe closed her eyes, sighed forlornly, then opened her eyes again and nodded assent.

'Okay, do it,' Cusack said, sounding more harsh than he felt, feeling like a pimp. 'Please do it, Chloe.'

*I'm doing what Prince did,* he thought. *I'm now down at his level. This isn't what I expected.*

'Okay,' Chloe said.

She picked up the phone and dialled a number. 'Prince?' A pause. 'It's me, Chloe.' Another pause. 'Can I come and see you?' A third pause. 'I can't sleep. I think I'm scared, Prince. I'm worried about what's going to happen. I just need . . . I mean . . . I need to *talk*. To . . . *You* know . . .' A fourth pause. 'Yes? Oh, good. I'll come over right now . . .' She put the phone down and turned back to Cusack. 'He's going to take me to bed to console me. Is *that* what you want?'

'That's what I want,' Cusack said, gritting his teeth.

'You're just like him,' Chloe said.

Cusack wanted to die. His shame and pain were unbearable. It was almost as if she had read his mind – his conviction that he was, like Prince, making her whore for him – and this thought came close to destroying him, right there and then. He didn't show it, however, because this job had to be completed, so he shrouded himself in ice and kept his voice steady.

'Do what you've promised,' he said. 'When you go in there, don't change your mind. I'll keep my promise if you keep yours; otherwise there are no rules. Is that understood?'

'Yeah,' Chloe said, reverting to the way she had spoken when she was whoring around King's Cross Station. 'Anything you want, mister.'

'Let's go,' Cusack said.

Chloe got out of her chair and walked straight to the door, brushing past Black Stealth without even looking at him. Black Stealth held Chloe's weapons up, shrugging, asking what he should do with them. Cusack nodded to Chloe's chair, indicating that Black Stealth should place them there. When Black Stealth had done so, Cusack repeated his original orders: 'Stay glued to my back, keep your mouth shut and do just what I tell you.'

'No sweat,' Black Stealth said.

Cusack followed Chloe to the door and Black Stealth fell in behind him. Chloe opened the door and peered out, her head moving left to right as she scanned the compound.

'Okay,' she said. 'There's no one out there. Let's get over there quickly.'

'We're right behind you,' Cusack said.

They all left the Portakabin, going down the steps, then Chloe turned right and led them along the front of the other Portakabins until she reached the end of the row. Prince's Portakabin was isolated from the others, a lot bigger than them, located across an open stretch of mowed, moonlit lawn, between the accommodation for the general community and the motor pool. Chloe looked about her, checking that all was clear. Seeing no one, she nodded at Cusack and then started across the lawn. Cusack and Black Stealth followed her. When they reached the steps of Prince's Portakabin, Chloe turned back to face them. She looked directly at Cusack.

'You *promise* not to kill him,' she said, 'if he doesn't resist?'

'I promise,' Cusack replied.

Chloe stared steadily at him for a long time, her brown-eyed gaze questioning, filled with doubt, perhaps fear. Then she nodded, as if answering her own unvoiced question, and walked up the steps of the Portakabin to ring the bell by the door.

'Yes?' Prince called out from within.

'It's Chloe.'

'Come in.'

Chloe glanced back over her shoulder at Cusack. He nodded. Chloe opened the door and entered the Portakabin. The door closed behind her.

Turning to Black Stealth, Cusack signalled for silence. Then he went up the steps until he was standing right in front of the closed door. Black Stealth came up behind him. Once standing there together, they froze.

It took a long time. It seemed to take an eternity. Cusack kept checking the luminous dial of his wristwatch, but the minute hand was moving so slowly that it seemed to be frozen. He was imagining that, of course. Time moved on, as it always did. Ten minutes later – though it seemed like decades – he heard music playing inside. It was the prelude to Charpentier's *Te Deum*. Cusack kicked the door open.

# CHAPTER THIRTY-ONE

Rushing into the Portakabin, Cusack saw the thick-pile carpet, black leather couches, a wide-screen TV with video recorder, and a Panasonic music centre that was pumping religious music into the bedroom, located on the far side of the living room.

'Find the computer!' Cusack bawled at Black Stealth as he raced to that door, which was unlocked, and pushed it wide open. Prince and Chloe were in there, both still fully dressed, and Prince, having heard Cusack's noisy entrance, was already rolling across the bed to reach the handgun resting on the bedside cabinet. Cusack went for him as Chloe jumped out of his way. He grabbed Prince by the hair and jerked him backwards, away from the handgun. Prince bellowed and fought, but Cusack thumped him with the barrel of his MP5 and sent him rolling off the far side of the bed to hit the floor with a solid thud. Cusack aimed his gun at Prince as the Millennialist pushed himself on to his knees. Prince shook his head to clear it, then looked up, blinked a few times, and grinned.

'Well, well,' he said. 'My good friend, Sergeant Cusack.' His grin disappeared when he looked at Chloe. 'Is this your doing, my angel?'

'I gave her no choice,' Cusack said.

'Is that true, Chloe?'

'Yes.'

'I truly hope so, Chloe. For your sake, I hope so.'

'Shut your mouth,' Cusack said.

'I found it!' Black Stealth called out from the study. 'I'm here at that fucker's workdesk!'

Keeping his MP5 trained on Prince, Cusack nodded in the direction of the bedroom door. 'Out,' he said, 'and don't make a false move or I'll chop you in two.'

'Where are we going?'

'To your study. I'll be right behind you and I'll shoot at the slightest sign of trouble. Okay, get moving. You, too, Chloe.'

Prince glanced left and right, calculating every angle. But seeing that he really had no option, he stood up to leave the bedroom.

'Put your hands on your head,' Cusack said. Prince smiled, but did as he was told. 'Okay, start walking . . . but slow . . . no fast movements. You get me?'

'I get you,' Prince said.

With Cusack close behind him, keeping his MP5 pointed at him, Prince left the bedroom, crossed the living room, and entered his study on the other side. Black Stealth was in there, standing at Prince's cluttered desk, staring at his computer. Black Stealth gave a low whistle of appreciation.

'An old Dell,' he said admiringly when the others had entered the study. 'This guy may be living in the dark ages, but he sure has some class!'

'Stop admiring it and do the fucking job,' Cusack said bluntly. 'We're not here for your pleasure.'

'He's here to deactivate the bombs, is he?' Prince asked sardonically.

'Yes,' Cusack said.

'Why waste his time?' Prince said. 'Since you've caught me – since the game is all over – I might as well *give* you the code. I mean, I've nothing to lose.'

'Yeah, right,' Black Stealth said. 'You're real generous,

right? Don't listen to a fucking word he says, Cusack, 'cause he's going to shaft you.'

'How come?' Prince said.

'Because you'll give me a code that's supposed to deactivate those bombs when in fact it's the code that'll set 'em off. Don't fuck with me, Prince, I'm not that dumb. I'll find the code for myself, thanks.'

Then Black Stealth took the chair in front of Prince's computer and went to work, his fingers flying across the keyboard.

'We'll be in the living room,' Cusack said to Black Stealth. 'Call out when you've completed the job.'

'Aye, aye,' Black Stealth said.

'Okay,' Cusack said, still aiming his MP5 at Prince while indicating the doorway with the briefest flick of the barrel. 'Into the living room.'

Prince glanced left and right again, always calculating the odds, but then nodded and walked out of the study with Chloe beside him. When they were back in the living room, Cusack indicated one of the black leather settees. 'Sit down there.'

Prince sat on the settee. Cusack remained standing where he was, his gun still pointing at Prince who looked up at him, smiling slightly, though his green gaze was unusually intense. Cusack knew without a doubt, from that steady gaze, just how dangerous Prince was.

'A bright boy you've got there, Cusack,' Prince said, nodding to indicate his study where Black Stealth was working enthusiastically. 'Where on earth did you find him?'

'Like you, he's an Internet wizard. They call him Black Stealth.'

'Oh, my God,' Prince said, smiling disdainfully. 'I've seen his name so many times. In fact, he's one of my heroes. A criminal, of course, just like me. How *could* you sink so low, Cusack?'

'Alas, to clean up shit, you sometimes have to go down on your hands and knees.'

'You've certainly done that, my friend. And now Chloe here,

having already betrayed you, is betraying me. How are *your* hands and knees, dear?'

'Prince, please, I . . .'

But Chloe didn't know what to say. She was too confused to deal with this. She turned away, trying to hide her tears, not knowing to whom she belonged.

'Are you going to kill me, Cusack?' Prince asked.

'I'm taking you prisoner,' Cusack said.

'And what if I *don't want* to be taken prisoner? Which I certainly don't. What then, Cusack?'

'Then I'll have to kill you.'

'Did you hear that, Chloe? He's going to kill me if I refuse to be taken in and I *won't* let myself be taken in. Prince will *not* rot in prison.'

'Prince, *please* . . .' Chloe said, sounding choked, backing away from where she'd been standing beside Cusack.

'Kill me, Cusack,' Prince said with a sneer. 'Do what you came here to do. Do what you know you're going to do, despite any promises you made to Chloe. You're an SAS man – so was I – and we both know what that means. You've come here to neutralize me, so neutralize me, as you've been ordered to do, and put an end to our mutual misery.'

'I just might do that, you shitheap,' Cusack said, his hatred and anger blinding him to everything else around him.

Something hard touched the side of his head and he froze instantly.

'No, you won't,' Chloe said. 'You made me a promise.'

Cusack glanced sideways without moving his head. The hard thing touching his head was the barrel of a handgun, Prince's pistol, which Chloe must have picked up from the bedroom when she had backed away from him. Black Stealth, being otherwise engaged in Prince's study, could not see what was happening.

'Chloe . . .' Cusack said.

'Don't move an inch,' Chloe responded.

'You can't do this, Chloe,' Cusack said. 'If you do, you'll regret it.'

Prince smiled. 'Don't listen to him. The devil speaks with a forked tongue. Think of everything I've taught you here, Chloe, and take your faith from it. What were you before you came here? What would you be without us? Who, apart from us, offered you help when you desperately needed it? No one. Not a soul. They didn't give a damn, Chloe. The only family you ever had is right here and they're trying to wipe it out. That's what Cusack is here for.'

'Oh, Christ,' Chloe said. 'Jesus Christ. Tell me what to do, Prince.'

'Do what your conscience dictates, Chloe. Do what you think is right. Just consider why Cusack is here and decide upon that.'

'I can't think. *I can't think!*'

'Think!' Cusack insisted.

'He's in the SAS,' Prince said. 'You know what that means, Chloe. The SAS are assassins, paid killers for the Establishment, backed by Freemasonry and the Illuminati, the disciples of Satan. Where were *they*, dear Chloe, when you so desperately needed help? When you were drowning in the gutters of King's Cross, your veins heavy with heroin. They were *elsewhere*, Chloe. Attacking the people who could have helped you. They're renowned – the SAS, represented here by our good friend Sergeant Cusack – for their skill at eliminating Millennialist communities such as our own. And who helped you, Chloe? Certainly not the SAS. You were helped, Chloe, by the very community they now wish to destroy. And who'll destroy us, Chloe? This man here. Sergeant Cusack. He'll do it if you don't put a stop to him. So put a stop to him right now.'

'You fucker,' Cusack said.

'Fucked your wife,' Prince responded.

'*What?*' Chloe said.

'You bastard,' Cusack groaned.

'Fucked your wife and your daughter,' Prince said, 'then put them into their graves. How does *that* grab you, Cusack?'

Cusack, ignoring the gun at his temple, cocked his MP5.

Chloe's choked sob held him back. 'What he's saying,' he told Chloe, not turning his head, 'is that his thugs raped and then murdered my wife and our fifteen-year-old daughter on his orders. I never got around to telling you about it. Did *he* tell you about it?'

'No!' Chloe said, sounding strangled, her eyes haunted and glistening.

'The wife and daughter of SAS filth,' Prince clarified. 'It was repayment for what Cusack had done to us – to our Millennialist friends. It was the start of our righteous war.'

'Oh, God!' Chloe exclaimed, lowering the handgun, her cheeks streaked with tears.

Cusack turned slightly towards her, pushing the handgun lower. Then Prince leaped from the settee and raced to the front door. Cusack saw him slapping his hand down on a button beside the door, saw him jerking the door open and fleeing as sirens began to wail outside.

'Shit!' Cusack exclaimed, realizing that Prince had set off those sirens to alert everyone in the compound. He raced to the door and saw Prince fleeing across the compound while other people spilled out of the Portakabins, all bearing arms. 'Shit!' Cusack exclaimed again, raising his MP5 to shoot at Prince. Then he changed his mind, pulling his transceiver from his webbing belt and hitting a button.

'It's Cusack,' he said into the transceiver. 'Launch the assault.'

'Wilco,' Jack Lewis replied.

'Over and out,' Cusack said.

Turning off the transceiver, he glanced back into the room to see Chloe's wide-eyed, startled gaze and Black Stealth framed in the doorway of the study.

'What's happening?' Black Stealth asked.

'Get back to that fucking computer,' Cusack said, 'and don't stop until those bombs are deactivated. I'm staying here to protect you.'

'No shit!' Black Stealth exclaimed, then disappeared around the side of the doorframe, back into the study.

'Oh, God,' Chloe said, sounding distraught, her large brown eyes filling with tears. 'Jesus Christ. What have I –?'

But she never finished the sentence. She was cut off by the thunderous roaring of many different explosions as the SAS men, still outside the compound, detonated the Claymores with explosive MEMS to make safe paths through the mined perimeter and gain entrance. Glancing out of the front door, Cusack saw the explosions, great jagged sheets of white light in the midst of boiling smoke, erupting from all around the compound. He also saw the Millennialists racing across the compound in all directions, and heard the roar of sub-machine guns as some of them fired blindly in the direction of the perimeter. Realizing that his time was running out, that Prince would alert some of his men and either send them or bring them to his Portakabin, Cusack raced across the living room and stuck his head through the doorway of the study. Black Stealth was still at the computer, his fingers racing over the keyboard.

'How's it going?' Cusack asked.

'I'm getting there,' Black Stealth said.

'You better get there quickly,' Cusack said, 'because they're soon going to be hammering on the front door.'

'A few more minutes,' Black Stealth said, sounding incredibly cool.

Cusack turned back to the living room just in time to see Chloe fleeing through the front door, still gripping the handgun, sobbing wretchedly.

'Chloe!' he bawled.

But Chloe was gone before he could stop her. Cursing to himself, Cusack ran to the door and looked out. The Claymore mines were still exploding, ripping the night sky apart with massive blinding flashes and filling the air with smoke. Two SAS troopers – he could not recognize them from this distance – were running at the half-crouch along the safe paths created by their exploding MEMS, straight through the mined perimeter, shooting on the move at the Millennialists now racing towards them who were also firing as they ran.

The machine-gun on the watchtower was roaring in staccato bursts as the gunner aimed first this way, then that, trying desperately to cover the whole perimeter. Up ahead, about fifty metres away, a whole bunch of Millennialists, led by Prince himself, now armed with a sub-machine gun, were heading straight for Prince's Portakabin.

'Time's running out!' Cusack bawled at Black Stealth. 'What the fuck's happening back there?'

'Another minute!' Black Stealth bawled back. 'One more minute, for Christ's sake!'

Cusack stepped into the doorway, spread his legs and braced himself, then fired an extended burst from his MP5 at the group, led by Prince, advancing towards him. Some of them fell and the rest of them scattered, with Prince haring off at an angle, obviously planning to come in from the side.

*That fucker's got guts,* Cusack thought. *I'll give him that.*

He jumped back into the living room, twisting sideways as bullets ricocheted off the doorframe. Slamming the door shut, he hurried to the nearest front window, smashed the glass with the butt of his MP5, then proceeded to fire in sustained, savage bursts at the people, men and women, advancing towards him, all firing while on the move.

'*Voilà!*' Black Stealth yelled.

'What?' Cusack responded.

Black Stealth came running out of the study, looking pleased with himself. 'Those bombs have been deactivated,' he said. 'You can stop sweating, Sarge.'

'Jesus Christ!' Cusack said.

Bullets were ricocheting off the walls of the Portakabin and exploding through the other windows, filling the room with flying glass. Dropping low, Cusack raced to the front door and attached a small Semtex charge to it. He set the timer for two minutes, then spun away, grabbed hold of Black Stealth and raced him back into Prince's study, which was at the back of the Portakabin and had one large window. Cusack smashed the window with the butt of his MP5, kept hacking at it until the remaining pieces of glass were cleared away, then shoved

Black Stealth at the window and said, 'Get the hell out.'

Black Stealth was clambering through the window when the front door burst open and the first of the Millennialists swarmed into the living room. Cusack fired at them, swinging his MP5 in a wide arc. His bullets flew everywhere, tearing the black leather settees to shreds, pulverizing the walls, as the Millennialists screamed out in pain, doubling over and falling to the floor. Cusack slammed the study door closed and turned away to start scrambling through the window. He was just dropping down to the ground outside when the charge attached to the front door exploded with a fearsome roar that made the whole Portakabin shake. Cusack fell to the ground beside Black Stealth, grabbed him by the shoulder and pushed him forward, bawling, 'Run for it! *Go!*'

Black Stealth started running, though he didn't know where to go. Cusack leaped on him and pushed him down to the ground as the Portakabin behind them burst into flames.

'Stick with me!' Cusack bawled. 'Don't leave me for a second! My job's to get you out of here, no matter what happens to my men, so stay with me every inch of the way and try nothing foolish. Now get up and *go!*'

They jumped up and ran, with Cusack at the front. He led Black Stealth around the blazing Portakabin and out into the main compound, glancing sideways to see the front of the Portakabin, half blown away, the other half on fire, with dead bodies sprawled all around in ungainly poses under a curtain of smoke. Cusack ran on towards the main gate, towards the sangars where machine-guns were roaring. He blazed away at anyone wearing overalls, brutally shooting his way through. As he advanced, he saw Bill Stubbs and Mel Grant racing towards the watchtower, crouched low and weaving to avoid the machine-gun bullets, intent on planting Semtex bombs around its base to bring it all down. At the same time, Jack Lewis was leading Chris Mapley, Ben Wiley and Norman Carter on an assault against the sangars, obviously planning to neutralize the machine-gun crews.

Cusack couldn't help them. He had to get Black Stealth out.

He knew that Stubbs and Grant would have cleared the main gate as they entered the compound, dispatching the guards, leaving a safe exit for Black Stealth, so that was where he was heading. When he had fought his way to twenty-odd metres from the gate, he saw, with relief, that the run would be a clear one, with no Millennialists blocking the path.

'Run for it,' he said to Black Stealth. 'Get the hell out of here. When you get through those gates, hike all the way back to the RV. You'll be taken back to Hereford in the van – with us or without us. Thanks for everything. *Go!*'

Black Stealth ran for the main gate.

Turning back the way he had come, Cusack saw that Stubbs and Grant had made it as far as the watchtower and that Stubbs was planting Semtex bombs around the base of the tower while Grant gave him covering fire with his MP5, picking off the Millennialists attacking them. By now, however, a lot of the Millennialists were throwing down their weapons and fleeing from the compound, some driving away in cars, vans and trucks, others making it through the safe paths created by the SAS, while others stupidly ran straight through the minefields and were blown up.

Wondering where Prince was and also concerned for Chloe, Cusack headed back towards the centre of the compound. As he advanced, shooting back at any Millennialists firing at him and blazing away at those who simply got in his way, he saw that Jack Lewis and his team were attacking the sangars with the M203 grenade launchers attached to their sub-machine guns. The grenades were exploding inside the sangars, blowing men over the low stone walls, shredding others with shrapnel and filling the air with billowing black smoke reeking of explosive. Before Cusack had advanced another fifty metres, the sangars were wiped out.

Exultant, Cusack increased his pace, wanting to help his men. But at that moment the Semtex bombs placed around the base of the watchtower exploded.

Cusack froze where he was. He felt the whiplash of the explosions. A jagged flash of brilliant light, the screeching of bending, breaking metal and wood, and then the base of the watchtower was blown outwards in all directions in billowing clouds of black smoke. The whole edifice collapsed, the struts bending and snapping, and the men in the watchtower screamed, sounding like nothing remotely human as they plunged down through the flying debris – lumps of wood, pieces of metal, disintegrating machine-guns – to smash into the ground far below and die writhing in a hell of boiling smoke and spiralling dust. This smoke and dust gradually covered the whole compound, rendering everyone within it ghostlike – silhouettes, apparitions. Nothing seemed real at this point.

Cusack released the breath he'd been holding in, then started forward again.

He didn't get far.

Bullets smashed into Cusack's left shoulder, making him spin around, and he caught a glimpse of Prince – that unmistakable golden-blond hair, that intense bright green stare – as his numbed fingers released his MP5 and he followed it down to the ground. He fell forward on to his belly, involuntarily sucked in a mouthful of dirt and spat it out, then rolled onto his back to see the vast sweep of the star-filled, moonlit sky. Then Prince's head blotted out those stars. He was looking down at Cusack, standing over him, holding a sub-machine gun across his chest and smiling thinly, maliciously.

'You Satanist bastard,' he said. 'Did you *really* think you could beat me?'

'I've beaten you,' Cusack replied. 'Your bombs won't go off and your computer's been destroyed, and soon there'll be nothing left in this damned compound. You're fucked and you know it.'

'Not as fucked as you are,' Prince said. 'You're about to take your last breath. What's it feel like to know that?'

'There's nothing you can do to me that could be worse than what you've already done. Go screw yourself, Prince.'

'Alas, I can't manage that. What I *can* do instead is check just how brave you are when you stare into the barrel of this gun that's going to blow your head apart. Here it comes, Cusack. Look at it.'

Prince leaned down over Cusack, smiling at him, his green eyes brilliant. Then he lowered the sub-machine gun until the barrel was mere inches from Cusack's eyes. Cusack studied the black hole of that barrel: it looked like eternity.

'Fuck you,' Cusack said.

He saw Prince squeezing the trigger, preparing to fire. He saw his thin, humourless smile and his brilliant, demented green eyes. He saw the barrel's black hole.

*I won't let him see my terror,* Cusack thought. *I'll deny him that much, at least.*

Prince increased the pressure on the trigger.

'Drop the gun,' Chloe said.

Cusack moved his gaze sideways and saw Chloe standing there, pointing her handgun at Prince. She was wreathed in the smoke swirling over the whole compound, but he could see the tears staining her cheeks and his heart went out to her.

Prince, still smiling slightly, mirthlessly, looked directly at her, though he kept his own gun aimed down at Cusack and did not move an inch.

'Drop the gun?' he said to Chloe.

'Yes, Prince, drop the gun.'

'You'll shoot me if I don't drop the gun? You'll really pull that trigger?'

'Yes, Prince, I will.'

'Do you know what you're doing, Chloe? Do you recall who I am? Without me, where would you be, Chloe, and what would you do? I'm your saviour, Chloe. I'm the man who resurrected you. Without me, you'll go back to the gutter and almost certainly drown there.'

'Drop the gun,' Chloe repeated tonelessly.

Prince's smile broadened. He didn't believe her for a second. 'If I don't kill him,' he said, referring to Cusack, 'he'll kill me and you'll end up in prison. You're an accessory,

Chloe, one of mine, and you'll be punished for that.'

'He's lying,' Cusack said. 'You've done nothing wrong, Chloe. As long as you don't do anything wrong, you won't be sent to prison. Don't listen to him.'

'*He*'s lying,' Prince said. 'They'll find something to pin on you. They'll look at the mayhem created here and find something to get you for. Remember what I said about prison, Chloe, how you'd never survive it. Stick with me, Chloe. Trust me. Find your only salvation.'

'Drop the gun,' Chloe said again.

Prince sighed and smiled, but he didn't drop his weapon. 'You won't squeeze the trigger,' he said. 'It's just not in your nature. Also, you need me too much. I'm where it begins and ends for you.'

'If you don't drop your gun,' Chloe said, 'I'm going to kill you. Believe me, I will.'

'Don't,' Cusack said. He felt the blood draining out of him. 'You'll only go to prison if you kill him, so don't shoot him, Chloe. Let him kill me instead.'

His declaration of love.

'There you are,' Prince said to Chloe. 'Cusack's just said it himself. You have to let me kill him instead of you killing me, and then we can both start afresh. Why threaten *me*, Chloe?'

'You raped and murdered his wife and daughter,' Chloe said, sounding remarkably calm. 'That was the thing I didn't know about Cusack – the *secret* thing that you suggested was something I'd rather not know. You made it seem that if I knew it, I'd hate Cusack. But now I hate you. You bastard. You shit.'

And she fired the handgun.

Prince was bowled backwards, the bullet striking his heart, and the MP5 flew out of his hands as he fell to the ground. He landed a few feet away from Cusack and did not move again.

'Oh, Christ!' Chloe exclaimed.

She dropped her handgun to the ground and then knelt beside Cusack. Her brown eyes were wet with tears and she was visibly trembling. She looked steadily, intently, at

Cusack, then bent lower to kiss him tenderly on the lips. Cusack felt the kiss. It enriched him. Then Chloe withdrew her lips and gave a sad, tender smile.

'I loved you,' she said. 'I really did. Don't ever forget that. Goodbye, Cusack. Remember me.'

'Jesus, Chloe, I . . .'

But Chloe was gone. She disappeared into the smoke. Cusack lay there, too weak to move, wondering what would become of her. He certainly knew that she wouldn't be coming back and that thought broke his heart.

Her declaration of love.

He felt himself weakening. His blood was draining away. He tried to sit up, but he couldn't, so he just turned his head. The smoke was thinning over the compound. The dead were scattered far and wide. The Millennialists not killed had fled and the battle was over.

Someone loomed over Cusack. He looked up and saw Jack Lewis. Jack knelt beside him on the grass and studied his wounds. He nodded and smiled.

'You're a bit of a mess right now,' he said, 'but it's not as bad as it looks. You need bandaging up, though.'

'What about the others?' Cusack asked.

'No gains without losses,' Jack said. 'Carter down. Mapley down. Wiley wounded worse than you. We won't be hiking back to the RV; I called the driver and he's coming to collect us. Now let me patch you up temporarily. Grit your teeth. This'll hurt.'

Trained in field medicine, as all of them were, Jack cleaned and bandaged Cusack's wounds. Cusack winced, gritted his teeth and turned his head to the side. He saw Prince stretched out on the grass, his chest covered in blood. Prince was dead. It was done.

Cusack closed his eyes and passed out.

He was out for a long time.

# CHAPTER THIRTY-TWO

'I can't imagine you being retired,' Lieutenant Colonel Blackwell said as he and Cusack had drinks in Cusack's house in Redhill. 'It just doesn't seem real to me. What the hell do you do these days?'

'I travel a lot,' Cusack said. 'Mostly France at the moment. I've always wanted to speak French, so I started taking lessons and I go there as much as I can to speak with the natives. I'm also boning up on wine and good food – I really enjoy cooking – so France is pretty good for that as well. I also go fishing and I eat the fish I cook. I like to be alone with my thoughts and a river is good for that. Otherwise ... well, what can I say? I cruise along. I do nicely. I don't miss the regiment.'

'It misses you,' Blackwell said. 'It's not the same with you not there. Of course, it's not the same anyway, as you can imagine, but at least it's still there. We've you to thank for that, Lenny. Operation Millennium. If you'd failed to pull that off, the regiment would have been finished. There were people waiting out there in the wings, waiting for us to fail. We didn't fail and the regiment endures, and you're the one to be thanked for that.'

'I didn't do it alone,' Cusack said. 'I just survived it, that's all.'

'You and some others,' Blackwell said. 'But they're still with the regiment. How long has it been now?'

'Two years,' Cusack said.

'Seems like only yesterday, right?'

'Not right. It seems like a hundred years ago. I feel older and wiser.'

'And are you?'

'What?'

'Older and wiser?'

'Certainly older,' Cusack said.

Blackwell grinned. 'We learned a lot from that one. The regiment's modernized since then – new technology, new weapons. Those little toys you and the QRF team were playing with – it's *all* computers these days.'

'Prince certainly was a wizard with those – him and Black Stealth . . . So whatever happened to *him*?'

Blackwell grinned again. 'That kid is incorrigible. He got his early parole, went straight back to his old business and was caught hacking into a major bank to transfer cash electronically to an account in Switzerland. So now he's back in Pentonville Prison with a lot of other hackers. Normal criminals don't go to Pentonville any more; it's full to bursting with hackers like Black Stealth. He'll get out in another year or so and start all over again. You can't keep a good hacker down.'

It was Cusack who grinned this time. He'd had a soft spot for Black Stealth. 'You're going to need a few like him in the regiment, just to keep abreast of the times.'

'Don't I know it?' Blackwell said. 'So what about that other one – the girl – the one who was originally on Prince's side, then put out his lights?' He suddenly looked embarrassed. 'I'm sorry. Is this still a sensitive area? I didn't mean to –'

'No, it's okay,' Cusack cut him off. 'It was a short-lived affair two years ago and I'm certainly over it. As I said, I'm older and wiser. It's all in the past now.'

Though it wasn't *quite* over. He still had memories of love and pain. It was over in the sense that it could never start again, not even if she turned up, because too much had happened between them, both good and bad. It wasn't over because it had never properly ended, and it lived on in his heart. The beating of that heart quickened slightly at the very thought of her. The heart could not be denied.

'Well, you know,' Blackwell said, 'she just vanished into thin air, not a trace left behind, and I just wondered if you'd heard anything about her – in the newspapers or on TV or wherever. A police report, say, maybe back at her old trade and found dead in some alleyway, murdered by some deranged client. Or, perhaps, gone back on drugs and found in a rehab clinic or hospital. I never picked up a damned thing. You heard nothing either?'

'No, not a thing. Want another drink, boss?'

Blackwell smiled. 'I'm not your CO any more. And thanks, but no, I'll do without another one. I'll have to be going now and I'm driving.' He checked his wristwatch and looked up again, rolling his eyes. 'An afternoon meeting in the Kremlin,' he explained, 'to discuss new ways of beating the cyber-terrorists, who grow in numbers each year. Would you like to sit in?'

'Absolutely not,' Cusack said.

Blackwell chuckled and pushed his chair back to get to his feet again. He looked through the living-room window at the small garden out front. Then he buttoned up his jacket and glanced about him. 'I remember you were going to sell this place,' he said. 'You only stayed on before Operation Millennium in the hope of snaring Prince. What made you change your mind and stay on afterwards?'

Cusack stood up too and ran his fingers through his hair, also glancing about him. 'Memories,' he said. 'What else is there in the end? The instant I left the regiment – or, rather, was discharged – I realized that if I was going to live alone, I wanted it to be where I felt that my real life had been – here, with Mary and Jennifer. Being here isn't painful any more. Quite the opposite, in fact. This place gives me solace.'

'A *medical* discharge,' Blackwell reminded him. 'An

*honourable* discharge. So how's the bad arm these days?'

Cusack raised his formerly wounded arm experimentally and smiled ruefully before lowering it again. 'It's not too bad. I can use it for most things. I wouldn't try fencing, and I don't think I could hold an MP5, but otherwise it's okay.'

'And the rest of you?'

'Fit as a fiddle.'

'Good,' Blackwell said. 'Excellent.' And he nodded affirmatively. 'Now I must be off.'

Cusack walked him to the door. The sun was shining outside. Blackwell held out his hand and Cusack shook it.

'I'll call again,' Blackwell said.

'You're always welcome, boss.'

Blackwell smiled, turned away and walked back down the garden path. Cusack watched him as he climbed into his car and drove off. When he turned the corner at the end of the street, disappearing from sight, Cusack continued to gaze after him, thinking of the small white lie, the necessary lie, that he had just told his former boss.

It was true that he hadn't seen her for two years and didn't know where she was. But he did at least know that she was alive. He knew this because, only ten days ago, a small van had come along this very road and had stopped outside his door. Cusack hadn't seen it coming, but he had heard the doorbell ringing and when he opened the front door, he found a middle-aged woman standing there, holding a bunch of flowers in her hands. Cusack had thought that it was a mistake, that the woman had come to the wrong door. But the woman, after checking the name and address, had insisted that the flowers were for him. Cusack took the flowers from her and thanked her, then went back inside. Removing the card that was tucked into the flowers, he saw only one word, written in a delicate, shaky scrawl. That word was:

*Chloe.*

Cusack had put the flowers in a bowl and kept them there to watch them gradually wilting. By now, they had wilted entirely, though they were still in the bowl. The card had been tucked back into them, but that hadn't wilted. Cusack stared at that card every night before he went to his lonely bed.